Rambunctious Buccaneers

By now the grappling lines were fixed and the pirates had begun to reel us in like a big fish. I glanced up and saw their flag—against a black background, a human skull grinned while a strangely flexible-looking hoof poured green goo over it from a jar clearly labeled "mint sauce." I got a better grip on my blade. . . . The wall of planks dropped.

"They're repulsive!" Anisella gasped.

"They're vicious-looking!" Scandal cried.

"They are clearly without mercy," Rhett observed.

"They're *sheep*!" I was so stunned, I dropped my sword. "They're all a bunch of big, fat, fluffy, cuddly *sheep*!"

And while I was still gaping, the sheep charged across the plank bridges and showed us why you should never call a pirate *cuddly* to his face.

Ace Books by Esther Friesner

DEMON BLUES
HERE BE DEMONS
HOORAY FOR HELLYWOOD
GNOME MAN'S LAND
HARPY HIGH
UNICORN U.
MAJYK BY ACCIDENT
MAJYK BY HOOK OR CROOK

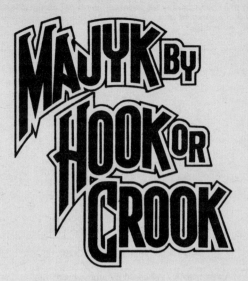

MAJYK BY HOOK OR CROOK

ESTHER FRIESNER

ACE BOOKS, NEW YORK

This book is an Ace original edition,
and has never been previously published.

MAJYK BY HOOK OR CROOK

An Ace Book / published by arrangement with
the author

PRINTING HISTORY
Ace edition / May 1994

All rights reserved.
Copyright © 1994 by Esther M. Friesner.
Cover art by David Mattingly.
This book may not be reproduced in whole or in part,
by mimeograph or any other means, without permission.
For information address: The Berkley Publishing Group,
200 Madison Avenue, New York, NY 10016.

ISBN: 0-441-00054-1

ACE®
Ace Books are published by The Berkley Publishing Group,
200 Madison Avenue, New York, NY 10016.
ACE and the "A" design
are trademarks belonging to Charter Communications, Inc.

PRINTED IN THE UNITED STATES OF AMERICA

10 9 8 7 6 5 4 3 2 1

This book is dedicated to
Ian Kinkade and Jim McDonald
"Sheep May Safely Graze"

CHAPTER ——————— 1

"A WIZARD'S GOT TO DO WHAT A WIZARD'S GOT TO do." I pulled up the hood of my black cape. "Don't try to stop me."

"Who, me?" The big cat sat in the palace doorway and yawned. "You're the one who wants asparagus for dinner, *you* go into the garden and pick it. You're not getting me out in this weather."

"Oh, it's not that bad," I scoffed, and stepped outside. Shading my eyes with one hand, I looked up into the stormy sky. "There's hardly anything coming down at all any m— Ow!" A parrot the size of a layer cake smacked me right in the eye.

I grabbed it by the throat and glared at it while a tempest of robins, finches, and larks pelted me. Far out over the swamp it was raining albatrosses and hens.

"Oh, nice one, boss!" said Scandal. The cat licked his chops. "Lotta good eating on that one. Parrots go great with asparagus, trust me. Wring its neck and pitch it right over here."

"Rrrawk!" The parrot objected, flapping its wings wildly in my face. Canaries, parakeets, and a few cockatoos were coming down hard all around us. Puddles of chickadees were everywhere. The parrot knocked my hood off, and I was getting pummeled. I couldn't hold onto one mad bird, even if I wanted to. The beast bit my finger and flew away.

"You rotten—!" I pointed my wounded finger at the escaping parrot, and a sizzling bolt of Majyk shot after it.

I missed. I usually do. More wizardly fizzle than sizzle, that's me.

"Awwww." Scandal was disappointed. "Try again."

"No." I stepped back inside the palace and shook off a few sparrows. I tried to look grave, dignified, and mysterious, the way a great wizard is supposed to be. If you do it right, everyone's afraid to bother you, just in case you're working on a blow-up everything spell. My old teacher, Master Thengor, always used that look when he didn't want to take out the garbage.

It doesn't work on cats.

"Pleeeeeeze, Kendar?" Scandal rubbed up against my ankles, pleading. "C'mon, look, there went a whole *turkey*, I swear! We could *all* eat that one."

"No," I repeated. "My mother always said that only a fool goes outdoors in fowl weather."

"Aaargh!" The cat fell over and stuck all four legs up stiffly in the air. "It's a deadly *ninja* throwing pun!" he cried, twitching from tail to whiskers. He made a loud choking noise and went limp.

"I don't know what you're talking about, Scandal," I said. "I meant what I said."

The cat came back to life. "You did?" He blinked at me with huge green eyes. "You mean, having birds fall out of the sky like this is a *normal* thing here on Orbix? What, your weatherman gets up in the morning, looks out the window, and says, 'Cloudy with a chance of buzzards'? 'Light snow, mixed with occasional chickens'? I mean, I knew this world of yours was screwy when I got here, but this is one for the books."

I sighed. It wasn't easy, helping Scandal get used to Orbix. For one thing, the place Scandal hailed from was so—so—*weird*! It was actually shaped like a rapidly spinning ball, and the people all walked around on the *outside* of it. And they didn't get spun off into space! No wonder he called it "the Whirl'd." (The one time Orbix turned ball-shaped at least it had the common sense to keep all of us safe on the *in*side. It's good to live on a smart planet.)

"You've been living here long enough to know that we don't have this kind of weather all the time," I told him.

"Hey, *you* haven't been living *anywhere* long enough to know from *nuthin'*," Scandal replied. "Except you're a teenager, so you think you know everything!"

"All right," I said, my teeth clenched. "Fine. If you don't believe me, let's ask someone else." I cupped my hands and concentrated.

A blue-green light began to glow through my fingers. A bright bubble swirled with streaks of gold formed itself out of thin air. Only Scandal and I knew it wasn't thin air: It was Majyk.

My fingers itched. I'd become a lot better at using Majyk since King Steffan gave me Master Thengor's old palace to live in. The Academy of High Wizardry went out of business and partially to pieces when Master Thengor died and I had my . . . uh . . .

little accident at his deathbed, but the Academy library was still in good shape. You can learn a lot about magic from books, if you can stop your Majyk from setting fire to them.

A face formed in the ball, the face of a beautiful woman with long blond hair and eyes the color of the sea. I blew on the bubble and it went floating off into the palace, up the stairs, seeking her.

"All that fuss to call Mysti, bwana?" Scandal asked. "Geez, she's in shouting distance, in the doorkeeper's apartment down the hall."

I looked down my nose at the cat. "You'd probably like it if I just hollered *Yo, Mysti!* or something."

"'Yo, Mysti, *c'mere!*' is more like it," Scandal replied calmly. It's no use; you can't use sarcasm on a cat. It only makes them laugh at you.

I stiffened my spine. I was going to be a proud, dignified, respected wizard if it killed me. As coldly as I could, I told the cat, "As *Master* Kendar, Chief Wizard to His Majesty, King Steffan, I do not yell *Yo!* at anybody. And as *wife* to King Steffan's Chief Wizard, the lady Mysti would never in a million years dream of responding to such a rude, crude, barbaric—"

A loud crash sounded somewhere in the palace, followed by a musical voice raised in very un-musical rage. "Son of a dirty, rotten, stinking tree-toad's moldy gizzard! Stop floating in my *face*, you miserable ball. I *said* I was coming! Don't I even get to finish one blue-bleeding *chapter* in peace? Kendar? Kendar! Kendar Gangle, what in the name of the sixteen-and-a-half gods of skin blemishes do you want *now*?"

There came another crash and the message-bubble flew back down the hall a lot faster than I sent it. It whizzed past my right ear and smashed into a hundred glittering pieces against the wall. I threw myself flat on the floor just in time. Shattered Majyk can make some nasty cuts.

Heavily booted footsteps rang through the hall. Tall and slim and lovely—except she had a look in her eye that would broil a basilisk—Mysti clomped in. She was dressed for voondrab hunting—swampproof boots, leather trousers, loose tunic, short cape—but the sudden change in the weather had canceled her plans. She planted her fists on her hips, tossed back her thick mane of golden hair, and shouted, "*Yo!* I asked you a question."

I was still hugging the floor. Scandal stepped gracefully over to purr in my ear, "Tell me, *maestro*, do Welfies get P.M.S.?"

I think I just had time to reply, "Huh?" when there was a flash of lightning, a crump of thunder, and a gust of wind that drove straight through the still-open door.

Twenty-eight wild geese, two dozen sea gulls, six dodo birds, and one royal messenger blew in, knocking Mysti off her feet, boots and all.

Mysti killed two of the geese and one dodo on the spot, using her bare hands. She would have done the same thing with the royal messenger if he hadn't been so fast on his feet. Scandal and I shooed the surviving birds out the door and shut it tight, then tried to convince the messenger it was safe to climb down off the coat rack.

"Not until you banish the fiend," he said.

"What fiend?"

"That one." He gestured at Mysti with the royal scroll he carried. (You can always tell one of King Steffan's royal scrolls: It's so tied up with ribbons and sealing wax and tassels that it looks like a parchment bundle of soggy noodles. I wish he'd send postcards like everyone else.)

I glanced at Mysti. She did look kind of fiendish, standing there in a cloud of flying feathers, her hair all wild and her hands covered with blood. Still . . .

"That's no fiend," I said. "That's my wife."

"The devil you say!" the messenger replied. He clung to the coat rack. "No, no, I'm sorry, I can't take your word for it. This is my first time carrying a message to a wizard, so I did my homework. It says plain as day in the Messengers, Heralds, and Postal Workers Handbook (Part V, Section D, Sub-section 201a: Delivery Service to Wizards, Witches, Warlocks, and Sundry Select Sorcerers) that most of you don't like to be disturbed. That's why you guard your home with all kinds of traps, pitfalls, and monsters."

"It cuts down on the junk mail," Scandal said.

The messenger stared at Scandal, and his eyes got big as cartwheels. "Another fiend!" he gasped.

"No, that's a cat," I said. "His name's Scandal."

The messenger gave me a suspicious look. "Cats don't exist," he said in a stony voice. "Except in myths and fairy tales. They are unnatural creatures who have nine lives, always fall on their feet, steal the breath from sleeping babies, bring bad luck when they cross your path—"

"Booga-booga," Scandal remarked.

"This cat is real," I said. "He's just not from around here." I was willing to tell the king's messenger the whole story of how

Scandal came to Orbix through a strange one-way passage the size of a rat hole. I was even ready to show him the very rat hole itself, down in the kitchens of Master Thengor's palace.

Unfortunately, before I could offer, the messenger's weight pulled the coat rack right off the wall. The king's scroll went flying one way, the messenger the other, both of them landing with a sickening *crunch*!

A little while later, the messenger awoke in one of the guest bedrooms. Mysti was patting one side of his face with a damp towel, Scandal was licking the other. He took one look at the two "fiends" bending over his helpless body and fainted away. They snickered.

A slightly longer little while later, over a delicious dinner of roast dodo, I read the king's message.

"He wants me to come to him at once," I announced, putting the scroll down in my salad.

"Any particular reason?" Scandal asked. "Or does he just miss your pretty face?"

"If it's about those Raptura Eglantine books of his I borrowed, tell him I'm still reading them," Mysti said. "Whenever I get a little time off from housework, *some* people I could mention interrupt me." She jabbed the roast dodo viciously with the carving knife.

The messenger jumped. "Um, er, I assure you, my lady, His Majesty is in no rush to get his old books back. He is quite content with the divine Eglantine's latest novel, *My Dragonlord, My Destiny*."

"The sequel to *My Sorcerer, My Soul?*" Mysti asked eagerly.

"My God, my stomach," Scandal muttered, making little here-comes-a-hairball noises.

"Sshh!" I scowled at him. He should know better than to say one word against Raptura Eglantine around me. I tapped my wineglass with a knife to get everyone's attention. I broke the wineglass. "If you really want to know what the king said, I'll read the letter."

"Please do." Mysti settled back in her chair.

I cleared my throat and began: "My dear Master Kendar, everyone complains about the weather but no one does anything about it. These stupid birds have been falling out of the sky on and off for three weeks. I can put up with a few bluejays and a sprinkling of finches now and then, but on days when it rains titmice we can't get any business done because everyone goes around giggling and telling nasty jokes. Last week my Minister of

Finance got clobbered by a penguin. He hasn't been the same since. When I asked him for new ideas to raise the royal revenues, he suggested *taxing the money people earn!* Do I really *need* a revolution? Clearly the man has lost his mind. This has gone far enough. As my Chief Wizard, I call upon you to put a stop to this. Come to me at once, on pain of death. Your friend, King Steffan."

"A reasonable request," Mysti said. "When do we leave?"

"We leave tomorrow morning." I took a deep breath. "*We* being me and Scandal. Not you."

"*What?*" Msyti's lovely face twisted into an ugly mask. Her hand closed around the hilt of the carving knife.

"I said—"

She yanked the huge blade out of the roast dodo.

"—not—"

The king's messenger gave a strangled scream and dived under the table.

"—you."

The knife whipped through the air, straight for my heart.

CHAPTER ——————— 2

"HI," I SAID, PICKING UP THE TABLECLOTH AND LOOKING underneath. The king's messenger crouched in the shadows, shivering. I waved to him. It seemed like the friendly thing to do. "It's all right, you can come out now."

"Is the fiend—your wife—dealt with?" he asked, staying where he was.

"Oh, yeah, sure, you bet, uh-huh."

He gave me a suspicious look. "I heard a loud explosion. Was that—?"

Scandal trotted under the table to join the messenger. "You were expecting maybe a *quiet* explosion? Look, buddy, if the boss tells you it's O.K. to come out, then it's O.K. to come out."

"Certainly, certainly, no disrespect intended." The messenger crawled out from beneath the table and brushed himself off. He glanced at Mysti's empty chair. "I am truly sorry it came to violence, my lord Master Kendar. The lady was quite fetching, for a fiend, but even the best of husbands has his limits."

"Yeah, this wasn't the first time she lost her temper like that," I said. "But that's part of being a Welfie."

"An ex-Welfie," Scandal corrected me. "She got booted out of the corps when she married you, remember?"

"Well, was that *my* fault?" I demanded. "It's not like I *wanted* to marry her or anything. They forced me!"

"He talks like that all the time." The cat spoke to the messenger as if the two of them were old friends. "Maybe she hears him, maybe she doesn't. With pointed ears, you pick up a lot of what you shouldn't, know what I mean? Nudge, nudge, wink, wink?" He twitched his own ears at King Steffan's man.

"Er, yes," the messenger replied, edging away. "To be sure. An ex-Welfie, just as you say."

7

I sighed. "Welfies are hard to live with, ex or not. I guess when you're born immortal, beautiful, and loaded with natural Majyk, you can get a little spoiled. I had to do *something*." I had an afterthought. "You won't tell King Steffan about this, will you?"

"Domestic quarrels can be so indelicate." Still staring at the vacant chair, the messenger shook his head. "If you chose to explode your wife for attempting to thrust a knife through your heart, it's none of my bus— "

He looked at my chest for the first time. The carving knife was sticking out by only half the handle. The rest was sunk deep into my flesh. Mysti never knew her own strength. There was no blood, just an eerie green glow oozing from the hole in my shirt.

"Could you give me a hand pulling this out?" I asked. "I can't get a good grip on it."

The messenger was not helpful. He fainted again.

Mysti came back from the kitchen, carrying a tray. She looked at the messenger. "Can I have his dessert?" she asked.

"You can try," I told her. "But you know what it's going to taste like."

"I know: nectar and ambrosia and honeydew and all the traditional Welfie slop I had to guzzle when I was living in the jolly greenwood with those other pointy-eared losers. *Those* were the days." She gagged. "Oh, what I wouldn't have given for a nice, rare, juicy beefsteak back then." She stuck out her lower lip at me. "Except now if I eat a beefsteak, it'll taste like—like—Ohhhh! That was just *mean,* Kendar."

"And *this* wasn't?" I pointed at the knife.

"You big baby, it won't *kill* you."

I knew that. "It *can't* kill me. My Majyk won't let anything this simple kill me. But it *can* ruin my favorite shirt, and for all I know, there's going to be this big open wound left in my chest when you pull the knife out. I don't want to have a knothole!"

"Dammit, Jim, he's a man, not a pine tree!" Scandal rasped from the floor.

Mysti just shook her head, grabbed the handle, and yanked. The knife came out with a wet-sounding *shlooooorrp*! I looked down and saw that the hole in my chest had sealed itself. The hole in my shirt had not.

"I'll mend it for you," Mysti said without being asked. "And I'm sorry I did it. I lost my temper. It won't happen again. I promise, Welfie's honor." She kissed her pinky. "*Now* can I come with you to the city?"

"No."

Mysti's knuckles turned white around the knife handle.

"I mean," I said hastily, "that you'd only be bored. This is a business trip. I'll be locked up in a stuffy old council room with the king for hours. Then I'll have to go down into the palace cellars to work up a spell to stop this awful weather. I'll probably have to meet with a lot of other wizards, too, and you know what they're like: always showing off their latest tricks, or talking about how hard it is to housebreak their familiars, or telling the same old jokes about the traveling merchant and the sorcerer's daughter."

"I've never heard that joke even once," Mysti said, her eyes getting harder and smaller. I felt the temperature in the room go up, and I didn't like it.

"There's nothing for you to do in Grashgoboum at this time of the year," I went on desperately. "No markets, no festivals, no—"

"Never mind." Mysti dropped the knife on the table.

"What?"

"I said forget it." She turned her back on me. "You go, I stay. Have a nice time." She started to leave the room.

"Wait a minute!" I caught up with her in the doorway. "Where are you going?"

"To pack some things." She looked at me indifferently. I went from hot to cold, and I liked it even less.

"Things—?"

"Your things. For the trip. Will you be taking the carpet?"

"Um, er, well . . ."

The carpet was the Welfies' wedding gift to Mysti and me. When we first met, Mysti had a pair of the biggest, softest, most beautiful wings you ever saw. (All Welfie women can fly, which Mysti says is great because that way they can get away from Welfie men.) When we were forced to get married, the chief Welfie tore them off her back as a sign that she was now no longer part of the tribe—uh, herd—um, gang. Well, whatever you call too many Welfies living together in one place, she wasn't part of it anymore. The minute the wings came off, they melted like rainbow sherbet all over the white carpet we were standing on during the wedding ceremony.

The result was a flying carpet. Most of the time.

"No, I think I'll just ride Nintari," I told her. Nintari was my horse, a gift from good King Steffan. I don't know why he gave him to me. I never did anything nasty to him.

Mysti looked dubious. "You think you'll be able to stay on top of the beast long enough to reach Grashgoboum?" she asked.

I took offense. "Nintari hasn't thrown me in three whole weeks!"

"Uh-huh," she said.

Translation: *You mean you haven't* ridden *Nintari for three whole weeks.*

"That's not true!" I shouted. And it wasn't. I hadn't ridden Nintari for two and a half weeks, and when I finally gave it a try, he didn't throw me off, he lay down in the mud and tried to roll on me. Only my Majyk saved me from becoming a pancake.

"I don't know why you won't take the carpet."

"I like to ride. And besides, the king's messenger came on horseback. It would be rude to leave him behind."

"Uh-huh."

Translation: *You're afraid that you won't be able to make the carpet fly without me there to help you.*

"I *love* to ride," I insisted. "I get along wonderfully with horses. If my sister was here, she'd tell you how all the horses at Uxwudge Manor always used to follow me around." That was true. I ran away screaming and they followed, snapping their big ugly teeth at my head. "Horses and I understand each other." Also true. They understood that they could fracture my skull with one kick, and I understood that they were just waiting for the chance to try.

"Well, suit yourself." Mysti shrugged. "I'll bring your bag down to the stable. You saddle up Nintari."

I caught her by the hand a second time. "Look, why don't you saddle up Nintari and I'll pack? I know what I need to take with me."

"I've got an even better idea." She pulled her hand away. "You pack *and* you saddle Nintari. I've got other chores to do." And she was gone.

"Bad call," said Scandal.

"Oh, shut up." I scowled and kicked the table leg. Then a happy thought hit me. "Say, do you think I could persuade the messenger to saddle that monster for me?"

"Why not?" The cat switched his tail. "You're the big *kahuna* around these parts. Now if only you could get him to *ride* the horse for you, you'd be set."

We revived the messenger, who agreed to saddle my horse. He was so eager to get out of the palace that he would have agreed to saddle a fire-breathing dragon. As I stood by the mounting block in the stable courtyard, watching King Steffan's man lash my pack to Nintari's rump, the weather took a kindly turn.

"Terns," Scandal said, observing the latest type of bird tumbling from the cloudy sky. "Great fliers. I especially like the way they can pull out of a nose dive and zoom away before hitting the ground—and me."

"They're sea birds," I said. "I guess they don't like falling this far inland." An old boyhood dream made me get all sentimental. (Well, all right, so I was just a couple of years out of boyhood, but it was still a dream!) "I wonder if I'll ever get to go to sea?"

Scandal made a noise I didn't think a cat could make at that end. "What are you, crazy? Why would anyone in his right mind—or even you—want to go to sea? It's wet, it heaves around all the time, it smells like very *old* dead fish, and once you fall in, *hasta la vista*, baby!"

"Have you been to sea, Scandal?"

"Are you kidding? The ship's cat is a tradition on Earth going back almost to the days of the first ships! We caught rats and ate 'em, when the rats weren't as big as three cats put together. Then they ate us. We drank the same slimy water as the crew. If we did a good job, maybe the captain wouldn't use us for fish bait. When we ran out of lives and luck, we'd get washed overboard during a storm and drown. Gee, Kendar, with all *that* to look forward to, I just don't know why I didn't rush right out and sign up with the Navy!"

I thought about what he said. "So you don't want to see strange new worlds on another shore? To seek out new life and new civilizations just over the horizon? To boldly go where no cat—?"

"Ready, my lord," the messenger called. He stepped back, holding Nintari's reins. My horse was the picture of docility. He batted his eyelashes at me and whickered happily as I edged nearer. The messenger was impressed. "Goodness, how fortunate you are, my lord Master Kendar, to have such an affectionate steed."

"Oh, yes, Nintari just loves me," I said. Why bother telling the man that what Nintari really loved was getting another chance to try mashing me like a potato.

"Beam me up, boss," Scandal directed.

"What?"

"Okay, *pick* me up and put me on top of your pack."

"I thought I'd carry you in front of me, in the saddle," I said.

"Think again. You're riding a four-footed member of Murder Incorporated. If he bucks, you'll jerk forward and I'll get squashed. But if I ride on your pack, I can hold onto it with my claws. Besides, the minute I see Mr. Dead act up, I can use the same claws to teach him some manners. *Capeesh?*"

I had my doubts about Scandal's plan, and said so. If I were a beast the size of Nintari and I felt something jab my rump, I wouldn't behave, I'd do my best to get that annoying little pincushion off me by bucking, rearing, rolling, biting, or any combination of the above.

"Hey, you don't want to do it, you don't have to," the cat said. "*No problemo, kemo sabe.* But I'm not riding with *you.* My mama didn't raise me to be pavement pizza."

"Couldn't you just *ask* Nintari to behave?" I suggested.

"What do I look like? Dr. Dolittle? *No hablo* horsie-worsie."

"I thought—" Actually, what I thought was pretty stupid, when I stopped to reconsider. And since Scandal never did have a very high opinion of any human's mental abilities, I decided to shut up.

Too late. "I can guess what you thought." Scandal pounced on my words like they were mice. Fat, stupid mice. "You thought that all animals speak the same language."

"They don't?"

"Do all humans? Gimme a break, bwana. I don't know how it works on Orbix, but back where I come from I only understood what other cats were saying."

"Gee, that's too bad."

"No, it's not." Scandal was firm. "When a big dog's chasing me, I don't want to know what he's calling my mother. And when I'm closing in on a mouse, I don't care if she can sing *opera*; she's still lunch. But you'd think it was *cute* if you could understand the language of animals. Yeah, I'll bet you would! Out for a little stroll in the pasture and up comes Mrs. Moo-cow who says, 'Good morning, Master Kendar. I have some lovely fresh milk for you today,' right? Well, if you *could* talk the talk, the odds are a whole lot better Mrs. Moo-cow would grab you by the neck, shake you until your brains rattled, and shout, 'What the hell did you do with my calf and why does your breath reek of veal scallopine?' "

I sighed. "I wonder if it's that bad on the Underside."

"The underside of what?" Scandal asked.

"You know, the *Underside*. The last time the planet changed, it changed the animals living on the Underside." The cat was staring at me like I was crazy. I looked around for a way to illustrate what I meant. The king's messenger was already mounted on his own horse, so I dropped Nintari's reins, taking a chance that he'd stay put. He did. He was biding his time. I found a length of worn-out bridle strap cast aside in the dirt near the stables. Perfect. Stretching it out flat, I gave it a single twist, then brought the ends together. I now had a pretty good model of the funny bow-tie shape my planet was in. For the time being.

(Ages ago, Orbix was an ordinary place to live until a pair of wizards got into a Majyk duel. By the time they were through, they'd left the planet with a bad case of the geological hiccups. No one knew when the next shape-shift was coming, or what shape we'd be in after it came. Mothers liked to scare bad children with stories about how if they didn't behave, one day they'd wake up and the world would be *round* with everyone trapped on the *outside* until they were flung off into space. But that's just a fairy tale.)

"Oh, yeah!" said Scandal, recalling what I'd shown him before. "Like that bear we once met on the road; the one driving a porridge-wagon pulled by those cute little goldy-haired girls. He could talk, and he even dressed human. *He* was from the Underside."

"Right," I agreed. "So were they. There were people living on the Underside when the change hit. I wonder if all of them get treated like animals and all the animals act like people? And if not, do they use nonhuman animals the same way we do? *Can* they? And what about—?"

"Humans." The cat always sounded tired when he talked about us. "Top of the food chain and bottom of the brain barrel. The king's waiting to see you, you got your wife so mad at you I could broil a mouse on her forehead, you've got whooping cranes and kiwis falling out of the sky, and *you're* worried about how things are on the Underside? *Priorities*, Kendar; get some. Now get on the horse and let's go."

Scandal swaggered away, tail high, and bummed a ride from the king's messenger. I picked up Nintari's reins. The horse batted his eyelashes at me again, then lunged for my arm. I jumped away before those teeth could take a chunk out of me. The horse laughed, and I grabbed the chance to scramble onto his back.

"On to Grashgoboum!" I announced in triumph.

Nintari did a casual little sidestep and I toppled off.

"The journey of a thousand miles begins with a single pratfall," Scandal said solemnly.

"Oh, shut up."

"BEHOLD, THE ANCIENT AND HIGH-TOWERED ROYAL city of Grashgoboum!" The king's messenger raised himself in the stirrups and made a sweeping gesture at the horizon.

"We've seen it," Scandal said. "Also called the City of Towers, yippee. I *still* say it looks like a lot of pencils stuck in the ground." The cat was walking alongside the horses. He claimed it was to stretch his legs. I knew it was to be right there, ready to laugh in my face every time I fell off Nintari.

"The palace towers in all their splendor are built only of a rare and valuable stone whose deep amber hue is richly flecked with gold," the messenger replied. "No other sight can equal them for beauty."

"If you like pencils," the cat maintained.

The messenger got grumpy. "Hmph! I can see how *some* clods would not appreciate our fair capital." He gave Scandal a disdainful stare. During our trip to Grashgoboum, he'd gotten used to the cat. He no longer thought Scandal was a nasty, dangerous, mythical monster; he just thought he was nasty. "Ah, truly it will be a pleasure to savor once more the exquisite delights of yon fabled town: the beautiful women of the court, the tasty morsels of the king's own cooks, the sweet melodies of the happy minstrels—"

"The flush toilets?" Scandal asked innocently.

"The what?"

"Never mind. As long as you can scare up a box full of clean sand, I'm a happy kitty."

I fell off Nintari again.

When I got back on, we rode towards the city. Maybe I should say the *cities*; King Steffan's capital was equally divided between the towers of the palace and the cluster of slums surrounding it. The first time we saw Grashgoboum, Scandal said the low, crumbling slum dwellings looked like a lather of dirty soap bubbles washing the feet of the golden towers. In Grashgoboum, either you had a palace address or you were nobody.

You were also probably sharing a room with rats, roaches, and rubbish. The palace or the slums; that was it as far as choices went when you lived in Grashgoboum.

The messenger led us through some of the cleaner streets to the main palace gate. The clustered towers of King Steffan's home shot up behind a curtain of gray stone raised by my old teacher, Master Thengor. The wall itself wasn't much taller than a man on horseback. I remember Master Thengor saying, "It won't stop an army, but it will keep the riffraff out. And since there are always more riffraff than armies, I do believe I gave His Majesty his royal money's worth."

He loved to lecture us about how he was the first wizard to perfect the "riffraffproof" spell. I didn't know what he was talking about; all I knew was he spit between his teeth every time he said "riffraffproof."

I didn't suspect it, but I was about to witness my former teacher's spell in action, minus all that spit.

As we trotted up to the palace gate, I saw a number of callers ahead of us. Some were the king's own servants, clad in Steffan's official black-and-blue livery. Some were ambassadors dressed in the gaudy, startling, often silly-looking costumes of faraway lands. Some were successful merchants, many of them better dressed than the ambassadors or the king's men, come to sell expensive wares. Some were the better class of bards, dressed in good plain traveling garb, with perhaps a silver ring or two on their fingers to show they were doing well.

But most of the people knocking at the palace gate were wandering jugglers, tumblers, singers, and assorted entertainers whose clothing was rags and air. The only way they'd get a silver ring to wear was if they could find a high-class bard so drunk he never felt them slip it off his finger while he snored at the tavern table. This was riffraff with a capital *riff* and very raffish. But that didn't matter; no law said they couldn't come try their luck at the palace gates.

No law at all; just Master Thengor's spell.

We pulled up our horses behind a troupe of raggedy mountebanks. There were six of them, wearing only enough clothing to keep four people warm. They had a rickety wooden cart full of battered juggling equipment and costumes for a play. A little girl sat on top of the pile, holding a sad-eyed monkey. She looked as

if she could have done with a good meal, but for the moment she
forgot her hunger. She was gazing up awestruck at the magnificent
carvings over the gateway. There was one figure of a wide-winged
gryphon at the very top of the arch that was particularly impressive. Meanwhile, the leader of the troupe was having words with
one of the eight gateway guards.

"I tell you, King Steffan will have your head if you delay us any
longer," he said, shaking his fist under the foremost guard's nose.
"We have come here at great trouble and expense, across vast
deserts, through dark forests, over trackless wastes, broiled by the
sun, soaked by the rain, battered by an unexpected storm of herons
and egrets—"

The guard yawned. "I tol' yer, if yer name ain't on the king's
list, I can't let yer in this gate." He leaned on his spear and called
to the guard nearest the gate, "Yer find 'em on the list yet, Verix?"

Verix was scrawnier than any guard I'd ever seen. He had a long
parchment scroll in his hands, which was giving him a lot of
trouble. He kept trying to unroll one end while rolling up the other,
except both ends kept unrolling all over the place. He probably
could have handled it better if not for the fact that he also had an
official palace guard's spear to manage at the same time.

(Why do they always give the guards at the gate those
extra-long spears with the gilded points and the tassels hanging
down? A spear is all right if you've just got to fight a single
horseman or a lone foot soldier, but the only way an enemy attacks
the palace gate is by throwing lots and lots of troops at it all at
once. A plain short-sword would be better. That way the guards
could kill two or three attackers before they got crushed to jelly
and rivets. And those tassels—! Maybe they're good for making
into tourniquets afterwards; I don't know.)

Aside from the spear and the scroll, Verix had other problems: His
helmet didn't fit him well. It kept slipping forward over his eyes,
knocking his wire-rimmed glasses down to the end of his beaky nose.
By the time he got the spear balanced against his shoulder, the scroll
reeled in and unrolled to the right place, his helmet adjusted and his
glasses up, he was in a rotten mood.

"No, I *haven't* found them!" he snapped. "I didn't find them the
other four times you asked. Now, are you going to do your job and
send them packing, or do I have to do everything?"

The first guard snickered. "Yer heard Verix," he drawled.
"Don't go gettin' him mad. He's a real tiger when he's got the wind
up him. Best go round to the city gate and find some tavern work.
Market day's comin' in a bit; yer won't starve."

"Bah! What do we care for your catchcoin markets and taverns?" the troupe leader declared. "I tell you, we were sent for by His Majesty's own word! Is it our fault if some overpaid royal scribe forgot to make a note of it on that list? Melina!" He clapped his hands briskly. "Fetch me the king's letter!"

A thin woman hurried to join him. She pulled up the top layer of her tattered skirts and pulled out a dirty piece of paper. "The king's letter," she said, handing it over to the guard.

"And bought by the bunch from any penman-for-hire who wants the price of a beer," the guard replied. "Wish as how I had a day off for every one of these I've seen. I could retire."

"I assure you, *this* one is real," the chief player persisted.

"And I assure *yer*, yer time's up. Now move along. There's others waiting."

The player folded his arms across his chest. "We are not moving until you let us in." All of his people did the same, even the little girl in the cart. The sad-eyed monkey just sat there, too travel-worn to even chatter.

"All right," the guard said. "If that's how yer want to play it. I don't like havin' to do this—" He said it in a way that let everyone know he didn't *like* to do whatever "this" was, he *loved* to do it! "But yer don't leave me no choice. Hey, Verix!"

Verix snorted angrily and his helmet clipped the bridge of his nose again. "What is it *now?*"

"Tell the other fellas: It's time to say *the word.*"

"What wor—? Ohhhh! *That* word." Verix shoved his helmet back on his head. He had an ugly smile. "Right you are." He turned and hollered at the six other guards, "Hoi! Men! Guess what time it is?"

"Lunch time?"

"Nap time?"

"Gawfee-break time?"

"Hamster ti—?"

Verix threw his scroll at them. "No, no, *no,* you overmuscled idiots! It's say-the-magic-*word* time! On the count of three—"

"What magic word?" one of the guards asked.

"What do you mean, 'what magic word,' Simbert? You know very well what magic word! The magic word what that old wizard gave us all to say whenever there was stubborn riffraff knocking at good King Steffan's door just as if they were real people!"

"Oh." Simbert was big enough to make three of Verix. Heck, the muscles he had on one arm were enough meat to make a Verix and a half. He could have snapped Verix like a twig, but instead he just stuck out his lower lip and looked embarrassed. "I forgot it," he told his boots.

"How could you forget it?" Verix was in a red rage by now. "It's written on the inside of your helmet, for Wedwel's sake!"

"Oh?" The guard started to undo his chin strap.

"What do you think you're doing?" Verix bawled.

"Just takin' off me helmet to have a look-see at the magic word what we've all got to say so's this riffraff'll shift off," Simbert replied.

Verix lifted his nose a little higher. "Rule Number 437d of the Palace Guards Rulebook clearly says that no guard is to remove any part of his uniform while on duty."

"Yeah, but I don't remember the magic word I've gotta say an' you just told me that it's writ inside me helmet an'—Oh, blazes take it. I'll just let the other lads say it, then."

"No," said Verix.

"Huh?" Simbert replied, as who wouldn't?

"When the late, great Court Wizard, Master Thengor, gave our good King Steffan that spell, he specifically stated that it must be uttered by at least eight guards at the same time for it to work."

"Oh. Orright." Simbert reached for his chin strap again.

"Stop!" Verix shouted. He sounded angry, but I was starting to notice the ghost of a really nasty leer playing around his lips. He was *enjoying* this! If this guy wasn't up to something mean, I'd eat a voondrab. "Step out of uniform, Simbert, and I'll have no choice but to place you under arrest."

"Yeah, but if I don't get a look at the word what I'm supposed to say, I can't *say* it, can I? And then what?"

"And then"—Verix's nasty leer came out into the open—"you will be guilty of not doing your official duty and I will have to arrest you for *that*."

"Well, clip my tail and call me a schnauzer," Scandal murmured. "It looks like Ichabod Crane's got an axe to grind with Simbert's name on it."

"I wonder why?" I said.

"Gosh, just a wild guess, but have you ever heard of *envy*? I mean, take a look at the two of them! Not exactly the Doublemint twins. I bet when Saturday night rolls around, all the girls tell Verix they're sorry, but they're washing their hair. Only it's Simbert's hair they're washing, and it's all on his chest, and they're washing it with their—"

"I get the idea!"

"You wish." Scandal chuckled. "Most of the king's guards look like they were raised on milk 'n' steroids, but Simbert's got enough beef on him to feed Texas."

"Who's Texas?" I asked. I loved Scandal, but I don't always follow everything he says.

"Texas is a very big, very loud, very friendly giant who lives on my home world. He only eats barbecued beef and Democrats. Once he tried to swallow a televangelist's line and it made him break out in armadillos."

I winced. "That sounds painful." Scandal grinned. "It also sounds like a load of what Nintari's been dropping all the way here."

"You?" the cat asked sweetly.

Scrawny little Verix had poor Simbert backed into an imaginary corner. The muscular guardsman was reaching for his helmet, dropping his hands, reaching for his helmet, dropping his hands, and at the same time trying to hang onto that awkward spear of his. His six other companions stood around impatiently, watching Verix have his fun. The people waiting in line at the gate were starting to grumble. Ugly scowls and angry words were flying, most of them aimed right at the troupe of traveling players. The little girl in the cart began to tremble at some of the things the crowd was saying.

"Why are they picking on the actors?" I asked, thinking out loud. "This delay isn't their fault."

"They've got to blame someone," the king's messenger replied. He sounded bored and annoyed. At the palace gate, everyone from lowest acrobat to highest diplomat had to wait his turn with the guards. That included royal messengers and Court Wizards. "If you shout awful names at a piece of tatterdemalion road-trash, what's the worst that can happen? Nothing. They're used to worse insults. But if you raise your voice to one of the king's own guards—" He shrugged.

"*F-thannnnng!* Goooosh! Ooops," Scandal said.

"What?"

"That's the sound of a spear going off by accident," the cat told me. "And that's what happens if you mouth off to one of the Godzilla Brothers, I betcha."

I guess he was right. Scandal was usually right about such things. Still, it didn't seem fair to me. Maybe that's because for most of my life I was always the safest one to blame for anything that went wrong. If one of the better students at Master Thengor's Academy of High Wizardry stole some cake from the kitchen, would Velma Chiefcook punish him? Not unless she wanted to be turned into a toad. (A toad would have been an improvement on her looks, but she refused to believe that.) But Velma had to punish *someone*, so even if the real thief was sitting there munching the stolen cake right under her nose, guess who she whacked with her ladle?

Right.

I hated that, but I was too powerless to do anything about it. Then I accidentally got hold of most of Master Thengor's Majyk, and everything changed.

Not everything: I still hated it when people picked on someone who didn't deserve it. Only now I *could* do something about it.

The question was: *What?*

I leaned forward enough so that I could whisper in Nintari's ear. "Okay, horse," I said. "For once, I really need you to play nice. I've got to make an impression on these people. A *good* impression. Throw me off now, and the first chance I get, I'm going to look up the right spell for turning you into a horse chestnut. Got it?"

I don't know if horses can understand human speech, but I'm willing to bet they do. Nintari got it. When I touched my heels to his flanks, he gave the most gorgeous, awe-inspiring, bugling call. Everyone turned to look. He reared up just enough for effect without making me slide off, and flailed the air with his forefeet, snorting loudly.

I heard the troupe leader breathe, "Egad! What a performance!" I swear Nintari must have heard him too, because the beast actually made a little bow before gathering his hindquarters and leaping forward, light as a sparrow. He landed neatly between the players and the guards, his nostrils flaring, tossing his mane.

"Enough, enough," I whispered to him. No good; he was a born ham. He snorted and pawed the ground and tossed his mane some more. I'll bet he would have gone on like that for hours if the little girl hadn't put down her monkey and come over.

"Nice horsie," she said, grabbing his bridle and stroking his nose.

"Awwwwwwwww!" said everyone, guards included (except Verix).

I lifted one hand in a heroic gesture. "In the name of good King Steffan and the great Council of Wizardry, I command you all to be silent!"

They obeyed, sort of. They were all (except Verix) still going "Awwwwwwwww!" over the little girl and the horse. It would have to do.

"I am Master Kendar, His Majesty's duly appointed Court Wizard!" I declared.

"Never heard of you!" came a cry from the back of the crowd.

"What? That baby, the king's Court Wizard?" a second voice chimed in. "He doesn't look old enough to change a tadpole into a frog!"

"Not old enough ter change 'is own diapers!" a third hollered.

"Not old enough to change his mind!"

"If you're a wizard, do the one where you pull a rappid outa yer hat!" someone demanded.

"Ha! He hasn't even *got* no hat!"

"Say, that's right. If he's a wizard, where's his pointy hat?"

"And his robe!"

"And his whatd'youcall'em—his stick thing!"

"*Wand,* you moron."

"Right! Wand! Where's that, then?"

"Nice going, Fearless Leader," Scandal remarked. He had crept through a forest of legs to claim his usual place at Nintari's feet. "Now they've got someone else to blame."

I dropped the reins and stretched out my arms like I was getting ready to cast a spell. I knew I was putting a lot of trust in Nintari, but the horse was so busy being adored by the little girl that he forgot about dumping me. I put on my blackest scowl and said, "I will prove to you that I am a wizard! I will make that man"—I pointed at Verix—"rise high into the air before your very eyes!"

Verix squinted at me through his glasses. "I'd like to see you try."

"Very well." I began to make complicated motions with my hands. "You asked for it." I made it sound like I was really saying *Where do you want the body shipped?*

(You see, I may not know how to use all the Majyk I've got, but I have learned one thing: It's not what you know, it's what you *pretend* you know. Act like an all-powerful wizard, and nine out of ten people will treat you like an all-powerful wizard. Act like yourself and you'll get hit with a ladle.)

I added some fancy finger-wiggling to the hand gestures and muttered strange words under my breath. They didn't mean anything, but they sounded very impressive. "Gorbaduc-gammer-gurton-coriolanus-buchanan-cambyses-beowulf!" I growled. I heard a strange sound from the ground: Scandal was laughing. "Lhasa-apso-calypso-shuttup-oryouradead-pussycat-Imeanit!" Scandal got the message.

So did Verix. He started to look nervous and kept shifting his weight from one foot to the other, checking to see if they were still close to the ground. "Um, I say, this really isn't necessary!" he exclaimed at last.

I let my hands drop and continued to glower at him. "Oh?" I said as coldly as I could. I sat even taller in the saddle. "And why is that?" (It's hard to sound like a still-angry all-powerful wizard when what you really want to do is jump around yelling *He bought it! He bought it! Thank all the gods, he bought it!* You see, I can actually do a levitation spell, but there have been a few times when it didn't work *quite* the way I wanted it to, if you know what I mean. I've got the bruises to prove it.)

"Well, Your Wizardliness, *I* never doubted for a moment that you are who you say. But you know how it is—" He nodded towards the crowd, many of whom were still howling taunts at me. "Some people wouldn't believe they were dead if you handed them their own head on a platter."

"Is that what you suggest I do to prove my identity?" I made my smile as hard and thin as the edge of a sword. "Cut off your head?"

"Nononononono. I wouldn't want to bother you with that. Something simple. Nothing messy. Your choice."

"Very well." I tried to sound reluctant about the whole thing, even though I was just as much in favor of "Nothing messy" as Verix was. I turned halfway round in the saddle to address the crowd. "I shall now use my magical powers to determine once and for all whether these people have any right to enter good King Steffan's palace!"

I motioned for the skinny woman, Melina, to approach me. "Where is the letter?"

She pointed to the first guard at the gate, but before she could say *He's got it*, the paper was in my hand.

As I read the letter, I felt a soft paw poke into my mind. *Well, what's the verdict, Perry Mason? Is it the real McCoy?*

I wish you'd stop doing that, I thought at the cat.

Hey, I don't do it all the time. On my world, lotsa people think cats can read minds. Is it my fault if on your world it works?

I don't care. I want you out of my mind!

Hey, being out of your mind is your job. O.K., O.K., I'm going, but first I wanna know if that letter's real or not.

Oh, it's real.

How can you tell, Mister Wizard?

This is an official royal invitation to perform at the palace. It's written in the king's own handwriting on the back of a crumpled-up fan letter to Raptura Eglantine. Poor King Steffan never got up the nerve to send it, so he used it for scrap paper.

Yep, that's King Steffan, all right, Scandal admitted. *But not everyone in the crowd knows what his handwriting looks like, or that he's the biggest Raptura Eglantine romance fan on Orbix. How are you gonna convince them?* He nodded towards the grimly waiting throng.

I winked at the cat. *Watch me.*

I held the letter over my head so that everyone could see it. "In the name of high wizardry, may the all-seeing and all-knowing forces of Goodness and Honesty reveal unto me whether this document is genuine!" I shouted, and threw it into the air.

The paper didn't go very high. It didn't need to. As soon as it was airborne, it hovered right where it was and began to glow with an eerie pink light.

"Oooooh!" said someone in the crowd.

"Aaaaah!" said another.

"Ohhhhh!" said a third.

"All done with mirrors," said a troublemaker.

The glowing paper began to spin. Faster and faster it twirled, the corners shooting off short bursts of silver sparks. When it became a racing, glittering pinwheel, I heard more gasps from the crowd and even some applause.

"Nice stunt, bwana." It was Scandal. "Good thing you do fireworks better than you do floating. But what are you gonna do for an encore?"

"Wait." I whispered the right words under my breath (Oh, please, please, *please* let them be the right words!), and pointed dramatically at the spinning letter.

One by one, the words leaped from the page. They weren't just ink anymore; they were green flames that burned tall against the sky. Everyone in the crowd could see them, but in case that wasn't enough, King Steffan's unmistakable voice boomed out of the clouds, reading the words aloud.

I threw in a couple of giant singing butterflies and called it good enough.

The whole mob in front of the gate stood there with their mouths hanging open. Even the wandering players were stunned. "All I did was tell His Majesty I'd give that play of his a read-over," their leader was muttering half to himself. "It wasn't even original, just his version of Raptura Eglantine's *My Pixie, My Passion.* He gave me a copy that time we were all stuck in the Mole and Firkin tavern on the road to Vicinity City, and said if I was ever in Grashgoboum to look him up and tell him what I thought of it. Blessed Buskin, god of stage-trash, now I suppose we'll have to *perform* that stinkeroo!"

Verix stumbled forward to tap him on the shoulder. "Uh, by a marvelous coincidence I just happen to have found your name on the official royal entry list. Won't you please go right in? And if there's anything you need while you're here, don't hesitate to call on me."

As the troupe started to file through the gate, I turned off the Majyk. The letter stopped sparkling and drifted down into my hand. "Here," I said, smiling as I gave it to the little girl. "I think you'll want this back."

She took it and thanked me without a word. Dropping Nintari's bridle, she curtseyed quickly and scooted after the rest of the company. Nintari uttered a disappointed snort and sat down, mule-style.

I think you can guess where that left me.

"Are you dead, Jim?" Scandal asked, standing on my chest.

A well-dressed man walked by us, pausing only long enough to look down his snub nose at me and sneer, "Huh! Some wizard. Some magic. I knew it's all done with mirrors." I sat up in the dirt in time to hear him tell the guards, "Open up. The king is expecting me. I am the royal fishmonger, Pilchard Porbeagle, purveyor of fine finned fare to His Majesty." He waved at the train of servants behind him. There were a dozen of them, each groaning under the weight of a huge wicker basket strapped to his back.

The cat's nose quivered. "Salmon," he breathed. "Trout. Sword-fish. Lemme at 'em."

I sniffed the air. "I can't smell a thing."

"That's because it's *fresh* fish and you're only human. Kept on ice, I bet. Look at how the baskets are leaking. Those poor guys are getting their backs soaked *and* frozen. Howzabout you do another good deed and, uh, make some of that fish disappear?"

"I can't do that," I whispered, getting to my feet.

"I could," Scandal said wistfully.

In the meantime, Verix was fumbling with his scroll again. The royal fishmonger tapped his foot impatiently. It was obvious that he hadn't caught any of his own wares. Real fishermen know how to wait.

"Give me that!" he snapped, snatching the scroll out of Verix's hands. "*There's* my name! Right there, big as life!" He jabbed a finger at the parchment, then shoved it back into the guardsman's arms. "Why did the king ever hire a near-blind sludgebat like you for this job? If you can't see to read the entry list, what good are you?"

"I, um, I—" Poor Verix pushed his glasses up his nose a few times. He looked miserable. To make matters worse, a light sprinkle of loons began to fall from the sky. It didn't help Porbeagle's temper at all.

"Oh, who cares for your excuses? I'm a businessman, my lad. I don't have time for your Oh-I'm-so-sorry's and Oops-pardon-me's. Do you see these wretches? *Can* you see them?" He waved at his train of shivering servants. "Every one of them was once the master of his own fishing boat, each manned by a full crew. And every one of them was always *sooooo* understanding whenever a crewman showed up with some silly excuse like *Oh, please, can I have the day off, my wife's having a baby,* or *Could you let me have my pay a little early, my child's sick and we need to buy medicine."* He curled his lip. "This is where listening to excuses got them. Now I own their ships and their crews; they work for me."

"Oh, I'm—I'm so sorry," Verix stammered. "I mean—I mean, oops, pardon me. That is—"

At this worst of all possible moments, a loon hit Porbeagle right on the head. "If you don't open the gate and let us in out of this awful weather, I'll see to it that the king himself fires you!" he roared.

"Yes sir, at once, sir." Verix fumbled with the scroll. "I just have to check your name off, sir—"

The loon shower grew heavier. Now there were sea gulls and sandpipers mixed in. They hit the ground and immediately took wing, but they didn't fly away.

"They're after the fish, boss!" Scandal exclaimed. "They're dive-bombing the baskets!" He licked his chops "Mmmm, do I help them eat the fish or do I wait until they're so stuffed they can't fly, and then eat them? Decisions, decisions."

Porbeagle had no trouble with decision-making. "That does it!" he bellowed in Verix's face. "Not only will I have King Steffan fire you, but I'm going to take the price of every fish I lose out of *your* last salary!"

"But—but, sir—sir, all a royal guard gets paid is room and board and uniform and—and a little walkabout money."

The fishmonger showed a mouth full of small, pointy teeth. "In that case, I'll take *you."*

"Scandal, we've got to help him," I said softly.

"Yummmmm, fresh raw sea gull stuffed with—Oh, sorry, Kendar; you say something?"

"I said Porbeagle's already got too many slaves."

"Slaves?" The cat looked at the line of basket-bearers. The unlucky men were dancing around, flapping their arms, trying to keep the sea birds from getting at the fish.

"What would you call someone who's forced to work for Porbeagle?"

"Gotcha. I guess even Verix doesn't deserve that. So you gonna zap Porbeagle into a bunch of fish sticks?"

I bit my lower lip. "I can't do that."

"Why not? They're good with tartar sauce."

"I can't use my Majyk to destroy anyone."

"You mean you *won't*," the cat corrected me. "You're just an old softy. Lucky for you I like softies. Okay, tellya what I'm gonna do."

Only he didn't tell me, he *thought* it at me.

"Scandal, that's—that's *wicked*," I said as soon as I "heard" his idea.

It is, isn't it? He looked proud. *Well, shall I?*

"Be my guest."

It was just a moment later that good old Simbert blinked, looked around, and exclaimed, "Hoi! Verix! I got it!"

"Not now, you big oaf!" Verix called over his shoulder. "Can't you see I'm busy?" He went back to trying to placate Porbeagle.

"But Verix, I *got* it!" Simbert insisted.

"Got *what*?" Verix sighed.

"The *word*, Verix. I got the magical word. Honest. It come to me all of a sudden, it did." He raised his eyes to the heavens. "There was this mysterious voice inside my head an' it told me the word, plain as plain."

"Huh!" One of the other guards was skeptical. "As if Simbert ever had anything inside his head but air!"

"Now, now, could be it was one of the gods talkin'," another guard said. "You know the gods are fond of shouting things where they get a nice echo."

"Five copper *gabors* sez it ain't the right word," a third guard offered.

"Ten sez it is!"

"Twenty on Simbert forgetting it even if it *is* the right word!"

"Fifty he don't!"

"Fifty he gets the word right, then gets his *name* wrong after!"

With all that talk of money flying around, Porbeagle forgot

about the king and the fish and the sea gulls and Verix. "Did you say *fifty?*" The guards all nodded as one man. "Fifty over whether or not he knows *one word*?" They nodded again. The fishmonger grew suspicious. "What's so special about this word?"

"It's a magic word," Verix said. "If we all say it together, something very magical will happen."

"Is that so? All right, then." Porbegale dug into his belt pouch. "Here I have *one hundred* newly minted copper *gabors* that say your friend says that word right. I wager we'll have the proof of it if this so-called something very magical does happen." He dropped the money into Verix's cupped hands.

The startled guard dropped his spear and the scroll as he tried to catch the clinking coins. "Errrr—very well, sir. But it'll have to be all of us saying it at once, or else the spell won't work. Simbert, ready?"

Simbert's face was beaming. "Ready, Verix!"

"All right, then, lads, on three: A-one, a-two, a-three—"

"Paellyaalavalenciana!" all eight guards shouted in unison. Simbert shouted loudest of all.

"Well?" Porbeagle demanded. "Did he get it right?"

A deep rumbling filled the air. Everyone waiting for admission to the palace looked up automatically, checking the sky for thunderclouds. There wasn't even one to be seen, but the noise did frighten off the sea birds.

The rumbling sounded again, louder. I heard a pitter-patter, too. It wasn't rain—raindrops don't make such a solid-sounding noise. It was more like someone dropping handfuls of gravel from very high up.

And that's just what it was.

With a creak and a crack and a resounding POP! the huge carved gryphon over the palace gate broke free of the stone holding him. He flapped his wings once or twice, to get the kinks out. He yawned, opening his eagle's beak wide; then he stretched his lion's paws and arched his back just like Scandal waking up from a nap.

Then he looked down.

A bright golden spark flashed in his eyes. I know he had a beak, but he still seemed to smile. It was a scary smile. I was glad he wasn't smiling at me.

He was smiling at Porbeagle. Porbeagle wasn't smiling back. "Uh—" the fishmonger said. He started to back away from the palace gate.

The gryphon shook his feathery mane and let out a cry that was half lion's roar, half eagle's scream. He leaped into the air, wings beating, and circled overhead once. Then he dropped, talons reaching for the luckless fishmonger. Porbeagle squeaked just like a fieldmouse and ran, shoving his servants out of the way. The servants scattered in terror. The rest of the crowd thought this was a really good idea. Minstrels made tracks, merchants fled, horses stampeded, carts were overturned, actors fainted, women threw things, ambassadors screamed.

The king's messenger shouted, "I'll get help!" and galloped into the guards. Simbert tripped over his spear and stumbled into Verix. Verix lost his glasses and dropped Porbeagle's hundred copper *gabors*. The rest of the guards dived for them. "Stop! Stop! You'll step on my glasses!" Verix shouted, and began swatting anything he could reach with the official royal entry scroll.

Baskets full of fish went tumbling all over the road. Scandal growled and bravely pounced on a salmon twice his size.

The gryphon didn't care about all that. It didn't matter to him how fast or how far Porbeagle ran. He knew who had the wings. The last I saw of Porbeagle and the gryphon, the fishmonger was still running and the monster was still flying after him just fast enough to keep the unhappy little man in sight.

When I looked back towards the palace gate, I saw that the only three left waiting in line were Nintari and Scandal and me.

"Well, I guess that's riffraffproof, all right," I said.

"Glomph," said Scandal, his mouth full of salmon.

Nintari bit me in the shoulder.

CHAPTER —————— 4

INSIDE THE ROYAL PALACE, MY INTERVIEW WITH GOOD King Steffan was short.

"Oh, there you are, Master Kendar," he said, looking up from his copy of *My Hobgoblin, My Hero*. "So glad you could come."

"It was the least I could do, Your Majesty," I said.

"Yeah, on pain of death, it sure was," Scandal added. He marched right up to the throne and jumped into the king's lap. "Okay, King, you know where it itches: Scratch!" (They were old friends. Not so long ago, it looked like Scandal was going to become King Steffan's pet. Not every king can boast that he owns a legendary monster. Most of them have to be content with unicorns. But even though the king could give him anything he wanted, Scandal stayed with me. Sometimes I wondered why.)

"Ooza widdle woozums kitty den?" King Steffan asked, scratching Scandal under his chin. (All right, so maybe I knew why.)

"Cut the cute," Scandal snapped. "You got us out of a warm palace for this, so put 'em on the table: Whaddaya want?"

The king looked puzzled. "I thought I said that in the letter. I want this fowl weather stopped."

"And you expect him to do it?" Scandal nodded at me.

"Yes."

The cat laughed so hard he fell off the king's lap and rolled around on the floor, waving his paws in the air.

"I don't see the joke," I said stiffly.

"Neither do I." King Steffan agreed with me. "Although if you don't change the weather, I'll have to have you executed, and the royal hangman always tells a few humorous stories in dialect just before he pulls the trap."

"Oh, my aching fur," Scandal gasped, getting to his feet. "If I don't teach you guys some Abbot and Costello routines before I find a way back home, I'll never forgive myself."

"Why can't I do what the king wants?" I asked, holding onto my dignity with both hands. "I do own the biggest chunk of Majyk on Orbix. It's just a matter of finding the right spell to—"

"And who owned that chunk of Majyk before you?" Scandal asked.

"Master Thengor."

"And when you had your little accident, did you get *all* of Master Thengor's Majyk?"

"You know I didn't. It shattered and shot off in a hundred different directions when you and I ran over his deathbed. Most of it stuck to me, some of it stuck to you, and the rest burst out through the roof of Master Thengor's bedchamber. The only other piece of it we ever found was attached to Graverobber, the sword of Grym the Great."

"Oh, yes," King Steffan joined in eagerly. "That nice barbarian chap. One of the best lawyers I ever met. Not the man you'd want to split hairs or chop logic with, but he does get right to the heart of a case."

"What does all this have to do with me changing the weather?" I asked.

"Simple, sport. You only got *most* of Master Thengor's Majyk, but Master Thengor had it *all*. So tell me, in twenty-five words or less: In all the time you knew him, was Master Thengor, the most powerful wizard on Orbix, *ever* able to change the weather?"

I thought about it. The memories crowded into my mind. Most of them were wet and gloomy, or hot and sweaty, or icy and snowy. I saw Master Thengor fighting with his chief wife, Lady Inivria, because they'd gotten caught in a sudden downpour and her gown was ruined. I saw him sitting in front of the fire, sneezing and cursing the blizzard outside. Most of all, I saw him staring out the classroom window at the rain, sulking because he had to call off the annual Academy of High Wizardry field day. (He always won the egg-and-spoon race because he made his opponents' eggs hatch into dragonlings that bit their noses off.)

"Oh," I said.

"Well, I suppose that if the great Master Thengor couldn't do anything about the weather, Master Kendar can't either," King Steffan admitted. He looked sad.

"Right, Your Kingness," Scandal said, pleased with himself. "So how about you give us a nice square meal, and we play a few friendly games of strip poker with the kitchen wenches, and you send us home in the morning? Besides, when Master K. left the house, he had a little spat with the Welfie wifey. I think he oughta go back and tell her he's sorry, bring her a big bouquet of roses, maybe some candy, a priceless diamond necklace or two, and—"

Then something dangerous happened: King Steffan had a thought.

"You can't change the weather," he said. "But you can use your powers to find out what's causing this awful situation, and you can change *that*!"

"We-e-e-e-ll . . ." I wished I was as confident as he was.

"Of *course* you can! Oh, how exciting! It will be a challenge, a mission, an adventure—"

"Oh no." The cat cringed. "He's gonna say it. I know he's gonna say it! He's gonna say the q-word!"

"—a *quest!*"

Scandal yowled.

"Well, that was stupid," the cat said. He batted a couple of thirty-two-sided dice out of our path. We were walking through the Dregs, the worst neighborhood in Grashgoboum, a city that had nothing but bad neighborhoods. The dirt streets were littered with all sorts of rubbish.

"I don't think it was stupid to give Nintari to the king," I replied, trying to sound haughty. I hated it when Scandal criticized everything I did. "Didn't you see how thrilled he was to get him? Jumping up and down, clapping his hands, looking in Nintari's mouth—Let *him* get bitten for a change."

"Good thing for you that King Steffan's got the memory of a poached oyster or he'd've remembered that *he* gave *you* that horse first. And whaddaya wanna bet that he forgets *you* gave *him* Nintari now, so he sends it back to you in a couple of months? Man, that's no horse, that's a Christmas fruitcake with legs!"

I licked my lips. "I like fruitcake."

"Good. You should always like your relatives." Suddenly the cat froze in his tracks, his back arched. Tiny sparks of Majyk sputtered from the tips of his whiskers.

"What is it, Scandal?" I asked.

"I don't like the look of that dark and sinister alleyway," he said, growling low in his throat.

I scratched my head. "We're in the Dregs; there's nothing *but* dark and sinister alleyways here."

"Oh yeah, I forgot." The cat relaxed a little. "Now, if you'd listened to me, you'd've held onto that dumb horse and we'd be riding through this dump."

"What's so great about riding?"

"For one thing, it puts more distance between your nose and the street-stinks."

"A little walking is good for you," I maintained. "It makes you healthy."

"It makes you an easy target," the cat countered. "This looks like a place where they like easy targets."

"Oh, stop whining. You know that my Majyk won't let anything kill me, and you've still got eight lives left."

"Big comfort." Scandal switched his tail angrily. "All I need is to run into some creep with a sword who's stubborn enough to cut my head off *nine* times. Hey, what else is there to do around here? And as for you, Mister Nyah-nyah-can't-kill-me, death's one thing, pain's another. Suppose some hotshot thug bashes you a good one in the head, just for giggles? Maybe you're not dead, but your brains get scrambled enough so you're a rutabaga the rest of your life. You like that idea?"

I thought it over and shook my head. "I don't like rutabagas."

"Me neither. So let's go back to the palace while we still can, and this time let's say yes-please-thank-you to the nice kingie when he asks us if we want some armed and mounted guards to come with us when we go visit Master Williwaw. Okay?" He turned around and started trotting back the way we'd come.

He didn't get very far. Someone flung open one of the upper-story windows on the street and dumped a full chamber pot right on top of him.

"Scandal! Scandal!" I cried, falling to my knees and digging my friend out from under. "Are you all right?"

The cat came up spluttering out of a pile of cards, dice, and copies of *Ye Onlee Authentique Guide for Ye Compleat Palace-Master*. "What *is* this stuff?" He shook himself, and tiny lead figurines went flying.

"This is what gets dumped on you if you don't watch where you're going in the Dregs," I told him, picking crystal pendants out of his fur. "This part of the city is where all the mystics live. That's why it's so dangerous. The good mystics use their powers to sense and avoid danger, so they can live here safely and still take advantage of the cheap rents. The *bad* ones think they're good enough to do the same. That makes them careless, and *that* makes them easy pickings, and *that*—"

"—that makes this neighborhood a good hunting ground for

any goon who wants to make an easy living. Gotcha." Scandal licked his shoulder, then spit out a tiny lead dragon. "What I don't get is how come a big-shot wizard like Master Williwaw lives here when he could have an apartment at the palace like the rest of the parasites—I mean, like all the other wizards."

"Master Williwaw?" came a voice from on high. We looked up and saw a fat-armed maid with an empty chamber pot in her hands. "You want that old geezer, you just go two doors down, one flight up, and you're there." A gentle shower of shrikes began to fall and she slammed the shutters.

Following her directions, Scandal and I dashed down the street to get out of the birds. We found the wizard's address, sure enough. There was a big sign posted outside the street entrance:

MASTER WILLIWAW, WHETHERMAN
ONE FLIGHT UP
MIND THE DICE

"I hope he's a better wizard than a sign-maker," Scandal said. "He can't spell for beans."

"Why, what's wrong?"

"The king said Master Williwaw was the best weatherman wizard in the business, and he can't even spell it right on his sign, that's what."

I studied the sign closely. "Oh, I see." I chuckled. "You thought the king said *weather*man, but he really said *whether*man." I patted the cat's head.

He jabbed me with his claws.

"Talk down to me again and I'll slice your other hand, bozo," he snarled.

"Sorry." I sucked my bleeding hand a bit, then said, "Around here, whenever you've got an epic quest for something, the first thing you do is go to the *whether*man. He's a very special kind of wizard who can tell you whether or not your quest has a chance of succeeding. I mean, if you want to seek the ancient Lost City of Emessdos, first you've got to know whether it's still lost, or you're going to feel mighty silly when you get there and they've already set up the official Lost City souvenir stands."

Scandal just snorted and walked into Master Williwaw's building.

"What is it with these dice?" he complained as we climbed the narrow stairs to the second floor. The steps were littered with hundreds of dice in all colors, shapes, and sizes.

"I'm not sure, but I think Master Thengor once taught us that they're a way for mystic wizards—instead of practical wizards, like him—to work their spells. They hold the secrets of man, woman, birth, death, infinity, law, chaos, charisma, and if you put enough of them in a sack, it makes a pretty good weapon."

"Man, not much light on these stairs," the cat remarked. "Good thing I can see in the dark. With all this junk underfoot, I'll bet it hurts like crazy if you step on 'em."

"Ow," I said, doing just that. "Do you think you could maybe knock them out of my way? Since there isn't a lot of light and you can see in the dark and I can't."

"You know the story about the rhinoceros steak, bwana?" the cat asked.

"No, what?"

"Tough."

There was no reasoning with Scandal when he got cranky. I had a choice: either stumble along in the dark or make my own light. I cupped my hands and concentrated. Majyk pooled in my palms and began to glow. When a trained wizard wants to see where he's going, he summons up a fire-sprite or conjures a globe of *illuminum*. Plain Majyk doesn't always give a steady light—it's best for fireworks and stage flashes—but it was the best I could do.

"Hey, what's keeping you?" Scandal called from the top of the stairs.

"Oh, shut up," I mumbled, focusing on the Majyk in my hands. There was a tiny flash and then the whole stairway filled with blinding white light. I yelled and threw my arms up to shield my eyes.

As quickly as the light came, it was gone. I lowered my arms slowly and blinked into the darkness. From somewhere up ahead, I heard Scandal sigh.

Then a slice of warm, golden light fell over the stairs as the door on the second floor opened. "There is an eighty-three per cent chance that someone is out there," said a rich, plummy voice. "Considering this neighborhood, there is a seventy-five per cent chance that he is still alive. There is a one hundred per cent probability that he will not stay alive unless he tells me who he is right now."

"It's me, Master Williwaw!" I called up. "Kendar Gangle—I mean, *Master* Kendar. King Steffan sent me."

"You come from the palace?" A plump shadow blocked off part

of the light. "There is a fifty per cent chance I'll be glad to see you. You might as well come in."

A little while later, Scandal and I were seated in a pair of overstuffed armchairs, watching Master Williwaw as he waddled back and forth in front of a big chart. No, it was more than big, it was huge—huge enough to cover one whole wall of the whetherman's den. Strange signs and symbols were scrawled all over it, but underneath them I thought I recognized a map of Orbix.

"So you see," he said, using his magic wand as a pointer to slap the chart, "the prevailing winds are bringing a strong sorcerous front into our area. That means that this spell of fowl weather will get worse before it gets better. *If* it gets better at all." It was grim news, but he was smiling. Master Williwaw never *stopped* smiling. It got on my nerves.

"But you did call it a *spell* of fowl weather," I said. "So the cause is magical?"

"Oh yes, definitely. That is, there is a ninety-seven point two per cent probability that this was caused by sorcery. What's started by sorcery can be ended by sorcery. Therefore I feel safe in telling you that you've got a ninety-eight per cent chance of fixing it—"

"Great!"

"—as soon as you find out what caused the spell in the first place."

"Oog. How am I going to do that?"

"Cheer up, lad!" Master Williwaw looked cheerful enough for all of us. He couldn't look anything *but* cheerful, with that smarmy smile glued across his face. "You're in the right part of Grashgoboum for getting answers. This neighborhood is crawling with fortunetellers, seers, prophets, oracles, and assorted visionaries."

"That's not all it's crawling with." Scandal scratched himself energetically.

"Do you have any money?" the whetherman asked me.

"Maybe he does and maybe he doesn't." Scandal lowered his head and stared at Master Williwaw with suspicious eyes. "Who wants to know?"

Master Williwaw's frozen smile got a little colder. "The seers will, for one. They don't just give away their visions. Why do you think they're called prophets?"

"King Steffan gave me this." I opened my belt pouch and took out a jingly little silk bag. I loosened the drawstring and peeked inside. "I didn't count it, but there's plenty of copper *gabors* and even a few silver *ivanas.*"

"Very good, very good." The whetherman bobbed his head.

"More than enough to buy you the services of a first-class soothsayer. You'll find out what's at the bottom of all these birds, never fear."

"Tail feathers?" Scandal cocked his head.

Master Williwaw gave us the names of several reliable soothsayers and told us where we might find them. "Try the Wand and Crystal Balls tavern," he suggested. "There is a forty-five per cent chance that if you get them drunk, they'll lower their prices." We thanked him and left.

Too bad he didn't tell us that there was a ninety-nine point nine per cent probability that we would be attacked by a gang of cutthroats before we'd gone twenty paces from his front door.

CHAPTER ———————— 5

THERE WERE FIVE OF THEM, ONE WITH A QUARTERSTAFF, the rest with knives or short-swords. "We want money," said the spotty-faced man who had his blade only a finger's width from my throat.

"Not *that* way, Dawlish!" His skinny companion in crime gave the spotty-faced man a strong thump on the back. "Of course we want money! Everyone in this part o' town wants money. The gent knows *that* much. I'll wager he's lots smarter than he looks. Do it how we planned."

"Uh . . ." Dawlish was momentarily puzzled, but he tried again. "We want *your* money." He got another thump on the back. "We want *all* your money." Thump. "We want all your money *now*." Thump. "*We* want *you* to give us all *your* money right *now*." More thumps, accompanied by the mocking snickers of the three other thugs. The one with the quarterstaff leaned on it and brayed like a donkey.

Dawlish began to flounder badly. "You have to give us all your money *right* now? Oh, wait, I forgot the threat part, didn't I? That's right. Now I've got it. *We* want *you* to give us all of the money you've got that belongs to you right now—I mean, not the money that *belongs* to you right now, but *right now* is when you should give us all the money that belongs to you or—or—or—"

"The threat part, Dawlish," one of his friends hissed. "Do the threat part!"

"—or else?" Dawlish finished lamely.

"I don't know why I bother." The skinny man yanked Dawlish aside and stuck his pug nose in my face. "*Your money or your life!*" he snarled. Then he turned to Dawlish and demanded, "There! Was that so hard? Now you try it."

"Aw, Master Strelblig, why's Dawlish got to do it again?" the

37

man with the quarterstaff complained. "You already done it for him. Let's take the brat's coin and get going."

"You shut up, Fenmore!" The skinny man—now obviously the leader of this gang—jabbed an equally skinny finger at his underling. "I'm not getting any younger, and when I go, I don't intend to leave you lot unprepared. Your folks signed you up to be my apprentices, and by the holy name of Usirs—god of thieves, pickpockets, and tax collectors—I'm going to give each of you equal training and an equal chance to make good!"

"Lovely," I heard Scandal murmur. "You're not just a mugging victim, you're a midterm exam."

"All right, now Dawlish, you just ignore Fenmore and the rest," Strelblig said. "Try it again and don't be shy. He's more scared of you than you are of him."

"Wanna bet?" Scandal remarked. Without looking down, I somehow got the feeling that the cat had vanished. It was uncanny, the way he could melt into thin air without using any Majyk at all.

"Coward," I said half aloud. I meant Scandal, but Dawlish overheard and thought I meant him. It made him mad.

"We'll just see about that!" he announced. His blade was back at my throat. "*Your money or your life!*" he bellowed as bravely as any apprentice-master could wish to hear.

"Oh, excellent, Dawlish, excellent!" This time the pounding on Dawlish's broad back was by way of congratulation, not punishment. "Now take it from there."

"Take it from—?" That bewildered look was back on Dawlish's spotty face. "Uh, I think it's *his* turn now, Master Strelblig."

"So it is. You're right, Dawlish; forgive me. Carry on."

Dawlish gave his master a proud smile, stuck his tongue out at the other apprentice goons, then turned to me with a ferocious expression. "Well? You heard me and you heard Master Strelblig. Your money or your life!"

"No," I said.

"No what?"

"No nothing."

Dawlish's shoulders slumped a bit. "No you won't give me your money or no you don't want to lose your life?"

"Just plain *no*." I wasn't saying that to be mean—although Wedwel knows, it was cruel to confuse Dawlish any more than he was already confused—but to buy time. While I kept Dawlish and his comrades waiting, I was busily trying to call Majyk to my rescue. The trouble was, I'd never been formally trained to use the stuff, and the spells I'd taught myself didn't always behave the

way the instruction books promised. The only time I could be sure
my Majyk would jump to answer me was when something scared
me or enraged me or put me over the edge somehow.

Watching Dawlish, the only edge I was going to go over was the
edge of laughter. Too bad that wouldn't help me take care of this
gang of footpads-in-training. If I wanted to use Majyk on them, I'd
have to take my time summoning up just the right spell for the job.

Meanwhile, Dawlish was getting to the end of his rope fast.
"You can't just say *no*," he protested. "I gave you a choice; it's got
to be one or the other. So which is it?"

"I chose already," I replied very calmly. "I chose *no*."

"No *what*?" he wailed.

"No *thank you*."

Dawlish howled at the moon until Strelblig stepped in and
gently pushed his pupil to one side. The master-thug leaned one
elbow on my shoulder and laid the point of his short-sword right
at the base of my neck. "Now look here, lad," he said in a friendly
way. "You don't strike me as the village idiot type, nor suicidal
neither, so what's your game?"

"I'm not playing games, sir," I said, doing my best to copy
Scandal's famous *Who, me?* expression.

I guess it only works for cats. Strelblig took a step back and
slapped me across the face with his free hand. It wasn't a loud
slap, but it shot off a few stars behind my eyelids and made my
ears ring.

"Now let's try it one more time," Strelblig said. "And *this* time,
Dawlish, if the client don't give you a proper answer when you ask
him the question, you stab him. All right?"

"*Really* stab him, Master Strelblig?" Dawlish was excited. "Stab
him *dead* and all?"

"Aw, that's no fair!" one of the other apprentices whined. "You
never let none of us stab anyone."

"Shut your mouth, Lurp. That's on account of as how all of you
took care of clients what wasn't smarty-pants," Strelblig responded, sounding reasonable. "Not even that married couple
what you robbed, Pendis." He nodded at the shortest of the
apprentices, a fat boy who was almost smaller than the big clumsy
knife he carried. "And believe me, the husband had lots of
opportunity to make silly jokes."

"How d'you figure that?" asked Pendis.

"When you asked him the *question*, don't y'see?"

"The question?" Pendis frowned. "I'm very sorry, Master
Strewbwig, but I reawy don't see what's so funny 'bout going up

to a man in a dark awweyway and saying, 'Your money or your—'"

"Yeah, all he said was 'Take my money . . . please!'" Fenmore interrupted. "How come that means Dawlish gets to kill someone and we don't?"

"Because—" Without warning, Strelblig leaped forward and gave his three discontented apprentices the back of his hand. He hit Lurp hard enough to give him a bloody nose. "—I said so," he finished.

"Thad's good enuv for be," Lurp said, trying to stop the bleeding. The others agreed.

"It better be," Strelblig said. "Now, we haven't got all night—there's still your pickpocketing lesson to do—so let's wrap this up. Dawlish?"

Grinning widely, Dawlish aimed his knife at my heart instead of my throat. You could see he was praying I'd give him a hard time. I'm not a spoilsport, but this was a special case.

"Your money or your life!" Dawlish cried.

"Here," I said, giving him the little silk purse from my belt pouch.

"Uh." Dawlish stared at it stupidly. You could tell I'd ruined his evening. He glanced up at me. "Are you sure about this?"

"That's my money," I said. "All of it. What's the matter? It's real. Test an *ivana* if you don't believe me." I rooted around in the purse and pulled out one of the silver coins for him while he just stood there, watching me.

"Do what the nice man says, Dawlish," Strelblig instructed. "And don't mope! You're young yet. You'll get your chance to kill lots of people."

"I should test the coins?" Dawlish asked.

"To see if they're genuine. Yes, do. Don't let the client go free until you've tested his money. If it's fake, you're within your rights to kill him for that."

"I am?" Dawlish took the *ivana* I gave him and licked it. "Well, it's fake!" he announced happily. "You're dead."

Strelblig grabbed his arm before he could stab me. "You don't *lick* the money to test it, stupid; you *bite* it. A pure silver *ivana* should show your toothmarks."

"Toothmarks," Dawlish grumbled as he raised the coin to his lips. "Huh! Who cares about toothmar—*Yeeeeooooowww!*"

Dawlish shot straight up into the air, screaming with pain. He dropped his knife and my coin purse. I pounced on the knife—not as a weapon, but as a focus for my Majyk. I felt the power respond inside me, pouring down my arms and into the blade. I raised and aimed it, trying to get a clean shot at Dawlish, all the while thinking *frogfrogfrogfrogfrog*. It wasn't original, as spells go, but sometimes it's best to stick with the old favorites.

Hey, Annie Oakley, hold your fire! Scandal's voice exploded in my head. *At least let me shake loose first, okay?*

I looked all around, seeking the cat. I didn't see him anywhere. *Where? Where are you?* I thought desperately.

Here, dope! I'm right here, hanging onto Dawlish's rump! Or did you think the big slob grew his own tail? The cat's unvoiced laughter rang through my skull. *Betcha he's gonna care about toothmarks in the morning.*

"Aaiiiieee! A monster!" Pendis exclaimed, pointing at the whirling Dawlish.

"A fiend!" Fenmore cried, trying to hide behind his quarterstaff.

"A debon!" Lurp shouted, still holding his nose.

"In a bushpig's eye," Strelblig said, coolly sheathing his sword. "Fenmore, the stick." Fenmore tossed him the quarterstaff. "Dawlish, stand still." Dawlish didn't obey, so his master gave him a hearty thunk on the head. Dawlish folded over peacefully.

Immediately I heard Scandal's mental distress cry. *Help! Help! The big ape landed on me!*

Hold on, Scandal, I've got the Majyk warmed up now. I'll just turn him into a frog and—

And the kind of control you've got, you'll probably turn me *into a frog along with him! For gosh sakes, don't shoot!*

While I stood there, too scared to act, Strelblig didn't have any such problems. He shifted the quarterstaff and used it to lever Dawlish over onto his back. Snake-tongue quick, he grabbed a half-crushed Scandal by the scruff of the neck and held him high.

"What in Usirs' holy name is this?" he asked.

"I'm your worst nightmare," Scandal growled. He took a swipe at Strelblig's face with his claws. The master thief just held him a little farther away.

"No, my worst nightmare has naked people and talking broccoli. Now answer me! What are you?" Strelblig shook him.

"Put down that cat!" I shouted, aiming the Majyk-charged knife blade at the master thief.

"A cat?" Strelblig was mildly interested. "I don't believe it. I thought they was legendary monsters."

"They are," I told him. "But I'm Master Kendar, the greatest wizard on all Orbix. I used my magical powers to summon him. He's my familiar."

"Be afraid." Scandal fluffed out his fur. "Be very afraid."

"No," Strelblig said, drawing his sword and laying it across Scandal's throat. He met my eyes. "*You* be very afraid. I know all the old stories about cats. If you don't drop that blade, I'll see if the one about them having nine lives is true."

I dropped the knife. It made a fierce, fizzling sound when it hit the dirt. What else could I do? If I turned my Majyk against Strelblig, I might use it all in one shot. Then where would I be if Strelblig's apprentices jumped me? They couldn't kill me, but like Scandal said, there was always pain. As for Scandal, I couldn't risk Strelblig carrying out his threat about taking the cat's nine lives. Besides, Scandal was already down to eight.

"That's better," Strelblig jerked his head at the fallen blade. "Pendis, pick that up before it rusts. Good steel don't grow on trees. Not in this kingdom, anyhow." The fat boy scuttled in to grab the knife and then get as far from me as possible. "So you're the greatest wizard on all Orbix?" He looked me up and down. "Where's your pointy hat, then?"

"And your robes?" Fenmore asked.

"Ad your wad?" Lurp added.

"Wet's see you do the one where you poo a rappid out of a hat!" Pendis demanded.

Playing the all-powerful wizard had worked for me once today already. I decided to give it a second try. I crossed my arms and scowled at them. "If you don't release my familiar at once, I'll do worse than pull a rappid out of a hat. I will split open the very heart of the world and pull out a fiend so deadly, so ferocious, so powerful, that you will all be torn to pieces and eaten alive whole!"

All the apprentice thieves crossed *their* arms and scowled right back at me.

"Like to see you try!" Fenmore sneered, speaking for all of them.

Strelblig smacked him with the cat. "No you wouldn't! I know he don't look like much, lads, but suppose he is what he says? What then, hey? Just like them wizards to go wandering through the Dregs in disguise, pretending they're fool boys, tempting honest scum to attack them just so they can whip out their magic wands at the last minute and shout 'A-*ha!*'—nasty like they do—and turn a hardworking man into a frog for his troubles."

"I never was!" I protested. But I blushed, remembering what I'd been about to do to Dawlish.

"Will you swear to it?" Strelblig asked.

"I'll swear by anything you name," I replied. "And you can keep all the money, too. Only let the cat go."

"Awww, boss, not the *money*," Scandal objected. Strelblig shook him again. Scandal gave him a vicious glare and hissed, "You shake me once more, and I swear, if it takes me a thousand years, I'm gonna find out where you live, and I'm gonna get inside your house, and I'm gonna pee in every single pair of shoes you own."

"I don't need your oath, fiend," Strelblig said. "Just your master's. And I'm wearing the only pair of shoes I own, so there."

I raised one hand. "I swear by Wedwel, the one and only true god my mother says nice people worship, that I didn't come into the Dregs to trick honest thieves into attacking me so I could turn them into frogs."

"Or toads," Fenmore put in.

"Or toads," I agreed.

"Or durdles," Lurp piped up.

"Or turtles."

"Or wizards!" Pendis didn't want to be left out.

"Or wizards—I mean, lizards. There." I lowered my hand and looked at Strelblig. "Good enough?"

"Not so fast." He gestured with his sword for me to raise my hand again. "Do the threat part." He saw me hesitate, and added, "You know, the part where you say, 'And if I'm lying, then may Usirs—'"

"Wedwel. He really is the only god."

"Says you. Don't interrupt. '—then may whichever god strike me down where I stand!'"

THUD!

One minute the master thief was standing there, waving his sword and my cat; the next minute he was struck down by a dark shape that plummeted onto him from the roof of the nearest building. Scandal and the sword both flew in opposite directions, but only the cat landed on his feet. The caped and cowled figure leaped up lightly and unsheathed a shining length of steel. I saw bright eyes glittering with bloodthirsty glee behind a black mask.

"I'll give you all until the count of three to run," said a husky voice. Strelblig's apprentices didn't even wait for the count of two; they were gone. It was fantastic; even Dawlish came to his senses and fled. Strelblig tried to join them, but the caped figure stopped him with a twitch of the sword.

"Not you, cur. Not just yet. Speak: You seem to know your way around this part of the city, not so?"

The master thief was a different man in defeat; he sniveled. "Strelblig the Slippery, humbly at your service. Yes, born and raised in the Dregs, I be, if it please you."

"What would please me would be to see these two"—the caped figure jerked a thumb at Scandal and me—"out of danger, and that means out of this neighborhood as fast as possible. The sooner they get what they came for, the sooner they can get gone. They seek a mystic who might give them the answers they need. I assume you know one?"

"Oh, yes, aye, truly." Strelblig's head was bobbing like a cork in a storm. "Not none of these fly-by-day fortunetellers, but the real thing."

"Excellent. Take them to a reliable visionary and you will have your reward."

"Reward?" Strelblig perked up.

"Yes. I'll let you live," came the dry reply. With a flash of steel and a dashing flourish of cape, our mysterious helper was gone.

"Where's Robin?" Scandal asked, scanning the rooftops.

I picked up my coin purse and Strelblig's sword. "We'll get you something to eat later," I promised.

CHAPTER ———————————— 6

THE WAND AND CRYSTAL BALLS IS THE BEST TAVERN IN
the Dregs if you want to be sure of what the future has in store for
you. It's also the best place if you want to be sure your future is
real short. This tavern is the favorite haunt of gypsies, seers,
oracles, and sometimes an elder god who's down on his luck and
doesn't mind having to find his own human sacrifices.

It's also where the local gamers hang out.

"This place sounds like a rattlesnake convention," Scandal said
as we entered the tavern. "What's all the racket?"

"Dice," I told him.

He sighed. "I had to ask."

"It's not always this loud, gents," Strelblig explained. "You just
happen to have come during the last round of our annual contest."

"Can't be a beauty contest," the cat said. "So what is it?"

"What is it?" The master thief was astonished at the cat's
question. "Why, it's tournament-level Palaces and Puppies, is all!"

"Palaces and . . ." Scandal's whiskers corkscrewed up and
twitched violently. "What's the object of the game?"

"Gee, Scandal, even *I* know that," I said. "We used to play it at
Master Thengor's Academy of High Wizardry sometimes. You
make up a fantastic character, then you team up with the other
players and you make your way through a huge, complicated
palace with a litter of mongrel puppies. The object of the game is
to force the palace-dwellers to take the dogs off your hands. It's
the Palace-Master's job to make it difficult by doing things like
covering all the floors with white carpets, or putting a No Pets
clause in the family curse, or—"

"Y'know, I don't like to brag," Strelblig interrupted, "but in my
younger days I got the trophy four years running."

"Really?" I looked at the thief with new respect. "I used to play a dwarf dentist. What was your character?"

"What character? I didn't *play* the stupid game. I told you: I got the trophy four years *running*. Away with it. Fast."

"And that, Your Honor, is why I killed him," Scandal said.

"Maybe we should get on with the business that brought us here," I suggested to the thief. He nodded.

"Rhett?" Strelblig called into the low-ceilinged, smoke-filled room. "Rhett, are you in here?"

"Who are you bleating for?" Scandal asked, keeping close to my ankles.

"You said you wanted the best, so that's what I aim to get you," the master thief replied. "The Dregs is full of charlatans and quacks. Every two-*gabor* lout who's ever had a bunion twinge before it rains thinks he can predict the future, so he moves here, buys himself a crystal, and goes into business. None o' them'll do you any good."

"And this Rhett will? Why is he any different?"

"He's my cousin," Strelblig said proudly.

"Look, if he's anything like you, maybe we'll take our chances with the charlatans and quacks," Scandal said.

Strelblig wasn't listening. "Go take a seat and I'll see if I can find him."

"How do we know you won't run away?" I asked.

He gave me a funny look. "First off, I gives you my word as a criminal and a gentleman that I won't. Second, if you're half the wizard you say, you shouldn't have no trouble finding me again if I do run out on you. And third, Cousin Rhett pays me a little something for every bit o' business I throws his way."

"We'll treat you to a beer when you come back," Scandal said.

Strelblig grinned. "That'll guarantee it," he said, and melted into the crowd.

All of the tables were taken, mostly by strangely dressed people throwing dice, moving little lead figures on game boards, and mumbling things that made no sense. We finally found a table with four empty places. "Mind if we sit here?" I asked the lone man already there.

He didn't answer, just sat there muttering, "Now, if I make all the palace-dwellers vegetarians, they won't want the puppies because they don't like anyone eating meat and—"

"Thanks." Scandal jumped onto the chair.

A serving wench sashayed over to take our order. Instead of asking us what we wanted, she reached into her bosom, pulled out a small crystal ball, gazed into it and announced, "You'll have a mug of gawfee, extra sweet, and your familiar wants a bowl of milk. I'll bring a beer for Strelblig the Slippery, even though if he drinks it, it'll make him so tipsy he won't notice he's being followed home until his throat's cut. No, we don't serve doughnuts." She glanced at the stranger sharing our table. "Any minute now," she told him. "Better get set up."

"—curse on the palace that says no animal living there can ever be housebroken unless—" Still mumbling, the men bent over and started unloading the big black sack next to his chair. We watched, fascinated, as he piled one huge, heavy book on top of another in front of him. They all had titles like *Ye Booke of Binding Arbitration, Palace-Master's Manual,* and *Player's Guide to Freshman Geometry.*

The wench shrugged and walked away. I decided that our tablemate wasn't going to be interested in a friendly chat, so I looked around the tavern instead. Mom would've dropped dead if she'd seen me in a place like the Wand and Crystal Balls. It was full of every kind of wickedness, vice, and sin she'd ever warned me about, plus a couple she'd never imagined. There was drinking and gambling and wenching and name-calling and people using the wrong fork to eat their salad.

Over by the bar, a couple of fortunetellers were having a fist fight. One took a swing; the other ducked, then said, "Nyaaahh! I *predicted* you'd aim for my head!" Then he tried to land a punch, but the first one sidestepped it and said, "Ha! I *foretold* you'd try for my belly!" It went on like that for a good while until the bartender reached under the bar and pulled out a dead chicken. He slit open its stomach, looked inside, sighed, then picked up a *puija* board and clonked both of them in the head with it. As they slid senseless to the floor he remarked, "The entrails said you wouldn't be expecting that."

An elder god slithered across the floor and tried to carry off the unconscious fortunetellers. The bartender threw the dead chicken at him and told him not to eat any customers until they'd paid their bills. The elder god slunk away in a sulk, dragging his tentacles and sucking on the chicken neck.

The serving wench came back with our order. "You're going to leave a big tip," she told me, still staring into her crystal. "Also you will soon meet a mysterious stranger and go on a long voyage. But not before you leave that tip. You'll have a nice day."

"Monkey paw, sir?" said a voice behind me. I turned and saw a peddler with a tray full of weird relics. "Nice fresh mummified monkey paws, special today. You still get your full three wishes, but at half price. Satisfaction guaranteed."

"No thanks."

"Sure, sir? Lovely and plump, they are, and as a special bonus I'll throw in this handy little pamphlet telling you how to talk your way around the curse when you make those wishes."

Scandal fixed the peddler with a cold green stare. "You are going on a long journey," he said. "Now." His whiskers shot off sparks.

The peddler grabbed one of the paws from his tray, looked at a funny device strapped to the hairy wrist, and exclaimed. "Why, would you look at the time! I must be going. Good evening to you, gents." He ran off.

"How do you do that?" I asked Scandal.

"Do what?"

"That trick with the sparks. It's Majyk, right?"

"Darn tootin', sonny boy. What's the flap? You've seen me do it before." He lapped his milk. "Hmmm, mighty tasty. Must come from contented unicorns."

"Yeah, but it always just *happened*, before. I never knew you could do it on purpose. You didn't used to be able to do that—to use your Majyk on command."

Scandal raised his face from the bowl. "Hey, it's only sparks. Don't make a federal case out of it."

"Gosh, this is great! You know what this means?"

"I don't get to drink my milk in peace?"

"No, it means that you've got *talent*, Scandal! Master Thengor always said that you needed talent to become a wizard."

"Master Thengor also never bothered to tell you that you needed Majyk, too," the cat said with a lift of his whiskery eyebrows.

"Right, you need Majyk, but you also need talent and training. Boy, this is exciting! You've got the Majyk, you've got the talent, now all you need is the training and—"

"No way, José." Scandal was firm. "No way am I going to become a wizard. My mama always told me, 'Don't go to a lot of trouble; it'll be happy to come to you.'"

"What trouble? Being a wizard's no trouble."

Scandal gave me *that* look. "You speak from vast experience, O Master of the Mystic Arts with a capital F? I've had some fleas longer than you've had your Majyk."

We were still arguing about it when Strelblig came back to our table. He was followed by a tall, awe-inspiring person wrapped head to foot in a dark green hooded robe. The hood wasn't pulled all the way forward, so I could see the man's face. He had skin so pale it looked like moonlight, hair the color of midnight in a dragon's belly, high cheekbones, a hawk nose, and green eyes that seemed to glow with their own fire. Stick a pair of pointed ears and a furry tail on him and he could have passed for Scandal's cousin.

"Good evening," he said in a voice that *meant* something. I didn't know what it meant, but just the deep, rolling sound of it made me feel that there were mysterious things afoot. Big things. Lurking things. Things with long claws, sharp teeth, purple scales, and an appetite for me.

"G—g—g—good evening," I replied, chills creeping up my back.

Strelblig chuckled. "Right, Rhett, pay me." He stuck out his hand, palm upward. "I told you as how you'd make him shiver like all the rest. Huh! Some wizard!"

The hooded man turned slowly towards the thief. "Who are you to judge the hidden qualities of another?" he asked. The words reverberated through the tavern like thunder, silencing all talk. Even the dice stopped rattling.

Scandal gaped at the man, a drop of milk dangling from his chin, and breathed, "Wow. Cool sound effects. You use an echo chamber or what?"

Strelblig just blushed. "C'mon, Rhett, turn it off. You're embarrassing me. Pay off the bet and have a sit-down with the boy. You won't miss the money. Besides, he's got plenty, and he wants to throw some of it your way."

Rhett's lanternlike green eyes narrowed until they were glowing slits of contempt. With a magnificent gesture he reached inside his robe and produced a coin. It was only a copper *gabor*, but he made such a spectacular show of giving it to Strelblig that it might as well have been a golden *leona*. The thief bit it, checked it for toothmarks, grinned with satisfaction when it turned out to be genuine, and popped it into his pouch. Then he reached for his beer.

"*Don't drink that!*" sixty-two separate psychics, including Rhett, all yelled at once.

"*Damn!*" snarled a sinister-looking man over by the front door. He jammed his dagger back into its sheath and stalked out of the tavern.

Strelblig sadly eyed the beer before putting it down, untasted. "Well, I've done like I was asked," he said. "And small reward

I've got for my troubles. I'll leave you gents to your business." He drank my gawfee before he left.

"So . . ." I tried to give Strelblig's cousin a friendly smile, but it probably left me looking weak-minded. "You must be Rhett."

"Must I?" When he smiled, it was just a stiff grimace of the lips. "Who would have thought that you are Kendar Gangle, called Ratwhacker?" he added. "Your favorite color is blue, you don't like rutabagas, and your sister Lucy is in reality the celebrated romance writer, Raptura Eglantine. If your father, Lord Lucius Parkland Gangle, ever found out, it would not kill him, but he would yell a lot. He thinks it is bad enough that the girl is reading books, let alone writing them. *His* favorite color is red." He glanced at Scandal. "And this must be your cat."

"Must it?" Scandal shot back. "Okay, Houdini, you impressed us. I suppose we don't have to ask you what we want to know, either. You'll just tell us."

"It is the job of every good oracle to answer both the questions his clients ask and those they dare not," Rhett said, sitting down beside the cat. "For example, you want to know how one human can be such a—what is that alien word you're thinking of?—a *snot*?" A tiny flicker of warm good humor showed in his eyes, then promptly died of frostbite.

"*Scandal!*" I gritted. I didn't want the cat to insult Strelblig's weird cousin. It was pretty obvious by now that Rhett was the real thing when it came to mind reading. If he was half as good at finding the reason behind the bird baths we'd been having, we needed him on our side.

"Let him speak, Kendar." Rhett raised one hand, and half the tavern stopped talking again. "It is good to meet one who does not fear me. Besides"—his green eyes mirrored the cat's emerald gaze—"are not he and I kindred spirits of a sort when it comes to mind reading?" He reached for Scandal's head and scratched him gently between the ears. "That *is* the itchy spot, is it not?"

"Ohhhh, *baby!*" Scandal purred loudly until the oracle stopped scratching, then said, "Hire him."

"Hire—? Scandal, I don't even know yet if he's got the answers we need!" I objected. "So he reads minds—"

"Not very well," Rhett admitted. He drank Strelblig's untouched beer. "It is just a hobby. Like your cat, I can not always count on being able to enter every mind I meet. Some are more open than others. An oracle's true skill lies in accurately predicting the future for his clients; his *art* lies in being able to make it sound better than it is."

"The unvarnished truth's got too many splinters, huh?" The cat clicked his tongue in sympathy and polished off his milk. "Mmmm, now *that's* some kinda dynamite moo-juice." He hiccuped.

"You are a creature of wisdom," the oracle said, setting down the empty tankard. "I wonder why your former master ever called you a pain in the keister—whatever a keister might be."

"My former master was a dork," Scandal said. Talk of his previous life always made him cranky. "Also a nerd, a geek, and a wiener."

"Fascinating." Rhett raised one eyebrow.

"Oh yeah, and a trekkie. And I stuck by him through it all. If I had a catnip mouse for every Saturday night he told me, 'Mittens, you're the only friend I've got in the world,' I'd be higher than the cost of living." He hiccuped again and his eyes got a funny look. This was beyond his usual crankiness. "Then a miracle happens: Some normal woman actually finds him *attractive* and moves in. Nice, right? Stay tuned for Part Two, in which the bimbo sneezes her bleached-blond head off every time she gets near me! So what does Ol' Faithful do to the only friend he's got in the world? Kicks me out, that's what! Gives me the heave, place-kicks me into next Christmas, says the A-S-P-C-A word, tells me so long and thanks for nothing, hands me my diploma and—"

"Let us go to my dwelling," Rhett said abruptly. "If the cat does not cease his jabber, he will soon disturb the players at all nearby tables and they will throw things at me. Moreover, this gentleman's friends"—he indicated our still-muttering tablemate—"are coming through the door and will want their table."

"Rotten, lousy, treacherous, disloyal skinballs," Scandal growled. "They can *wait*. Hic!"

"Scandal, come on, let's go with Rhett," I pleaded. "If he says something's going to happen, I'll bet it is. We don't want any trouble."

The cat's head swayed side to side like a snake's. "Oh sure, stick together. That's just like you hairless yobbos. Well, I'm mad as hell and I'm not gonna take it anymore. Arise! Arise, you downtrodden mammals!" He jumped from the chair to the table to the top of the stack of books. "Throw off your leashes, kick over your litterpans, bite the hand that feeds you! Comes the revolution!"

I picked up his empty bowl and sniffed it. Uh-oh. "Just as I suspected," I told Rhett. "It's not milk; it's cream."

By now the tavern had fallen silent for a third time, but it was different from the awed silence Rhett commanded. This was a brooding, threatening kind of silence. This was silence that promised violence to follow. This was silence with warts. To make matters worse, I became aware that our table was surrounded by four rather large and muscular men, all of whom were carrying gaming sacks. Two of them wore funny hats, the third held a basket full of toy puppies, and the fourth wore a long, blond, curly wig. Aside from that, all they had on were loincloths, sword belts, and sweat.

"Hullo, Morgan," said the one in the wig. "Thought we told you to save us a table."

"We were just leaving," I said, making a grab for Scandal. The cat evaded me easily. His eyes were a little unfocused, but he could see well enough to make out the blond wig.

"Homewrecker!" he spat. "You think he's so great? Just wait until you cough up one lousy little hairball on his computer keyboard, then you'll see the real him! Yeah, or—or tape a rerun of *The Brady Bunch* over one of his *Star Trek* episodes! Serve him right, the stinker. And don't think I wouldn't do it in a second, if I had opposable thumbs!"

"You'll have to forgive him," I said to the man in the blond wig, grinning so hard I felt the corners of my mouth meet at the back of my head. "He's a legendary beast and he's not used to straight cream. Sit down, sit down, set up your game. We'll be out of here before you can say—"

"He will not believe you," Rhett intoned. "He will pick up the cat and throw him all the way across the room. If you go now and stand in front of the fireplace, you will be in the best spot to catch him. If you do not, he will land right in the fire. I will meet you outside."

He left without another word just as Scandal sat back on his haunches, stared the wigged warrior right in the eye, and sneered, "I'd like to see you try it, Blondie!"

CHAPTER ——————— 7

"ANY RESULTS?" SCANDAL ASKED, ANXIOUSLY GLANCING over his shoulder at me. He was seated on my lap and both of us were comfortably placed near the crackling hearth in Rhett's consulting room.

"No, nothing yet."

"Maybe the oracle's got some ideas."

"All he can do is predict the future and read minds. That's talent, not Majyk. If you don't believe me, you can ask him when he gets back from brushing partridge feathers off his cloak."

The cat sighed and looked up at the rafters. The stuffed slimegrind hanging from the ceiling looked back. "You'd think that a simple little spell like making new fur grow on a cat's tail would be easy for a big-shot wizard like Master Kendar Know-it-all Gangle," he told it. "But noooooooo."

"Look, I'm *trying*, all right?" I snapped. "I never had to use my Majyk for something like this before. Anyhow, it's your own fault."

"Oh, like *I* was Mister Butterfingers so I almost let *me* slip all the way into that fire at the tavern? I'm lucky it was just my tail that got singed furless." The cat sniffed disdainfully. "You couldn't catch a cold using both hands and a bushelbasket."

"You wouldn't have gone flying into that fire in the first place if you hadn't opened a big mouth to that gamer," I reminded him.

"It was the cream talking," Scandal said, pulling his dignity around him like a cloak. "And I think it's stinky of you to remind me of it."

"But you just—But I didn't—Oh, forget it." If I'd learned anything from my friendship with Scandal, it was that cats are never bad losers because cats never lose. I went back to concentrating a grow-spell on his tail.

It was an old Welfie enchantment, which was why it was giving me so much trouble. Because they're creatures of Majyk, Welfies can be any size they like. Sometimes they're tall and elegant, sometimes they're tiny and cute, depending on the fashion set by the nobility. (Most mortals prefer Welfies when they're tiny and cute because it's easier to stomp them.) The only problem is that Welfies live in little blue mushroom houses, so every time the fashion is for tall, elegant Welfies, they have a housing shortage.

"That's when the male Welfies use the grow-spell," Mysti explained when she was trying to teach it to me.

"Can't the female Welfies use it, too?" I asked.

"Yes," she said, blushing. "It's not just for mushrooms, you know."

I wondered what she meant by that. I also wondered how she was, all alone back home in the palace. Was she unhappy? Was she lonely? Was she all right? Did she miss me? Part of me answered, *Don't be silly. She's probably thankful to have you out from underfoot. Now she's got all the time she wants to read her books.* Another part of me hoped she missed me just a little.

Scandal's tail-fur wasn't reacting to the grow-spell. Maybe I was doing it wrong. It was Welfie Majyk, after all, and I never was much good with foreign accents. Finally I gave up.

"I guess you're just going to have to get used to this," I said, holding up Scandal's hairless tail.

"Never!" The cat twitched it out of my hand. "It makes me look like a freakin' *rodent*."

"Perhaps this will help," said the red-haired woman in the itsy-bitsy teeny-weeny chain-mail kilt and halter. She had stolen up on us so softly and gracefully that not even the cat knew she was there until she spoke. Her voice was like smoke and burnt honey, her skin the color of the cream that had undone poor Scandal, and the look in her amber eyes made me feel like I was trying to swallow fire. She held out a small blue bottle in her hand.

"Haggahaggahaggahagga," I said. That's the trouble with words: There's never any around when you need them.

"Oh, I'm sorry," she said, a delicate pink flush traveling from the soles of her dainty bare feet to the roots of her waist-length hair. "I didn't mean to interrupt your spellcasting, Master Kendar."

"You—you—you know who I am?" She ducked her head and gave me a sideways smile that melted all my bones into a puddle of warm syrup. I had a frightening thought: "You're not a mind reader, too, are you?" If she was, I didn't need Rhett to tell me I was about to get my face slapped.

Her laughter was the only thing about her that was less than divine. She tittered. "Of course not. I just asked Rhett. What have you people been doing, visiting a henhouse? It took me forever to get all the feathers off your cloaks."

"We got caught in a cloudburst of canaries on the way back from the Wand and Crystal Balls," Scandal said. "It only started coming down partridges a block from this house." He passed his pink tongue over his fangs. "Delicious weather we've been having, huh, toots?"

The lady tittered again. It was sharp and shrill, but as soon as she stopped, it was hard to imagine such a nerve-grating sound had ever come from that petal-perfect mouth.

"You really didn't have to clean my cloak too," I said.

"Yes, I did." She pulled up a tall stool and sat down with a motion that made water look stiff. "I don't mind. I'm supposed to do all that kind of work around here. I'm a slave-girl, you know."

"A slave!" Scandal and I exclaimed in unison. It was hard to say which of us was more horrified. Then the cat turned an accusing look on me and said, "I thought there were no slaves in King Steffan's realm!"

"There aren't," I protested.

"Yes, there are," the girl replied. "One, at least. Me. My name is Anisella. My daddy sold me to Rhett when I was thirteen. Wasn't that nice of him?"

"*Nice?*" This time Scandal and I tied for Most Horrified.

"Certainly. What else could he do? Because of the curse. My curse. But enough about little old me. We've got to take care of your problem first, don't we?" She puckered up her lips at Scandal and added, "Yes, we do, we do got to take care of dear li'l pussums what's he's got no more fursies on his tailums." She scooped him out of my lap and hugged him to her, um, her, ah, her chain-mail halter. "Did dat naughty man throw pussums in dat mean ol' fire? Well, don't you be sad, pussums, Auntie Anisella make it alllllll better."

If King Steffan used that kind of language to Scandal, the cat would have been out of his lap and halfway home before he uttered the second *pussums*. If I was fool enough to talk baby talk to the cat, I'd be shredded meat. But all he did in Anisella's arms was close his eyes, snuggle into her embrace, and purr.

A brief thought flashed from his mind to mine: *Eat your heart out, skinball!*

Anisella uncorked the blue bottle with her teeth and spat out the stopper. "Now pussums just hold still and we'll see if dis nice li'l potion work, yes?" She held it carefully and let a few drops fall on the cat's singed tail. "'Oo's a good bwave pussums, den?" she asked.

While she was rubbing in the potion, Rhett rejoined us. Even though he had shed his cloak and was just wearing a plain white shirt and close-fitting black breeches, he still managed to look powerful and mysterious. He ran his fingers through his raven hair, which hung in loose waves halfway down his neck, and announced, "I have been in my workroom, using all the tools of my trade to confirm the answer my visions already gave me. I can now say without a doubt that I have found the answer to your problem." His green eyes slued towards the lissome slave-girl, still cooing over the cat, and he added, "I see that you have met mine."

"Your . . . problem?" It wasn't the word I'd choose to describe Anisella.

Rhett's expression was rich in irony. "No, to the unknowing eye I will wager that she does not look like a problem—except perhaps the problem of how to make one day contain enough hours to adore her sufficiently—and yet—"

"*There* it is, pussums!" came Anisella's delighted cry. She held up Scandal's tail so that we could see the fine fuzz of new fur covering it. "Does ums darling pussums be happy now?"

Scandal regarded his quickly recovering tail with joy. "Hallelujah, Lordy, I *believe!*" he caroled. "How much Majyk do you have, anyhow?"

"Magic?" Anisella repeated the word in a way that as good as told me she'd never heard of *Majyk*-magic. "I don't know anything about silly old magic. I just know where to shop. I bought this from a wandering bear and his dancing gypsy." She showed him the blue bottle so he could see the label.

"'Fur-Back,'" Scandal read. "'Guaranteed to bring back that youthful pelt or we'll skin ourselves! Restores fur damaged or destroyed by moths, mange, or man. Another fine product of Brother Bruin Enterprises, Kingdom of Wingdingo, the Underside.'" He looked up at her. "The Underside—That's the part of this cockamamie planet where everything's reversed: The animals can talk and the people can't, right?"

"Well, not *all* the animals there talk, and not *all* the people can't," she replied. "It's just that the talking people and the non-talking animals never leave the Underside. Why should they? They wouldn't be anything special here. It's the talking animals that can make their fortunes, so they're the only ones who make the long, long journey. When I was studying for my Slave-girl

First Class examinations, I wrote my dissertation on the Underside Effect and its impact on the ecology of Orbix." She showed more dimples than any woman is entitled to, and added modestly, "I got the top marks in my grade."

"Wow, all that beauty, and brains to match!" Scandal said what I was thinking.

"Oh, such a *sweet* kitty to say dat! Yes, it is!" She lifted the cat high in the air and gave him a big kiss. Rhett and I both sighed aloud with envy, then realized what we'd done and looked away from each other, embarrassed.

The oracle cleared his throat loudly. "Perhaps you would care to accompany me into my workroom, Master Kendar? I feel that what I have discovered ought to be discussed in private."

"Don't mind me, fellas!" Scandal called, curling up in Anisella's lap. "Just forward all my mail care of Heaven."

As soon as we were in Rhett's workroom, he threw a heavy bar across the door. I heard it fall, even though I couldn't see it. The room was pitch-black, the darkness full of alien smells and sounds. "You want to know why I own a slave-girl," he said. "You also want to know why I call such an enchanting creature a problem."

"I figure it must have something to do with the curse on her," I said.

"Indeed, that is so. Wait. I will explain all as soon as I strike a light."

I heard a *tap-tap-tap*, then saw a glimmer of flame as a fire-sprite stepped into a clear glass globe beside the door. The sound must have been Rhett rapping on the door of the elemental's dwelling, a miniature house of *aswurstos* (the fireproof sausage made by the dragon wranglers of Ignall) that rested on a shelf just above the globe.

"No, I do not possess a true wizard's power to command fire-sprites and other elementals," Rhett informed me before I could ask. "This was merely a gift from a somewhat grateful client. Please follow me." He led me to a table covered with a green silk cloth. On it rested a *puija* board, a handful of toss-bones, and a deck of Tarhona cards.

"At least you gave my question the full treatment," I remarked.

"What true oracle needs such crutches to read the mysteries of the universe?" Rhett demanded. Like most of his questions, he didn't want an answer to this one either. He yanked the cloth off the table with a brisk snap. The fortunetelling tools remained where they were. He made a disgusted sound and swept them all to the floor. "Mere toys, all of them, and yet they mock me by confirming what I already know."

"If you don't use any of those, how do you get your answers?"

He looked at me as if I'd grown horns. "I ask."

"Sure, I know, but *what* do you ask? A crystal ball? A bowl of water? The inside of something dead?"

"I will show you." Rhett folded his hands, twiddled his thumbs, didn't bother making any mystic gestures or uttering any hair-raising invocations, and simply said, "Why are there birds falling out of the sky?"

I was about to remind him that that was *my* question to him, when all of a sudden the whole room shook with the force of a Voice more dreadful than any I'd ever heard, including Dad's.

I THOUGHT I ALREADY TOLD YOU WHY, it said impatiently.

"My client wants to hear it for himself." I was shaking in my shoes, but Rhett looked as if hearing the Voice of doom was nothing much to him. He even sounded a little bored.

VERY WELL. ONLY THIS TIME PAY ATTENTION. JUST BECAUSE I HAVE ALL ETERNITY DOESN'T MEAN I LIKE TO REPEAT MYSELF. THE FOWL SHALL TUMBLE FROM THE SKY SO LONG AS THE MYSTIC BALANCE REMAINS UPSET. THERE.

I gathered all my courage and piped, "What Mystic Balance?" I meant my question for Rhett, but the Voice obviously had an Ear to go with it because it answered me directly:

WHAT MYSTIC BALANCE, DOES THE MORTAL WORM DARE TO ASK? DO YOU DOUBT THE EXISTENCE OF THE MYSTIC BALANCE?

"N—no, it's just—just that this is the first time I heard of there being a Mystic Balance."

WELL, THERE MUST BE A MYSTIC BALANCE BECAUSE *SOMETHING* IS SURE AS HELL UPSET! YOU DON'T JUST STEP OUTSIDE, LOOK UP TO CHECK THE WEATHER, AND GET AN OSTRICH IN YOUR FACE IF EVERYTHING IS HUNKY-DORY WITH THE MYSTIC BALANCE, NOW DO YOU?

"Could you—could you tell us why the Mystic Balance is upset?" I asked in a squeaky little voice. "If it's not too much trouble? Please?"

"*I* can tell you that," Rhett said.

BUT I WILL TELL HIM MYSELF, SINCE HE ASKED ME SO NICELY, the Voice cut in. ONE THING THAT UPSETS THE

MYSTIC BALANCE WORSE THAN ANY OTHER IS INJUS-
TICE. YOUR WORLD HAS MORE THAN ITS SHARE OF
THAT, BUT AS FAR AS I CAN TELL, THE WORST INJUS-
TICE CURRENTLY GOING ON IS THAT THE RIGHTFUL
KING OF WINGDINGO WAS WRONGFULLY SLAIN BY HIS
WICKED BROTHER, WHO THEN USURPED THE THRONE.
FORTUNATELY, THE KING'S HEIR WAS SPIRITED OUT OF
THE CASTLE TO SAFETY. UNTIL THE TRUE HEIR OF
WINGDINGO IS ON THE THRONE ONCE MORE, THE
EARTH SHALL WEEP, THE SEA SHALL MOAN, AND THE
SKIES SHALL DRIP POULTRY.

"That's awful!" I gasped. "The kingdom must be in an uproar!"

HARDLY. IT ALL HAPPENED EIGHTEEN YEARS AGO,
SO THE PEOPLE HAVE HAD LOTS OF TIME TO GET USED
TO THE IDEA.

"Eighteen years ago, and the Mystic Balance is only upset by
the injustice of it all *now*?"

WOULD YOU BE HAPPIER IF THE MYSTIC BALANCE
STARTED DROPPING TURKEYS ON YOU EIGHTEEN
YEARS AGO? THE HEIR WAS ONLY A BABY WHEN THE
USURPER TOOK OVER. IF YOU PUT A BABY ON THE
THRONE, RIGHTFUL HEIR OR NOT, YOU'RE GOING TO
HAVE MORE TROUBLE THAN IF YOU BIDE YOUR TIME
AND RESTORE THE TRUE RULER OF WINGDINGO AFTER
THAT RULER'S BEEN PROPERLY HOUSEBROKEN AND
HAS GONE THROUGH ALL THAT PUBERTY NONSENSE.
THE MYSTIC BALANCE KNOWS BEST.

"Ummm," I replied doubtfully. "Well, at least now we know
what's wrong. I'll tell King Steffan, and he can send an army to
Wingdingo and restore the true heir to—"

WHAT TRUE HEIR? the Voice asked. If it had a Face, it would
have been smirking.

"Don't tell me there's no true heir to restore!" I cried. "We'll be
up to our ankles in albatrosses forever."

OH, THERE'S A TRUE HEIR, ALL RIGHT. RAISED BY
FOSTER PARENTS AND LIVING IN COMPLETE SAFETY. I
COULD EVEN TELL YOU WHERE TO LOOK. BUT I WON'T.

"Would it help to ask why not?"

I'M NOT BEING MEAN ABOUT THIS. I AM VERY GEN-
EROUS WITH INFORMATION, REALLY. I AM MERWAL-
LOW, THE FORTUNETELLER'S FRIEND AND GOD OF
LITTLE WHITE LIES. I AM THE REASON WHY RHETT IS
SUCH AN ACCURATE ORACLE. YEARS AGO HE TOOK A

MIGHTY OATH OF RENUNCIATION ON MY ALTAR THAT
HE WOULD ALWAYS TELL HIS CLIENTS THE TRUTH
ABOUT THEIR PROBLEMS AND THEIR FUTURES. I MUST
SAY, I WAS QUITE IMPRESSED. I THOUGHT HE WAS
SMARTER THAN THAT. IN EXCHANGE FOR THIS OATH, I
AGREED TO ANSWER ANY QUESTION HE ASKED ME, AS
LONG AS IT DIDN'T UPSET THE MYSTIC BALANCE OR
MAKE HIM GET TOO BIG FOR HIS BREECHES OR I
DIDN'T FEEL LIKE IT FOR REASONS OF MY OWN THAT
ARE NONE OF YOUR BUSINESS. HE GAINED THE POWER
OF PERFECT PREDICTION AND LOST ALL BUT HIS BRAV-
EST CUSTOMERS. WHY DO YOU THINK HE LIVES IN THIS
DUMP?

"I like it here," Rhett said between clenched teeth. "It is
picturesque."

A VERY TRUTHFUL WAY TO SAY IT'S RUN-DOWN AND
OLDER THAN MY GRANDPA. NO, KENDAR, THE REASON
I WILL NOT REVEAL THE TRUE HEIR'S IDENTITY IS
PRECISELY BECAUSE I DON'T WANT YOU BRINGING AN
ARMY TO THE UNDERSIDE. AN ARMY IS NEVER SUBTLE.
HUGE MASSES OF MEN WITH SWORDS AND SPEARS
AND CATAPULTS CAN'T KEEP A SECRET. AS SOON AS
YOUR TROOPS COME IN SIGHT OF THE UNDERSIDE,
WORD WILL FLY TO KING WULFDETH THE USURPER.
THE MOMENT THEY REACH WINGDINGO, HE WILL
KNOW ALL ABOUT THE TRUE HEIR. BEFORE YOU SAY
"SENSELESS VIOLENCE," KING WULFDETH OR HIS SPIES
WILL FIND THE HEIR, DRAW STEEL, AND CHOP OFF—

"I get the point."

BUT THE HEIR MUST NOT.

"So the best thing to do would be to go find the true heir on my
own." I hoped Merwallow would say no, but he didn't. Rats. "And
once I'm sure of the heir's safety, I can call in King Steffan's
troops to depose King Wulfdeth. I understand. You're right," I
admitted.

OF COURSE I'M RIGHT. NOT MUCH USE BEING A GOD
IF YOU CAN'T BE RIGHT OCCASIONALLY.

"I'm sorry, I don't want to sound ungrateful, but I can't think of
you as a god, Merwallow. My family has always been strictly
Orthodox Wedwellians."

I KNEW THAT! I'LL BE SURE TO GIVE WEDWEL YOUR
REGARDS.

The room suddenly seemed bigger. Merwallow was gone. It was easier to breathe, but all I could do was sigh.

"You wonder how you will manage to fulfill this quest," Rhett said. "Do not fear; you will not voyage to the Underside alone. I will go with you."

"You? But why——?"

"Would I not be a fool if I let you leave Grashgoboum without paying me for my services?" Rhett almost got his lips to turn all the way up into a human smile. "You have had the answer to your question, and now you must pay the price."

"That won't be a problem." I reached for the money King Steffan had given me.

Rhett's hand closed on my wrist before I could pull out the silk purse. "Did I say I wanted money? You are a wizard, and I would have you reward me with Majyk." He pronounced the word as if he knew *exactly* what it meant.

"I'm not very good at——"

"I know. I do not want a share of your Majyk, Kendar Gangle. Since I have used my skill to help you with your problem, you must use your Majyk to help me with mine."

His problem . . . "Anisella?"

"Anisella."

"Well, since you like the truth so much, Rhett, I'll give you some: I think your first problem with Anisella is that she's your slave. I don't know much about women——"

"I know."

"——but I doubt they enjoy being anyone's slave. If you want her to fall in love with you——"

"I want her to marry me. I have wanted her to marry me for years. It can never be. The curse prevents it." Some of the light went out of his eyes. I almost pitied him. "Do you think I *wanted* her to be my slave, Kendar? It was her father's idea. He brought her to me when she was thirteen. I was only seven years older, but I took Merwallow's Oath of Renunciation of Fibbing when I was fifteen, just out of Seer School, so my reputation for accurate prophecy was already well established.

"To this day I cannot believe that such a man as *that* could have fathered so marvelous a creature as Anisella! He commanded me to pronounce the girl's future. I consulted Merwallow and was the first to hear the dreadful verdict: There was a curse upon her. Anisella would bring death, destruction, and hideous ruin to the first to wed her, likewise upon whoever gave her in marriage."

Now I did pity the oracle. "Anisella told me her father *sold* her to you. I guess that was so he could avoid the part of the curse about *giving* her in marriage."

"Yes, the coward. The only reason I agreed to it was to save her from being sold to a worse master. You have seen how beautiful and kind she is, you have heard how smart she is—except when talking to your cat, I admit—but you do not know how noble she is as well. As soon as she understood her fate, she too took a mighty Oath. She swore by Dul, goddess of unicorns, to let no man be more than just a good friend until the curse was broken."

I could feel the blood rising to my cheeks, but I went ahead and said, "I thought the curse was just on the first to marry her, not the first to, uh, um, er, ah—"

"She is also a very *sensitive* girl," Rhett told me. "Sensitive both in body and spirit. I assume you noticed what she is wearing?"

I swallowed hard, bit my lower lip, and whispered, "Maybe."

"She does not dress that way by choice. She can't wear too many clothes—they smother her, she says—and what little she wears must be chain mail because she is allergic to cloth. She is also sensitive to the fact that curses are sneaky things. Although her curse promises death, destruction, and hideous ruin to the first to marry her, certain tribes on Orbix consider it a marriage if the man and the woman only, uh, um, er, ah—"

"Ah. I see. Well. That was noble of her," I said.

"Very noble." Rhett looked miserable. "Oh, so very, very noble!" If Anisella had been any more noble, he would have burst into tears.

CHAPTER ——————— 8

"I HOPE RHETT WILL COME BACK SOON," ANISELLA SAID.
"This place makes my skin crawl." The way she was dressed, you
could see every inch it crawled, too. It was kind of fun. I didn't
blame her for being nervous. Dockside taverns are no place to take
a sensitive woman, but the dockside taverns of Port Laverne are no
place to take a fully armed barbarian swordsman.

"Don't worry," I said, trying to comfort her. "He's only gone to
find us passage to the Underside. The sea route's quicker than the
overland way. The only thing is, there aren't that many ships
making the voyage at this time of year."

"What I don't get is how come old Sees-All-Knows-All didn't
just predict where to find us a ship," Scandal said. He was
occupying his favorite spot, Anisella's lap. He said she'd hired him
as a bodyguard, and she was too nice to call him a bald-faced liar.
(Now that his tail-fur had grown back, he wasn't bald-anything.)

"Rhett can't predict everything," Anisella said, stroking the cat.
"He only gets his answers by asking Merwallow, and sometimes
through spontaneous visions. He can't control what the visions tell
him, and he can't bother Merwallow about every little thing."

"You like Rhett a lot, don't you?" I coaxed. Ever since we'd
taken the road to the Underside together, I'd used every spare
moment alone with Anisella to try to find out if she felt the same
way about the oracle that he did about her. (It was one question
Merwallow refused to answer.)

The slave-girl shrugged. "We're just good friends." I couldn't
tell whether she meant that or not. She sighed and gazed around
the tavern. "I still wish he'd hurry back."

I agreed. Secrecy was important to our mission, and we were
making a bad start by sitting around a dive where we all stuck out
like lips on a chicken. We just didn't blend in with the other

drinkers. We had no tusks. I'd seen more human-looking customers at a troll convention. I didn't like the way they were looking at Anisella. I didn't like the way some of them were looking at *me*.

And then the door was flung open. A blast of salty air flooded the tavern. The customers opened their eyes wide in astonishment— those of them that had at least two eyes, I mean—for there in the doorway stood a tall, lithe, striking figure in a flaring black cloak, gleaming black boots, fine black breeches, a well-stocked black sword belt, a loose-fitting black shirt, and a black mask covering the top half of his face. I knew that costume. I knew that sword. I didn't know the man's name, but I recognized the accessories.

"Scandal, that's the swordsman who saved us from Strelblig's gang," I whispered.

"No fooling. I thought he'd be back to the Bat Cave by now."

"How do you know where he lives?" That cat would never stop surprising me.

"I rented the movie. Never mind. At least now you've got a chance to say thank you to the nice caped loony."

It was true; he had seen us and was coming towards our table. He moved with such grace and self-confidence that all the wharfside scum eyed him with a mixture of hate and envy. One of them picked up a tankard and threw it at him for no other reason. He didn't stop, turn, or even pause to meet the attack, just drew his sword and used it to bat the flying mug back in the face of its thrower.

"Ooooooh." A gush of hot breath seared my ear. I glanced over my shoulder and saw Anisella, her mouth hanging open prettily, her lips moist and trembling, her amber eyes glazing over, her halter heaving. She was looking right at the figure in black. She didn't sound like she wanted to be his just-good-friend; she sounded like she wanted to be his just-*very*-good-friend.

The masked swordsman reached our table and fixed his steely gaze on me. "So," he rumbled. "We meet again."

Scandal leaped from Anisella's lap to mine and put his paws on my shoulder. "A word to the wise, boss," he whispered. "If he tells you his name is Inigo Montoya and that you killed his father, don't argue; run like Hades."

"If he says his name is Hades I should do what—?" I whispered back.

"May I join you?" the swordsman asked.

"Oh, *yes!*" Anisella burbled. "*Please* do."

"Yes, please," I repeated, although not as eagerly as Anisella. "This is lucky, running into you here. Let me buy you a drink. I never got the chance to thank you for your help back in the Dregs when—"

"Don't mention it." He took a seat beside me and threw back his hood. Short curls of pale gold hair glittered in the dim light of the tavern. Anisella announced that she was allergic to her chair and moved into the one nearest our guest.

It wasn't easy buying the masked swordsman that drink. There were no psychic serving wenches to take our orders in this tavern. For one thing, once you figured out how to tell the difference, you saw that most of the servers were male. (The ladies' tattoos were done in pastels and they could spit with better aim.) For another, the female servants carried daggers instead of crystals. For a third, the only prediction they needed to make was when the next brawl was going to break out. If you wanted to get the servers' attention, you threw something at the bartender.

I was still looking around for something to throw, when our guest stood up, slung one slim leg onto his chair, and snapped his fingers. Immediately we were surrounded by every (probably) female server in the place.

"A round of Delphinium-brand mead for all," he said. "Yes, Delphinium, mead of champions." The servers raced off and he sat down again.

"I just knew you were a champion," Anisella said, purring worse than Scandal. She folded her arms on the table, rested her heavily laden halter on top of them, and squeezed her shoulders forward on purpose. Three sailors at the next table happened to look in her direction. Poor men, they weren't prepared for the sight. They all seized their chests (not being able to do better), exclaimed "Awkgh!" and keeled over with smiles on their faces. The tavern's resident pickpocket fumbled through their belongings while doing his best *not* to look at Anisella.

"Whoa, mythology news flash!" Scandal exclaimed. "It *wasn't* Medusa's hair that turned men to stone. Not unless she had hair on her—"

The serving women began a loud argument over by the bar, trying to decide which of them would get to serve our mysterious guest. It didn't take long for the debate to get painful. From where I sat, I soon learned that around here trays, tankards, and small pieces of furniture were the popular ways to make your opponent see your point of view. Also stars. By the time our order was ready, the honor of bringing it to our table went to the lass smart and swift enough to have unscrewed her pegleg and used it as a club on her rivals.

She hopped over to our table and set the tankards of mead down. I heard a sizzling sound when the wench took longer than necessary to serve our guest. It was Anisella, doing a slow burn.

"Thank you, dearie, you can go now," she told the wench. Maybe she thought she was smiling, but to me it just looked like someone had glued her teeth together and stripped her lips away.

"I'm a trained perfeshunul, sweetie," the server replied. "I'll be th' judge o' when I've served 'im enough." She went back to spoon-feeding our guest his mead. The masked man did nothing to stop her, although he didn't look like he was enjoying it much.

"Oh, I don't mean to tell you your job, *honey*," Anisella said. "I can see that you've been doing it for a long, long, long, *long* time. Just years and years and years and years and—"

"Why, bless yer heart, *precious*," the wench snarled. "You make it sound like I been working since back when you still had your *natural* hair color."

"This is the hair color I was born with, *darling*." Anisella rose from her place, fists on the table, and tossed her mane of auburn hair. Nintari used to do that right before he tried to bite me.

"Is it, now!" The serving woman leaned forward and squinted her one good eye at Anisella. "Well, isn't that amazing. So purty, 'tis. Y'know, *lovey*, I think it's grand the way them wig-makers can take care of the worst cases, fix up any color they want at—"

Anisella took care of that good eye with one punch.

"Hot dog!" Scandal gloated in my lap. "Cat fight, cat fight!"

He was disappointed. Anisella threw punches with the same perfection she did everything else. One was all it took. The serving wench crumpled across our guest's lap, to the cheers of her defeated co-workers.

"Oooh, just look at the mess. Let me brush that off for you." Anisella was the only person I ever knew who could flutter while wearing chain mail. Now she fluttered around to shove the stunned server off the masked man's lap with one dainty touch of her boot. "Whoopsie!" she exclaimed as she pretended to lose her balance and toppled right into the space her rival had just vacated.

"Goodness, this isn't right," Anisella said, blushing. "Here I am, sitting in your lap, and I don't even know your name."

The masked man lifted his chin and told the chandelier, "You may call me . . . a Blade for Justice."

"Kendar Gangle," I said, sticking my hand between him and Anisella. It wasn't easy. "*Master* Kendar, actually, Court Wizard to—"

"—good King Steffan."

Not another mind reader! I thought. *My brain is starting to feel like a public notice board.*

"You see, it was King Steffan himself who sent me to your aid," the swordsman explained. "Although no one doubts your wizardly skill, least of all our king, there are times when a good, clean length of steel is a more faithful friend than the greatest spell." With a smooth maneuver he managed to slip out of his seat, leaving a bewildered Anisella warming the chair alone. He took a wide stance and whipped his sword from the scabbard. All the nearby tables emptied in a rush. In Port Laverne, if you stand too near cold steel, you could catch your death.

"Then you've been following us?"

"Aye." His sword slid back into its sheath with a vicious hiss. "As is my duty, I have taken care not to let you out of my sight. Until this moment, I was able to do so secretly. However, now that you are about to embark, I can no longer cling to the shadows. Your cause is mine. If you sail, I sail at your side."

"What if I don't want you to sail at my side?" I was a little annoyed with this masked man. I didn't like finding out that King Steffan thought I needed a protector. It reminded me too much of Dad—although to be honest, what Dad always bellowed at Mom was, "Abstemia, what this son of yours needs is a bloody *keeper!*"

"But Kendaaaaar," Anisella whimpered. "I don't think you're being faaaaaair. If King Steffan went to all the trouble of hiring a Blade for Justice—"

"You may call me Blade for short," he said gallantly.

"—then it wouldn't be right to send him baaaaack."

I chewed my lip in thought. "If I tell you to go away and leave us alone, will you do it?"

"I am a Blade for Justice. Wherever there is injustice, it is my calling to seek it out and right all ancient wrongs. I know that you voyage forth to undo a serious injustice. How can I ignore so great a call to arms? The king paid me in advance. I'll promise you to go away and leave you alone, but I won't do it. I'll sneak after you instead." He had a nice smile. "I'm a very good sneak."

"In that case, I guess it's better to have you out where I can keep an eye on you keeping an eye on me. All right, Blade, you're in." We shook hands. He had smooth skin and fine bones, but a strong grip.

When Rhett returned to tell us he'd found a ship, I introduced him to Blade.

"Charmed," said the oracle, who wasn't. He could see how

Anisella was eating the swordsman with her eyes. "I only paid the captain for three passages."

Blade tossed back his cloak to reveal a bulging leather purse. "I like to take care of my own expenses."

We paid the tavern owner for our mead and for damages to the waitress, then followed Rhett down the wharf to where our ship was docked.

"Uh-oh," I said when I saw the craft.

"What is wrong?" the oracle demanded. "It is going where we wish to go, and it is entirely seaworthy. There were no other ships sailing for the Underside."

"Yes, but—"

"I know, I know: To your eyes, she is crewed by monsters. Perhaps you have never met the animal residents of the Underside before—the transformed ones, that is. It is said that during the last shape-shift of Orbix, during the Great Wrench, some of the internal wizardly forces which caused our world to assume its current shape were thrown into the atmosphere through a rift in the ground. This cloud of power settled over the Underside, giving to certain beasts the ability to speak."

"Hey!" Scandal objected. "I'm a beast, I can speak, but I sure as Shirley MacLaine don't look like any of *them*." He eyed the Undersider crewmen—crewbeasts—slowly going about their business aboard the ship. "Ug-*lee*!"

"Scandal, we've met Undersiders before," I reminded him. "Remember that time we ran into the itinerant porridge vendor? He was a bear driving a wagon pulled by a team of matched Goldilockses. You didn't think he was so ugly."

"A bear is a bear, so there, so there, but some of what's crawling around that deck looks like what you find in all the best noses." Scandal made a hairball-alert sound.

"I confess, the change was not equally kind to all the animals it touched," Rhett said. "Some grew out of all proportion without being able to speak. These were either captured and put to work, or else they ran away and became legends. To this day in the kingdom of Wingdingo they sing of the great hero, George the Gerbilslayer. It does not sound like much if you did not see those gerbils."

"Do they still have any of those giant gerbils running around loose?" Scandal asked, his mouth watering. "And if they do, did we remember to pack the mustard?"

The oracle was wise; he ignored him. "Not only did certain beasts receive the gift of speech, but their bodies were also changed just enough so that they could use man-made things such as tools, vehicles, clothing—"

"You mean you got them some nice clothes and they grew into them?" Scandal asked. "Four legs, good; two legs, pretty silly-looking on some of 'em."

"Nevertheless, it is how they are," the oracle pronounced. "It was while the newly transformed beasts were growing used to the changes that certain humans took advantage of the situation. First, they noted that some of their fellow-humans had lost the same gift of speech the animals gained, and along with it, a measure of intelligence."

"Huh!" Scandal was skeptical. "Most humans I know always sound *smarter* when they shut up."

Rhett let the comment pass. "These same schemers immediately confiscated the property of their stricken friends, relatives, and neighbors and took them into custody. They said it was for their own good. Later they sold them as slaves to the transformed animals, who never had been taught that slavery was evil. It was a time of grave injustice."

"I should have been there," Blade said. "I would have stopped it."

For once, Scandal didn't give *that* look to me. "Hey, Zorro, you're a sweet kid and all that, but Rhett's talking major cosmic and political disaster. In case you haven't counted noses lately, you're only one—*uno, un, eins, ichi,* singular, solo, the cheese stands alone."

"Silly kitty," Anisella said, wagging a finger at Scandal. "If Blade says he would have stopped it, I *know* he could have." The poor cat shivered in the draft from her rapidly batting eyelashes.

"Finally," Rhett said, staring at Blade and Anisella with his jaw clenched and white. "Finally the enslavers of their fellow humans went to the transformed animals. They gained their trust and friendship by giving them clothes and equipment with which to start new lives, and by teaching them how to adapt to the human way of life. In spite of this, there have never been any wars on the Underside. The animals do not seem to care about things like leadership and power. As long as they have good health, happy children, and enough to eat, anyone can be king."

"Which is why only humans rule on the Underside," Anisella finished. "The animals outnumber them, but no animal wants to be king. Most of them are still too busy working off their debts to the people who first sold them their clothes and land and property and slaves, even though it's been centuries. Animals don't understand contracts or compound interest, either. I learned that when I did my dissertation." She gave Blade another of those warm and gooey smiles.

"So *that* slimy thing on deck is—?" Scandal gestured with his paw.

Rhett peered at it. "A slug, by my guess. They do look most odd when given legs and grown to man-size, I admit."

"If we ever get back to my world, I've gotta take you to see Congress. How about *that* refugee from a bad cartoon?" Scandal pointed out another crewman, this one green.

"A transformed turtle. Or perhaps a tortoise. I find it hard to tell them apart."

I looked up into the ship's rigging and saw a long-armed crewman snoozing upside-down from a crossbeam with a happy smile on his face. "What about him?"

"A sloth. Now, shall we board? The tide will be with us in six hours, and this ship needs every instant to get under way."

With that crew? No wonder. Still, I hesitated. "Look, I don't have anything against talking animals," I said.

"Some of his best friends," Scandal put in. "But when I wanted to marry his sister, he talked about getting me fixed." The cat winked at me.

"Come on, I mean it! We've got a long voyage and this ship just doesn't look seaworthy. It doesn't even look like a ship!"

"It is not a ship," Rhett said. "Any fool can see that."

"Any fool just did," Scandal remarked.

"It is a snail. A goodly giant four-masted snail."

"A snail?" I repeated.

"What else did you expect?" Rhett shrugged. "This ship belongs to the Postal Service."

CHAPTER ———————— 9

DELICIOUS SMELLS CAME FROM THE GALLEY OF THE good ship *Eventually*. They lured me away from the bridge to see what was wrong. Our ship's cook was slow (he came by it honestly, being a tortoise), but he made up for it by being terrible. The only smells I ever expected to find coming from the galley were singed scales and burned food.

I found Anisella in the little cookhouse built high on the giant snail's shell, her hair tied back with a thin copper wire. She wasn't wearing an apron—allergic to cloth, remember? But a chain-mail halter and kilt get very hot when you're working near cook-fires, and so . . .

"Oh, hello, Kendar." She looked happy to see me. Happy all over. "I hope you don't mind that I've taken over the cook's job. I love to cook almost as much as I love to clean house and do the laundry. Sometimes I get so sad when it seems like there aren't enough chores in a day. But then I just go and make clothing for orphans and I feel much better, even if working with cloth does make my hands break out in hives. It's for a good cause. How long have you been standing there?"

"Haggahaggahaggahagga."

"Dinner's almost done. I'll serve it just as soon as I slip back into my clothes. I hope you like it."

"Oh yeah. Oh boy. Like it. Oh boy. Oh yeah."

She tittered. "Silly Kendar! I haven't even told you what we're having yet."

"Look! A walrus!" I cried, and used it as an excuse to tear my eyes away. "Uh, no. My mistake." I continued to gaze out to sea, though. Mom always taught me that it's good manners to look someone in the eye when you're having a conversation, but Mom never met Anisella. "So, um, have you seen Rhett anywhere?"

71

"No," came the answer from behind me. "He spends most of his time in his cabin. I hope he's not seasick." Anisella sounded genuinely concerned about Rhett's health. I wondered if she really cared about him, or if it was only something just-a-good-friend would say.

"You could go and find out," I suggested. I knew what was making Rhett sick, and it wasn't the sea. The sea was very beautiful, but it couldn't wear a chain-mail kilt and halter like Anisella. Or *not* wear them, in this case.

"Maybe later," she said in a way that meant *No*. "He might be having a vision or talking with Merwallow. He wouldn't want to be disturbed."

"Maybe he's trying to find out how to break the curse on you," I said.

"Oh, that." (I was still looking the other way, but I bet she shrugged when she said it. I could picture how she'd look, wearing what she wasn't wearing and shrugging her shoulders. Her soft, white, curved, rounded—*Argh!*) "Honestly, there are times I wish someone would publish a book to tell people how to get along with wicked fairies. It would save everyone an awful lot of troubles and curses and misunderstandings."

"You were cursed by a wicked fairy?" This was a surprise. "I guess your parents forgot to invite her to your Naming Day party, and when all the other fairies gave you their gifts, she showed up and put the curse on—"

"No, that's not it." (I heard her moving around the galley, stirring pots.) "The wicked fairy was the only one my parents *did* invite to the party. She had a wonderful time and she gave me a pink stuffed rappid that played the 'Go To Sleep, Your Mommy's Tired' lullaby. And after that she always remembered to send me a birthday present: one year, a doll; the next, eternal beauty; the third, some pink chain mail. Once I asked her for a pony, but all I got was a stupid dragon's egg. They take forever to hatch, they're impossible to house-train, and you have to wait years until they're big enough to ride. I didn't have the patience to take care of it, so I gave it to—"

I thumped the cookhouse doorjamb. "What does that have to do with your curse?"

"That's just it; I don't know." (I'll bet anything she was pouting. She had the perfect mouth for pouting: so red, so soft, so—*Stop* that, Kendar!) "One day, soon after Mama had that funny little talk with me about where babies come from, I was up in my room when I heard people arguing in the kitchen. The door was open just a crack when I came downstairs, so I spied through it. There she was, screaming at my parents. Before I could figure out why, she shouted, '—and if I can't, then neither shall you! I place a curse on her from this day forward!' Poor Daddy asked, 'What curse is that, O terrible Acerbia?' She sneered and said, 'That's for me to know and for you to find out. But I promise you one thing: It's a pip.' Then she vanished and I never saw her again. It was a few days afterwards that Daddy took me to see Rhett. You know the rest."

What can you say when one of the most beautiful women in the world has just finished telling you her troubles?

"So, uh, what are we having for dinner? No more baked molasses and cheese, I hope."

"Perish the thought!" This time her shrill giggle was accompanied by the chinking sound of chain-mail clothing being put back on. "That was all the real ship's cook ever seemed to serve us. I don't know about you, but I'm relieved the crew all declared an eternal gawfee break as soon as the captain jumped ship."

"Poor Captain Lupe," I said, remembering the unhappy, frustrated jackrappit. He was always darting here and there around the ship, trying to get his men to work faster. He was lucky if he got them to work at all. "How did someone like him ever get into the Underside Postal Service?"

"He told me it was a mistake. He was supposed to work for the Department of Taxation as a collector. When he was sent to the Postal Service instead, he tried to get out. They said they were sorry and told him they'd get him transferred right away. That was seventeen years ago." Anisella sighed. "I'm surprised the poor bunny didn't go crazy. It's a good thing all he did was stow away aboard that merchant ship we passed two weeks ago."

"A good thing for all of us," I agreed. "Maybe now that the crew's not sailing the ship, we'll reach the Underside in less than a year."

Another sigh. "Oh, *I* wouldn't mind that."

I knew what she was thinking: Blade. Ever since we'd come aboard, Anisella had spent every free moment following him around, seeing if he needed anything. Usually Blade said he needed to be alone with his thoughts of justice. Then Anisella offered to help him think of some.

Right now Blade was up in the ship's rigging with Scandal. The cat loved it up there. He called the mainmast the world's biggest scratching post, whatever that was. He was good at leaping from timber to timber, and he could yank the ropes with his teeth. As for

Blade, the masked swordsman was also a pretty good seaman. Between him and the cat, I had a fine crew.

Captain Kendar! I liked the sound of that. I wished Dad and my brother Basehart were here. If they could only see me now, in full command of an entire ship, they'd have to respect me at last. Dad never thought I'd do anything useful with my life because I didn't like to ride around the forests killing things. Basehart didn't bother thinking about me at all, if he could help it.

They were both really impressed when I became the king's Court Wizard. Too bad that it wore off after a while. Dad went back to saying things like, "Magic, *huh*! I'd like to see where your parlor tricks get you when you come face to face with a savage, cunning, vicious, bloodthirsty, man-eating deer!" Basehart went back to burping and agreeing with him and falling asleep. Or maybe he fell asleep first. With Basehart, it's hard to tell.

Ah, but with a title like *Captain* Kendar—! They'd have to be impressed then. And stay impressed. True, no one gave me the title, but I think I earned it. Blade and Scandal helped out a little, but I was doing most of the actual work of sailing the Underside Snail Ship *Eventually*.

Just because I was doing it with Majyk shouldn't mean it didn't count.

Speaking of Majyk, it was about time for me to give the ship another nudge. "I've got to go do something. Call me for dinner," I said to Anisella as I hurried away.

There were two hatches cut into the snail's shell, fore and aft of the cookhouse. If you wanted to go below, you could choose either one, or you could go all the way forward to where the snail's head stretched out of his shell and slip under that way. Not too many of the crew did, though, because it was . . . well . . . *yucky*. The only ones who liked to go that way were the transformed slugs. Under the hatches it was a different story. Inside, the snail's shell was divided into cabins and holds and passageways, like a regular ship.

To reach my cabin, I had to go past the crew's quarters. They all lived together in one big area with lots of hammocks and comfy cushions and more gawfee-making supplies than most taverns. They never closed their doors—too much work—so when you walked by, you couldn't help overhearing whatever they were up to. Mostly you heard snores, but this time I caught a little bit of conversation.

"—never forget that terrible day. Oh, the blood, the blood! I was all alone at my post. No one could hear my screams. It was cruel, the pain. And all around me, others were bleedin' just as bad."

"I thought you said you were all alone at your post?"

"I was. My post was right next to Leonardo's post; ain't that right, Leo?" Leo didn't answer, so the storyteller went on. "Anyhow, the bloodshed—! Happened right in these waters, it did. Pray you never see anythin' like it. I'm lucky to be alive. Oh, cruel and wicked, they are, and they don't know the meanin' o' mercy."

Mom always taught me that eavesdropping was rude (unless she was doing it to me for my own good), but I didn't care; I had to know what was going on. Bloodshed? Pain? Cruelty? On the high seas it could mean only one thing:

"Pirates?" I cried, bursting into the crew's quarters. "You mean there are pirates in these waters?"

Twenty pairs of eyes turned to meet mine. Very slowly.

"Pirates?" the storyteller drawled. (It was our former cook, a tortoise named Flash.) "Dunno nothin' 'bout pirates."

"Then what were you talking about?" I asked. "Blood and pain and screams and—"

"Paper cuts." Flash nodded his head. It took four heartbeats to go up and five to come down. "Twenty years ago, back before I was ship's cook, when I was still a lively young sprat, I used to sort mail. One year they started makin' a new kinda paper. Nasty stuff. Not safe. Sharp edges." He rubbed his wrinkled brown cheek. "Goin' to write in a complaint 'bout it some day real soon now."

I left the crew guzzling gawfee and trading war stories. I'd wasted enough time. In my cabin I had the peace and quiet I needed to concentrate on Majyk. I also had the privacy I wanted in case the spell I tried didn't work. So far I was getting the results I wanted about two times out of five, which wasn't bad for a mostly self-taught wizard.

My cabin was pretty large because it slept two. Blade insisted on being my roommate. Either he wanted to be there to protect me from unknown perils, or he wanted me to be there to protect him from Anisella. All the furniture was built into the walls or anchored to the floor, and the smaller things were also tied down or otherwise attached so they couldn't be tossed around during rough weather.

I sat down on the edge of my bunk and untied the tankard attached to the side rail. Swaying with the motion of the ship, I held the big drinking vessel out at arm's length, closed my eyes, and concentrated.

When I was first getting the hang of my Majyk, Mother Toadbreath the witch gave me helpful books of spells and instructions. Mother Toadbreath also let me borrow her enchanted gravy boat so I'd have a focus for my Majyk. Using the gravy boat and the spells, and with a little help from Mysti—Oh, all right, a lot of help from Mysti—I managed to make a carpet fly. I hadn't packed the book, the gravy boat, or the carpet for this trip, but I didn't want to make the *Eventually* fly, just go a little faster. I discovered that I could do that by using almost any piece of hollow kitchenware to focus and hold my Majyk, then trying the levitation spell. We never got off the ground—I mean the water—but we did pick up speed.

Two times out of five.

It was pretty easy this time. Too easy. Had something really happened or was it just my imagination? I felt the ship shudder the way it always did when it changed speed, but it wasn't a big shudder. I secured the tankard and went topside. It was hard to judge if we were going any faster than before. You can tell you've picked up speed on land by seeing if you pass things like trees and houses and piles of horseflop any faster, but when you're at sea, what is there? Waves. Water. How can you tell if you're passing water faster? (I asked Scandal that question once and he laughed so hard he fell out of the rigging. Stupid cat.)

Fortunately for me, Rhett was on deck for once. The oracle leaned against the rail and stared out to sea. Maybe he could tell me if my Majyk had done the trick.

The real trick was getting a straight answer out of the oracle. Even though his oath to Merwallow guaranteed he'd tell the truth, the whole truth, and nothing but the ugly truth, he still had his ways of sidestepping if he didn't want to help you. Ever since Blade had attached himself to our expedition and Anisella had attached herself to Blade, Rhett blamed me for the whole thing.

"Nice day," I remarked casually, taking a spot beside him at the rail.

"What is there to dislike about it?" he replied.

"Nothing like a good ship under full sail," I went on. "I know that speed isn't the *Eventually*'s specialty, but I do think she's going a little faster."

"Can you tell?" Rhett arched an eyebrow at me.

"No," I admitted. "I was hoping you could."

"I can."

"Well, are we?"

"Are we what?"

"Are we going any faster?"

"Does it matter?"

"I'd like to know."

"Why?"

"I'm using Majyk to speed us up and I want to know if the spell's working right, that's why." I was starting to get annoyed.

"Can't you tell?"

And there we were, back where we'd begun. It was too much for me. I grabbed Rhett's collar and jerked him forward, even if he was older than me and had a god on his side. "No, I *can't* tell and I *want* to know and if you don't tell me I'll throw you overboard and we'll figure out how fast we're going by how long it takes us to sail past *you!*"

His eyebrow twitched again, just like Scandal's. "Fascinating." (Scandal said that a lot, too.) "But what if I refuse to stay in one place? I can swim, you know."

I sighed and let go of his cloak. "Fine. Don't tell me anything. For all I know, my Majyk's making the ship go slower instead of faster. Great. We'll take even longer to reach the Underside."

"Long enough for you to learn some manners?" Rhett smirked.

That did it. "Long enough for Blade to stop running away from Anisella!"

Rhett's eyes snapped back in his head. He sank to his knees in the fastest trance I ever saw. His lips mumbled at top speed; then he was back on his feet with the happy news that my Majyk speed-spell was working this time, we were almost to the Underside, and we should be sighting land within three days.

"Thank you," I said.

"Pirates permitting," he added.

"What pirates?"

"Those pirates." He pointed dramatically off to the right—I mean starboard. A black ship flying a black flag was racing over the waves right for us. "Merwallow refused to tell me whether we could outrun them or outfight them. He is a little bored at the moment, and he thought it might be fun to watch our pitiful mortal struggles. Of course *he* knows how it will all turn out, but he wants a few cheap laughs. Gods. You cannot live with them and you cannot live—"

"*Pirates!*" I cried, clinging to the rail. "*Pirates!*" I shouted, cupping my hands to my mouth and bellowing the word up into the rigging at Blade and Scandal. "*Pirates!*" I gasped, shoving

Rhett towards the galley to warn Anisella. "*Pirates!*" I howled, leaning over the hatch and thumping on the deck so the crew would be sure to hear, grab their weapons, and muster to defend our ship.

"Aye, sir, just a minute 'til we finish this last cup," came a voice from down below. "Then we'll show those fiends how a postal worker fights!" A rousing cheer followed.

Blade, Scandal, Rhett, and I were the only ones on deck and ready for battle by the time the pirate ship caught up with us an hour later.

CHAPTER ——————— 10

FLASH STUCK HIS HEAD OUT OF THE HATCHWAY AS THE first grappling hooks flew from the black ship to our own. "Pirates, all right," he said to the crewmen still below.

"Of course they're pirates!" I yelled. "Now get *up* here!" One by one, they did. Slowly.

Blade raced up and down the deck, slashing at the pirates' lines and tossing their grappling hooks into the sea. "To the galley, men!" he cried. "I've stacked weapons from the ship's armory there for every able-bodied fighter among you!"

The crew stood around muttering about how they didn't feel so well; the weather was too cold, too damp, too hot, too dry; when they signed up to serve on the *Eventually* no one ever told them they'd have to fight pirates and they had all these paper cuts—

"Whoever does not do his part to save this ship shall perish on the end of my good sword!" Blade told them. I never saw turtles, tortoises, slugs, and sloths move so fast.

While the crew crowded into the galley, the rest of us took our places for the coming battle. More grappling lines arced through the air, and Blade couldn't be in a dozen places at once to cut them away. The pirate ship closed with us even more. I stared over the rail, trying to see the face of the enemy. All I could see was what looked like a plank fence. The boards parted only to let another grappling hook fling through at us.

"What's that they've got there? Shields?" I asked.

Blade shaded his eyes. "Gangways," he said. "They'll pull us closer and then let the boards fall to make bridges from ship to ship."

"No wonder they call it boarding," Scandal said from somewhere up the mast.

"Gee, in all the stories I ever read, pirates just throw ropes into the other ship's rigging and swing over."

Blade's eyes shone cold with scorn through the slits in his mask. "*One* episode about nectar pirates from a Raptura Eglantine romance does not make either you or her an expert on the subject."

"Hey! How did you know it was—?"

Before I could finish my question, someone tapped my shoulder. I turned around fast and nearly cut off my nose on the cutlass Anisella was holding straight up in front of her. "Well, I'm ready," she announced.

"What are you doing here?" Blade snarled. "Get below."

"Nonsense," the girl replied. "We're going to need all the able-bodied fighters we've got."

Not even Blade could argue about the able-bodied part, but he did ask, "What do you know about sword-fighting?"

"Oh, not nearly so much as *you*," Anisella simpered.

"Claptrap," Rhett said curtly. "She is being modest. From the moment she was placed in my care, I saw to it that Anisella received the best education I could afford. In view of her allergy—and therefore the way she must dress—I insisted that she learn self-defense first and foremost."

"Goodness, yes," Anisella agreed. "I couldn't begin to do the shopping without it, especially when there's a sale in the fruit market. The way some people behave, you'd think they never saw cheap melons before. I don't even need a sword, really. I have a black belt in *helo kiti* and a green barrette in *po kipsi.*"

"Very well, I suppose we can use you." Blade turned his back on Anisella and strode across the deck to see what was keeping the rest of the crew.

By now the grappling lines were fixed, and the pirates had begun to reel us in like a big fish. I glanced up and saw their flag—against a black background, a human skull grinned while a strangely flexible-looking hoof poured green goo over it from a jar clearly labeled "mint sauce." I got a better grip on my blade. I was going to use it as a Majyk focus, because frankly, Scandal (who was still up in the rigging) would be a better swordsman than me. There was a terrible grinding noise as the wooden hull of the pirate ship rubbed against the giant snail's shell. The wall of planks dropped.

"They're repulsive!" Anisella gasped.

"They're vicious-looking!" Scandal cried from above.

"They are clearly without memory," Rhett observed.

"They're *sheep!*" I was so stunned, I dropped my sword. "They're all a bunch of big, fat, fluffy, cuddly *sheep!*"

And while I was still gaping, the sheep charged across the plank bridges and showed us why you should never call a pirate *cuddly* to his face.

It was a furious battle. Like all transformed Underside animals, the sheep still had hooves, but hooves that could hold a sword and use it well. They ran on two legs, which was bad for us all, and Rhett was right when he said they had no mercy.

I went to my knees to grab back my sword and just missed losing my hand to one of them. His blade *chonked* into the deck at my fingertips. Chips of wood spun through the air. "Back, laddie!" he shouted, making several false jabs at my face. "One o' them's like t' put out yer eye." (He must have known what he was talking about. He had only one; the other was covered with a black patch.) He planted one hind hoof on my wrist and sneered at me.

"Baa'aaarrrrh, ye fleeceless noddy! Not so high and mighty now, are ye?" The point of his sword held steady between my eyes. "Who'll be wearin' them fancy little paper pantaloons on whose chops before this day is done, eh?" He pulled the blade back for the killing blow.

"MROW!" Scandal dropped on the sheep's head, claws out, and dug in. The cat had long claws, Wedwel be praised—long enough to pierce the pirate's bright red bandanna, the fleece beneath, and make themselves felt. Even better, Scandal's weight pushed the bandanna over the sheep's eyes—bad and good alike—blinding him. He dropped his sword right into my waiting hands and waved his hooves around wildly. Scandal kept screeching and hissing and scratching as the pirate stumbled towards the rail. The cat leaped off just before the unlucky sheep went plunging over the side and into the briny water.

"Piece o' cake," Scandal remarked, licking his paw as he perched on the rail.

"What flavor?" I asked, kind of nastily. I was feeling a little cranky. My left hand was bleeding (Well, *you* try catching a falling sword with your bare hands and see if you can do it without getting cut!) and it made me impatient with the cat's smugness.

Scandal didn't even bother to look at me. "Chocolate sheep," he replied, and swarmed up the mast again, ready to pounce on more pirates.

I pressed my left hand against my trousers to make it stop bleeding, and struggled to hold onto the blade with my right. A pitched battle isn't the best place for the quiet concentration I needed to work my Majyk, but it didn't look like anyone cared. They were too busy.

Most of the pirates were gathered around the cookhouse, fighting our crew. Well, maybe *fighting* is too strong a word. *Putting up with* our crew comes closer. Putting up with one crewman after another surrendering, I mean, and they had their hooves full doing it.

According to Raptura Eglantine—who does *too* know plenty about pirates! Lucy told me she always does her research because all romances must be strictly accurate—there is something called the Law of the Sea which every pirate obeys. Part of it says that if someone surrenders to you in a battle, you have to let him say a few last words before you stab him, clap him in irons, or look for a handy shark.

Now guess how the crew of the U.S.S. *Eventually* was surrendering. Uh-huh. Sloooowwwwwly. The poor pirates were nodding off left and right.

"Wouldja look at that!" Scandal's voice drifted down from the rigging. "I always wondered what sheep counted when they couldn't get to sleep, and now I know: Postal workers! Too bad there's not more of them, or we'd have this fight all sewn up."

Yeah, too bad. Even with so many of their men tied up with our crew, the sheep still had us outnumbered, and there were more coming aboard every instant. I saw Anisella holding off three at once. Rhett was right again: She was good. At one point she leaped at the pirates from the ship's rail, squealing "Hiiiiiiiiya!" Whirling in midair, she caught one under the chin with her heel, the second in the windpipe with her elbow, and the third had to settle for a hefty bash on the skull with the butt of her sword. She looked at the fallen pirates. "Oooh, did I do that?" She tittered, and flounced off to find some more.

Meanwhile, Rhett wasn't doing so well. He took a few swings and slashes at the pirate fighting him, then paused. An ordinary man would've gotten himself stabbed then and there, but Rhett was an oracle. Everything he did seemed important; important enough to make the pirate pause too, just in case this was a trick.

"No, it is not a trick," Rhett said. "If you desire tricks, you had better see Master Kendar over there; he is the wizard. I am not going to fight you anymore."

"Baa'aaaarrrrh, d'ye mean ye surrenders?" the sheep demanded. He was a crusty old ram with a dirty yellow fleece and two big gold earrings.

"I suppose I do. What is the point of continuing the battle? We are going to lose it. Merwallow has spoken, although I must say,

I do not like his sense of humor. If he had told us earlier, we might have saved ourselves the bother of hoping for the best."

"'Oo be this Merwaller, eh?" The pirate frowned. A frowning sheep is an awful sight. "Friend o' your'n?"

"Hardly," Rhett replied in his dry way. "Now, do you want to accept my surrender or not?" He thrust out his sword suddenly. Good thing it was hilt-first or the ram would have been shish kebab.

The beast jumped, then looked—sorry, there's no other way to say this—sheepish. "Gi' that here!" he bawled, trying to save face as he snatched the sword from Rhett's hands. "Ye'll be spendin' yer days in irons, me lad!"

"I know." Very few things came as a surprise to the oracle. He sat down on a keg of herrings.

"Rhett, you coward!" I shouted, forgetting that I was only going to use my sword as a Majyk-aiming device. I stalked towards him, waving it around, cutting a lot of space between me and the nearest pirates. "How can you just give up like that?"

"Merwallow has spoken," he repeated, with a shrug. "We are doomed. So why prolong it?"

"We are not!" I maintained, taking a swipe at the nearest pirate. He bleated with pain as my blade accidentally drew blood. "Look there, Anisella's doing just fine!" I gestured, stabbing another pirate on the backswing.

Anisella was indeed doing just fine—until the next pirate she punctured fell forward instead of backwards. He was a fat one, with a thick fleece, and he landed against her leg. She froze in mid-swordstroke. Her face contorted in a horrible expression. She kicked away the body, but it was too late: Big red blotches were already starting to creep up her shin. When they reached the thigh, she began to scratch. When they spread to the other leg, she began to claw. When they climbed up to her belly, she dropped the sword and scraped at the blotches with both hands.

"Oooh! Oooh! Oooh!" she yipped, dancing around the deck in agony. "I am soooo *allergic* to wool!" They captured her with little trouble after that.

"Yeah, well, uh, look at Scandal!" I exclaimed, fending off the fleecy fiends who were closing in on me. "He's not even human, but he's putting up a good fight!"

He was, he really was. No wonder we always thought cats were legendary monsters on Orbix. How else could something so small and cute-looking turn into something so vicious and bloodthirsty so fast? Every sheep he landed on got his face scraped raw. The ones wearing bandannas got the same treatment he'd given his first victim. Whether your eyes are covered with blood or a bandanna makes no difference: You still can't see. The deck under the mainmast was a mob of blinded sheep. They milled about, bumping into one another, sometimes falling overboard, sometimes getting pushed. The few too stupid to drop their swords were slashing their own comrades. Scandal was enjoying himself.

Until a furious barking came from the pirate ship and a beautiful collie came bounding across the boards. The beast wore a single hoop in one ear, a plumed hat, and dark green plaid trousers. Scandal took one look at her and flew straight up the mast. The dog snarled and threatened him with a cutlass, then set to helping the wounded sheep.

"You see?" Rhett was resigned. "Victory is impossible."

"It is *not!*" I don't know why I said that. Inside, I agreed with Rhett: There wasn't any hope. Blade and I were the only two left on board the *Eventually* who could still fight, but we were only two. It didn't matter how good a swordsman Blade was—and right then I could see he was mighty good—we couldn't win. It was impossible.

Just like my father always told me: *You'll never make something of yourself, boy! It's impossible!*

Just like my brother Basehart always sneered: *You, do anything right, Kendar? Haw! That's impossible!"*

Just like my old teacher, Master Thengor, always said: *Kendar Gangle, a wizard? Impossible!*

There's just something about that word that makes me mad.

How mad? a little voice in my head whispered. I began to tingle all over, then to burn. *This mad?* My whole body shuddered as a surge of power shot from my hands. It sped down the sword and exploded from the blade in all directions, a sunburst of Majyk. The smell of singed wool and roasting mutton filled the air. It was pretty strong. I didn't know whether to drool or throw up.

"Would you like to be a little more careful with that?" Rhett's flat voice intruded. The oracle pointed to a heap of blackened bones and slagged steel beside him. "That very well might have been me. Now I suppose I shall have to find another pirate to whom I may surrender. I hope he will believe me without the sword."

I seized Rhett's shoulder and yanked him off the herring keg. "We're not giving up, understand?" I growled.

"Merwallow has—"

"Merwallow might be lying," said Blade, swinging across the embattled deck on a ship's line, slicing pirates all the way. He landed easily on the rail beside me, cut himself some space to stand, then leaped down. Four sheep swarmed towards him, bleating for blood. Steel clashed and clanked, but that didn't stop Blade from keeping up a polite conversation.

"The gods do lie to mortals," he said, driving his attackers back. "It's their privilege."

"It is their entertainment," Rhett admitted. "But Merwallow would never—"

"And when they're not lying to us outright," Blade went on, skewering the first sheep to get careless, "they tell us things all twisty."

"Right," I said, stepping in and launching a couple of Majykal fireballs. "If you think they mean one thing, they can laugh when it turns out they meant another. Like the famous prophecy the oracle gave to King Bukrich of Yonda that goes, 'If you attack your enemy, you will destroy a great empire.'" My fireballs hit their targets. Two pirates stopped dead in their tracks, suddenly aware that every bit of fleece and clothing on their bodies was frizzled away. They retreated to their ship, and knocked a few more of their comrades into the drink when they tried to push past them on the boarding planks.

"King Bukrich *did* destroy a great empire," Rhett put in. "And it was not his own. How do you think he came to be *King* Bukrich? He was a mere shepherd before that."

"Oh." I shot off some more fireballs, but they fizzled out. It's hard to work when you're embarrassed. "Well, yeah, but how about that other famous prophecy? You know, 'If you build it, he will come'?"

"Exactly!" Blade was on my side. He took a moment to slash the sword from one sheep's hoof, along with the hoof, then added, "A very sad tale. King Bukrich died, leaving the throne to his son, Prince Fin." He kicked another sheep somewhere unfair, but it worked. "But Fin was young, and his evil uncle took all the royal power. The prince was angry and asked an oracle for help." Blade ducked a swordstroke and grabbed his fourth attacker by one hind hoof, then tossed him into the sea.

While four more sheep came running up to replace the first group, the masked swordman was able to say, "When he heard the prophecy, Fin assumed the gods meant that his father would come back from the dead and destroy his wicked uncle if only he used the right bait. So Fin spent all his treasure on building a great playing field for eight-hand *roxi*. It was King Bukrich's favorite game. In fact, he died while playing a match."

By now the four fresh pirates were close enough to be a nuisance, so Blade turned his attention to them. I did my part with a few more crackling stings of Majyk from my sword's point. I scored two bull's-eyes, except they weren't bulls, I didn't hit their eyes, and I don't think my mother would like me to say where I *did* hit them.

"So then what happened?" I gasped, swinging my sword in the normal way. The Majyk was getting fainter. I wanted to hold onto it and use it for one final, deck-clearing blast. "Did he build it? Did King Bukrich come back?"

"Yes"—Blade stabbed one pirate—"and yes again." He stabbed the other, but there were plenty more where they came from. "But things didn't turn out the way Prince Fin had hoped. The king's ghost walked into the middle of the *roxi* field, looked around, saw his son waiting for him and stretched out his arms. Fin ran to his father, but instead of embracing the prince, King Bukrich's ghost clenched his hands around the boy's neck, shook him like a dust rag and yelled, 'You idiot, I was *killed* playing this stupid game! If this is how you waste the treasure I broke my back stealing from the peasants, I say my crummy brother Bakskar *deserves* the throne more than you!' It was lucky for Fin that the ghost vanished before he could choke the prince to death. Bakskar became King Bakskar and Fin ran away to be a shepherd like his father."

"I am not surprised," said Rhett, which went without saying.

By this time, all of the *Eventually*'s crew had finished surrendering. The pirates herded them below and slammed the aft hatch, then turned to us. Not even Blade could hold all of them off alone. Scandal was still treed in the rigging. Anisella was nowhere to be seen. It was now or never.

I gave Rhett a grim look. "You want to be surprised?" I gritted, calling all my Majyk up from inside me and shaping it with my mind. "You're going to be surprised."

The oracle yawned. "So are you," he said.

"That's what you—"

A sheep stumbled forward, impaled on Blade's sword. With his last, dying effort he groped for the masked man's throat. He missed his grip and clung to Blade's shirt. There was a loud tearing sound as the sheep's weight ripped the cloth. I glanced over without thinking and got a momentary glimpse of Blade's bare chest before the swordsman clutched his torn shirt closed again.

Swords*man*?

His torn shirt?

My jaw hit the deck. I followed it. One of the pirates must have grabbed the keg of herrings and crowned me with it, because all of a sudden everything went dark and fishy.

Just before I lost consciousness, I thought I heard Rhett's irritating voice say, "Surprise."

CHAPTER ——————— 11

A ROUGH, MOIST TONGUE WAS LICKING MY CHEEK when I came to. "Whozat?" I muttered.

"Anisella," said a familiar voice. "You wish." I opened my eyes and saw Scandal laughing at me. The cat was in my lap, his forepaws resting on my chest while he scoured the last pieces of herring from my face. "I gotta tell you, boss, I really like your taste in after-shave lotions."

I petted the cat. I mean I tried to. I couldn't move my hands. I was fully awake now, and I saw that I was chained to a heavy wooden chair. Shackles held my wrists and ankles. "Where am I?" I asked.

"You're dead last in the Original Wake-Up Lines contest," Scandal told me. "Other than that, you're aboard the bad ship *Golden Fleece*, a pirate vessel commanded by the dreaded Captain Lan and his almost-as-dreaded brother Ramses. You're in Ramses' cabin right now."

I looked around. There was a blackwood table bolted to the floor near me, a second chair on the other side of it, a blue brocade curtain that was pulled back a little to show a bunk hidden behind it, and a couple of portholes. I'd never been on board a real pirate ship, in a real pirate's cabin. I was a little disappointed. Aside from the furniture being sheep-sized, it wasn't that much different from the cabins on the *Eventually*.

Which reminded me . . .

"What happened to our ship?"

"The pirates chopped some holes in the snail's shell below the waterline, set fire to it, and cast off. I managed to jump over to this one while they were doing it."

"They sank the *Eventually*!"

"Wow, you're a regular Einstein. Maybe even an irregular one.

They *tried* to sink her, but they found out that the *Eventually* goes down about as slowly as she used to go forward. It'll take a week before that hulk goes under all the way. The pirates didn't have the time to hang around and wait for it."

"What about the crew?"

"They're still aboard. Hey, don't worry about them, *kemo sabe.* The holes are small, the fire isn't much, and the pirates didn't tie the crew up or lock them away. They can save themselves and the ship, but—"

"But—?"

"—but only if they *hurry up*." The cat shook his head. "Torture your victims instead of making a clean kill; isn't that just like a sheep? You can't trust 'em. And speaking of things you can't trust . . ." His eyes narrowed. "I'm not naming any names, but a certain skinball whose initials are Kendar Ratwhacker Gangle once told me that there are *no dogs* on Orbix."

"There aren't," I agreed.

"Then what the hell chased me up the mizzenpoopboom-mast before? A bad dream?"

"Not on *our* side of Orbix," I corrected myself. "I didn't know they had them on the Underside. I never saw one before, except in books. It sure was, um, a noisy beast."

"Better watch your mouth, fella. That noisy beast is Lodda, First Mate aboard the *Fleece*, and from what I've overheard, she's a real bi—"

"I still don't understand. Why wasn't I left behind on the *Eventually*? Why am I here, in this cabin? And where are—?" I stopped. There was something else I wanted to know, only maybe I didn't. I was afraid I might not like the answer. "Scandal . . . where are Rhett, and Anisella, and—and Blade?" If that was his—*her*—real name.

Scandal jumped out of my lap and swaggered back and forth across the floor, holding one hind leg stiff. He squinched his left eye shut and said "Arrrrh!" a lot, for no reason. For instance: "Arrrrh, matey, 'tis a yarn long in the tellin', aye. Ye be here because 'twas the will o' Ramses, an' no sailor aboard this vessel dares to question that, arrrh. Not if he's fond o' livin'. Yon lubber Rhett's in the brig, aye, and yon sweet pippin Anisella's worked her wiles on Cap'n Lan. She's his *personal* prisoner, if ye gets me drift." He winked at me, which is hard to do if you've got one eye closed already.

"With a *sheep*?" I squealed.

"Arrrrh, if 'tis good enough for a certain senator I could

name— Nay, but 'tis none o' that. Wi' these very ears I heard the cap'n say as how Mistress Anisella reminded him o' a wench he were fond o' once, when he were but a lambkin in his old home village, Port O' Lyn. A sweet shepherdess who went by the name o' Bo, she did, aye. 'Tis a right odd world we live in, salt me fer a codfish if it ain't."

"And what about—what about Blade?"

Scandal paused and hung his head. "Blade's gone."

I felt a sharp pang in my chest. "Gone?" I repeated stupidly. "Who killed—?"

The cat looked up. "Killed? I said nowt o' killin'. Now why'd ye be thinkin' anyone was man jack enough t' slay such a one, eh?"

"You said—"

"I said Blade was *gone*." He went back to his stiff-legged pacing. "As far as ye be concerned, that is. Blew her cover the lass did, aye. *Tore* her cover's more like it. And hard goin' she had t' fight on wi' one hand holdin' her shirt together, so the pirates overwhelmed her an' brought her here wi' the rest."

"So you know Blade's a girl, too!" I was glad to hear it. For a while I was afraid my eyes had tricked me.

"Better'n that, laddie-buck: I know *who* she is besides, tie a rope t' me tail an' use me fer an anchor else." He chuckled. "I wager as ye never knew yer wife was such a fair hand wi' a sword."

"*My wife!*"

"Aye, yer Welfie wife an' none other. Only none but we knows it. I doubt anyone else save ye an' me saw them—it—those— arrrrh!—else they'd never have shackled her below in the brig wi' Rhett, aye." He stalked back and forth, back and forth, singing "Fifteen Men on a Welfie's Chest, Yo-ho-ho and a Barrel of Herring."

"Why are you walking like that?" I demanded, eager to shut him up. "Did you hurt your leg?"

Scandal sat down and opened both eyes. "Naaaah."

"And why are you *talking* like that?"

"I was just trying to get you in a pirate-y mood, that's all. It'll make it easier to deal with the captain and his brother if you can speak their language. Pieces of eight, pieces of eight, awk, awk!"

"Pieces of eight what?"

The cat sighed and waved a paw at me. "Skip it."

I strained against my bonds again. "Scandal, help me get loose."

"Isn't that a little like Godzilla asking a termite for helpful housewrecking hints? You're the one with the hog's-load of Majyk, big guy."

"Yeah, but I can hardly move my hands to cast a spell."

"That didn't stop our pal Zoltan, remember? When the Council brought him to trial, he could move his fingers just a little, but it was enough to cast a little spell to summon a little demon. One with little poisoned fangs." The cat frowned at the memory. He'd been one of the demon's victims.

"I'm not Zoltan."

"Nooooo. Tell me another one, Daddy."

"What I mean is, he had more practice using Majyk than me. Anyway, these shackles are iron."

"Really puts a crimp in the old cauldron, huh?" The cat clicked his tongue. "So what do you want me to do?"

"You've got Majyk of your own, and you're not tied up. Use it to set me free."

"An' den? Just because someone hands you a bowl of fruit doesn't mean you can juggle apples."

"I'll help you."

His whiskers twisted. "Giving me the benefit of your vast experience, huh? Yippee. Also, yahoo."

I let my head loll back. Arguing with the cat was tiring work. "Look, at least you can *try*. I don't know what this Ramses wants from me, but I don't want to face him trussed up like a chicken."

"This is all a plot, right?" The cat raised an eyebrow. "Misery loves company. You won't be happy until I study wizardry, too. And then what? You want me to hang up my shingle and settle down in this cockamamie world, I betcha. Well, it won't work. People have been trying to trick cats into honest jobs for centuries. Besides, I never promised I was gonna hang around forever. I still wanna go home."

"I know." I couldn't help sounding sad. I liked Scandal.

"Hey, nothing personal against Orbix, but you also told me I'm the only cat in this world, outside of stories to scare the kiddies. Unless you were wrong about that, too?" He looked hopeful.

I shook my head. "I forgot about Underside dogs, but I'm sure about cats: Legendary monsters. Master Thengor taught us that lesson, and he was never wrong."

"He was human; how could he never be wrong?"

"Because a wizard only gets to be wrong once. Then he gets to be dead."

"Oh." Scandal's whiskers drooped. "So if that's the way it is, then *I'm* all there is as far as cats go."

"I know," I said, because I did. "No female cats."

"Yowzah. And unlike you, I don't want to stay a bachelor all my life—especially not a married bachelor, which is what you are, and don't deny it."

"Scandal, I've done my best. I've tried and *tried* to find a female for you." I'll say. If I had a grain of salt for every hour I'd spent on my knees going *Here, kitty, kitty, kitty,* and dangling anchovies in front of the "rat hole" that brought Scandal from his world to mine, I could start my own ocean.

"I know you have, boss; no one's blaming you. It's just the way it is." The cat sighed. "Okay, I'm no ingrate. Tell you what: I'll try to help you, but this is a one-shot deal, got it?"

"Got it. Now rub against my ankles."

"Not unless you buy me dinner and a movie first."

"*Scandal!*"

The cat chuckled and did what I asked. While he rubbed against my ankles, I searched my memory for any Spells of Freeing I might remember from the big book Mother Toadbreath gave me. A dim cloud of sparks like a halo of fireflies formed around the cat. That was Scandal's Majyk, rising to the surface and making itself visible. My own was trapped inside me by the power of the iron shackles.

(The Council used iron shackles on Zoltan too—you don't get to be on the Council if you're stupid—but iron doesn't *destroy* Majyk, it just makes it harder to reach, harder to use. You know, like when you want to stir a cauldron full of soup, only someone's hidden all the ladles? A good cook—an *experienced* cook—can still manage to stir it a little, using only a teaspoon. An apprentice cook will just burn his fingers and drop the teaspoon in the cauldron.)

So Scandal provided the Majyk and I provided the words. It didn't work.

Scandal stopped rubbing. "No reflection on your talents as a wizard, big guy, but my chin's going bald. Shouldn't we be seeing some results?"

"I'm trying," I growled. "I'm pretty sure the shackles feel a little looser. You just keep on doing your part."

"Okay." Scandal shrugged, which is a pretty good trick when you don't have shoulders. "It's no skin off my—Oh, wait, yes it is. Ahhhh, what the heck." He rubbed against the shackles some more.

"Well, isn't this a pretty picture?" The voice was low and menacing, with only a hint of bleat. Scandal stopped and lifted his head, his Majyk-charged fur bristling. His lips curled back in an angry hiss, but I bet he was more afraid than angry.

You'd be frightened too if you suddenly saw a giant sheep with a sinister black hood over his head. He stood in the cabin doorway, one black-gloved hand resting there for a moment. Then he entered the room as its master and threw his thickly fleeced body into the other chair. "So, what have we here?" he asked, swinging his booted hind feet onto the table. His boots were black too, and so were his trousers. It looked like he and Mysti shopped for clothing in the same places.

I admit it: I was scared. But there was no reason he had to know that. In my mind I pictured our family dinners when Mom would serve a thick roast of mutton. We raised big sheep on the Gangle lands. The leftovers went on for days and days.

"I am Master Kendar Gangle, Chief Wizard to His Majesty, good King Steffan of Grashgoboum," I replied haughtily. "And I eat your kind for breakfast." Several breakfasts.

"Do you, now?" The hooded sheep seemed amused. "Then perhaps I ought to protect myself and my dear brother by throwing you into the sea right now."

"Try it." My stomach sank down to knee-level, but I had to see this through. Once you start out acting brave, you can't say *Oops! Just fooling. Actually I'm a professional coward* all of a sudden.

Besides, Mysti was on board, chained in the brig. I couldn't just leave her there. She was my wife, after all, even if I never wanted to marry her. *A Gangle always does what's right, like it or not, lads,* Father taught us. *Or I'll give you a smack in the head.*

The sinister sheep tilted his chair back and crossed one leg over the other on the table between us. "You are in a hurry to die, Master Kendar?"

"I didn't say that." I tried to look mysterious and all-knowing. Sort of like Rhett, only not so snotty.

"Then what did you mean by it?"

"Come now, Ramses," I said. "You're a sheep of the world. Let's not play games. There's a reason you had me brought to your cabin instead of locking me in irons below with my friends. I'm betting it's because you need me."

"Why would I need you?" The hint of a sheepish bleat went right out of Ramses' voice when he taunted me.

"Because like I said, I'm a wizard." It was my best guess. It was my only guess. "You saw a sample of my work during the battle for the *Eventually*." I nodded at Scandal. "And you see my familiar right here."

"Arrrrh," said the cat politely.

"Good, very good," the hooded sheep drawled. "A fine bluff, at any rate. But don't flatter yourself. You and your companions are here simply because you are obviously Topsiders. I don't know what brought you into our waters, and I don't care. What matters to me is that there might be someone you left behind on the Topside who'll be willing to ransom your worthless hides."

I don't know why, but Ramses' words just seemed to ring false. "Then why pick me for questioning? You could have used any of the others."

He hesitated a little before answering; then he talked too fast, too glibly. "That was impossible. My brother has taken a fancy to the female—don't ask me why—and won't allow me to question her. As for the other males, one is too fierce a fighter to be trusted out of irons and the other refuses to tell us anything except 'You are going to be sorry, but not until we reach land. Merwallow has spoken.'"

I was relieved to hear the sheep call Mysti a male. That meant her secret was still safe, and a safe secret can sometimes be turned into a surprise to throw your enemies off guard at the right moment. Wedwel knows, it worked on me.

"That's Rhett, all right. I understand why you wouldn't try to question him. But I do find it hard to believe Captain Lan would let a mere human girl take his mind off business," I said smoothly. (I *hoped* it sounded smooth.) "If you wanted to question her, you could always give her back to him after you were done. And as for that fierce fighter you're so afraid of—" Where *did* Mysti learn to use a sword like that? "If you managed to capture her— herrrrrumph! Sorry. Something in my throat—if you managed to capture him and bring him aboard the *Golden Fleece*, surely you could manage to bring him into your cabin. Or you could have gone down to question him in the brig. No, no, Ramses; you wanted to speak with me, and you wanted it only because I'm a wizard."

"You *say* you're a wizard, anyway." I didn't know sheep could snarl. He was angry that I'd outsmarted him.

"What kind of proof do you want? I know the name of this ship and your brother without being told."

"That monstrous familiar of yours might have told you," Ramses pointed out.

"Mint sauce," Scandal said. "Rosemary and mint sauce. Call *me* monstrous, will you? Souvlaki. Shish-kebab. So there."

"I will have First Mate Lodda attend to you later," the sheep told him. "After I reveal your master for the charlatan he is."

"Could a charlatan command enchanted fire the way I did on board the *Eventually*?" I asked, pulling my shoulders back so my chest would look larger. (Well, it was a good try.)

"'Enchanted fire'? Hmph!" I swear the sheep was sneering at me, even if that hood did cover his face. "Everyone knows it's all done with mirrors."

"Free my hands and I'll show you if it's done with mirrors or mutton!"

"Threats, Master Kendar? I don't need threats; I need proof that you are a true wizard. It must be a test of my own choosing, of course. If you pass it, I will free you and your companions. What's more, I'll do everything in my power to put this ship, my brother, and all his crew at your service."

"Zowie, Captain Leotard, just what we needed," Scandal said. "A boatful of sheep pirates to call our very own."

Ramses chuckled. "You could do worse, little familiar. And you do need help of one kind or another, or you wouldn't be here. No one travels to the Underside for pleasure. They either have something to sell, something to buy, or something important on their minds. A quest, perhaps? A mission? A desperate mission, I'd say, but not an emergency or you never would have traveled on the *Eventually*."

"Anyone ever tell you you're real sharp, for a sheep?" Scandal replied.

"And what if I won't take your stupid test?" I asked.

"Then I assume you are not a true wizard and you are afraid my test will expose you. In that case, we go back to Lan's original plan."

"What's that?"

"We throw you and your friends overboard—all except the girl—and see if a few lengths of stout chain wrapped around your bodies will make you sink any faster than that cursed Postal Service ship." He leaned towards me. "Well?"

What could I say? What could I do? "All right. I'll take the test. I *am* a true wizard."

"We'll see." The sheep got up and went to a cupboard built into the wall of the cabin. He came back holding a tiny glass vial in one gloved hoof. "Here is your test, O wizard." He tilted the vial back and forth so that it sparkled in the light. It was full of golden liquid.

"What do I do with it?" I asked.

"You drink it."

"So it's not a multiple choice test," the cat remarked.

"But it is!" the sheep responded. "This vial contains poison. His choices are simple: Drink it and live or drink it and die."

CHAPTER ———————————— 12

SCANDAL RAISED HIS PAW. "ABOUT THIS TEST . . .
Do you give partial credit? Like if he drinks the poison and just
gets sick on the rug?"

"There are only two choices." Ramses was firm. "A true wizard
has the power to transform things. He can turn a bird into a bell,
beer into broth, beef into broccoli."

"Why in heck would he want to?" the cat muttered.

"In this case, he had better be able to turn poison into something
harmless. If he lives, I will know he is a true wizard."

"I'll do it," I said. As if I had any real choice! I couldn't let the
pirates throw my friends overboard. "First you have to free my
hands. If I'm going to work a spell of transformation, I must—"

"The *best* magicians on Orbix don't need to wave their hands
around as if they're shooing chickens," the sheep said. "All the
fancy gestures and mystical words are just there to make the
wizard's tricks seem harder to do than they are. The *best* wizards,
that is. If you are one of the best, you don't need your hands free.
And if you are *not* one of the best, I don't need you."

*Whoa, baby, where'd a sheep learn so much about magic? He
knows what he's talking about!* Scandal's voice was inside my
head again. *No way we're gonna pull the wool over his eyes.*

It doesn't matter, I thought back. *Maybe I can transform the
poison into something else. Even if I can't, I've got to try.*

Where do you want the body shipped?

*Scandal, there isn't going to be any body. My Majyk protects
me, remember? The poison won't be able to kill me. The worst it
might do is make me sick, but sick isn't dead.*

*Spoken like a skinball who's never had a nuclear hangover.
Okay, bwana, it's your ball game. Bottoms up.*

I looked Ramses in the eye. "Well? If you won't free my hands,

97

you're going to have to feed me the poison yourself, you know."

"You really do intend to go through with this." I thought I heard reluctant admiration in the sheep's voice. "So be it." He approached my chair, the vial ready. I could hear my heart beat as he pulled the stopper out. Scandal wound himself nervously in and out between my legs as the sheep brought the vial closer and closer to my lips.

Kendar, are you sure—?

I'm sure. I trust my Majyk. The vial was under my nose. I felt the cool glass press against my lower lip.

Majyk didn't save Master Thengor's life, the cat reminded me. *And he had the complete set, in mint condition.*

It was Master Thengor's time to die, and his Majyk knew it. It couldn't interfere then.

The way you talk about it, it sounds like you believe it's alive.

Aw, come on, you know I don't mean it to sound that way. Majyk's just—Majyk. It's one more wizard's tool, like a wand or a crystal ball, except a lot more useful. I could smell the poison. It had a bitter, yeasty tang, like stale beer. *When I sleep, something nasty can sneak up on me, but as long as I'm awake, my Majyk won't let me get killed.*

Just hurt. And remember what happened that time you ran into Graverobber?

Grym the Great's sword. I wrinkled my nose. Ramses was having a hard time with the vial. I guess he'd never tried feeding anyone poison before. He was probably afraid he'd spill it, or clink the edge of the vial against my teeth. *That blade picked up a share of Master Thengor's shattered Majyk—the fragments that flew off in all directions when you and I had that little, uh, accident.*

A sword like that, with Majyk of its own—could something like that kill you in spite of your Majyk, boss?

I don't know. It sure did hurt when he smacked me with the flat of it, though. Majyk meeting Majyk . . .

A sharp pain made me break off that train of thought. Ramses had clinked the vial against my teeth. My whole face tingled. Then he snapped, "You *could* help me with this," and gave the vial a quick upward tilt.

I didn't see the sparks or realize what that tingling was until I'd swallowed the whole thing. Then it was too late.

Majyk.

Spit it out! Spit it out! I heard Scandal scream inside my skull.

Good advice. I would have taken it, if I could. But like I said, it was too late. The poison was halfway down my throat. It hit my stomach like a thunderclap. I gasped with the pain and doubled over as much as my shackles would let me. Every part of my body was being bathed in fire. I could see the flames themselves dancing before my eyes. They gleamed like dragon's-eye stones, a thousand colors I couldn't name. Then, with a slam like a blow from a giant's croquet mallet, everything went dark for me again, this time without the fish.

A tool, am I?

I lifted my head slowly. I wasn't bound to the chair anymore. My hands and feet were free. So was the rest of me—free of the chair, of the cabin, even of my clothes. I was drifting through a deep red light that carried me along like a river. Somewhere, I could hear a huge drum sounding a slow and regular beat. There was no sky, no shore, no riverbed. There was only the crimson light and me . . . and Majyk.

Well, it took you long enough to recognize me.

It had a voice that reminded me of Scandal's.

And why not? He didn't have a voice to call his own until he met me! It floated along beside me in the light, an unformed mass of glowing gold. Spider webs of rainbow colors held it in a flexible net that stretched this way and that, changing with the Majyk's changing shape. When it talked about Scandal, it made itself into a blobby cat for an instant, then relaxed. *Except to say meow. What kind of word is meow?*

I was dying. They say that people who are dying see and hear all kinds of crazy things. I knew I had to be dying. Maybe my Majyk could have protected me against ordinary poison, but Ramses' stuff was Majyk-laced poison. All bets were off. I wondered where he'd gotten it. Still, in spite of that, I just couldn't let this blob make fun of my friend.

Scandal would tell you it's a pretty good word, I replied. *It got him almost everything he wanted. How many other one-word languages do you know that can do the same?*

My Majyk twisted itself into a fat tube, then shot out five branches. One became a knobby-looking head without eyes, nose, ears, or mouth; two turned into legs that ended in flipper-feet; two became arms with hands like mittens. The human-ish thing sat back in an invisible chair, crossed its legs, and said, *You know, Kendar, I just can't figure you out. Master Thengor had the most Majyk on Orbix, and he started collecting when he was much older than you. You've got the ligron's share of his hoard and the power to absorb more. You could be the biggest thing to hit this world since Master Uvom if you wanted to.*

Master Uvom was the reason Orbix is a planet with no fixed shape. Every so often there's a big shake-up and the whole world goes into contortions. People die, civilizations fall, map makers lose their minds, and no one gets a passing grade in Geography for years.

I don't want to be another Master Uvom, I said.

Yeah, I gathered that when you didn't harvest the cat's share of Majyk. A few smears surfaced on my Majyk's "face" and turned into eyes and a mouth. The eyes were sly and the mouth was twisty. *I hear you even want him to learn how to use what he's got. Kendar, I've been around since the day before forever, but that was a new one on me.*

He can do it, I maintained. *Scandal's smart.*

Smarter than you. For soon you will be dead, boo-hoo, and who's going to look out for Scandal then? Or Mysti? Or Rhett and Anisella? Ramses will probably be so mad you lied to him about being a wizard that he'll throw them all overboard the first chance he gets. You'll be dead, they'll be dead, and it will never stop raining storks and popinjays on the Topside, all because you were too much of a loser to put up a fight.

A fight? I frowned. *What fight?*

'What fight?' he asks! A sigh shook my Majyk back into its original formless form. *Just the only kind of fight that means anything to a wizard: a battle of Majyks! That poison's packing a share of Master Thengor's old powers—I'd recognize the scent across an ocean—and now it's inside you. All you've got to do is hunt it down, find it, and show it who's the boss. Make it a part of me again. Make it a part of us. Unless . . .* It got a nasty, insinuating tone in its voice.

Unless what?

Unless you're afraid.

Afraid? I didn't know the meaning of the word fear! No, wait, *fear* I knew. It was *trepidity* I didn't know. Afraid or not, I had to do something. More lives than mine were riding on it.

Can you help me find this other Majyk? I asked grimly. *And can you help me fight it once we've found it?*

I saw a curving chasm split the blob. It was a lot like a smile. *Can I? Can I ever!* It rippled and shimmied itself until it was about the size and shape of a stout, sturdy pony. *Hop on.*

Soon we were galloping through the red light. It was like trying to run through water. Every move we made slowed down, but it still felt like we were getting somewhere fast. My Majyk ran with the current, its mane whipping my face. Sometimes we had clear going, sometimes there were obstacles.

Yuck! What are these things? I asked, pushing away the hundreds of tiny blobs that we were running through.

Majyk filled my head with laughter. *Never mind what they are, just be glad you've got 'em. And while you're at it, slap a coupla dozen onto you. They make the best armor you'll ever own.*

Put them on? The thought was disgusting. I expected them to feel slimy, like jellyfish, but when I actually touched them it was more like handling patches of very thin, very wet leather. I held onto Majyk with my knees and used both hands to gather enough of the strange things to slap a full suit of flexible armor onto my body.

No, not that one! Majyk said when I reached for one peculiar-looking glob. *Can't you see it's different?*

I guess it was. When I gave it a second look, I saw that it was fuzzier than the others, with thousands of tiny hairs sticking out all over it and a dingy green color.

Boy, are you gonna have one nasty cold in a few days, my Majyk chuckled. It ran on.

And then, when my armor was starting to get heavy and it felt like we'd be running and running forever, we found it: the alien Majyk. It looked like mine, only much smaller and not as brightly colored. It was sitting on top of a big brown mountain whose sides were slippery as glass. It was making itself at home. Every so often it would stick out a tentacle, plunge it into the mountainside, tear off a hunk, and stuff it into a mouth it made just for that purpose. It looked lazy and greedy, but not dangerous.

Hah! Shows what you know. Not only did my Majyk have Scandal's sharp tongue, it also seemed to share the cat's talent for popping into my mind uninvited. It took back its first shape, dumping me off without warning (See? I *never* have any luck with horses!), then sailed halfway up the mountainside and hollered at the other Majyk, *Hey! You! Yeah, I'm talking to you, bubblebody! Lay off the kid's liver before you kill him!*

My liver? That's my *liver?* I peeped.

And a nice healthy one it is, too, my Majyk told me. *It comes from living a clean life. Or a really dull one.*

Ugh, I remarked. The only livers I'd seen were what Velma Chiefcook used to rip out of chickens in Master Thengor's kitchens or what Mom used to force-feed us three kids when we'd done something awful but Dad thought it was funny so she couldn't spank us.

Listen, no one's asking you to marry it, my Majyk said. It turned back to the other Majyk on the mountain—I mean on the liverside. *Yo! Squatter! Make yourself a pair of ears and use them! What do you think you're doing?*

The other Majyk didn't have a head to raise, but it still managed to look like it was paying attention. *I'm part of a poison. Poisons are supposed to kill people,* it drawled.

Well, in case no one told you, poisons never kill people when they get a visit from relatives.

Huh? The smaller Majyk was puzzled. *You're a relative of mine?*

You bet I am! I'm your auntie. My Majyk kept climbing.

Auntie? Auntie who?

Auntie Dote!

The smaller Majyk dug out a fat chunk of liver and threw it at my Majyk so hard the larger blob slid all the way down to the bottom again. If that mountain wasn't a part of me, I would have picked up a handful of it and done the same. Instead I did my best to help my Majyk to its feet—which wasn't easy, because it had no feet at the time.

There you go, Kendar, the shining blob said. *It's all yours. I softened 'im up a little for you.*

That thing doesn't look like it could get any softer, I said. *What am I supposed to do?*

I'm the Majyk. You're the magician. Magicians use Majyk. Three guesses.

Yes, but—how?

However you want. I can help, but you've got to make all the decisions.

I looked up the liverside. The smaller Majyk was chewing on several pieces of me at once, using half a dozen mouth-openings that weren't there before. It could probably make half a dozen more if it felt like it. The faster it ate, the faster I died. The red light around me began to fizz and bubble, the way I always felt when I was near part of Master Thengor's scattered Majyk. But more than the bubbling, I felt mad. How dare that—that greedy blob help itself to me? My Majyk was right: *I* was the magician, and magicians use Majyk, not the other way around.

Fine, I said, my fists and my jaw clenching. And I let my Majyk know what I wanted.

Whoa! That's a tall order, my Majyk said.

Just do it, all right?

Look, it's not so easy. A wizard doesn't simply tell *his Majyk*

what to do, he makes *it serve him. The harder the task he wants
done, the harder he's got to work to convince his Majyk that—*

Was I going to stand for this? One Majyk devouring me, the
other giving me arguments? I didn't have time for arguments. I
had to live, because if I didn't, Mysti and Scandal and the others
would die. I fixed the shimmering blob with a look that caused its
golden body to break out in dark patches.

Just . . . do . . . it, I growled in a voice that didn't sound
even close to my own.

My Majyk quailed. I saw a shudder run over its ever-changing
curves. Then it began to shift shape, sticking out more here,
tucking in more there, until I was face to face with a royally
saddled and bridled battle-horse.

Of course the saddle had a tall back, like a throne, and a clever
system of straps to hold me in once I mounted. I'd ordered my
Majyk to make it so. I wasn't going to take any chances on falling
off *this* horse.

Secure in the saddle, I stuck out my right hand and said, *Well?
Where's the weapon I asked for?*

Are you sure I couldn't interest you in a nice sword? my Majyk
asked.

I know what I want. Give it to me.

Suit yourself. The horse's back rippled, and a portion of the
rainbow net holding the blob together tore away. It floated through
the red light to my waiting hand while the tattered edges of the
original net quickly spun out new threads to replace it.

Now go, I commanded. The horse reared, pawing the air. I fell
back in the saddle, but the straps held and the cushioned backrest
was nice and soft. *Better luck next time,* I said with a smirk.

The horse glanced over its withers at me. *You can't blame me
for trying.* Then he flung himself into the charge.

The other Majyk never had a chance. It was too sluggish to
escape us and too small to fight. I cast the net over it and dragged
it in. The closer it got, the more excited I felt my Majyk become.
Its horse-shape was melting out from under me. When the smaller
Majyk was near enough, I could almost hear my Majyk drooling.

Hey, be nice, I told it, giving the net another pull. *You two are
going to have to work together from now on, you know.*

Oh, we will, we will, it promised, and threw itself onto the other
one like a wave crashing down on a sand castle. Spouts and
streamers of Majyk leaped all around me as I fell through the light.

I landed with a bump on the floor of Ramses' cabin.

"Alive?" was the first word I remember hearing. That was Ramses. He sounded startled.

"You bet your argyle cardigan he's alive!" That was Scandal. He sounded just as startled as Ramses, but he was doing a better job of hiding it. "I told you: Real magic takes time. It ain't over 'til the fat lady sings or the skinny kid croaks."

I sat up, rubbing my wrists and ankles. It appeared that, as a favor, the pirate sheep was willing to let me die unshackled. "Well, Ramses?" I sounded shaky, but so did he. Maybe he wouldn't notice. "Did I pass your test?"

The hooded sheep bowed so low to me that his mask fell off. "A true wizard!" he told the floor. "After so long, my prayers are answered. I am not worthy." He raised his head.

"You're no sheep!" I squawked, pointing an accusing finger at the handsome man's face surrounded by woolly curls. He did have sheep's ears, but the rest of his features were as human as mine. And he didn't even have pimples. Life's not fair.

"Or else you are a very, very ugly one," Scandal said deliberately.

"You have discovered my shameful secret," Ramses admitted. "I am not a trueborn sheep." Now there wasn't even the ghost of a bleat in his voice. He waved me towards a chair and brought me something to drink. I sniffed at it cautiously; watered wine, nothing more. It was sour. I drank only enough to get the taste of the poison out of my mouth. While I sipped, Ramses told us his whole sad story.

CHAPTER ———————— 13

"I WAS NOT ALWAYS AS YOU SEE ME NOW," SAID RAMSES.

Scandal jumped into my lap, then climbed up my chest to perch on my shoulder. "Oh, please let me guess: You were a poor-but-honest something or other, weren't you?"

The man-sheep was astonished. "Why, yes! How did you know?"

"Because you're going to tell us a sob story about how you got to be half-man, half-mutton. Then you're going to beg for Master Kendar's help and expect him to forgive and forget the fact that you threatened the lives of his friends and flat-out tried to poison him. If that's what you want, you're going to have to earn his sympathy in a big way. Very few people are sympathetic to folks who start their tales of woe with 'I was a rich-but-crooked' whatever."

"Scandal, give him a chance," I murmured.

"Did I say anything?" The cat settled himself more comfortably on my shoulder and started kneading with his paws.

"It is as your familiar says," Ramses said with a sigh. "Except that in my case, it is the truth: I was a poor but honest shepherd."

"You've come a long way, baby," the cat commented.

"*Scandal!*"

"Not a word, boss; I didn't say one little word."

"A shepherd's life is never easy anywhere," Ramses continued, "but it's harder here on the Underside. We raise sheep for their meat and their wool, just as your people do, and sell the products to the cities. No one minds the wool part—there are even some shearers who are so famous for their artistry that their services are sought out by the *intelligent* sheep as well. Oh, but as for the meat—" He shook his head.

"I began herding sheep from the time I was old enough to stand on my own two feet and hold a crook. My parents may have forced me into the family business a little early because they were very old and I was their only child. Sometimes I wondered how they came to have me when most of my friends' parents were so much younger. Still, a child generally accepts what he sees. I admit, though, I also wondered a good deal about why I didn't look like either one of them. You get a lot of time for pondering things when you're herding sheep."

"I was just saying the same thing to Master Kendar about watching rat holes," Scandal put in pleasantly. I reached up and gave his tail a light tweak. He just kept kneading my shoulder, only this time with his claws out.

"Some people think a shepherd's life is boring," Ramses said. "That may be true in other lands. Here, we shepherds always prayed for things to *stay* boring. There were three or four of us sent out to mind the herds, so we banded together for our own protection and took turns standing lookout against the threat of dangerous animals."

"Wolves?" I asked.

"Sheep," Ramses replied.

"No, I know you had to look out for the sheep, I mean were you in danger from—?"

"I know what you mean, my lord wizard," he said, looking grave.

"'My *lord* wizard'? Uh-oh," Scandal remarked. "When they start calling you by titles you haven't earned, they're gonna try to get you to work for free."

Ramses was offended. "I am more than willing and able to pay Master Kendar generously for his help. If you don't believe me, go look under my bunk, in that curtained nook. You will find a treasure chest marked 'Do Not Open Except In Case of Wizard.'"

Scandal wasn't going to take Ramses at his word. He leaped down from my shoulder and trotted off to check on the chest. The man-sheep snorted. "He doesn't trust me."

"Is there any reason why he should?" I asked.

"Why shouldn't he? Why shouldn't you? I may have offered you poison, but I didn't try to sneak it over on you. It was all done on the up-and-up. I am still honest, even if I'm no longer poor."

"Go back to your story," I directed. "What's all this about wolves?"

"Wolves were no danger to us. The upheaval that gave speech, intelligence, and other human traits to most of the Underside's animals did not give them to all. That was how my friends and I herded sheep like any other sheep, while at the same time Caltrop, the wool merchant, always sold most of our clip to a sheep named Pringle. The wolves, however, were *all* rendered intelligent. They may get stuck in chimneys or be arrested for teasing small children in the woods—and some of them have an, er, embarrassing habit of dressing up in nightgowns belonging to elderly ladies—but they haven't bothered with sheep-stealing for ages. No, we never worried about wolves. It was the sheep that scared us."

"Your own?"

He laughed at me. "Our sheep were good plain country sheep. It was the *city* sheep we feared: the smart ones, the ones who could speak—" he lowered his voice to a whisper, "the ones who took lamb chops *personally*."

"Well, I can't blame them."

For a moment, Ramses seemed to forget that he wanted a favor from me and should agree with everything I said. Instead he responded testily, "Yes, yes, it's all very well and good for you to talk about it so nobly from a safe distance. *You* never saw your parents' livelihood scattered over four counties by a band of fleecy revolutionaries. Down they'd swoop on our herds, terrifying the poor beasts into a stampede. 'Be free, enslaved brothers and sisters!' they'd cry. 'Be free!' Then they just rode away—if we were lucky and they didn't beat us with our own crooks before they left."

"They *rode* away?"

"Yes, on ponies. They didn't seem to mind about the *ponies* being enslaved, for some reason. Afterwards, it always took the better part of a week to find all the animals they'd spooked. Half a dozen at least would be dead by then. They either ran themselves to death, or raced over a cliff, or ended up in the barren upslopes where no grass grew, so they starved. And *you* never got the blame for all that, or had to go to bed hungry because without those half-dozen sheep your parents couldn't afford to put food on the table, oh no!"

"Please don't get so upset," I said, trying to soothe the indignant Ramses. "If I'm going to help you, I need to know the rest of your tale."

That brought him around. "Well, there's not much more. I grew up and so did my friends. Sheepherding's a job for boys, not men. Most of my old comrades passed the task on to their younger brothers as soon as they could, and found better work. Before I knew it, the only two of the old crowd left were me and Bertram. I couldn't quit because my parents didn't have anyone else who could do the job, and Dad was too old. Bertram couldn't quit because sheepherding was all he had the brains for."

A fond smile stole over Ramses' face. "Good old Thickskull Bertie! I wonder if he remembers me? It's been about a year since I left. I wonder if he ever figured out how to use a belt? Loosest tunic in all the hills, that was Bertie. We used to tease him all the time: 'Hoi, Bertie, how's the breeze?' we'd ask. He just smiled. He was a chatty child, but when we all grew up, wild sheep could hardly pull a word out of him."

At that moment, Scandal came trotting back to announce, "Take the job, Master Kendar; he wasn't lying about that treasure chest. The sheep's loaded!"

"It's a long way from herding sheep to being a pirate," I said. "And it's a longer way from being human to being—whatever you are now. How did that happen?"

"I'm coming to that. One year, Pringle got the gout and had to send an assistant to call on Caltrop. The assistant drank too much of the local ale and began to talk. First he told us about how King Wulfdeth had just renewed the reward."

"What reward?"

"That's what all the sheepherding folk asked. News doesn't reach the mountains fast, but it gets there eventually. The fellow rummaged through his pack and pulled out a tattered old poster with Wulfdeth's smiling face on it. No one in our village could read except Caltrop, and he claimed the marking on the poster said that because King Wulfdeth so loved his subjects, and because he would sooner die than make us suffer the horrors of a civil war, he was once again renewing his offer of a reward for anyone who could produce the one surviving member of the old king's family. Even though sixteen years had passed with no word, all infants are born troublemakers and you never knew when this one might show up and want to start something."

Ramses got up and walked over to a large, gilt-framed mirror bolted to the cabin wall. "Do you see this, Master Kendar? I never knew there were such things as mirrors until I left home, but in spite of that, I knew what my own face looked like from reflections in ponds and puddles and the one metal ale mug at the village tavern." He gazed into the mirror and sighed at what he saw there now, then turned away.

"Later that night, I sneaked back into the tavern and stole the poster. I stared and stared at the picture of King Wulfdeth; then I found a full rain barrel, to double check. It was as I'd thought from the moment I laid eyes on the king's picture: We looked alike.

Wulfdeth was the old king's brother, you know. I added that to the fact that I was sixteen years old, more or less, and there was just one answer I could come up with."

He wasn't the only one. I couldn't stop a grin from spreading clear across my face. To think that we'd had such wonderful luck! Here was the true heir to the realm of Wingdingo, the rightful king we'd come all this way to find. Now that we had him, we'd just get him back on the throne and—

Well, first we'd have to get him a haircut, but then—

"King Wulfdeth looks like a Whiffenpoof?" Scandal asked.

"A what?"

"One of the legendary monsters of *my* world, half man and half sheepskin," the cat explained. He leaped back into my lap and sat there like I was his human throne. "My former human used to be one, in fact. They haunt the moldy dungeons of the kingdom of Yale and gather together to give their mating cry: 'We are poor little lambs who have lost our way, baa, baa, baa.'"

"In Wedwel's name, why?" I asked.

The cat lowered his eyelids. "By doing so, they hope to attract and deceive their prey: charming though gullible females. Most women think lambs are adorable, but are too smart to let a Whiffenpoof within brick-throwing range."

Ramses and I exchanged a look. "I could drop him overboard for you, my lord wizard," he said. "It wouldn't be any trouble."

"Maybe later. Please go on."

Ramses returned to his chair. "At first I was thrilled. It was as I'd always suspected: I was too special a person to have been born to such common people as my parents. In reality, I was a prince, heir to the throne. I even showed King Wulfdeth's picture to Bertie, and he agreed that we looked a lot alike: curly blond hair, blue eyes, a strong chin— My skin was darker than the king's and I was much more muscular, but that was on account of all that healthy outdoor living. Yes, we agreed, I was the long-lost heir. But what to do about it?

"Bertie suggested raising an army of shepherds. We could march on Loupgarou, the capital city of Wingdingo, and demand that I get back my crown. An army of shepherds? Good old Thickskull Bertie. As kindly as possible I told him that would never work, but to leave it all to me. I'd think of something. Eventually. After a bit. Real soon.

"Unfortunately, someone else thought of something first. That someone was Pringle's assistant. He'd been drunk, but not blind drunk. He saw me well enough, and when he woke up the next morning and discovered the poster missing, he suspected something. Never a word he said, though; not while he was still in our village. He must have waited until he got back to Loupgarou before he told anyone about the shepherd boy with the king's own face. And what a someone he told!"

"The king?" I asked.

"Geraldo?" Scandal suggested. He was back on my shoulder.

"What a strange name," Ramses said to the cat. "It certainly *sounds* evil enough to have been hers. But I never got her name, you see. I was out on the hillsides, tending my sheep and trying to think of a good way to take back my kingdom, when suddenly the air was filled with the thunder of dragon's wings. It was only a small green dragon, the size of a milk-cow, but she was a very small fairy. She came soaring over the mountains on dragonback, her scarlet and purple and gold robes streaming out behind her like an army's banners. The sheep bolted, with my loyal dog racing after them. I stayed rooted to the spot. I don't know whether it was some spell of hers or just shock that did it to me."

"If she was riding a dragon, you couldn't have escaped anyhow," I said, trying to console him. "They're fast."

"True. She flew towards me until she was less than the length of my crook away, then tugged at the dragon's jeweled reins to make him hover in place. She was very beautiful but very wicked-looking, if that's possible."

"Sure it is," Scandal reassured him. "Where I come from there's plenty of pretty people—male *and* female—who look like their idea of a good time is pulling the wings off flies. And moths. And sparrows. And chickens. And Air Force colonels. And 747's. And—"

"She stared at me awhile," Ramses went on, "and then she laughed. 'You are a handsome one, Borith,' she said. 'And to think, here you were all this time, being raised as a simple shepherd boy. I should have known: In all the stories the hidden heir to the throne always turns out to be a simple shepherd boy in disguise. I see that country life agrees with you. Why would you want to give it up just to wear a silly old crown on your head and spend the rest of your life cooped up in a stuffy old castle? I can't allow it. And yet, you *are* so very handsome. Perhaps we can work something out so that I don't have to kill you.'" Ramses turned his head away from us and added, "That was when she made me a very naughty business proposition."

Scandal pawed my ear. "What did she call him? Borith? I thought his name was Ramses."

That was my question exactly, so I asked it for the both of us.

He replied, "I wondered about that too, so I asked her. She told me that Borith was the name given to the newborn heir by the queen herself before her faithful servants whisked the infant to safety. King Wulfdeth was slaughtering everyone in the palace at the time, so she was in a bit of a hurry. Ramses is just the name my foster parents gave me later. Unfortunately, they also gave me a strong sense of right and wrong."

"What's so unfortunate about that?"

"I knew it was wrong to agree to the evil fairy's naughty proposition, so I said no." He struck a noble pose, which was not so easy when you're sitting down and covered in wool. "That was when she did *this* to me."

"You're lucky she didn't kill you," Scandal said.

"She said I was no threat to King Wulfdeth this way," Ramses explained ruefully. "And since she was the most powerful magician on this side of Orbix, the only way I could be changed back was if I changed my mind about her offer first. But I won't!" Ramses was on his feet, slamming his fist on the tabletop. "I refuse!"

"Mmmmm, I see." I tapped my chin in thought, but the pimples hurt when I tapped them, so I stopped. "I guess that explains why you got so excited when you found out I was a wizard."

"It still doesn't explain how he got to be a pirate, though," Scandal reminded me.

"Ah, that's the tail-end of my story. The evil fairy departed, laughing cruelly. I was left behind, helpless and ashamed. In my sorrow, I whistled for my good dog, Lodda, to come with me, and together we ran away to Port O' Lyn, the nearest harbor."

"It couldn't have been too near if you were up in the mountains," Scandal said.

"That's so, but our adventures on the road were pretty evenly divided between meeting folk who wanted to roast me, shear me, or exhibit me. Lodda bit them and I hit them on the head with my crook. It got to be fairly monotonous after a while."

"Why did you want to reach the sea?" I asked.

"The sea is the fastest route to the Topside, and a seaport is the best place to gather news. I hoped to find a wizard there, or to learn where I might find one. Alas, my search was hopeless! Few *true* wizards come to the Underside. Oh, we get our share of quacks and fakers and phonies, but they could not help me. And thus it was that Lodda and I came to be sitting by ourselves at a dirty table in a dirty tavern in the dirtiest part of a very dirty town when"—he paused for effect—"*it* struck."

He fell silent. He must have been waiting for Scandal or me to ask *And what was "it"?* But we both figured he'd explain that anyway, so we didn't bother asking. Which meant the three of us sat there, staring at one another.

Just then, the door to Ramses' cabin burst open and in swaggered the biggest, blackest, most sinister sheep I ever saw in my life. And it takes a lot for a sheep to look even a little bit sinister. Gold earrings the size of bangle bracelets dangled from his ears. He wore scarlet trousers with a black and green sash stuck full of daggers, sword, belaying pin, and a short whip with multiple lashes. His head was covered with a high-crowned black hat decorated with diamond pins and gaudy *owmytush* feathers. When he walked, it was to the uneven rhythm of one thick boot and one stout pegleg. Scars crisscrossed his muzzle, and his single eye glittered coldly. His eye patch was black silk sewn with tiny diamonds in the shape of a human skull, and his left forefoot was gone, replaced by a shiny hook.

Anyone who had to ask this sheep what he did for a living must have spent his life in a sealed barrel.

"Ahoy, Brother!" the black sheep hailed Ramses, clapping him on the back (with his good hoof, fortunately). "How fares yer questioning o' th' wizardly landlubber, eh?"

"Brother?" Scandal murmured to me. "That merino marauder's as much Ramses' brother as I am."

"I heard that!" The black sheep rounded on us angrily. He jabbed his hook at the cat, stopping just short of Scandal's whiskers. "I'll have ye know that Ramses here is me *long-lost* brother, aye! Come near t' never knowin' him, I did. I was sittin' in the Frisky Ewe tavern, down Port O' Lyn way, when I seen him come in wi' that dog o' his. Thought no more of it, did I, but drank me rum an' minded me own business, arrrh. Then sudden-like the whole tavern shook to her foundations! A great bolt o' brightness shot through the open door, but 'twas no color o' lightnin' as I ever saw, nay. Struck *his* table, it did." He gestured dramatically with the hook and almost impaled Ramses.

"Er, yes, Brother Lan." Ramses slid his chair back, out of harm's way. "I was just about to tell them about that very thing."

"That was the *it*?" Scandal asked. "A bolt of lightning hit you? So that's where you got such *divine* naturally curly hair!"

Ramses stood up, glowering. "That *it* hit my table and everything near it. It was what transformed Lodda from a common dog to what she is today. Would you like a second introduction?" Scandal hissed at him. Ramses ignored the cat and turned to me.

"That *it* was also what struck the mug of ale I was drinking and turned it into the deadly poison with which I tested you, Master Kendar."

That explained everything: Ramses' *it* was one of the stray fragments of Master Thengor's shattered Majyk. It had flown far, but it had landed at last. Knowing Master Thengor, I wasn't too surprised to hear that it had landed in a mug of ale in a tavern.

"Nay, 'twere more'n that, laddie!" the black sheep interrupted. "'Twere a sign from the gods theirselfs what was meant to wake up a daft old pirate like me. 'Course it had t' knock me senseless first. Aye, wake I did at last, in a happy hour, an' recognized ye straight off fer me long-lost brother, arrrrh." He embraced Ramses, this time being careful with the hook. Ramses gave us an embarrassed look, and shrugged.

"He's serious," Scandal whispered. "He really believes the guy's his brother!"

"It must've been a splinter of the Majyk that planted that idea in his head," I whispered back. "It does the weirdest things."

(I'll say it did. It *talked*, for one. But no; all the things I saw and heard after drinking the poison were just part of an hallucination. They had to be, I was sure of it.)

(I hoped.)

"Do tell." The cat grinned and made a few sparks dance on the tips of his eyebrows. "Well, now we know how Ramses got to be a pirate."

I rose from my chair carefully, so that Scandal wouldn't dig his claws into my shoulder to hold on. Offering the black sheep my hand, I said, "Captain Lan, I presume?"

The black sheep eyed me mistrustfully. "Aye?"

"I'm Master Kendar Gangle, true wizard. And this is my familiar, Scandal. Your brother has just hired us . . . *and* our friends. You know, the ones you've got chained up *by mistake?*"

"Hired ye?" Captain Lan echoed, even more suspicious. "Fer what?"

"To break the spell, Brother," Ramses said quickly.

"He *knows* about the spell?" I was taken aback. If Captain Lan knew Ramses had started life as a human until the wicked fairy's spell hit, how could he still believe they were brothers? Majyk was strong, but Master Thengor always taught us that the minor illusion spells always melted away in the heat of reality. ("So if you're going to cast a love-spell, for pity's sake make sure you're not wearing anything with a lot of buttons!")

"Oh, yes, certainly, of course." Ramses spoke faster and faster.

"The spell I just told you about, Master Kendar, remember? The one that transformed me from a *normal* sheep into what I am now, remember? The reason why my long-lost brother almost didn't recognize me, *remember?*" He winked at me so hard and so rapidly that I felt a little breeze.

"Did ye believe any trueborn brother o' mine would look like *that* if he weren't under an evil spell?" Captain Lan demanded, waving casually at Ramses' human face with his hook.

I folded my arms and gave the black sheep my best I'm-the-wizard-and-you're-not look. "I charge extra for working with sarcastic sheep," I said.

Captain Lan fell all over himself apologizing. "Any friends o' me brother be mates o' mine," he told us. "An' I'll just be havin' the crew fetch yer comrades up from below, aye. All a mistake, o' course, an' no hard feelin's, now is there, arrrrh?"

"Arrrrh," I replied coldly.

CHAPTER ———————— 14

IT WAS DARK AND CRAMPED IN THE BRIG, AND IT STANK. Scandal had no trouble finding his way—cats can see in the dark—but I kept banging my head on the beams.

"Why don't you strike a light, sport? Candles are cheap and Captain Lan gave you a lantern," the cat said from somewhere in the blackness ahead.

"Shh! I don't need a lantern; I've got my Majyk."

"Oh, yeah? Where?"

"You know I've got to concentrate if I want to use—OW!" It was another one of those cursed beams. It sure was cursed after I got through with it.

"Kendar, cookie, baby, sweetie, angel, listen to papa," the cat wheedled. "You've been trying and trying to make with the sparklies. Used to be, that was the one part of your Majyk that was always on tap. It turned itself on with or without you. Remember how you'd sometimes light up like a Christmas tree in your sleep, wake everyone else up?"

I grumped and refused to ask what a Christmas tree was. That'd show him!

"Things are different now," I said, sounding stuffier than Dad when he gave the Hunting Lecture. ("The deer *want* you to kill 'em, lad! They're *grateful* for it. And it doesn't hurt 'em at all to get all stuck full of arrows. Rather a pleasant experience, if truth be told. Every deer I ever killed died with a smile on its face. It was the high point of their day.") "I'm in complete control of my Majyk."

"Yo mama."

"Aw, Scandal, no one's in complete control of my mama; not even Dad."

"I mean I don't believe you. If you're in complete control of your Majyk, prove it. Get lit."

"I *said* I have to concentrate."

The cat made a rude noise I didn't think he could do without human lips. "Kendar, give it up. Admit it: Something's mucking up your Majyk."

"Yeah? Like what?"

"Maybe we're in a No Majyk zone." The cat paused. A moment later I saw a small eruption of rainbow sparks ahead of me in the dark. "Mmmmm. Nope. Mine still works, so I guess that's not the reason."

"It doesn't make sense," I complained. "I should be able to do even more stuff since I captured that other chunk of Majyk from Ramses' potion."

"Oho! Comes the dawn."

"Where?" It was still pitch-black all around me.

"I think I know what your problem is, ace—aside from no grasp of figures of speech, and thinking it's a bad thing to be married to a gorgeous Welfie like Mysti, and your weirdo family, and—"

I barked at the cat.

"Okay, okay, don't get your wand in a knot! Your problem is now you've got more Majyk than before."

"That's a problem? I thought the more I got, the better a wizard I could be."

"Look, I'm not saying you're wrong. I mean it's like a woman who's got one baby in the house. It's hard at first, but after a while she gets the hang of motherhood. So then she figures it's safe to have another kid because she knows the routine. Except then— ta-daaaah!—it's twins. Bingo! System overload. Next thing you know, she's sitting in a corner with a Big Bird doll on her head, playing patty-cake with a bowl of strained peaches and singing the theme song from *Mister Roger's Neighborhood* to the goldfish. *Capeesh?*"

I blinked in the dark. "You're saying that when I absorbed the other Majyk, it was more than I could handle."

"For the time being, boss," Scandal said, trying to pacify me. "Maybe you can't make it jump through hoops now, but you'll get the hang of it. You just gotta practice some more, that's all. Meanwhile, strike a light and come on."

When Scandal was right, he was right. I turned around, felt my way back to the door (three *ow!*s straight ahead, then two *dangthathurt!*s to the left and one *yeep!* to the right), and lit my candle from the lantern burning there. Once I had a lighted lantern to guide me, it was easy to avoid the low-hanging beams and to thread a way between the crates and barrels. I spied Scandal's eyes shining ahead. "Move it, Flash; I found her already," he called. "We're waiting." Guided by the twin green glows I reached the place where Mysti was a prisoner.

"Uh . . . hello," I said, squatting down to pull off her mask.

"Hello yourself," she snapped. She was seated in a pile of dirty straw, her back to the wall, her hands chained above her head. Heavy shackles weighed down her ankles. "It took you long enough. Do you know how hot it gets under that stupid hood? They released Rhett ages ago and left me here. It's a good thing Welfies retain water."

"That's because the pirates are afraid to get near you," I said. And to be honest, they weren't the only ones. I took out the key Captain Lan had given me. "This won't take long," I said, fiddling with her chains.

"Why don't you just use your powers to set me free?"

"Iron shackles," I muttered.

"Oh."

"Also, right now he couldn't use his powers to open a bag of potato chips," Scandal piped up. He rubbed against Mysti's hip. "Didja miss me, sweetcakes?"

"Kendar! What's wrong with your Majyk?" Mysti exclaimed.

"Nnnungh." I was still wrestling with the lock. At last the key turned and something clanked. The first shackle fell open. I didn't give her an answer until after I'd taken care of the other three. "Never mind what's wrong with my Majyk. What's wrong with your *ears*?"

Scandal cocked his head. "Nothing much from this angle, bwana. There's trekkies out there would pay a fortune for a set like those." He lowered his gaze a little. "And for a set like *those*—"

"Didn't I tell you to stay home?" I demanded, helping her to her feet. She was a little wobbly and she had to lean on me. It wasn't too bad unless I stopped to think about it; then I got that funny feeling way down in the pit of my stomach. You know, the feeling that shouts, *Run away!* Then yells, *Run away from* this *and I'll kill you!*

"Not exactly." She pushed away from me and stood there, swaying. "You just said I couldn't go to the city with you. Well, I didn't go *with* you. I went on my own, and if I remember right, you were pretty darn glad to see me back there in the Dregs."

I made an exasperated sound. "And who gave you the idea to tag along dressed like a man?"

"Your sister." Mysti fluffed what was left of her hair.

"Lucy would never—"

"Raptura Eglantine would. She did it in *My Faun, My Fancy*. The heroine, Penetralia, is madly in love with Genghis, the warrior-faun, so when he goes off to battle she—"

"Mysti, I want you out of those men's clothes *now!*"

She looked at me, shrugged, and reached for the bottom of her shirt.

"Whoa! No! Not like—! I mean I want you to find some decent female clothing first."

She planted her hands on her hips. "We're on a ship full of pirates. The only thing female on board, aside from that twerp Anisella, is the First Mate. I refuse to wear hand-me-downs from a dog."

"Shouldn't that be paw-me-downs?" Scandal murmured.

"What have you got against Anisella?" I asked. "She's smart, she's pretty, she knows how to defend herself, she's a great cook, a wonderful housekeeper, she—"

"You can stop any time now," Mysti said between clenched teeth.

"She likes *you!*"

"She likes *Blade*, that's who she likes. If she knew I was female, she'd as soon shove me overboard as look at me."

"Aw, she would not!"

Mysti rested one hand on my shoulder. "Kendar, trust me. I've been alive a lot longer than you. I've seen girls like Anisella before. To them, the world's divided between two things: Men and The Competition. They just don't get along with their own kind."

"I think you're jealous of her," I said. "Once I introduce you, I'm sure she'll be your friend."

Mysti folded her arms and looked stubborn. "We've already been introduced. She knows me as Blade, and that's the way it's going to stay."

I folded *my* arms, just to show her two could play at this stubbornness game. "Do you want me to cast another spell on you so that everything you eat tastes like Welfie-glop *permanently?*"

Her smile was as sweet (and sickening) as Welfie-glop when she replied, "Do you want me to remind you that you *can't* cast any more spells until you learn how to handle your new supply of Majyk?"

"Hey! Who told you—?"

"A little birdie. A couple of loud little birdies who were yelling the whole story back and forth at each other in the dark." She touched the pointed tip of one ear. "There really isn't anything wrong with these." She changed her tone abruptly, going from smug to coaxing. "Think it over, Kendar dear: Until you can command your powers again, we need every weapon we've got. I can be one of our best, but you decide: Which is more impressive to have on your side—a frothy, fragile, frail little Welfie maiden or a daring, dashing, mysterious masked swordsman?"

"You're about as frail as a brick wall, Mysti."

"Why, thank you." She batted her eyelashes at me. "But I'm not talking about reality; I'm talking about images. You said it yourself: The pirates are afraid of *Blade*. How do you think they'll feel when they find out they were really scared of a Welfie? A *female* Welfie?"

"Uhhhh." It wasn't a comforting thought. Male Welfies are scary because they're excellent archers with bad tempers and no sense of right or wrong. They'll shoot you if they feel like it. But female Welfies are supposed to be dainty creatures who spend all their time gathering daisies, guzzling moonbeams, weaving spiderweb gowns, and running away from male Welfies.

"And what do you think they'll do when they find out?"

I remembered the single time I locked my brother Basehart in a closet and told him there was a fierce monster in there with him, for a joke. (He'd pulled worse ones on me.) He groped around in the dark and felt something furry, then something slimy. His shrieks brought every servant in the house running. When they got him out, he saw that I'd taken one of Dad's old fur cloaks and draped it over a chair, then dumped a bowl of cold noodles in oil on the seat.

I *really* remembered what he did to me afterwards.

I handed Mysti her mask without another word.

When we came out on deck, the sun was beginning to set. First Mate Lodda was barking orders at the crew. Captain Lan stood by the wheel, fondly watching Anisella try her hand at steering the ship. You could tell the sheep was smitten. Anisella had that effect on everybody.

"Hard-a-port!" she cried. "Whoopsie! I mean hard-a-starboard. Silly me." She caught sight of "Blade" and blew a kiss.

"Gack," said Mysti.

Almost everybody.

Scandal was riding my shoulder again. I felt him tense when Lodda caught sight of him. The dog growled low in her throat and started across the deck towards us. Scandal's fur stood out like a burr. Just as the First Mate was within snapping distance of my face, Mysti stepped between us.

"Down!" she commanded. "Down, I say!" Lodda snarled, but her heart wasn't in it. "Bad girl. Bad!" She gave the collie a short, sharp tap on the nose and repeated, "*Down.*"

Lodda jerked her head back, then gave a smart salute, grumbled, "Aye-aye, sir," and slunk away.

That night we all dined at the Captain's mess. Aside from the pirates who were standing the first watch, every member of the crew was there. It was a special occasion and a fine night, so instead of eating below, a long trestle was set up on deck. Captain Lan ordered the ship's cook to break out rum for all hands. (The crew on watch would get their share later, so there were no hard feelings.)

We all sat on benches, except for Ramses, who sat in a fine chair at the foot of the table, Captain Lan, who sat at the head, and Anisella, who had a place of honor beside the black sheep. Captain Lan raised his tankard high in a toast.

"Sheep! I give ye the health o' Master Kendar, greatest wizard o' Orbix, what's come all this way t' lift the curse off me own beloved long-lost brother Ramses!"

"To Master Kendar!" the pirates boomed.

One taste of the ship's rum was plenty for me. That stuff would peel the scales off a dragon. While everyone else was pouring a second round, I looked up and down the table to see how my companions were doing.

Obviously Scandal didn't have the same trouble with the rum that I did. The cat was standing on the table near my place, lapping up the leftovers in my tankard. He lifted his head, stared straight across the table at First Mate Lodda, and spat, "Yer mother wears a flea collar!"

It was a good thing that rum had a different effect on the collie. Lodda dropped her empty tankard with a thump, looked Scandal in the eye, then pointed her nose at the moon and howled. "My mother! What would she think if she could see me now?" She sprawled across the table. "Mama raised us to be decent, honest, working dogs. She—she always said I was the pick of the litter. She thought I'd grow up to win a medal for champion sheepherding, not for piracy on the high seas! Oh, how I've let her dooooowwwwwn!"

The cat padded over and patted her head. "There, there. Good doggie." Before long the two of them were swapping stories from their litter days and swearing eternal friendship.

Rhett was all the way down at Ramses' end of the table. Both the pirates seated next to him were busy talking to their other turnips. ~~ners,~~ ignoring the oracle. I had a pretty good idea why: ~~He'd~~ ~~wallow-has-spoken look again. He'd probably wondered why people a~~ of doom in the middle of the stewed ~~enough all by themselves. And he

Anisella, on the other hand, was ~~...~~ self. She and I shared the honor of places be ~~bright~~ and cheerful she wasn't neglecting her other dinner partner. Of ~~course,~~ ~~tain~~ Lan, but happened to be "Blade," so no surprise there.

For her part, the still-disguised Mysti was giving Anisella a shoulder cold enough to turn the Great Unseemly Desert into an ice slide. She was explaining to *her* other dinner partner how she was able to eat and drink with her mask on. The pirate acted like he'd never heard anything so thrilling in his life. That was because *his* other dinner partner was Lodda, and no one wants to talk to a drunken collie.

"Arrrrh, Master Kendar, be ye havin' a good time?" Captain Lan offered me the rum bottle. I waved it away. He shrugged and poured himself some more. Most of the crew were on their third round, but Captain Lan was a born leader. He'd had five and was sending a sixth down to join them.

So I wasn't too startled when he lowered his voice, drew closer, and told me, "I was not always as ye see me now."

"Oh," I said politely. "What were you before you became a pirate?"

The black sheep was puzzled by my question. "Why . . . a pirate, o' course! But not a *bad* pirate, nay. Ye see, 'twas once the way o' things here fer poor but honest folk t' put out t' sea in the good weather an' waylay innocent merchant ships, strippin' 'em of all their goods."

I thought a long time before I dared to say, "Sorry, Captain Lan, but where I come from we don't think plundering innocent ships is very honest."

Fortunately for me, the black sheep didn't take offense. He laughed and bellowed, "Arrrrh, away wi' yer finicky Topside ways! 'Twas but the custom. In the winter, d'ye see, the merchants would sell their goods for double price, t' make up fer what we took in the summer. An' all the towns did do the same wi' the first breath o' summer, aye, hoist sparklin' clean sails an' put t' sea.

'Twere almost a sportin' event. Right now we're bound fer Port O' Morph, what's the harbor fer Wingdingo's capital, Loupgarou. Time was, the *Bawdy Bellwether*—captained by me worthy opponent, Romney O' Morph—was the only serious rival me own home town, Port O' Lyn, knew."

Hey, bosh! Whadjer know 'bout that? Scandal's thoughts slurred and he let loose a mental hiccup inside my sk... blew my ears off. *If Cap'n Lan's fren'. Rat that makesh him? O' Morph, sho he'sh called R... comesh from Port O' L...* broke into sputtery giggles, then struck

Praise Wedw... "She Was Only a Shepherd's Daughter" with Lodda up a chorus of ... before he could utter the unspeakable answer to his drunken riddle.

"Then what you're saying, Captain Lan, is that everyone stole from everyone else during the summer and everyone cheated everyone else during the winter. Is that it?" I asked.

The sheep nodded vigorously. "Arrrh, aye. An' 'twould've done yer heart good t' see how eager the ladies looked for'ard to the summer white sails. But then Wulfdeth took the throne an' all was changed, not fer the better, nay. Greedy he be, old Wulfdeth. 'Tis said he's got magic on his side, but nary a spell there be strong enough t' give the wretch a feelin' heart. Dispossessed me, he did, o' me sacred ancestral grazin' lands. Did the selfsame thing t' full many o' the lads as sails the *Fleece* wi' me now. That be the whole sad tale o' how I come t' this." He sniffled and washed his tears away with another rum.

"I can see it hasn't been easy for you," I said, looking at the hook that held the rum bottle.

"Oh, this little thing?" He flourished it much too close to my nose.

Right then, Lodda collapsed under the table and Scandal came staggering back to me. He sniffed loudly at the hook. "Where'dja get the back-scratcher, lambie pie?"

"Scandal!" I reached for the cat, ready to carry him away before his mouth got us in trouble with the captain.

"Let be, let be," the black sheep said calmly. "'Tis but the drink talkin'. Yer familiar's not familiar enough wi' rum, I'd say."

"He's bad enough when he's got a skinful of cream," I admitted.

Scandal swayed back and forth. "Wait, don' tell me. Lemme gesh. You got it cut off by shome li'l boy, ri'? An' he threw it to 'naligayrer—eleva'rer—aggrava'er—Darth Vader—Aw, he threw it to a *crocodile*."

"Blow me down!" Captain Lan gasped. "'Tis the very way it happened! Aye, save only that yon wicked scalawag were more a young man than a mere boy, an' a sailor in vile King Wulfdeth's service. How'd ye come t' know o' all that?"

"'S a gif'." Scandal took a few sideways steps and fell into my plate. "Jush' tell me one thing, 'kay? Could thish kid fly?"

Captain Lan bleated evilly. "He flew well enough when I pitched him over the rail for the crocodile to devour, arrrrh. I'll tell ye true, from that day t' this I've hated all humans in me heart. But ye lot don't seem half so p'isonous as most, an' ye'll be the savin' o' me own dear long-lost brother, so I'm resigned t' let ye live."

"Gosh, thanksh." Scandal lay on his back in the turnips, his legs sticking straight up in the air. "Look! 'Nother use for a dead cat!" he hollered.

I decided it was time to put Scandal to bed. Captain Lan urged me to stay, but I insisted. "A wizard needs his sleep."

"Arrrh, well, begone t' ye. We'll make Port O' Morph by tomorrow noon an' then we'll share a finer celebration than this once ashore."

"Isn't it dangerous for you to visit the capital?" I asked. "You're a wanted sheep."

One side of Captain Lan's mouth curved up. "Port O' Morph an' Loupgarou be the safest places in Wingdingo fer an outlaw t' visit in these corrupt times, aye. A *successful* outlaw, that is; one what's got the magical power t' make the king's men blind an' deaf." He yanked a small purse from his belt and spilled shining gold pieces into his dinner plate. Coins twinkled among the turnip-tops. "Ye be not the only wizard aboard, Master Kendar." He leered at me, then shouted at one of the watch, "Take Master Kendar t' his cabin!"

I picked up the cat and slung him over my shoulder as we went below. "Ramses give ye two cabins, m'lud," our guide said. "One fer the males, one fer the cap'n's wench."

"You mean Anisella?"

"She be the only female 'mongst ye, aye." He stopped in front of a closed door. "Yer berth, m'lud." He only stayed long enough to open the cabin and touch his candle to the one fixed just inside the door.

Scandal began singing again. I got him inside fast and slammed the door after. The light the pirate had kindled for us was a stubby candle with a badly trimmed wick. It burned with a low, unsteady flame inside an amber glass holder. It was hard to see much of the cabin by such poor light. I could hardly make out the shadowy shapes of the narrow shelves that ran floor to ceiling against two of the walls. There were six of them, three to each.

Scandal stopped singing long enough to peer at them and announce, "I got newsh fer you, shport: Them's our bedsh. Hellooooo Shpanish Inquisition!"

"Oh, come on, Scandal, they're good enough," I said. I set him down on the lowest bunk on one wall and tried to fold myself into its mate on the other. It didn't work. "Maybe I'll try the top," I said. "More room up there." Scandal's only answer was a gurgly snore.

I used the two lower bunks to reach the top one. I never was a very good climber and I almost fell to the floor a couple of times before I hauled myself to safety.

"At last!" I mumbled as I rolled into bed.

"I'll say!" a female voice replied, and all the breath was sucked out of my body by a kiss that would have turned a Raptura Eglantine romance into a smoldering pile of ashes.

CHAPTER ———————— 15

"WHAT ARE *YOU* DOING HERE?" I GASPED, WHEN I WAS finally able to thrash free. I came near to falling out of the bunk, but soft, strong hands jerked me back. How strange: I thought we'd left Mysti on deck at the table, drinking like a sheep. Maybe she slipped down here ahead of me while Captain Lan was summoning our guide. I'd been too busy holding onto Scandal to notice much else.

"I know I shouldn't be here, but I couldn't help myself." The voice was sweet and husky. I'd never heard Mysti sound that way before.

"Look, wait. Rhett's supposed to sleep in here, too. If we carry on like this, aren't you afraid he'll find out?" And after her giving me that big speech about what a great secret weapon she'd be! You can't count on Welfies, not even ex-Welfies.

"Let him find out." Her low, urgent murmur sent a rush of warmth straight up my shins. "Let them *all* know. That's what I really want." She clamped her mouth over mine again.

"Myfdi! Myfdi, *pleef* ftop or—!" My hands flapped about and landed in her hair.

Her long, silky, uncut hair.

I stopped struggling so abruptly, it startled her into letting me go. My heart hammered out the rapid rhythm of a wild country reel (the Gangle galop, our family's hereditary dance) but not from passion.

From shock, yes; from relief, definitely. Long, silky, *uncut* hair? Mysti's hair was lopped off short. That was the shock. So while I'd been begging Mysti to stop it and get off me, it wasn't Mysti wrestling with me at all; it had to be Anisella.

I mean, she smelled too good to be Lodda.

The relief came in when I realized I'd been calling her by

Mysti's name, only her kisses had muffled and garbled my words. I wouldn't have to face any awkward Who's-this-Mysti-person? questions.

My relief didn't last. Anisella recovered in record time and flung herself back on me so hard I banged my head against the cabin wall. "Anisella, *please* cut it out!" I panted. "We've got a big enough job ahead of us without getting Rhett jealous and angry."

"Oh, poo." Her breath was a spicy breeze that made my face tingle. "I don't want to make Rhett jealous."

"That's good."

"I want to make *Blade* jealous." She dug her fingers into my hair, held my head motionless, and attacked. I could feel her chain-mail halter pressing into my chest, even through my tunic. I was going to have some strange black-and-blue marks tomorrow.

"Anisella, let me up *now!*" I got my hands on her shoulders and gave her a shove, then scrambled into a protective crouch. There wasn't much room between the top of the bunk and the ceiling, but I did what I could. "Now listen to me: You can *not* make Blade be more attracted to you by pretending to like me."

"Oh?" I could hear a tiny rising note of annoyance in her voice.

"It's the truth, I swear by Wedwel the All-Compassionate Destroyer. Anisella, there's something you should know about Blade."

"What's that?"

"Blade is"—uh-oh—"a Welfie." And I could swear to *that* in Wedwel's name too!

"I don't understand."

"Welfies can't mate with anyone but other Welfies."

"Ohhhhhh!" This time Anisella sounded like she got it. "That's right, I remember from my studies: All those stories about Welfies mating with beautiful mortal maidens, but only if the Welfie renounced his Welfinhood first. But if their *children* married Welfies, it was all right because they had a touch of their daddy's blood. That's why the motto of the Welfin Council of the Wise is: 'Once a Welfie, almost always a Welfie, as long as we feel like it and unless we say otherwise.'"

She'd learned her lessons well, I gave her that. I still recalled the chill, stormy night when Mysti herself explained the same Welfie rules to me. (It was either that or play our sixty-third match of Haxi-Chaxi, which had got to be the second-stupidest game ever invented. And when you've lost half the dice, most of the *You've Got a Rash!* cards and *both* blue groundhogs, it's even stupider.)

It's not just Welfies, Kendar, she said. *It's all creatures born of*

Majyk: trolls and fairies and pixies and hobbledehoys and mermaids and shenanigans and—well, everyone worth knowing. We have to mate with our own kind. That was why they tore off my wings when I married you, so I wouldn't count as a real Welfie anymore even if I can still use some of my old powers.

Then she started explaining the part about how it would be different for our children, with *that* look in her eye, and I made a fast grab for the Haxi-Chaxi board, babbling about how I was dying for just one more game.

"Well, Anisella," I said, trying to change the subject this time too, "since you do see it's impossible for you and Blade to have a future, why don't you forget all about him and pay some attention to Rhett. He's a good guy, and I know he likes—"

"Rhett is just a darling," Anisella purred. "He's the sweetest, dearest, kindest, most considerate man I've ever met."

"Then you're perfect for one another! Listen, I tell you what: As soon as we complete our mission here on the Underside I'm going to work night and day to get your curse removed, and then you and he can—"

"We're just good friends."

I groaned.

"Oh, please don't be unhappy, Kendar dear," Anisella crooned. "I want to be just good friends with you, too."

"Why don't you be just good friends with Blade as well? I know for a fact that he wouldn't mind."

In the dim light of the cabin, I could see Anisella's pretty mouth set into an ugly expression. My sister Lucy used to look just like that when she was a baby and Mom told her she couldn't have something she wanted. Then Lucy always opened up a big mouth and bawled her head off. Before the racket could bother Dad, Mom announced that the baby had a tummy-ache and gave Lucy a big gloppy spoonful of Master Dromion's Miracle Elixir, "Good for Man or Beast." It only took Lucy four doses before she got the idea and stopped shrieking any time she didn't get her own way.

I wished I had a bottle of Master Dromion's Elixir with me right then. A big one.

"Blade doesn't know what he wants," Anisella said in a tone that implied she knew what he wanted much better than he ever would. "That's because he's sooooo noble. If we left it up to him, he'd waste his whole life fighting for the rights of the poor and the oppressed."

I really didn't like the sound of that "we."

"Welfies live a long, long time," I said. "He's got plenty of life to waste. He'll never miss it, honest."

"Kendar, it's not *fair*." Anisella's mouth got even smaller and harder. "He's given so much to the world; he deserves to get something back."

"Anisella, you've hardly known him three weeks. How do *you* know how much he's given to the world?"

"A woman can tell," she replied decisively. There was no arguing with her; not unless you were tired of wearing your skin. "Well, I refuse to sit idly by and let a wonderful person like Blade throw his life away on silly things like truth and justice and rescuing the innocent. He's going to get what every good man deserves: *Married!*"

"Guh."

"And you're going to help me."

"Gah!"

"Pleeeeeease, Kendar?" Her fingers twirled and tangled my hair. "Pretty, pretty please?" She crept towards me in the tiny bunk. There was nowhere to run. There wasn't even anywhere to crawl. "Ussn't ums nicey-wicey Kendar want ums fwend Bwade to be all happy-wappy wif wittoo Anisella, humm?"

My screams woke the cat. "You know, *some* of us have the common decency to keep this sort of thing out on the back fence where it belongs," he said.

"Scandal, Kendar's being mean to me," Anisella whimpered.

"Howzat? Is he forcing you to read Raptura Eglantine books?"

She tittered; I saw the cat cringe at the sound. "Silly kitty, that would be *fun*. He won't help me make Blade jealous, that's what."

"Trust me, sugar, if our friend Blade catches you and Kendar together in that bunk, you're gonna see plenty of jealousy. Also blood, most of it yours."

"Scandal, I am trying to explain to Anisella that it's hopeless for her and Blade because Blade is a Welfie and Welfies can't mate with mortals," I said rapidly. I didn't want Scandal letting slip the real reason why it was hopeless for Anisella and "Blade." "Tell her she'd do much better to stick with Rhett, would you?"

"Whatever floats your boat, bwana. Anisella, you'd do much better to stick with Rhett"—Anisella screwed up her mouth again—"but if you'd rather have Blade, go for it."

With a squeal of delight, Anisella rolled out of the top bunk and scooped up Scandal, hugging him tight. "Who's the most wunnerful smart kitty inna world, den?" she cooed.

"Yeah," I growled. "Smart. Thanks a lot, Scandal."

"Don't mention it," Scandal said. "And for Bast's sake, *don't* squeeze me like that! My stomach feels like I swallowed a family of tap-dancing spiders. Hairballs are heck to get out of chain mail, toots."

"Sorry." Anisella put him safely back on the lower bunk.

"Now listen up, the two of you," Scandal directed. "It's not easy being the brains of this outfit, but someone's gotta do it. Kendar, I want you to do everything you can to make Anisella more attractive to Blade."

"But—"

The cat held up a paw for silence. "Stow it. I know what I'm doing. What's the lady's problem? A curse. The first one to marry her joins the Death-of-the-Month Club."

"And the same thing happens to whoever gives her in marriage," I reminded him.

"Pree-zactly. All the more reason for Blade to be the lucky bridegroom."

"But—"

"Ooooh, I don't know," Anisella put in. "I don't want Blade to die, just to get married." She showed her dimples. "Not unless he thinks it would be worth it."

"I bet he would, babe." The cat stretched out more comfortably. "But I don't think it's gonna come to that. Hey, it's simple: Blade's a Welfie. Welfies are Majykal. *Curses* are Majykal. You see what I'm getting at, or do I hafta bring out the sledgehammer?"

Anisella clapped her hands together with joy. "*I* see!" she chirped. "Blade's Welfin powers will be strong enough to cancel out my curse!"

Scandal closed his eyes. "Bull's-eye."

"So all I have to do now is make Blade fall in love so deeply that he's willing to renounce his Welfinhood for me," she concluded. "That will be easy—" Her eyes turned towards me. They were glowing brighter than Scandal's ever did, and for a moment I could've sworn I saw the glint of fangs between her rosy lips. "—if I have an eentsy-weensy little bit of help from a certain dear, sweet, darling, wonderful, generous wizard."

"Haggahaggahagga," I objected.

"You got it," Scandal announced. "Now go air out that bridal veil, honey; you'll be needing it before you can say 'Community property.' The boss and I have to have a little privacy to work on our battle plan. Poor old Blade will never know what hit him."

Anisella tittered again and scampered out of the cabin. I climbed down from the top bunk and glared at Scandal. "Are you crazy or just drunk? All that talk about Welfin powers overruling curses—What do you know about any of that? She can't marry Blade!"

"Well, at least I know *that*," the cat replied calmly.

"So then why—?"

"Ace, you are still so young, your ears are folded down and your eyes ain't open yet. Why do you think I promised her our help?"

"I don't know."

"Just stand there. You'll hear the answer."

I did what he told me. I stood there in the cabin listening, but all I heard was the creaking of the ship's timbers and the lapping of water outside the wall, and—

"Nothing. I don't hear a thing."

"Yeah." The cat smiled. "And you don't have Anisella the Octopus all over you any more either." He covered his nose with one paw. "Peaceful, ain't it?"

"You lied to her! You lied just to get her to leave."

He looked at me out of one half-open eye. "What's your point?"

"That was dishonest!"

"Lying generally is. Sure works like a charm, though."

"Scandal . . ."

The cat sighed and sat up again. "Kendar, get a grip. Get two, they're small. What are we here to do?"

"Get the real king back on the throne of Wingdingo."

"Also—?"

"Get Ramses turned back into human shape first. Although I bet no one on the Underside would mind having a king who looked like both kinds of his subjects."

"Very democratic. Plus—?"

"Help Rhett get Anisella to fall in love with him."

"And is all that going to be easy?"

"Nnnnnooooo."

"So what, pray tell, is it going to take to get all of those things accomplished?"

There was only one answer: "Majyk."

"Right. Which at the moment you don't got."

I was offended by the cat's attitude. "I've got plenty of Majyk!"

"Kendar, you got rhythm, you got music, you got the sun in the morning and the moon at night, but Majyk? Uh-uh."

"I do so!"

"Sure you do. And I really liked the way you were using it down in the brig before," he sneered.

"I'm going to regain control of my Majyk." I hated it when Scandal was right. "You wait and see."

"Oh, I'll wait, all right! Now for the washer-dryer combination, the living-room set, and the trip to Acapulco, what's the one thing you need so you can *get* control?"

"Mother Toadbreath's book? But we left that back in—"

"Wrong! Strike one!"

"Lessons? Maybe there'll be a wizard in Port O' Morph who can—"

"Wrong! Strike two!"

"Uhhhhh . . ."

The cat began to hum a very irritating tune and to make ticking sounds, lashing out the rhythm with his tail. "Be sure to write down your answer in the form of a question," he said, then went back to humming and ticking.

I couldn't take it. "Scandal, *stop* that! I can't come up with an answer unless I get a little peace and—"

"Ta-*daaaahhhh!*" The cat whistled shrilly and clapped his paws. "The kid scores and the crowd goes wild!"

"—quiet," I finished. I understood. "Anisella's going to be mad at us when she finds out we lied to her," I said.

"Yeah, she'll hate us. And she'll hate Blade, too. How dare he not fall madly in love with her? What a clod. So who does that leave for her to turn to?"

Realization crept over me. "Rhett! But Scandal, what if she finds out that Blade's really Mysti?"

"Even better. How dare he turn out to be a she? What a clod. And we're back to Rhett again. Face it, Kendar, Anisella's pretty as catnip pie and sweeter than cream, but there's a solid steel core underneath all the frills and fluff. When she decides she wants something, she doesn't care what she uses to get it . . . or who." He looked at me meaningly.

"You mean the way she tried to use me."

"Tried?"

He was right again, and I still hated it. I sat down next to him. "You know what, Scandal? For just a little while there—after I figured out she wasn't Mysti and after I stopped being afraid that Mysti would walk in and catch us in that bunk and explode—I liked having her kiss me."

"Uh-oh, better notify the Hormone Squad. This one's about to blow."

"I'm serious. It was nice. It was even nicer when I thought she was there because she *wanted* to kiss me." I sighed. "But all she wanted was to make Blade jealous. And the worst part is, if I didn't know who Blade really was, I probably would've agreed to help her just so she'd keep on kissing me."

The cat rolled over and pressed against my leg. "You know what, kiddo? Anisella's the kind of person who thinks she's always gonna get whatever she wants. Rhett's the kinda person who loves to tell people that they're *never* gonna get what they want. It's the Mystic Balance thing in a chain-mail nutshell: They were made for each other."

"Wedwel knows, they weren't made for anyone else," I muttered.

"Bingo," said Scandal, and got sick on the bunk.

CHAPTER ————— 16

"LAND! LAND HO! PORT O' MORPH IN SIGHT, ME HEART-ies!" The lookout's call from high up in the rigging transformed the *Golden Fleece* into a bubbling kettle of activity. In their peculiar boots, made to fit feet that were still mostly hooves, the sheep were as nimble as any human sailor. They scrambled up and down through the ropes and crosspieces of the vessel, unfurling or taking in sail as needed to capture the breeze that would bring them safely in to port.

I stood at the prow of the ship, drinking in my first real sight of the Underside. Water is water everywhere, but land has its own personality. I was a little disappointed; it looked remarkably like the Topside lands I'd left behind. I don't know if I expected to see any sights so different from the way things were back home. After all, to the folk of the Underside, we Topsiders were the foreigners, with strange ways and weird customs. Still, some part of me hoped to see Undersiders walking on their heads or wearing their clothing backwards or putting mayonnaise on their corned beef sandwiches. When you travel so far, you want to see monsters.

Port O' Morph was a jumble of run-down buildings that looked like a careless hand had sprinkled them all along the waterfront. Blue and yellow and green and white, the colorful shops and houses hid beneath a layer of grime that made them drab and muddy. There were all sorts of buildings: big warehouses meant to store plenty of merchandise; two- and three-story-high shops displaying signs for taverns or tradesfolk; run-down, shabby shacks that looked like all that was holding them up was a coating of greasy soot on the outside and a team of very determined rats on the inside.

And above all that dirt and disorder and life stood the pearl-gray cliffs that separated the proud city of Loupgarou from her ugly child, Port O' Morph.

A gloved hoof fell on my shoulder. "Well, lad, what think'ee o'

133

our destination?" Captain Lan leaned on me as he hung over the rail. His one good eye glittered brighter than the diamonds on his patch as he gazed at the port. "I'll wager ye've never seen the like before, baa'arrrrh!"

"It is a lovely city," I said, looking up at the shining bluestone walls of the castle. It was not as striking as King Steffan's palace, but it was still a wonderful sight. The round towers with their toothed tops and brave banners stood guard over both the city and the port. You couldn't help but feel safe with such a castle behind you.

You also couldn't help but feel like someone was looking over your shoulder all the time.

"Lovely, hey?" Captain Lan frowned "Many'n the word I've heard spoke o' Port O' Morph, but never the once was 'lovely' one o' they."

"I was talking about Loupgarou," I said, pointing at the city on the cliff.

The black sheep spat a thick wad of something brown and green into the water. "That fer yer Loupgarou," he said. "Call that lovely, d'ye? Like it were a female, aye?"

"I—I have heard cities compared to women, so I suppose I did mean—"

"Lad, the only ones fool enough t' compare a city t' a she-creature be poets wi' little in their stomach an' less in their brains. They says as how a city's a she solely 'cause they'll never learn their way round either one! Nor be let t' linger nigh neither, baa'arrrrh. Mark me words: If ever I did meet up wi' a female that was anyways like a city—all filthy an' noisy an' restless an' cold-cruel—I'd ship out so fast 'twould take the curl out o' me fleece, aye."

Still I gazed up at the heights of Loupgarou. The castle was flanked by neat rows of houses, all built of the same bluestone. Every one stood exactly two storys high and was topped with a roof of trim black shingles. Black shutters hung outside each narrow window and the sunlight reflected off a row of identical brass door handles.

I couldn't tell for certain at that distance, but I got the impression that the flower boxes beneath the windows all held exactly the same number and size and color of blossoms.

"Lovely . . ." I heard Captain Lan mutter. "Aye, if yer idea o' lovely's a stiff an' stony graveyard wi' every tomb the twin o' its neighbor an' all swept nasty-clean." He turned his back on the city and hollered up the mainmast, "Strike the colors, ye addle-headed lambkin! The king's guard may be as rotten a bunch o' apples as I ever bought an' sold at market, but we'd be fools t' taunt 'em. Even a toothless dog bites sometimes, ye know!''

"With all due respect, I resent that, sir!" First Mate Lodda snapped. She pulled down the *Golden Fleece*'s banner of piracy and ran up an innocent-looking flag. On a bright red background the black and white, almost human, face of a round-eared mouse beamed happily over the waves.

"Does anyone happen t' ask ye while we're in port, Master Kendar, we be cheese merchants, aye," Captain Lan instructed me.

"Aren't you afraid to dock here?" I asked. "This is the capital!"

"Nay, 'tis Loupgarou's the capital, an' a world away from Port O' Morph it be. Them as dwells on the heights 'ud sooner die than soil their pretty paws wi' the dust o' the dockside."

"But what if they come down from Loupgarou looking for you? You attacked a Postal Service ship and tried to sink her. If they were able to patch it up and reach land, the news must have reached King Wulfdeth by now."

"An' how d'ye think they gets news o' anything in these parts, lad?" the pirate asked, a twinkle in his eyes. *"They sends a letter!"* He slapped me on the back hard enough to ram my stomach into the rail while he roared with laughter. "We'll be long gone ere they hears a word o' our doin's with that cursed ship, aye. Waste o' time it were, too, boardin' her. 'Tweren't fer findin' ye an' yer friends aboard, the whole enterprise wouldn't have been worth an eel's whisker!"

"Did someone mention whiskers?" Scandal asked, strolling up to join us at the rail. I was still getting my breath back after Captain Lan's friendly pummeling. The cat jumped onto the railing and studied the view. "Nice town," he remarked. "Any dogs?"

"Oh, none so's ye'd notice," Captain Lan replied innocently. "Only the one pack o' wild ones that runs through the streets o' nights, barkin' an' howlin' an' tearin' to pieces anything they catches."

The cat gave the pirate sheep a cool look. "Mind if I borrow those boots, sport? It's getting a little deep out here."

Captain Lan guffawed, but fortunately he didn't pound me on the back again. (I was afraid he'd forget which hoof was which and pound me with his hook once.) "By the great starry Spindle, ye're a bold 'un! 'Twill be an honor if ye'll share a tankard o' rum wi' me this night in Port O' Morph's best tavern."

"Make it milk and you've got yourself a deal, lamb chop," Scandal responded. "I've learned my lesson with rum."

"Milk or rum or Wulfdeth's own blood, then!" The black sheep drove his hook deep into the railing. "We'll go ashore an' revel, but on the morrow ye'll call up yer wizardly powers an' free me beloved brother Ramses from his spell." By now we were almost at the piers, so he strode off to oversee the final docking of the *Golden Fleece*.

Scandal tilted his head towards me. "Any progress?" he asked.

"You mean with my Majyk? Mmmmmm, I did get it to light up this morning."

"Kendar, Captain Cutlet wants you to transform Ramses, not set him on fire."

"It wouldn't make any difference; he's going to be mad anyhow. Captain Lan wants Ramses turned into a full sheep and we have to turn him into a full human."

"What is this 'we' thing? *No hablo* 'we.' When it comes to Majyk, I thought I made my feelings clear: You do the tricks, I do the brain-work."

"Well, so far all I can do is make lights, so what does your brain say I should tell Captain Lan about that?"

"I say that before you tell Captain Lan anything he doesn't want to hear, you'd better let him know who Ramses really is."

"Do you think he's going to want to hear that?" I shook my head. "The only reason he took Ramses aboard his ship, freakish looks and all, was because he believed they were brothers. I don't think Lan's the kind of sheep who likes to hear he's made a mistake."

"Afraid to tell him, huh?" Scandal's whiskers twisted up in a half-smile. "Never fear; I'll handle that."

"He's not going to like it."

"He'll have to like it. Kendar, we need Captain Lan and his happy herd of broadtail buccaneers on our side. We've got to get Ramses back on the throne, and no way can we do it with the weapons we've got now."

"What weapons?"

"My point exactly. When it comes to cold steel we've got two, count 'em, two fighters who can handle a sword. That's if Anisella doesn't turn out to be allergic to the king's guards."

"We've got Rhett on our side too." Even as I said it, I knew it was foolish to count the oracle as a weapon.

"It won't take Rhett to predict what'll happen if just the four of us go up against that castle."

"Five," I said. "There's Ramses. He'd want to fight for his throne, even if he is a sheep."

Scandal rolled his eyes. "And how did Ramses get turned into a sheep?"

"Um . . . the fairy's curse?"

"And what was that fairy riding when she cursed him?"

"A dragon. A small dragon, but—"

"And what can dragons do? Even small dragons?"

"Fly? Growl? Breathe fire?"

"And what does fire—?"

"All right, all right, enough, I get the idea!" I threw my hands up in surrender. "King Wulfdeth's got guards and swords and even a vicious dragon-riding fairy on his side. All we've got on ours is an oracle, two swordswomen, an enchanted prince, you and me. And I'm not good for anything. Thanks, Scandal; you made me feel really hopeful about our chances." I turned my back on the port and sulked.

I felt the cat's triangular head nudge itself under my elbow. He was purring loudly. "Why the long face, bunkie? Back where I come from they tell a story about a kid named David who had to fight a giant named Goliath. Goliath was tall and strong and meaner than a sack full of weasels. He had swords and spears and shields and bazookas and hand grenades and nuclear spitballs and phasers set on 'kill.' All little David had was a sling and some stones from the river, but David killed the giant because he had something Goliath didn't have. You know what that was?"

"Faith?" I guessed. "Hope? Confidence?"

"Nope. A Jewish mother. He was so scared of what she'd say if he came home the loser that he *had* to win. Now we don't have any Jewish mothers on hand, but we're still gonna come out on top, sport. That's because we've got one thing King Wulfdeth doesn't have."

"What's that?" I asked eagerly.

"I dunno," the cat replied. "But we'd better have *something* he doesn't, or we're history. We've just gotta find it, that's all. Meanwhile, it wouldn't hurt to have a ship full of bloodthirsty pirate sheep to back up Ramses' claim to the throne. You know, the animals are in the majority here on the Underside. If we can get their support, maybe restoring the rightful king won't be that hard after all." He jumped off the railing. "I'm gonna have a word with Captain Lan in private. Don't worry about a thing."

The back room of the Cheese and Crackers tavern was the

grubbiest, greasiest, smelliest, smokiest place in all Port O'
Morph. Everyone except the toughest cutthroats, thugs, and
ruffians avoided it unless they were looking for trouble. If you
wanted to see the sparkle of ill-gotten gold or the splash of red-hot
blood and you didn't care whether it was yours or someone else's,
there were safer places to go for all that.

"What do you mean, we need a reservation?" Scandal snarled at
the tavernkeeper.

"Sorry, sir," said the lout. He was a fat gorilla named Marlon
whose silver-gray fur was starting to come off in patches. "It's
graduation night at King Wulfdeth's Academy for Future Guardsmen and all of our tables are taken." A loud crash shook the
smoke-blackened rafters. The tavernkeeper shuddered. "They're
having a wild time of it in there."

Scandal began to swear. The Cheese and Crackers was a small
tavern and we were a big group. After Scandal had his little talk
with Captain Lan, the black sheep ordered everyone aboard the
Fleece to accompany us ashore, with the exception of a skeleton
crew to guard the vessel. Lodda objected, insisting that it was not
wise to leave the ship so vulnerable to attack or burglary. Port O'
Morph teemed with thieves and rogues of all sorts. None of them
had any qualms about robbing their fellow outlaws. Captain Lan
replied that he had a startling announcement to make and he'd be
skinned for a scuppernong if he didn't have a mug of Marlon's best
rum in his hoof when he made it.

"That's that, then, sir," Lodda said. She sounded smug. "No
choice but to get back on the ship. We'll buy a keg of Marlon's
rum and bring it with us."

Captain Lan ground his teeth. "By cud and by carding combs,
I've been at sea fer too blasted long t' trudge back aboard me
vessel this night! I'll have dry land under me boots or know the
reason why." He reached for his sword and started for the door to
the back room.

"Please, Captain Lan, don't start anything," Marlon begged,
laying one huge hand on the sheep's pelt and lifting him easily off
his feet. "Those new guards were all given their official swords at
graduation and they're just dying to use them."

"Put me down, ye great gibbon," Captain Lan snarled. "I know
what I'm doin'. Pendleton! Harris! Bring the petty cash and follow
me!" He kicked down the door and swaggered in. Two burly rams
hustled after him, lugging a small chest between them.

Shortly afterward we were all seated around the same table as
King Wulfdeth's newest guards and their ladies. Most of the

Academy graduates were humans—there were two spotty-faced bushpigs in uniform and one short-horned bull—but the ladies were all the furry, feathery kind.

"You know, boss," Scandal told me in confidence, "back home we only *call* them chicks and foxes."

"Whatever you call them, they look like they're happy tonight," I said.

"Why should they not be happy?" Rhett commented. "They are each wearing enough gold and jewels to feed a family of four for a week." He flashed a warning look at Scandal. "And I do not mean that there are families of four who eat gold and jewels, so do not bother making your silly joke."

"Wow, with that sense of humor, no wonder the women can't keep their hands off you, big boy," Scandal mewed. Rhett scowled and sank back into silence.

"Sit down, sit down, me buckos!" Captain Lan waved us all to take our places at the back-room tables. The young guardsmen made room for us, their bejeweled ladies bustling to bring in fresh plates, mugs, food, and drink for all hands. The pirate sheep made themselves at home as if they hobnobbed with the king's men every day of the week. I looked around to see if I was the only one who felt bewildered by all this.

Anisella was enjoying herself too much to show any emotion but delight. The guards fell all over themselves for her, pulling out her chair, pouring her drink, giving her the best portions from all the platters. A few of the furry females gave her poisonous looks fit to boil her alive, but she didn't pay any attention to them. Between smiling and tittering at the smitten guards, she only had eyes for checking to see if Blade was looking her way and getting jealous yet.

What was it Mysti had said about Anisella? Her world was divided between Men and The Competition. Ah, yes.

And how was Mysti taking all this? It was hard to tell with that mask on. She had taken a seat as far away from Anisella as possible and already had a tankard in her hand. I heard her tell one of the new guards, "I am the strength of the weak and the help of the helpless."

"No kidding? Gee, what a coincidence; so am I! It says so on my diploma. So what's your name?"

"You may call me . . . a Blade for Justice."

"And you may call me . . . Elroy. Pass the wackamolie dip."

I edged my way around the packed back room until I was behind Captain Lan's chair. The black sheep sat at the head of the main table with Ramses to his right. "Sir, what's going on here?" I asked.

Before he could answer, Scandal sprang onto the table in front of us and said, "No sweat, Chet. Captain Lan's just gonna announce that Ramses is the true heir to the throne of Wingdingo. Then the pirates are gonna give three rousing cheers and get drunk. Then we're all gonna drag back to the ship and tomorrow we send out lots of messengers to tell the people the happy news. Then we toss Wulfdeth out on his—"

"*Are you crazy?*" I screamed. I must've screamed pretty loud. The whole room fell silent; everyone stared at me. "Uhhhh . . ." I've never felt comfortable talking to a crowd.

"Go back to your homes, folks; there's nothing here to see. Move along, move along." Scandal switched his tail and stared right back until they shrugged and took up their interrupted conversations.

In a *much* lower voice I hissed in Captain Lan's ear, "Who told you Ramses is the heir?"

The black sheep was surprised by the question. "Why, 'twere yer own familiar, o' course. An' I'd be lyin' did I say the news didn't fair knock me all of a heap. Me own dear brother, a prince! Mama would've been proud." He wiped away a tear.

I started to protest, but Scandal was there to cut off my questions before I could ask them. "Boss, you gotta understand: We're not in Kansas anymore. This is the Underside, dig? Down here the only things more complicated than restroom signs are family trees."

"What's so complicated about that? Either you're related to someone or you're not."

"Yeah, sure, like you're related to Basehart? Tell the truth: Did you ever think he wasn't really your brother? That he was maybe palmed off on your family by a mutant Easter bunny with a sick sense of humor?"

"I'm not sure what you're talking about, but— Mom always says it takes all kinds to make a family. Usually she says that when Dad's relatives come to visit and Uncle Hewlitt gets caught wearing a sausage on his head." I blushed. "It's a hobby."

"Well, from what my good pal Lodda's been telling me about Underside families, your Uncle Hewlitt could be related to that sausage. Their history books are full of dumb stuff like she-wolves raising human twins and storks giving out babies like they were free shampoo samples and bears running off with infants when everyone knows cubs smell better and never grow up to be half as vicious. With all that going on, plus adoptions all over the map, there's no reason why Ramses can't be heir to the throne *and* human *and* still be Captain Lan's brother. That's what I told Lan, anyhow."

"And he bought it?" My eyebrows went up.

"Yup. Then he bought the guards. Which is why they won't even blink when he stands up and makes his announcement."

I wasn't so sure about that, but I figured I was standing near enough to the door so that if one of the guards tried to get out and bring reinforcements, I could stop him. It would be easier if I had my Majyk back under control, though. Everyone was drinking and eating and making a lot of noise, so I figured I could get in a little practice without being noticed.

I cupped my hands and concentrated hard. A few sparks popped and fizzled out. I concentrated harder. The sparks kindled and stayed lit. I blew on them gently. They melted into a tiny pink and gold puddle that just lay there.

"Hmph!" I was pretty fed up with myself. The whole point to gathering the pieces of Master Thengor's old Majyk hoard together again was to make me a stronger wizard. (Originally the point was to get it all back together because I couldn't get rid of my share otherwise—except if I died—but I'd changed my mind since then.) How strong would I be if I had to go back and learn everything all over again each time I absorbed another portion of Majyk?

"Wedwel's sacred bassoon, that makes me mad," I mumbled.

The puddle in my palms wiggled. I brought it closer to my face. "I am *mad*," I repeated, aiming the hot words right at it. "I am *angry*. I am sore as a plucked voondrab. I am really, really, *really* furious. Honest."

The puddle split into a beautiful pair of wings, grew a body between them, and fluttered away. I let out a happy shout, but the racket in the room drowned it out. So that was it! My Majyk only worked when I got mad. Well, that was all right; I could get plenty mad if I wanted to. I leaned back against the door, grinning. Just let anyone try to get in or out without my permission. It would make me *mad* if they tried, and then I'd show them.

"I'm annoyed," I mumbled, and a cup of gawfee appeared in my hand. I sipped it. It was bitter. I guess I wasn't annoyed enough for sugar.

Meanwhile, Captain Lan banged his tankard on the table for attention. "Hark well, me hearties!" he cried, standing on his chair and resting his pegleg on the tabletop. "Fer too long has we suffered under the yoke o' Wulfdeth the Usurper! Yon black-hearted fiend kilt our own dear king an' all his family, an' fer that alone he must be brought down, aye!"

A chorus of excited bleats backed up the black sheep's speech. The pirate sheep thunked their mugs on the tables until the whole room echoed with the sound.

"Hear, hear!" one of the guards shouted. His comrade gave him a sharp elbow in the ribs.

"He didn't bribe us enough to *agree* with him, dummy. Just to let him say what he wants."

"Sorry." The first guard was ashamed. "It's just that—well, I don't much like King Wulfdeth."

"Who does? If more of the animals was like this sheep here, we'd have a chance of getting rid of him. They outnumber us something fierce. But as long as the king doesn't upset their comfy lives too bad, they don't care if a cabbage wears the crown."

"I hear that a cabbage does wear the crown Topside in a place called Vicinity City. But if I don't like King Wulfdeth, why can't I—?"

"That's not the point. The point is, if we start giving these folk services we haven't been properly bribed for, they're going to lose all respect for us as professionals." He gave the other guard a small red book. "Here. Take my copy of *A Young Guardsman's Guide to Graft Made Simple* and study up. I can't believe they let you out of the Academy with that attitude."

"A-*hem!*" Captain Lan glowered at the chatty guards. "If ye be quite done, there's more I've got t' say. The wicked days o' Wulfdeth be numbered. His hands may be stained wi' the blood o' his kindred, but one escaped. The true heir t' the throne be alive an' well, aye, an' ready t' lay claim t' what's rightfully his. Stand up, Ramses!"

Ramses stood up. Even in sheepskin he looked heroic. The guards and their ladies, humans and animals both, couldn't help but gasp in admiration. "Actually, as the rightful king, my name's Borith," he said. "But you can still call me Ramses until I'm crowned." Everyone cheered.

"Pretty neat, huh, boss?" Scandal was standing at my feet, rubbing his head against my shin. "The best way to get rid of Wulfdeth is a revolution. I don't care what kinda forces he's got on his side, he can't fight the whole kingdom. All any good revolt needs is a leader and a cause to bring all the people together. Ramses is the perfect guy for the job."

"How do you figure that?"

"Just *look* at him! The way he is now, he's got something for everybody."

I snapped my fingers. "Like Master Dromion's Elixir!"

"Huh?"

"Good for Man or Beast. You're right, Scandal, he's the perfect leader. The animals will follow him because he's one of their own, and the humans will follow him because——"

The back-room door exploded in a blast of flame. The force of it threw me into the air and onto the table. I slid on my belly through five platters of cold cuts, three pitchers of rum, a whole lot of cups and mugs and tankards, and landed in the lap of a large she-bear. She frowned, picked up a soup dish, and dumped it over my head.

"Hey!" I sputtered. "Why'd you do that? I was going to apologize."

"You were on fire," she grunted. (Bears are very practical creatures.) "I didn't think you'd want me to try dousing it with rum."

"On fire?" I sat up in her lap and sniffed. Black smoke was rising from my clothes. The back-room door was a blazing ruin. The other females were shrieking and running around looking for another way out. The males were just sitting there like——well, like a bunch of sheep. Even the ones who weren't sheep.

"Dragons will do that to you," the she-bear said. She shoved me off her lap and hid under the table. "Sorry about the noodles," were the last words I heard from her before the dragon leaped into the room with a heart-stopping roar.

CHAPTER ———————— 17

"MEEP!" ROARED THE DRAGON. WHICH IS A PRETTY heart-stopping sound if you're all braced to hear a real *arrr-grrrooowwwwllllsnortwoofgurgle*. Take my word for it.

It was about the size of a chicken. On its back rode a beautiful lady no bigger than my hand. I reached across the table, grabbed Ramses by the fleece, and said, "I thought you told us the fairy's dragon was as big as a milk-cow."

"It was," he said. He looked queasy.

"Don't tell me there's two of them."

"There couldn't be," he replied. The first shock was wearing off fast, the green tinge ebbing from his face. "Let me go; you're getting noodles in my wool." He shrugged out of my grip and drew a short-sword from his belt, his eyes flinty. "Yes, that is the same monster, and its rider is the same who cursed me. I don't know why they have become so small, but I would advise you, Master Kendar, not to let their size deceive you. Both are still formidable enemies."

As if to prove Ramses was right, the fairy swept her trailing blue and silver gown over one arm, pointed at us with the wand in her other hand, and commanded, "Capture the traitors!"

All at once the doorway filled with the biggest, ugliest, toothiest, hairiest brutes I'd seen this side of a bad dream. They wore brown and crimson britches and tunics, black gloves and boots, and dull steel helmets—no gold braid, no tassels, none of the pretty nonsense decorating the new guardsmen's uniforms. These ogres didn't look like they needed swords, but they carried them anyway. Their leader had a thick black moustache that hid his mouth, and shaggy eyebrows that did the same for his eyes. Seeing him, I understood family matters on the Underside. Any mama-wolf around would be proud to call him son.

He strode to the front of the troops and surveyed the room. "Traitors, Your Fairytude?" he asked, somewhat puzzled. "These are the new Academy graduates. That's my baby brother Melch over there."

A junior version of the big goon waved at him in a friendly manner. "Hey, Thukwad, I got my first bribe today!" he shouted. "Lemme buy you a new peasant-pounding club after you go off-duty."

"Thanks, Melch! That's good, quick work. Be sure you tell Mom when you get home," Thukwad yelled back.

The fairy sizzled, her doll-like face turning a dangerous shade of crimson. "*Captain* Thukwad," she gritted. "The traitors here are *not* the Academy graduates. If you will open your eyes to see something besides the end of your pimply nose, perhaps you'll notice that this room is a hotbed of outlaw sheep."

"Where?" Thukwad squinted hard. "Oh, *there!* Yes, Your Fairytude, I see them now. It was a little hard to tell them and the graduates apart because my baby brother Melch has naturally curly hair and—"

"Never mind. Arrest them all. The traitors for being traitors and the guardsmen for consorting with traitors."

At least two dozen of the new guards chimed in when Melch whined, "Awwwww, does he *hafta?*"

"Yes, he does *hafta,*" the fairy spat.

"But—but—but, Your Fairytude," Thukwad protested. "He's my baby brother and it's his first official bribe and he said he was going to buy me a new club and—"

"Captain Thukwad, *might* I remind you that as a member of my special Secret Police you are not supposed to take bribes from anyone?"

"I didn't take the bribe; Melch did. It's all right, he's a regular guardsman now and folks expect them to take bribes. It's a tradition. They'd be disappointed if a guard *didn't* take a—"

"Do you or do you not know my rules? If you accept any part of his bribe, even if it is a gift, it counts the same as if you took the bribe yourself."

"Awwww, Your Fairytude, I—"

"And if it counts, you die."

"How *dare* you try to bribe a member of the Secret Police!" Thukwad bellowed at his brother. "You know what you can do with that new club?"

Melch scratched his head. "I don't think we covered that on the final exams at the Academy."

The fairy tapped her dragon on the head. He spit a tiny fireball right at Melch. It seared a straight line dead-center along the top of his head. The stink of burning hair and the sound of his screams were sickening.

The she-bear came out from under the table long enough to put him out of his misery with another bowl of soup. "Porridge works better," she remarked as she ducked back out of sight.

Captain Thukwad swaggered towards the tables. "Give yourselves up, you miserable swine!" he roared.

"Hey! Watch your mouth!" One of the bushpigs snuffled in outrage. "Who you callin' miserable swine, you big bully?"

The bull-guard punched him right in the spare ribs. "Don't get personal," he snorted.

"Surrender, traitors, and it will go easier for you," the fairy cried.

"Meaning ye'll let us dance the airy hornpipe at the rope's end if we're fools enough t' trust ye, baa'arrrrh." Captain Lan climbed down from his chair and fell into a seasoned fighter's crouch, hoof on the hilt of his sword, hook on guard and ready.

"Compared to your fate if you do *not* surrender, hanging will be a mercy," the fairy replied, cold and queenly.

"I'll not be havin' me crew called traitors," the black sheep rumbled. "Faithful we be t' the lawful lord o' Wingdingo! Who calls us traitors fer that be false as yer promises o' mercy, aye."

The fairy's tiny red lips curled into a sour smile. "Faithful to the king, are you? When you break his laws?"

"We break none o' his laws, nay, fer he's yet t' make any." Captain Lan glanced at Ramses. "Ain't that right, Brother?" Ramses gave a curt nod. His sword was in his hand; he never took his eyes off the fairy and her dragonling. "Wulfdeth be no more our rightful lord than a tub o' monkeys," the black sheep went on. "Three cheers fer Borith—only he said we could still call him Ramses, baa'arrrrh—the true king o' Wingdingo!"

The rafters shook with the echoes of three mighty bleats.

The fairy pointed her wand at Captain Thukwad. "Kill them all," she said.

The Secret Police drew their blades. Captain Lan laughed in their faces. "D'ye fancy we're lambs fer the slaughter?" All around him, more than a dozen swords slid from their scabbards with a hissing sound like a nest of snakes. Lodda growled deep in her throat and herded the crew into place for open battle. The newly graduated guardsmen grew nervous as their recent drinking buddies turned into a pack of fierce, deadly, murderous, warlike sheep before their eyes. The ladies dived under the table with the she-bear and stayed there.

Rhett didn't move. "You do realize this is *not* going to work, do you not?" he drawled.

From out of nowhere, a ladle full of sauerkraut smacked him in the side of the head, good and hard. "I knew that was going to happen," he announced as he folded up and slipped out of his chair. It was getting mighty crowded under that table.

Mysti casually dropped the ladle and rose from her place. "Our fate and our future are in our own hands. Strike for justice, good sheep all!" she shouted, and leaped for the chandelier. Lodda bayed, Lan bleated, and the battle was joined.

It was a madhouse, even when seen through a haze of noodles (you wouldn't believe how hard it is to get those things out of your hair). Tables were overturned, chairs went flying, dishes smashed, sword met sword in a frightful clash. The air was filled with dust, curses, and tufts of wool. The Secret Police attacked the sheep, the sheep fought the Secret Police, and the Academy guards either attacked whoever was nearest or just stood there and got in the way.

"Hey! Whose side are we fighting on anyway?" I heard one ask.

"The sheep bribed us, so we're on their side!" came one answer.

"No, we're not!" a second voice chimed in. "They only bribed us to let them have their meeting here and not turn 'em in. We're fighting for King Wulfdeth on the Secret Police's side."

"But I never *liked* King Wulfdeth!"

"The Secret Police are supposed to arrest us, so we've *got* to fight on the sheep's side!"

"And give 'em something they didn't pay us for? Are you trying to ruin the whole bribery business for all of us?"

"Didn't you hear the fairy? She said kill 'em all! We've gotta fight on the sheep's side or the Secret Police will kill us, too."

"She just meant kill the sheep, not us."

"Want to bet?"

"If we fight *for* the Secret Police, maybe they'll let us go free."

"If we fight against the Secret Police, we can let *ourselves* go free!"

"I *can't* fight the Secret Police. Thukwad's my big brother!"

"All right then, Melch, you go fight anyone who's not with the Secret Police *or* the sheep."

"Like who?" Melch looked around, at a loss.

"Like that maniac who's swinging from the chandelier!"

Melch shuddered. I didn't blame him. No one in his right mind was going to get near Mysti. The chandelier was a big iron ring holding about a dozen lit candles. It dangled from the ceiling by a heavy chain. Mysti clung to the iron ring with one hand, slicing and slashing at anything her sword could reach with the other.

"Uhhhh, maybe I'll just fight the other one," Melch said, pointing at Anisella.

No matter what else I thought about her, I had to admit that Anisella knew her way around a sword. She was up on one of the tables, her glorious hair streaming free, fire in her eye, ready for anything. The only problem was, nobody was paying any attention to her. The Secret Police were hard pressed fighting Captain Lan's crew, and the few Academy graduates who did notice her said stuff like, "Gee, a girl in a chain-mail kilt and halter with a sword. Cute." Then they found someone else to fight.

Melch went up to her. "Er, 'scuse me, miss, but I couldn't help noticing you've got a sword in your hands. Would you care to fight?"

"I thought you'd never ask," Anisella replied, dimpling prettily. She glanced quickly over one shoulder to see if Blade were watching. Blade was hanging by "his" heels and flicking all the buttons off the uniform of any Academy grad dumb enough to stumble into range.

Melch and Anisella squared off, Thukwad's baby brother in the standard guardsman's stance, Anisella up on the table using a two-handed grip to hold her sword. It's a common fighting style—two hands on the hilt give you better control over the blade—but I guess it wasn't covered on the Academy's final exam either because . . .

"Awwww, you're holding it like it was a broom," Melch said, giving Anisella the kind of smile mothers give babies who stick strained beets in their ears. "I can't fight you. You're too cute!" He scampered off to find someone not so cute to fight.

Anisella stamped her foot. "Come back here!" she shouted. "I am *not* cute! Well, maybe I am, but that doesn't mean I can't fight you." She shook her sword at the ceiling.

Ramses and Lan fought back to back, cutting a wide circle of clear floor in the middle of the battle. They were outnumbered three to one, although two of their six opponents were Academy graduates who decided they were fighting the wrong people and dropped out of the fray.

Someone bumped into me. "Beg pardon," he mumbled, looking up from his copy of *A Young Guardsman's Guide to Graft Made Simple*. "Are you one of the Secret Police?"

"No."

"One of the sheep, then?"

I just looked at him.

"Oh, that's right. Silly question. Those noodles on your head threw me off. Well, I know you're not one of my classmates, so who are you?"

"Master Kendar Gangle, wizard."

"Hmmm. Don't have any wizards in our class. Secret Police don't need any wizards 'cause they work for the lady Acerbia—"

"The one on the dragon?"

"That's her. That means you're *with* the sheep even if you ain't one. That so?"

"You could say that."

"Good, I will." He closed the little red book, put it down, drew his sword and said, "Take that!"

He swung wide and wild. I ducked the stroke easily, smiling. This was going to be fun—not fair, not pretty, but fun. Oh, what this poor idiot guard didn't know he was letting himself in for! People swinging swords at me made me *mad*. He was going to find out it was a very bad idea to make Master Kendar Gangle mad. I could hardly wait. Already I felt my Majyk bubbling up inside me, getting ready to pounce. I stuck out my tongue and made a rude noise. "Missed me!" I wanted him to take a few more swipes at me, just to get me *really* angry. And then . . .

The guard threw his arms up in the air and uttered a piercing shriek of pain. His sword clattered to the floor as he hopped about, wriggling like a gigged frog. When he spun around, I saw Scandal attached to his back with all four paws' worth of claws.

"Hiya, boss!" he called out, grinning. "This is better than the Tilt-a-Whirl!"

"Scandal, you let go of him," I commanded.

"Why? You got"—the guard turned so that I couldn't see the cat—"the ambition"—the guard did a complete spin—"to be wizard-on-a-stick?"

"Just let go," I snarled. "This one's mine."

"Suit yourself, noodlehead." With one last jab, Scandal jumped away.

The guard had just enough time to catch his breath before I gave him a slap in the back of the head. "Hey, stupid, aren't you forgetting something?"

He had a good memory, even if he couldn't find his sword. The sauerkraut ladle Mysti had used on Rhett was handy. He grabbed it and tried to clobber me. A ladle's a terrible weapon—don't let anyone try to tell you different. I still have the scars from my days at Master Thengor's Academy of High Wizardry when they made me work in the kitchen as Velma Chiefcook's ratwhacker. When I didn't whack enough rats, Velma whacked me and she usually used a ladle to do it. This one was twice the size of hers, plus it looked like solid cast iron. It made an evil whistling sound when the guard swung it.

My fingertips crackled. I could hardly contain my glee. One more swipe with the ladle and I'd let him have it. I leaped onto a table and asked, "What's the matter, clumsy? Need a clearer target?" I stretched out my hands, palms forward, readying a gush of Majyk that would turn the ladle into black steam in his hands Or maybe a frog. Or else a snake. Two snakes. Half a dozen—

"Aaaiieeee!" I grabbed my shin and hopped around while the guard tried to smash my other leg with the ladle.

And he would have done it, too, if he hadn't slipped on a bunch of noodles that dropped from my head. He yelped as his feet shot out from under him. I got off the table, seized the ladle, and gave him what he'd been about to give me. His helmet didn't save him, but it did make a pretty sound when I bashed it.

"Nice work, Nicklaus," said Scandal, who appeared at my feet. He sniffed the unconscious guard. "Were you putting for par on that hole?"

"Impossible," I said, half to myself. I stared at my hands, still sparking and glowing with Majyk. "Why didn't it work? I was angry enough."

"You're just lucky these guards aren't big in the brain department. I think King Wulfdeth gets them from the same place that supplies expendable extras for old *Star Trek* episodes. You know, the ones whose last words are always: 'This looks like such a peaceful planet, Captain Kirrrrraaaaaaaggggghhh!'"

"Scandal, what am I going to do?" I pleaded, holding out my hands. "Won't I ever be able to use my Majyk again?"

"I wish I knew, bunkie." He licked my fingertips. "Yack! Sauerkraut."

I looked around the room. The battle was still going strong. "I feel so helpless," I said. "I can't do anything to help Captain Lan and Ramses."

"Why, 'cause the Great Cosmic Ooompah benched your Majyk?" The cat snorted. "So what! None of the sheep have any spells going for them, but they're doing all right."

They sure were. I saw Captain Lan cut Thukwad out of the crowd and engage him in single combat. Even with just one good hoof, the black sheep was mopping the floor with the Secret Police captain. A snick of the sword and Thukwud's moustache lay on the boards between them like a big, dead, hairy bat. Two more and his eyebrows sailed off in opposite directions. Then Lan's hook flashed three times, slashing a giant Z across Thukwad's tunic.

"Z?" Thukwad queried, glancing down. "What's that stand for?"

"It stands fer me own name, which be Captain Lan, as I'll thank'ee t' remember!" the black sheep declared, striking a dashing pose.

Thukwad frowned. "Lan doesn't begin with a Z; it starts with an L."

"Baa'arrrrh, make fun o' me 'cause I be illiterate, will ye?" Captain Lan roared. He renewed the attack.

"*And* he's drunk," Scandal put in. "Come on, Kendar, just because you're Majykless doesn't mean you have to stand there like a lump. You used to be a pretty good ratwhacker in the old days. Pick up the ladle and pretend these guys are rats. Trust me, it won't be hard to do."

I tested the weight of the ladle. It was a bit heavier than my old ratwhacking stick, but these were really *big* rats. "A Gangle! A Gangle! Victory or marriage!" I shouted, giving our family's ancient battle-cry.

(We Gangles didn't win a lot of battles, but we did marry into some of the best families in the kingdom during the peace negotiations afterwards.)

By now, the fighting had gotten more organized. The guardsmen who were still standing decided that they'd have a better chance of survival if they fought on the side of the Secret Police because the sheep were slaying any stranger they saw who didn't have fleece.

The pirates were driving the guards and the Secret Police back towards the door. Every time a pair of fighters dropped out of the main herd, Lodda was there to drive them back in. Anisella was still standing on her tabletop, stamping her foot and going "Ooohhh! Ooohhh! Ooohhh!" in frustration. Mysti took one more swing on the chandelier, let go, did a triple somersault in midair and landed on her feet between Lan and Ramses. I marched into the back of the crowd, bringing my ladle down hard anywhere I saw a dull steel helmet. Loud, musical *clonnng*s chimed out above the tumult of battle.

"On, on, me hearties!" Captain Lan bawled, gesturing with his hook. "Drive 'em before ye! I swear by me fleece, they'll rue the day they ever—"

A wall of flame rolled over the heads of the retreating guardsmen, a wave like none I'd ever seen. It split into countless smaller tongues of fire, each one dipping down to tag a pirate lightly on the shoulder. The stench of flame-crisped wool filled the room for an instant.

I plucked the last few noodles from my hair, just in case they were making me see things. No, I could believe my eyes. This was real. The fairy was human-size, the dragon big as the milk-cow Ramses had mentioned, and I was standing in the middle of a herd of naked sheep.

CHAPTER ——————— 18

THE FAIRY SLIPPED FROM THE BACK OF HER DRAGON AND waved her wand at Captain Lan, who was the only sheep left with his fleece intact. (Ramses too had been spared, but you couldn't really count him as a sheep.) "Greetings, outlaw," she said. "My magic has not touched you out of respect for your rank. Since you are the leader of this rabble, I thought I owed you that much. And as for *that* one"—she nodded in Ramses' direction—"I have reasons of my own for not harming a hair on his head . . . just yet. Well, will you surrender now?" she asked. Her smile was keen and nasty as a sickle-blade.

"An' what choice do we have?" the black sheep said bitterly. "'Tis a well known fact that no true pirate can fight his best when he be embarrassed, aye." He offered her his sword, hilt first.

She spurned the gallant gesture with a sneer. "I am not a scrap-metal dealer. You may drop that trash at my feet."

Captain Lan bared his teeth, but did as she said. One by one, under Lodda's sad but watchful eye, the other members of the crew lined up to do the same. The Secret Police quickly arranged themselves into two rows, flanking the pirates. The surviving guardsmen milled around blabbering congratulations at Thuk-wad's men and in general trying to look like they had been fighting on the same side all along.

Someone prodded me in the back. It was a Secret Policeman in a shredded tunic and a badly dented helmet. "Here! What're you waiting for, boy? Get in line with the rest of your cronies and throw down your weapons."

I held out the ladle. "Do you call this a weapon?"

"*I* don't," he said. "But *this* does." He pointed at a dent so big it made his helmet look like half a stomped-on melon. "Now get in line."

153

I did as I was told. If I'd put up a last-minute fight, they might have killed Captain Lan and Ramses then and there. I'd bide my time. Master Thengor always taught us, *Where there's life, there's hope, and the customers pay better if you can make them sweat first.* I let Lodda push me into line three sheep, an oracle, and one Anisella ahead of Mysti.

Anisella was in line right behind me, with a slowly awakening Rhett leaning on her shoulder. "How is he?" I asked her.

"I am going to be fine, although I will be seeing double until breakfast tomorrow morning. They will serve us stale bread and water, but we will have our choice of whole wheat or rye," Rhett spoke up, slowly and unsteadily standing on his own two feet. His normally gloomy expression melted into an affectionate gaze when he turned to Anisella and said, "You did not merely leave me lying under that table. I believe you are fond of me."

"Silly!" Anisella's dimples did their breathtaking work. "You mustn't give me compliments I haven't earned. I *had* to take care of you; you're my *master*. I couldn't just leave you there. That wouldn't be doing my job right."

"As, indeed, you do all things to perfection." Clouds of gloom fell back over Rhett's face. "How foolish of me to think that you might feel some tenderness towards me."

"Now, now, you know we're just good friends." She wagged a finger at him.

"It is as I feared," Rhett went on heavily. "For too long have I doubted a certain vision which Merwallow sent to me. In it he revealed that you would never think of me as anything more than just a good friend until the day you got your own way and discovered that you did not want to get your own way after all."

Anisella's satiny brows knitted into a frown. "Why wouldn't I want to get my own way? Is that a riddle?"

"It is. Merwallow is fond of riddles. They make mortals grouchy. The gods rejoice loudest when humans are most peeved."

"I don't like riddles. I do like getting my own way, though." Anisella was still adorable when she pouted.

"Merwallow could not care less for your likes and dislikes," Rhett replied. "Except perhaps if he is feeling especially bored. In that case he will pay close attention to your *dis*likes and make sure you get every one of those fulfilled twice over. He had certainly done so for me." He looked over his shoulder at "Blade" and scowled.

"Gee, this makes me kind of glad that we Gangles have always been Orthodox Wedwellians," I remarked. "Wedwel likes sending plagues and stuff as much as the next god—none of whom we believe in, so they don't really exist and please ask Merwallow not to report me for speaking to him, will you?—but at least when Wedwel visits us with misfortune, he's always got a good reason for it."

"Does he?" Rhett didn't sound convinced.

"Always. It's not his fault if we can't understand what his reason is. I mean, he *is* a god, you know, and we're just mortals. We must have done *something* to make him mad."

I didn't bother telling him one of the Fifty-two Unquestionable Truths we Wedwellians believe in—the one that goes: *And if it shall come to pass that the people do look deep into their hearts and see no taint of wrongdoing or sin, then they must accept Wedwel's punishment anyway, for it is a visitation of sorrow which they have brought down upon their heads for the sins that Wedwel knows they are going to commit any day now.*

The line of surrendering sheep kept moving at a good pace. I looked to left and right as I waited my turn to fling my ladle at the fairy's feet. The breath of the dragon and the smudge from all that burned wool hung heavy on the air. The bodies of the slain lay sprawled everywhere. Captain Thukwad found the ladies hiding under the tables and put them to work laying out the dead in neat rows.

"Awww, that one's crying," I said, watching a slender vixen struggle with the body of the dead bull-guard.

Anisella sniffed. "She just feels sorry for herself."

"Does she?" Rhett raised one eyebrow. The she-fox had found the body of a young guardsman. With a heart-rending howl, she threw herself across his chest, bathing his face with her tears.

The she-bear appeared behind her. "I'll do this one, dearie," she said kindly. "Don't worry, I know what he meant to you and I'll see that he gets proper honors. You go on along home now." The vixen didn't hear or didn't want to hear. The she-bear finally had to haul her off the dead man and send her on her way.

"What an awful sight," I said.

The sheep ahead of me in line shook his head. "No more than what's left after any fight. We pirates has a sayin' about battles: Some goes in lambs an' comes out sheep, an' some goes in what's doomed t' the big sleep."

"In other words, he knew the job was dangerous when he took it." Scandal stuck his head between the shins of the Secret Policeman on my right, wriggled through, and climbed me like I was the mainmast on the *Golden Fleece*. When he was safely perched on my shoulder, he added, "Whew! For a second there I thought I was gonna be one fried feline. I never knew you could fine-tune a fire-breathing dragon. If I were you, I wouldn't tell this fairy-babe you're Willie the Wizard. Not until we find out how she feels about the competition."

"But my name's not Willie," I protested.

"Then shut up until it is."

At last it was my turn. The fairy and her dragon stood behind a fair-sized pile of discarded pirate weapons. The sheep ahead of me was being herded out the door by a Secret Policeman who hit him with a club when he didn't move fast enough. Captain Lan and Ramses were still there, each one held captive by a couple of the fairy's thugs. They'd stuck a thick cork on the end of Captain Lan's hook to prevent him from using it on the ropes tied around his wrists. The poor pirate hung his head, humiliated and miserable.

"My! What have we here?" the fairy said as I stood there waiting to drop my ladle onto the pile. In an eye blink she shrank herself back down to hand-size, spread filmy wings that reminded me of Mysti's old ones, and fluttered across the heap of weapons to examine me up close. Her wings made a humming sound as she hovered near my face.

"A word to the wise, boss," Scandal whispered in my ear. "Never get involved with a dame who sounds like a mosquito."

"A mousekitter?" I repeated. They're the most dangerous flying pests on Orbix. They'll drink your blood and eat every crumb of cheese in the house if you don't stop them.

"Whatever. Keep your eyes open, okay?"

The fairy flew around my head twice, then flittered back to her old place and her old size. "You don't look like a pirate to me," she said. "You are very . . . young." She made the word sound like it was something good to eat. She was looking at me the same way Scandal eyed a fish dinner. "Can you speak, or are you one of these mute Underside humans? Hmmm, never mind if you are. My spells could make a turnip talk."

"So that explains King Wulfdeth," I replied boldly. On my shoulder, Scandal cringed so hard he drove his claws through my tunic.

Ix-nay on the artmouth-smay! came the cat's frantic thought. *Didn't anyone ever teach you not to tick off a fairy?*

And where did you *ever learn that lesson?* I countered. *You told me there aren't any such things as fairies on your world.*

You don't need to go one-on-one with Tinkerbell to know that you never, repeat, never press your luck when your opponent's holding all the cards and she owns the casino!

Scandal, she's smiling. I think she likes that I stood up to her!

A shark smiles his widest right before he bites your head off.

In spite of Scandal's fears, the fairy *was* smiling at me, and it didn't look like the cruel smile she kept giving Lan and Ramses. "You have spirit, young man," she murmured, reaching across the pile of weapons to pet Scandal on the head. "I see there is more to you than meets the eye. This creature *is* a cat, isn't it?"

"Yes, ma'am."

"How did you happen to acquire such a legendary beast?"

I tried to sound casual. "He followed me home one day."

"I don't blame him." Her laughter was low and sweet. "What is your name, young man?"

"Kendar Gangle." All right, so I listened to Scandal's advice about not revealing I was a wizard.

"Gangle? That is not a common name in Wingdingo. In fact, I don't think I've ever heard it anywhere here on the Underside."

"No, ma'am," I said, the picture of politeness. "That's because I come from the Topside. So do my friends." I pointed out Rhett, Anisella, and Mysti behind me in line. Anisella made a fancy curtsey, Rhett made a shallow bow, but Mysti just stood there, her knuckles getting whiter and whiter as she gripped her sword.

"My, my," the fairy mused, laying a finger to her lips as she studied my companions. "Here's something I never expected to see. From the Topside, you say? And what could possibly bring you nice young people all this way?"

"Oh, you know, the usual." I shrugged. "We wanted to see new sights, meet new challenges, have thrilling adventures."

"Really?" (I could feel the word slither all over my body like a snake when she said it.) Suddenly she was standing on my side of the weapon-pile, so close I could smell the mixed dragon-and-gardenia scent in her hair. "And just how thrilled do you want to be?" she breathed in my ear.

"*You leave him alone!*" Mysti knocked aside the three sheep, Rhett, and Anisella, then strode right up to the fairy. A Secret Policeman tried to stop her. There was a flash of steel and a screech.

The fairy bent down and picked up a severed hand. "Does this belong to anyone?" she asked. Mysti's unlucky victim whimpered. She tossed the hand in the air and batted it at him with her wand. It vanished in midflight, magically reappearing back in place on the end of his wrist. He gave a wordless cry of gratitude and fainted.

"You in the silly black mask, don't do that again," the fairy told Mysti. "Those who know me well can tell you that Acerbia is not famous for being a patient fairy."

(Acerbia . . . Now where had I heard that name before?)

"I'm not surprised," Mysti replied in her deepest, coldest Blade-voice. "My people have a saying about fairies: Short on patience, short on brains. I see now we left out the part about long in the tooth."

"Hey!" Captain Thukwad exclaimed indignantly. "You mind your manners, fellow. The Lady Acerbia's not *that* old." The fairy gave him a look fit to skin a lizard. "That is, I mean, what I should've said was she's not old *at all!*" the Secret Policeman added quickly. He was sweating.

Acerbia weighed Mysti with her eyes. "What do you hide beneath that mask, young man?" she asked. "Surely you can't be *that* ugly?"

"The face of justice is always ugly to a villain," Mysti replied.

"And you are justice personified, I take it?"

"I am . . . a Blade of Justice!" Mysti struck her favorite pose.

The fairy was unmoved. She flicked her wand once and a parakeet appeared on the tip of Mysti's sword. "Balderdash! Balderdash!" It chirruped, then flew away. The dragon snapped it up in one bite.

"A Blade for Justice," Acerbia repeated. "How quaint. How naive. How would you like me to turn you into a parakeet, too? I think Torquil is still hungry." The dragon grumbled a little, as if to say yes, he was.

Mysti planted her sword point-down on the floor and her other hand on her hip. "Your petty magic doesn't scare me. Do your worst! It can't touch me."

Acerbia's self-satisfied smile faded, but only for an instant. "Isn't this interesting?" she said. "A mysterious masked swordsman who isn't afraid of my spells. Let me see if I can guess your riddle, my fine friend. I suppose I could just make your mask vanish, but that would be too easy."

"That would also be impossible," Mystic countered. "I'd just make it *re*appear before your spell had time to cool."

"An expert with a sword, a hint of magical powers, high ideals, a tendency to overact badly, and a foolhardy tongue." The fairy laughed. "You make your riddles too simple for me. There's only one breed of creature on all Orbix *that* stupid: You're a Welfie!"

Before Mysti could respond, Acerbia grabbed my chin and kissed me hard on the mouth. I heard a roar of rage that made the dragon cover his head with his paws. Out of the corner of my eye I saw Mysti leap straight for the fairy, her sword poised, her whole body aglow with more Majyk than I'd ever guessed she had.

Acerbia's wand jabbed out, touching Mysti lightly just above the heart. White light blinded me. I heard Anisella shriek.

As I blinked away the last few swirling black dots, I heard Scandal gasp and felt him hop down from my shoulder. I rubbed my eyes and looked.

There at my feet sat a small white female cat with a mask of black fur covering most of her head. She raised her face to me and in a piteous voice said, "Mew?"

Acerbia linked her arm firmly through mine. "Fairies outrank Welfies," she told the black-and-white cat. "If you don't believe me, feel free to consult Master Droon's Handy Mystic Instant Reference Cards. I own the complete set." She snapped her fingers at Captain Thukwad. "I'm going back to my apartments. You and your men take care of the prisoners."

We were almost out the door when Thukwad hollered, "Your Fairytude, don't you want us to take care of that prisoner too?" He pointed at me.

"Ohhhh, no," she breathed. "This one's all mine."

Scandal! I thought desperately. *Scandal, come with me! Don't leave me alone with her.*

Huh? Wha—? The cat's answering thought was vague and muzzy. *Oh. Oh, sure, boss, sure. We'll be right behind you.*

'We'? I got no reply. Acerbia tugged my arm harder, dragging me away. The last thing I heard as we left the Cheese and Crackers was Scandal saying, "So, sweetie, what's your sign? Come here often? Can I buy you a bowl of cream? What's a nice kitten like you doing in a place like this? Wanna come up to my place and see my collection of fish heads?"

Who was he talking to?

Oh.

Oh, *no!*

CHAPTER ———————— 19

"MAKE YOURSELF COMFORTABLE, KENDAR," THE FAIRY purred as she opened the door to her apartment in the royal palace. "I'll be back as soon as I make sure that Torquil is nicely tucked in for the night."

I hesitated on the threshold. From where I stood, Acerbia's apartment looked like one huge bed with a little bit of room built around it. "How, um, how do you tuck in a dragon for the night?" I asked.

"Very carefully," she replied, laughing. She shoved me into the room and pulled the door shut behind me. I heard the bolt lock from the outside with a rumble like an ox-cart on a bumpy road. I tried jiggling the handle, anyway. Ha.

As long as I was trapped, I decided I might as well explore the place. Who knows? Maybe I could find a way out. Double ha. Acerbia's apartment had five other rooms, or at least five doors leading out of the central room. Every single one of those doors was locked. I took in the view from one of the point-arched windows. Through the diamond-shaped panes I could see the rest of the castle far, far below. With her wings and her flying dragon, Acerbia didn't have to worry about being up so high. Anyone else who wanted to reach the ground from up here without using the stairs was going to end up as three splatters and a goosh on the stones. It looked like my exploring was going to be pretty limited.

I made my way around the room slowly. It reminded me a lot of Master Thengor's bedchamber. Why was it that masters of Majyk always built themselves such gigantic, impressive beds? It's not like they slept more than other people.

Acerbia's bed was big enough for six normal human beings. Silver sea waves made a ring for the base. Out of the glittering water rose the ivory bodies of mermaids with sapphire eyes, ebony hair, and fish tails sheathed with leaves of turquoise. The headboard was the sea-king's own chariot, made from solid gold, drawn by a pair of giant serpents whose scales were shingles of emerald and pearl. All the carved figures gazed steadily at the center of the bed, with its blue-and-white silk sheets and green satin quilt. I thought I wouldn't be able to sleep a wink with all those jeweled eyes staring at me.

"I don't think Tinkerbell brought you up here to catch forty winks, bwana."

"Scandal!" I spun around and saw him sitting by the locked door. Mysti was huddled beside him. "How did you get in here?"

"I'm a cat. The only thing I can't get into's a can of cat food, and I'm working on that."

I knelt beside the black-and-white cat. "Mysti, is that you? Do you know me? Are you all right?" I asked.

"Mrow," she answered, head drooping. I looked to Scandal for the translation.

"She says that of course it's her, you dope; she knows who you are, and she's never been happier in her life. She wants to stay a cat forever. It's the best thing that ever happened to her and she's going to name our first litter after Acerbia, all of them, even the toms. It's just her little way of saying thank—"

"She did not say that!" I shouted.

"Nyow," Misty cried, as if agreeing with me.

"How would you know what she said?" Scandal challenged me. "You don't speak our language." He rubbed his head against Mysti's whiskery cheek and murmured, "Does he, my little catnip mouse *d'amour?*"

"RowrFFTZ!" Mysti lashed out at him with her claws and bounded away across the floor. She hid so far under a carved sweetwood chair, the only thing you could see was her glowing eyes. I laughed.

"Who needs to speak your language? I understood that just fine," I said. "And I hope you got the message, too."

"Look who's talking about getting the message," Scandal grumped. "The ding-a-ling who spent I don't wanna think about how many months living under the same roof with a gorgeous Welfie woman, and the closest he got to her was a hot game of Haxi-Chaxi. So now that she's finally in shape for a *real* male to appreciate her, he doesn't want to give her up. Tell me, bozo: Did your hormones finally kick in or are you just selfish?"

"I don't know what you're talking about, but I don't remember

getting kicked by anything. I just think you're not being fair to
Mysti. She doesn't want to be a cat!"

"What's not to want?" Scandal sat back on his haunches and
spread his paws. "Especially on this world. You get your seven
square meals a day, a warm place to sleep, not *too* many dogs, and
you're a legendary monster—a status symbol! The crowned heads
of Orbix will fight one another to the death for a chance to have
a cat around the castle. And no one here's ever heard of the
N-word."

"What's the N-word?"

Scandal dropped his voice and in a shuddery whisper said,
"*Neutered.*"

That was another word that meant nothing to me, but it seemed
to terrify Scandal. Maybe I could use it to make him behave. "If
you don't leave Mysti alone while she's got the fairy's curse on
her, I'll use my Majyk to neutered you."

The cat fell over on his side laughing. "He doesn't know what
it means, he doesn't even know how to use the word right, he can't
get his Majyk to work worth a plugged nickel, and *he's* threatening
me?" he told the ceiling. "Wha-ha-ha-ha-ha!"

While he was still rolling around on the floor, Mysti came out
from under the chair. She stalked across the room purposefully
until she was standing over the hilarious cat. "Nyaaarrrr," she
growled, and pounced on him with fang and claw.

Scandal was taken by surprise. He shrieked and dashed away
behind Acerbia's bed, his coat blazing with sparks of Majyk. Mysti
looked up at me, a chunk of Scandal's fur in her mouth. She
dropped it proudly by my feet. "Mew?"

I scratched her behind the ears. "I don't think you ought to do
that again," I said. "Scandal's learned his lesson. Besides, it was
your temper that got you into this mess in the first place."

She scowled sharply. "*Fffft!*" she spat, clawed my leg once, and
marched back to the sweetwood chair, tail straight as a lance.

Scandal waited until she was settled under the chair before he
came creeping back to me. "Okay, so she's the shy type," he said.
"I can take it. With female cats, it's all a waiting game anyhow."

"Didn't you learn your lesson after all that?" I asked, shaking
that tuft of his own ravaged fur in his face. "She's not a cat, she's
just Mysti in a cat's body."

"And what a body," Scandal murmured, eyeing the chair.
"Mama, you can share my catnip any time. Goodness, gracious,
great balls o' yarn!"

"Hey!" I scooped Scandal off the floor and made him look at

me. "Don't you understand? *She's not a cat!* She's not interested in you!"

Scandal half-closed his eyes. "Maybe not now . . ."

"What do you mean?"

"Didn't anyone ever teach you about the birds and the bees, sonny boy?"

"Mom and Dad did," I replied. "Dad taught me that birds are pretty good hunting, but they're not as much fun to kill as deer, and Mom taught me that bees do something nasty with flowers, but it's all right to eat honey if you don't think about it."

Scandal's eyes opened all the way. All he said was, "Oy."

I put him down. He licked his fur thoroughly, then told me, "Kendar, you're a big boy now. It's time you stopped putting the call of the wild on hold." And then he told me a lot of other stuff. For once he had trouble finding the right words. Sometimes he looked embarrassed by what he was saying. It was fun watching him squirm. When he was finally done I said:

"Oh, I knew all that."

"What." It came out too flat to be a real question.

"I learned it when I was at Master Thengor's Academy of High Wizardry. Sometimes Master Thengor had to go away on business trips. He always picked three or four of the youngest students to keep an eye on his wives while he was gone."

"Didn't he have professional guards to do that? Or spells?"

"Master Thengor never liked to use his powers when he didn't have to, and the wives could bribe the guards. They didn't dare try that when Master Thengor was in the house, but it was another story while he was away."

"So why couldn't these frisky ladies bribe you kids, too?"

"Well, for one thing, we were too young for some of the stuff they used to bribe the guards. And for another, we knew that if Master Thengor discovered us taking bribes from his wives, he'd kill us."

"Wouldn't he kill the guards, too?" Scandal asked.

I nodded. "But it costs less to replace a student than it does to replace a professional guard. Anyhow, before Master Thengor left us to watch his wives, he had to tell us the sort of thing we were supposed to be watching out *for.*"

"True," the cat sighed. "Very true. He only left out one thing."

"What's that?"

"Humans can turn it on and off. Animals got no choice."

"Turn what on and off?" I asked.

"The little light inside the big refrigerator of love," Scandal said. When I made a puzzled face, he added, "Master Thengor's wives might have had roving eyes, but they didn't do anything out of line when they knew they'd get fried for it. Lots of us animals have these certain times of the year when we've just *gotta* . . . you know. Cats, too. You could tell us a whole herd of wizards was gonna turn us into kitty cutlets and we'd still go for the gusto, prowl for the passion, howl for a little hubba-hubba—"

"I get it," I said. I glanced uneasily over at Mysti. "So you mean that now she's a cat, she's also going to—?"

"If she's a real cat, yep. It's just a matter of time until we find out for sure, and then . . ." I didn't like Scandal's grin one bit. It reminded me of Acerbia. "I'll make you a deal, boss. I'll keep my paws to myself as long as *she* wants. But if she gets flattened by the Ferrari of Doctor Love, she's mine. Okay?"

"If that's the way she wants it," I replied stiffly.

"Oh, it will be, it will be." Scandal licked his chops.

From under the sweetwood chair, Mysti uttered a half-hearted hiss.

Just then, the door opened; Acerbia was back. Her eyes lit on Scandal. "Well, well, who have we here? Did you miss your friend, puss?"

"Yeah, my heart was as broke as a politician's promise," Scandal drawled.

"It talks!" The fairy was startled. "None of my books of lore mention cats being able to talk."

"Only those of us lucky enough to be *born* cats. You won't get a word out of that Welfie makeover-job. By the way, nice work." The cat was pouring on the charm. "So whaddaya say? Can I hang around? For educational purposes."

"By all means." Acerbia looked thoughtful. "So cats can talk. Goodness. I'll have to make a note of this in my journal." She headed for one of the locked doors and touched it with her wand. I heard a click and the door drifted open easily. "Would you care to join me, Kendar?" she asked, too sweetly. She didn't seem to realize that she'd left the main entrance to the apartment open as well.

"Uh, no, no thanks. I'll just wait out here," I said, doing my best not to stare at the wide-open door to freedom.

"Forget it." Acerbia bit off the words. "There are some locks you don't need to see. You *feel* them." She entered the other room and left us.

"What do you think, Scandal?" I asked softly. "The door's open. Is she bluffing?"

"I don't think so."

"What's the worst that could happen if I walk out of here?" I sounded like I was trying to persuade the cat, but I was really trying to convince myself. "Even if I can't use my Majyk, it won't let me get killed."

"You want to find out if there's worse things than death?" the cat asked. "Tinkerbell's just the sort of sweetie who'd be glad to help you."

"But there's nothing *there*," I insisted.

Scandal padded over towards the open door and twitched his whiskers forward. Tiny fireworms of Majyk danced at the tips. "Aye, Cap'n, 'tis an invisible force-field these Klingon dogs have used here. Step through it an' I canna vouch fer the safety o' yer toupee." He looked back at me. "Do what you want, Kendar, but remember this: If you do get out of this room, how far do you think you can go?"

Score another one for Scandal. Getting out of Acerbia's apartment was nothing. I'd still have to escape King Wulfdeth's castle. And assuming I could do that, what would be the point? Ramses and the others would still be captive. I sighed and glanced at the other open door. At least if I went in there after Acerbia it would get me out of this room for a while. I could've sworn the eyes of the seafolk around the bed were following my every move.

Acerbia sat on a high stool no taller than my arm from fingertips to elbow. The desk at which she worked was of a similar size, as was she. In her hand was a sparrow-feather pen with which she was busily writing line after line in a book as big as a pack of playing cards. Light came from a single fat candle burning on top of an owl's skull.

"So, you've decided to join me after all," she said when I came in. "I'll be done in a moment. Amuse yourself."

With what? The room was full of books, bookcases, and bookshelves, floor to ceiling. They took up most of the floor space too, except for a path to the door and an empty area in the middle of the chamber. There was just room enough for one normal-sized human to stand, plus space for the fairy's desk and a table with a strange glass tank full of water and pin-point bubbles.

Ordinarily, I love to read, but these weren't ordinary books. Each and every one on display could fit neatly in the palm of my hand. I used my thumb and forefinger to pluck one off the nearest shelf. The writing inside was black spider-web and the pages were fragile as a moth's wing, so thin that I couldn't turn them. I soon gave up trying, afraid I'd crumple them past repair.

With nothing else to do, I clasped my hands behind my back and fidgeted, humming the old school song of Master Thengor's Academy ("We are the Wizards of Tomorrow"). Acerbia's head came up sharply, a tiny crease showing between her brows.

"Don't tell me you dislike books," she said. "You're a nice young man, but you certainly aren't handsome enough to get by on your looks alone."

"I *like* books," I protested. "I just can't read these."

"You can't—? Oh! Silly me." The fairy giggled. It sounded almost as shrill as Anisella's high-pitched tittering. "But of course, how could you read my books as they are? Well, I'll soon fix that. Kneel down and put out your hand."

I did as she told me. The fairy sat back on her stool, ran her gaze over the bookshelf nearest her, chose a volume and placed it in my palm. Then she leaned over, dipped her wand in the glass tank, and flicked it over the book. I thought I saw a droplet of water fall from her wand, but it was too small for me to be sure.

My doubts vanished in an instant. Acerbia had done something to that book, all right, because one moment it fit in my hand, the next it was crushing my hand to jelly. And flopping across the cover was a big, blue and purple fish with yellow lips and red spots over its eyes.

"Ow!" I yanked my hand out from under the book and shook it.

Acerbia giggled again. "I should have warned you that was going to happen."

"What *is* it?" I asked, pointing at the still-wiggling creature. "Where did it come from?"

"The tank," she replied. "There are hundreds more like him in there. Oh, don't bother squinting; you humans can't see them when they're their normal size. Even we fairies have a hard time doing that." She reached out with her wand and tapped the fish. It seemed to disappear, but the fairy made a great show of using the flat silver star on the end of her wand to shovel *something* from the cover of the book. She shook it off just above the bubbling tank and cocked her head as if she heard a faint splash. "Ah! Much better. Micro-fish can't live long out of water or off the books."

"Micro—?"

"They're *such* a help," she went on, waving at the vast array of miniature bookshelves and their contents. "I'd need a hundred rooms to hold my library of enchantment if I didn't use them."

"How do they work?" I asked, getting an idea. "Do you need to say a special spell, or do you just use the wand?"

"Isn't that cute!" Acerbia exclaimed. "You're interested in magic."

I lowered my eyes. "Just a little. You make it look so easy."

"That's because I'm a fairy, dear boy. It's second nature to us. I'm afraid you humans have to do a lot of studying before you can hope to learn a fraction of what we're born knowing."

Yeah, and run into some Majyk, I thought. I tried to sound casual as I asked, "Are there any books in here about, you know, getting started?"

The fairy waved her wand, and a stack of tiny books came fluttering off the shelves. She opened a drawer under her desk and took out what looked like a straight pin. I watched her rub it against her wand, mumbling words I couldn't quite hear. "Take this," she said, handing me the pin. "Don't lose it."

"What is it?"

"It's a borrower's wand," she said. "When you want to read one of my books, dip the point in the tank, touch it to the book, and stand back. The micro-fish grows as soon as it hits the book cover, and it makes the book grow with it. When the book's big, touch the micro-fish with the point a second time and it will return to normal. Then just shake the wand over the tank to put the fish back. Don't worry about making the book small again; I'll handle that. Now remember, the borrower's wand is only good for using on the micro-fish and books in here, so don't imagine you're a *real* wizard and go waving it around. It's all fun and games until somebody loses an eye."

I twirled the pin between my fingers, feeling the unmistakable prickle of Majyk. "I'll take good care of it," I promised, sticking it into the neckline of my tunic.

"Good." She was already back to her writing. "Now take that big book out of here and read it while I finish my work. I'll be ready for you shortly." I didn't like the sound of that.

"Whatcha got there, pally?" Scandal asked when I came out of Acerbia's library.

I hadn't even looked at the book I was carrying. "*A Raptura Eglantine Anthology,*" I read. I threw it out the front door. Green and orange flames devoured it, leaving nothing behind but a pinch of ash dancing on the air. So much for bluffing.

"Is that any way to treat a book?" Acerbia asked.

I whirled around and saw her standing in the library doorway, swinging her wand idly back and forth. She was big again, and her wings trailed after her like smoke as she glided towards me. Halfway there she raised her wand and touched it to her own head.

Her dress melted away, transformed into a glimmering robe the color of sunshine on water and just as transparent.

"Don't you like romances?" she breathed, slipping one arm around my neck. "Raptura Eglantine is my favorite author. I simply adored *Fairy Willful, Fairy Wild.*"

I tried to back off, but Acerbia had me in a hammerlock. "Isn't that—isn't that the sequel to *Goblin Master, Goblin Mine*?" I asked, desperate to buy a little time.

"Hmmmmm." She shifted her hold, pulling my face closer to hers. "No, I think it was published just after *Unicorn Beloved, Unicorn Bold*. You know, the one with that naughty enchanted sword?"

"Right, right!" I gasped. To tell the truth, I didn't know one Raptura Eglantine book from another, even if my sister Lucy did write them, but I wanted to keep the fairy talking. "I think the naughty enchanted sword was the best part."

"Oh, no," Acerbia said, batting her eyelashes at me. "*This* is the best part." She took one more step forward. I felt the edge of the bed hit the back of my knees and then I was tumbling over backwards onto the green satin quilt with Acerbia on top of me.

"NyowROW!" A black-and-white fireball leaped for the fairy's wings, hissing and spitting. Acerbia made a lazy backswing with her wand and Mysti was frozen in midair, fur on end and claws extended. She looked like a cross between a thundercloud and a puff-flower.

"You are a fighter to the heart, my Welfie friend, I'll grant you that," the fairy said, regarding the floating cat. "Your loyalty to your old shipmate is wonderful. Try anything like that again and I'll use your pelt for a purse and feed your liver to Torquil."

Scandal's head and forepaws popped up over the edge of the bed. "Cat livers are poison in months with A, E, I, O, U, and sometimes Y, in them. Let my fellow feline go, Your Sugarplum-miness, and I'll make sure we both stay on good behavior."

"Will you?" Acerbia shifted her weight, but not enough to let me get up. "Very well. You can begin by leaving Kendar and me alone." Her eyes met mine and she ran her tongue over her small, white, sharp little teeth. "We were discussing literature."

Another wave of the fairy's wand and a collar and leash appeared around Mysti's neck. The transformed Welfie was still up in the air, so Scandal grabbed the leash's end between his teeth and trotted off into the library, tugging her after him like a fuzzy balloon. As soon as they were inside, Acerbia's ever-present wand wiggled again and the door slammed behind them.

"Now, where were we?" she asked.

"You were about to be executed!" came a roar from the apartment doorway. A tall, muscular man with hair and beard the color of steel stood there, glaring at us. He wore crimson-and-cream velvet, a gold crown set with rubies, red leather boots, and Anisella.

CHAPTER ——————— 20

"HI, KENDAR!" ANISELLA CHIRPED, WAVING AT ME. SHE was riding the big man piggyback. "Have you met King Wulfdeth? He's awfully nice."

I was ready to believe the *awful* part. Have you heard of people so mad they're looking daggers? Well, King Wulfdeth's eyes were shooting javelins. It was a little comforting to know that I wasn't the only target.

"What is the meaning of this, madam?" the king demanded, striding into Acerbia's apartment and making a sweeping gesture over the bed. The destructive spell on the doorway didn't stop him. Either it only worked if you tried to get out of the room, or Wulfdeth had powers and privileges I didn't know about.

"That's Kendar, Your Majesty dear," Anisella said. She twined a lock of her hair through her fingers and tickled his nose with the end. "Remember? I told you all about him. He and I are just good friends."

The king's stormy brows rose, and sarcasm soaked his words as he said, "Obviously the lady Acerbia is interested in more than just his good friendship."

One moment I was pinned under the full weight of the fairy, the next I was free and she was buzzing furiously around King Wulfdeth's head like a rabid mousekitter. "How *dare* you!" she shouted, even if it came out sounding more like a squeak. "These rooms are *mine*! You gave them to me yourself, to do with as I liked. How dare you barge in here uninvited with that—that—" She zoomed right up to Anisella's nose and bawled, "—*spamini*!"

Even King Wulfdeth gasped. Anisella let go of his shoulders and burst into tears. I hurried over to put my arms around her and comfort her. The king and I gave the enraged fairy some extremely dirty looks.

"There's no need to use that kind of language, Acerbia," he said.

"Yeah!" I put in, forgetting that this was my enemy. "I never even heard my *dad* use that word. Or my brother Basehart, and he's got a mouth that would shock the scales off your dragon."

The fairy flashed back to human size, except this time she made herself taller than usual so that she and Wulfdeth were eye-to-eye. "I know you too well, Wulfdeth," she said. "You bluster and make a big noise about my . . . little hobby"—she blew a kiss at me—"while you go frolicking after every bit of female fluff that blows across your path. This isn't the first time you've cheated on me."

King Wulfdeth huffed and puffed and tried to look like she meant someone else. "I assure you, Acerbia, the girl and I are just good friends. You can ask her yourself, if you like."

"I will, if she ever stops sniveling." The fairy prodded Anisella on the arm with her wand. "Control yourself, child. I expected more backbone out of you."

"You called me a spa—spa—spa—" Anisella's sobs and gulps got in the way of her words.

"Spamini," I said, trying to be helpful and hoping Mom never found out I'd used that kind of language.

Anisella howled.

"I was in my bed—*alone*—when one of your Secret Police came trampling in, blabbering something about a nest of traitors all captured at the Cheese and Crackers," the king continued. "I'd had a very hard day, oppressing the peasants, and all I ask is a little peace and quiet, but your employees have no sense of kindness or mercy."

"They'd better not," Acerbia said through clenched teeth. "I pay them to have it surgically removed."

"Once the lout had me up, I had to go down to the dungeons to investigate his wild report." Wulfdeth's face went all goopy as he turned to Anisella. "That was where I met this exquisite child." He slapped a scowl back on to conclude, "So don't blame *me*; this is all *your* fault."

"Dear, dear Wulfdeth," the fairy murmured. "If I caught you with your arms plunged up to the elbows in the blood of your own brother, you'd find a way to blame it on someone else."

The king pursed his lips. "You *did* catch me up to my elbows in the blood of my brother," he objected. "You were the one who told me to kill him."

"You see? None of it's ever *his* fault," Acerbia said to us with a What-can-you-do? expression.

"Well, that *wasn't* my fault; not if you look at the big picture," Wulfdeth maintained. "I was perfectly happy being the second son until I met you. I was minding my own business, doing second son sort of things like riding through the forests, trying to find some deer to hunt that weren't taxpaying citizens, when I stumbled across that enchanted woodland fountain, and there *you* were."

"The enchanted woodland fountain was my home," Acerbia shot back. "Where else would you want me to be?"

"All I know is, this castle's *my* home and I don't go slouching around it without any clothes on!" Wulfdeth snapped.

Acerbia refused to meet his eyes. "It was hot. I was all dusty from work. I thought that any *real* gentleman who happened to come across me in my bath would have the courtesy to look the other way."

"Oh, I like that! 'Work,' is it?" King Wulfdeth grabbed me by the front of my tunic and yanked me forward. "Ask her what *sort* of work she did before I took her away from all that."

I chewed my lower lip. "Um . . . What sort of work did—?"

"What does that matter?" she spat at me.

"She's ashamed of it, that's what." Wulfdeth grinned.

"I am not! It was—honest work. The best I could get. I'm the youngest fairy on the Underside and all the others took the better jobs."

The library door opened and Scandal stuck his head out. "Hark! Do mine ears detect the jolly sound of a lover's quarrel?" he asked cheerfully. He trotted right between Acerbia and the astonished King Wulfdeth. "Scandal," he said, offering the king his paw. "Friend of Kendar's. I'm a legendary monster. Pleeztameetcha. Go ahead, you can talk in front of me."

"Are you—are you really—?" The king could hardly get the words out.

"He really is a cat," I said, answering the question he was having such trouble asking. "I, uh, I stole him from a powerful Topside wizard and brought him with me all the way from Grashgoboum. I thought I could, er, sell him for a profit and—"

"Pay no attention to Dick Witlesston, Your Majesty," Scandal told him. "I may be a legendary monster, but you're a man of the world. You know the legends."

Wulfdeth nodded. "A cat may look at a king."

"*Exactamundo*. Now we got that settled, I wanna hear what Tinkerbell was doing to bring home the nectar. It musta been *some* lousy job." He fixed Acerbia with a steady gaze. "Flipping ambrosia-burgers at McWelfie's? Selling Hamster Helper door-to-door? Fairy godmother for a used-car salesman? Writing science fiction? What?"

"Truth Fairy," Acerbia mumbled.

Scandal flicked an ear. "One mo' time, toots? If you don't mind."

"*I was the Truth Fairy!*" she hollered, and promptly shrank down to doll-size. I guess she was embarrassed. "Whenever a child forces his parents to tell him the truth about where babies come from, the Truth Fairy is supposed to leave him a piece of candy under his pillow."

"Candy?" Scandal sniffed. "Where I come from, we've got a setup sorta like that, only the kids get money. Shekels. *Dinero.* Cold, hard cash. Candy? Pfui!"

Acerbia's tiny cheeks turned red. "The candy I leave—*used* to leave—was an all-day sucker with a naughty joke written on it. If the child could get his parents to tell him the truth about why the joke was funny, I had to go back the next night and leave money. It was undignified, repetitive, tiring, and I had to make up the naughty jokes myself." She folded her arms. "The only good thing about the job was knowing all that candy would make the little brats' teeth fall out."

"That's not the way she made it sound when I met her," Wulfdeth said, folding his arms too. "All I heard from her was 'Oh, to think I gave up my career for this!' and 'It wouldn't be so bad, being just a housefairy, if you'd go out and *make* something of yourself.' So I *did* make something of myself. I made myself King of Wingdingo! Anything to stop her from yapping on about how she'd sacrificed *such* a glamorous job just to be with me, and how all the other fairies got to fly here and there on exciting business trips while she was cooped up in the castle, and how—Agh!" He turned his back on Acerbia.

Anisella tiptoed up behind the king and tapped him on the shoulder. "Please don't fight with the nice fairy, King Wulfdeth dear," she begged prettily. "She'll never agree to do that eentsy-weensy favor I asked you for."

"A favor?" Acerbia unfurled to her most preferred human size, the better to sneer at Anisella. "A favor for which you need *me*, am I right?"

King Wulfdeth slowly came around to face her once more. "Just a little favor," he said gruffly. "Not much magic to it at all, if truth be told. Something you could do in your sleep, my dear. It would make this sweet child very happy." He gave Anisella a look sure to make Acerbia's blood boil.

"Someone better teach ol' Wulfdeth about diplomacy," Scandal remarked under his breath. "Never rile a woman who's got a loaded dragon."

"Come, come, Acerbia," the king said, trying to brazen it out. "This delightful lass isn't one of those treacherous sheep you've got locked up downstairs. She's one of your little"—his lip curled when he looked at me—"*hobby's* friends. She told me that their group was attacked by the pirates through no fault of their own. They were coming to the Underside as peaceful travelers. You always did say that we ought to encourage Topside tourism. How will it look if they go back and tell everyone we treat our visitors so rudely?"

"We could solve *that* problem if we don't let them go back," Acerbia said, slapping her wand against the palm of her hand.

"My dear, you can't mean that." The king patted Anisella's cheek, then lifted her chin gently. "Although as far as I'm concerned, this charming girl is welcome to stay here as long as she likes."

A wicked twinkle stole into Acerbia's eye. "Why, Wulfdeth, I do believe you are genuinely fond of her," she said, her tongue dripping syrup. "And how gallantly you showed your affection, carrying her all the way up here on your back."

Wulfdeth became plainly uncomfortable. "There are too many stairs in this castle. She, um, she twisted her ankle on the way out of the dungeon."

"Of course she did."

"And she said I had to see you right away because you'd made a terrible mistake."

"I'm sure I must have, if *she* said so." The twinkle in Acerbia's eye was now the glow of a miniature blast furnace. Wulfdeth started to sweat.

"Er, of course I think she's a fine young lady, but I'm not *that* fond of her," he finished quickly.

"What do you mean, dear, by '*that* fond'?" The fairy put on a look as innocent and fake as a bad painting of a newborn baby.

"I mean I like her, but not enough to make you so angry you'll turn her into something ugly."

"Me?" Acerbia fluttered her wings and her eyelashes. "But Wulfdeth, darling, you know that everything I do, I do to please you. I knew you weren't *really* happy being the second son while your brother was king. I knew you could never hold onto the crown by yourself, so I organized the Secret Police just for you. When I heard that the true heir to the throne was still alive somewhere up in the mountains, I took care of the whole icky mess so that you wouldn't have to worry your dear little head about it."

"What!" This news clearly came as a surprise to the king. "Alive?" Acerbia nodded. "But—not any more, right? You killed the brat . . . didn't you?"

The fairy licked her lips. "Let's just say I settled matters so that he could never hope to claim the throne from you. Or so I thought."

"He? So Heskina had a boy! Well, well," Wulfdeth mused. "I always wondered about that. She'd just given birth before the, mmmm, peaceful transition of power took place."

"Before Wulfdeth killed anything in the castle that was moving," Scandal whispered the translation.

"The baby was gone by the time my men reached the queen's rooms, and there was no one left hanging about afterwards who knew anything about it, except that the child was named Borith. You finally caught up with him, eh?" the king asked.

"Maybe."

"What d'you mean 'maybe'? Either you killed him or you didn't!"

"There now, you see? This is just what I've been saying: I'm always thinking of your happiness before mine, but you never see it that way." Acerbia deftly stepped between Wulfdeth and Anisella. "When I heard there was a simple shepherd who was the spitting image of the royal house, my first thought was to kill him. But when I got a look at him—"

"Handsome, was he?" Wulfdeth shook his head. "I should have known."

"Yes, he was handsome, in fact," the fairy said, unruffled. "Not after I got through with him, though. If I spared his life, Wulfdeth, it wasn't because I hoped that someday he would seek me out, beg me to remove the spell I'd placed on him, and promise he'd do *anything* if I would."

"No?" The king sounded skeptical and I didn't blame him.

"No." Acerbia would not be moved. "It was because I knew you'd want the pleasure of killing him yourself. I flew right home as soon as I'd cast that spell—poor Torquil almost wrenched a wing, I made him hurry so—but when I tried to tell you about what I'd done for you, you were too busy with your silly government things to pay any attention to me. As usual."

There was something incredibly familiar about Acerbia's pout.

Wulfdeth rubbed his chin. "I don't remember you telling me anything about Borith."

"I never did tell you. By the time you could spare poor little me a moment, it was too late: He'd vanished. Not even my Secret Police could discover where he'd gone. I knew if I told you about finding him and losing him, it would only upset you." She patted his cheek the exact same way he had patted Anisella's.

"Did you ever happen to find out what became of him?"

"I did. He joined up with a band of bloodthirsty, cutthroat sheep pirates."

"Did he! The rascal."

"They sailed into Port O' Morph the other day."

"Really?"

"They went to the Cheese and Crackers to celebrate," Acerbia said slowly and carefully, watching the king's face for a reaction.

"The Cheese and Crackers? Fancy that. Someone woke me up to tell me something about the Cheese and Crackers only a few hours ago. What a coincidence," the king mused.

"She's trying to tell you that her goons captured Borith when they fought the sheep pirates and he's chained up in your stinking dungeons right this minute, waiting for you to kill him!" Scandal yelled. While he panted to catch his breath he said to me, "This guy couldn't catch a hint if you threw it at him with a catapult."

"Borith . . . in the dungeon?" Wulfdeth's face lit up with childlike joy.

"Just for you, my love," the fairy said.

"That's . . . very good of you, my dear," the king said. It's hard to sound as sincere as you can be while you're waiting for the other shoe to drop. It was plain to see that he knew Acerbia's ways very well. "Such a nice surprise. If there's anything I can ever do for you . . ."

Anisella whimpered.

". . . as long as this sweet, innocent, completely harmless girl isn't involved," he hastened to add.

"Not even if I'd like to grant her that favor she wants?" The fairy toyed with the end of her wand, making the silver star crackle and writhe.

"No, no, don't trouble yourself, my lady." King Wulfdeth backed off, trying to push Anisella ahead of him, out of Acerbia's apartment. In my heart, I prayed he'd take me along with him. "It was just a silly little request she made about one of your prisoners. I'm sure she understands that you know what you're doing when it comes to prisoners and that you have my best interests at heart and—"

"But Your Majesty—" Anisella's voice rose in protest. "Blade didn't do anything wrong! It was all a mistake! Can't you make her see—?"

"Hush, child, hush." The king hustled Anisella faster towards the door. "I'll speak to her about your friend later. She's in a bit of a mood right now. We'll just leave her here with Kendar and I'm sure she'll be much easier to persuade after she's had a nice, long—"

The front door slammed just as they reached it. "Going somewhere?" the fairy asked. "I won't hear of it. If the girl has a favor to ask of me, let her."

King Wulfdeth waved his hands. "No, no, all a mistake, she doesn't have anything to—"

"*Let her.*"

Anisella straightened her shoulders and cast off the king's grip. Tall and proud, she walked boldly up to the fairy and said, "I'm not afraid of you, you know."

"You're young yet," Anisella replied.

"I *do* have a favor to ask of you and I'm willing to pay whatever price it takes."

"This favor must be very important to you, child."

"You turned her friend into a cat, my dear." King Wulfdeth gave Scandal an inquiring look.

"Whoa! Not me, Your Regality. I was born this lucky," Scandal said.

"Yes, I did," Acerbia admitted. "Her friend is—*was*—a Welfie with a keen sword and a tongue to match. He was using the sword on the side of your enemies. He'd be down in the dungeons with them now if he hadn't opened up a fresh mouth to me and made me lose my temper."

"Blade fights on the side of justice," Anisella maintained staunchly. She turned to the king. "I'm sorry, Your Majesty, but you *did* kill your brother and his family. That isn't very nice."

"It's all her fault," Wulfdeth said, glaring at Acerbia.

"Well, I suppose it is." The fairy shrugged her wings and shoulders. "Whatever can I do to make it up to you both? I know!" She tried to clap her hands, but the wand got in the way. "I will grant *you* the favor you asked." She pointed at Anisella. "I'll return your Welfie friend to you just the way he was when I found him. And as for you, dear Wulfdeth—" Her smile sent chills through me.

"You've done more than enough for me, Acerbia dear. Really, you mustn't trouble yourself any further. Capturing Borith and his treacherous comrades is plenty for—"

"Not at all. There must be *something* I can do for you." I swear, you could see the king's skin crawl when she said that. "Ah! Why didn't I think of this before? What a splendid idea. I know exactly what you need."

"Do—do you?" Wulfdeth edged toward the locked door and tried pulling the handle without her noticing. It worked about as well for him as it had for me.

"You need a queen."

"A—?" His face was the color of chalk.

Acerbia floated across the floor to paste herself against the king's body. She placed a silencing finger on his lips. "I know what you're going to say, my sweet. Don't bother. What we've had together has been wonderful, but it is not a legal marriage. It can't be. You are human and I am a fairy with all my enchantments intact. You can't marry me as I am and I don't want to give up any of my powers to marry you. It's too bad, but those are the rules."

"What rules?" the king asked, struggling for breath.

"The rules of the great Mystic Balance. We mustn't break them or something awful might happen."

"Yeah, like a whole lot of birds falling out of the sky all the time," Scandal supplied.

"But just because you can't marry *me* is no reason for you not to get married," the fairy went on. "Admit it, Wulfdeth: You'd feel much more secure on the throne if you had a royal heir to leave the kingdom to after you died."

"Er, yes. My ministers have suggested marriage several times over the years for that very reason."

"They were all perfectly correct and I'm sorry I turned them into hamsters," Acerbia said. "Now I agree with them, and when you marry I promise I will do nothing to harm you or the mortal you choose for your bride." She held out her wand and placed her other hand on the star. "Fairy's honor. Now feel free to tell me, darling, *do* you have some lucky girl in mind?"

The king hemmed and hawed, but we all knew what his answer was going to be. To quote Raptura Eglantine: "His eyes sought hers—she for whom his soul hungered and thirsted with a mad, unbridled, searing passion—his gaze brimming with ardor and tenderness as his heart silently poured out all its desperate longing with an eloquence far beyond the ability of mere words to convey."

"I don't *wanna!*" Anisella wailed.

"But my dear, if you become my bride there will be nothing I can refuse you," the king said in a reasonable tone.

"Oh, Your Majesty dear, you're soooo sweet to offer," Anisella said. "But—but I can't marry you because there's a curse on me. I'm doomed to bring death and destruction to the first to marry me."

"I'm a fairy," Acerbia purred. "I can lift one hundred fifty times my weight in curses."

"Well then, I can't marry you because—because I don't love you!"

"You don't have to love him, child," the fairy said smoothly. "You just have to give birth to his children."

"I *won't* marry you!" Anisella stamped her foot. "I love Blade!"

"Fine." King Wulfdeth struck his stubborn pose again. "Acerbia! Find this Blade, bring him here, and lift the spell you put on him."

"Yes, dear," the fairy said meekly.

"Oh, thank you, Your Majesty!" Anisella exclaimed, bouncing for joy. "This is so good of you! I knew you were—"

"That will make it much more convenient for the royal hangman. He doesn't know how to execute a cat."

Anisella flung herself into my arms, sobbing wildly.

"Oh dear," Acerbia sighed. "Now you've gone and upset the poor girl. Really, Wulfdeth, you ought to be ashamed. Such a terrible fuss just because you want to marry your own daughter."

CHAPTER ———— 21

THE NEXT MORNING, I AWOKE WITH A COLD NOSE IN my ear. "Royal intrigue always give me a headache," Scandal said, wriggling under my arm. "Get up and rub that spot between my eyebrows, huh?"

"I *knew* I'd heard that name somewhere before," I said, sitting up. I planted the cat in my lap and rubbed that spot between his eyebrows.

"What name?" he asked, half asleep.

"Acerbia."

"Sure, me too. Bob Acerbia, a good, dependable southpaw, used to play shortstop for the Cubs."

"No, be serious. Anisella mentioned it when she was telling me about how she got cursed. Acerbia was the name of the fairy who came to her naming-day and gave her presents while she was growing up and—"

Scandal rolled over, showing his belly. "Now you know why."

"Yeah. I still can't figure out why Acerbia would put that curse on Anisella, especially since she's her mother."

"Mothers are always putting curses on their daughters and they all start: *Just wait until you have children of your own!* Fairies. Go figure. And where is the dear girl this morning? Having a nice family reunion with Mommy and Daddy while we're locked up in durance vile?"

I glanced around our prison. It was durance, but it wasn't very vile. It was just another of the rooms in Acerbia's apartment, and a nice one at that. Plenty of high windows let in the light of a new day. Beautiful wood paneling ran all around the room. Way down at the floor level, on opposite walls, were two perfectly fitted miniature doors. I wondered what they were for when I first saw them, but last night I'd been too sleepy to investigate.

The doors were the only small things in the room. Like Acerbia's bedchamber, the rest of the furniture here was also built on a human scale. Scandal and I sat on a plump divan shaped like a sleeping dragon, its curled-up golden body covered with scale-patterned pillows in black, gold, and green. I'd slept well on it. On the side of the room nearest the windows, two well-cushioned chairs flanked a round table, heavily laden with bread, fruit, cake, and jugs of strong, hot gawfee. It was good to know that Acerbia didn't intend to starve us to death.

"I don't know where they've taken Anisella," I said, setting the cat down. I was nervous, but I was also hungry. The food on the table looked good and the gawfee smelled great. I helped myself generously to breakfast.

Scandal hopped onto the table. "Just in case Acerbia decided to poison that stuff, what are your last words gonna be?"

"Snog bois'n," I answered around a mouthful of cake.

"It could be. Slow-acting poison. You saw how she likes to play with her victims instead of going for the quick kill. Disgraceful. The look on Wulfdeth's face when she told him who Anisella really was? Brother! So how about them last words?"

I chewed and swallowed. "Hey, if I die, just repeat the last thing I say."

"If you insist, boss. But 'Aaaaarrrrrgh! The pain, the pain! Holy *bleep*, that hurts!' doesn't look real classy in the history books. I could make up something for you, if you want. How's this?" He sat up on his haunches, raised a paw dramatically, and declaimed, "Good night, sweet Scandal, best of cats! Farewell, a long farewell to all my Majyk. Had I served my cat with half the zeal I served my king, he would not in my age have left me naked to mine enemies. *Et tu*, Acerbia? Then fall, Kendar!" He lost his balance and toppled off the table with a thud.

He was back in the blink of an eye. "Landed on my feet," he said, always smug about it.

"This is not poisoned," I said.

"It wouldn't make any difference to you if it was," the cat reminded me. "Not unless it's like that ringer Ramses gave you to drink. With ordinary poison you can get a bellyache to beat the band, but thanks to your Majyk—"

"What Majyk?" I was glum. "It's no good, Scandal; it's lost, all except the smallest traces. I've tried and tried, but I can't bring it back."

"I don't buy that." Scandal shook his head. "No way, José. You were getting good at that wizard shtick. You can't lose it all, *kablam*, just like that."

"Well, I did."

"Uh-uh. It's like falling off a horse. There's gotta be a way to get you back in the saddle."

I thought of Nintari and shuddered.

"Too bad Acerbia didn't lock you in the library," he continued. "Maybe there's something in there that could help you?"

"How's a Raptura Eglantine book going to help me get back my powers?"

"Don't knock it, *kemo sabe*." The cat grinned. "Nothing like a good romance to put the magic back in your life. Speaking of which, where's my little sugar cruller in the doughnut shop of desire? Come out, come out, wherever you are!"

"Mrowr." Mysti peered out from under the dragon couch. I broke off a piece of chocolate cake and held it out to her. She crept nearer, tail trailing, leash dragging, and sniffed it but refused a taste.

"But it's your favorite!" I cried. She just stared at me, miserable.

"*Was* her favorite," Scandal stated. "She's finding out that things are a lot different for her now."

"That's another thing," I said. "Why didn't Acerbia tell King Wulfdeth and Anisella that Mysti was here? She waited until they left her apartment before making all of us move into this room. She *did* promise to change her back to the way she was, didn't she?"

"Acerbia likes to give Wulfdeth little surprises. She'll 'remember' where she put the spare Welfie when she's good and ready, bet the ranch on it."

I groaned. "And then what? What will she do to Mysti then?"

The cat suddenly became somber. "Your guess is as good as mine, and probably a whole lot less scary. This fairy is one cold number."

I stroked Mysti's head. "Some help I am. I can't even get her collar off."

"Forget the collar," Scandal said. "There's gonna be a bigger one around Ramses' neck real soon now, made out of rope. King Wulfdeth will hang him, there goes the Mystic Balance, and we'll all be wading through whippoorwills Topside until the day we die."

He jabbed my arm with his nose and commanded, "You're gonna get your Majyk back, Kendar."

"I can't—"

"You can because you've *got* to."

"How? Just tell me *how!*" I smacked my hand on the tabletop.

"Hey, ease up!" Scandal skittered backwards. "Just 'cause you're upset, don't go busting up the joint. This table's priceless. Did you get a good look at it?"

He gestured and my eyes automatically followed the movement of his paw. The table *was* gorgeous, its top inlaid with a wealth of rare woods. Their different grains and colors formed a portrait of Torquil, Acerbia's dragon. I'd know those fangs anywhere.

"Where did she get him?" I wondered out loud.

"Where did who get what? Whom. Ahhhhh, you know what I mean. Cats don't do grammar."

"Where did Acerbia get that dragon of hers, Torquil?"

"Beats me." Scandal flopped onto his side and yawned, his tongue curling. "Army surplus? Green stamps? Crackerjack box?"

"Fairies don't own dragons," I said. "Not normally. I learned that during Master Thengor's class on Sprites of All Nations. He told us that fairies don't have the power to control any beast bigger than a hedgehog."

"He lied. Wulfdeth's lots bigger than a hedgehog."

I continued thinking aloud. "Master Thengor called it *power*, but now I know he must've meant Majyk. He didn't say a word about Majyk to us students until we showed that we had the skill and knowledge to handle it."

"He never told *you* about it at all, as I recall." Scandal was enjoying this.

I ignored the cat's barb. "Acerbia wasn't born with enough Majyk to command a dragon, but Torquil is definitely here and he definitely obeys her. That means that somewhere, somehow, Acerbia found the way to acquire more Majyk *and* to make it get along with the Majyk she already had. If she could do it, I can do it."

"Three cheers for our side," Scandal remarked. "Now *how* did she do it? And we are back at square one, do not pass 'Go,' do not collect two hundred dollars."

"Acerbia doesn't collect dollars," I said. "Acerbia collects *books.*"

A little later I was down on my hands and knees, peering through one of those little doors in the wall. "It's the library!" I cried.

"So?" Scandal was lapping up his second cup of gawfee.

"So remember what you said before? About how maybe there'd be something in the library to help me get back control of my

Majyk? Now I know there's more on Acerbia's shelves than *Centaur Tender, Centaur True*. The answer *is* in there! It has to be. Acerbia used it herself to add to her powers so she could control Torquil. All we've got to do is find it."

"Correction: First all we gotta do is look around for a bottle that says 'Drink Me.'"

I glanced over my shoulder. "A what?"

"Or else a cake that says 'Bite This.' Whichever one it was that made you shrink. It's been a long time since I saw *Alice in Wonderland*. Chief, Acerbia could have the Holy Grail in that room and it still wouldn't do you a lick of good. You can't fit through the fershlugginer door!"

"*I* can't. *You* can."

It took some doing and a lot of arguing, but before too long I had Scandal and Mysti going back and forth through the little doorway, fetching book after book from Acerbia's library. Scandal's reading skills were so-so, but Mysti helped him select books whose titles looked the most promising for what I had in mind.

"That proves she's not really a cat," I told him. "Real cats can't read."

"Who needs to read books when you can read minds?" he replied. "They've got better illustrations, they never go out of print, and you wouldn't believe the dirty parts. Hot-cha!"

Carefully I picked through the assortment of tiny books until I had four that might contain the information I needed. "Scandal, go back into the library and bring me the tank of water you'll see on a table in there."

"Thirsty, bwana?"

"Just do it, and watch out that you don't spill a drop."

The cat left, singing a song about toting that barge and lifting that bale. He came back with the tank of micro-fish carried delicately in his jaws. I took it from him and put it on the table with the books I'd chosen, then pulled the borrower's wand from my tunic.

Scandal jumped back onto the table. "Whatcha gonna do with that, bunkie? Let the hot air out of some lawyers?"

"Watch and learn," I said, flourishing the wand over the micro-fish tank.

Scandal sniffed at the bubbly water. His nose wiggled. "Ah—ah—ahhh—!"

"Scandal, *no!*"

"AHCHOO!" Drops of water flew everywhere.

The room shook with a sound like a billion giant roses all bursting into bloom at the same time. Before any of us could move, we were hip deep in books and fish.

"Isn't anyone gonna say 'Gezundheit'?" Scandal asked, wiping his nose with his paw.

CHAPTER ——————— 22

"DID YOU FIND IT YET?" SCANDAL ASKED, DESPERATE.

I waved him away. "I'm looking, I'm looking! Just keep stacking those fish."

"Where?" He flailed his forepaws. "There's too many books all over! Some of the fish are trapped *under* the books."

"For Wedwel's sake, you can't leave them *there*!" I looked up sharply from the book I was flipping through. "If we don't get them back in the water, they're going to die and stink up the whole room and then Acerbia will know what we've been doing."

"Oh, as if she won't figure it out when she comes back in here and finds half the Library of Congress blocking the door?"

"Scandal, leave me alone, I have work to do. I can't concentrate with you yammering at me. This whole mess is all your fault, anyhow."

"You sound like King Wulfdeth," the cat said coldly.

"Just . . . stack . . . the . . . fish."

"What do you want from me? It's a big job and I'm only one cat. I don't even have opposable thumbs!"

I sat back and covered my eyes. "Stack them, eat them, play Haxi-Chaxi with them; I don't care what you do as long as you get them out of the way. Why don't you get Mysti to help you?"

"Um, er, ah, well . . . Never mind. I can handle this. Mysti's asleep and I don't think she ought to be—"

"NYOWROWWWWWWW!" A mountain of books shifted and slid away as Mysti uncurled from her nap. She stretched lazily, arched her back, then stood tall.

She was as big as Nintari.

Mysti sat, crushing a few expanded micro-fish into a mass of scales, bones, and yuck-what-did-I-step-in. The rasping sound her tongue made as she washed her forepaws was like running a file over a leather saddle. She soon lost interest in washing, and fixed her glowing eyes on Scandal.

"YOWOWWWWW?" she said, tilting her head. "OROOOO-NYOW?" The words were different, but the wheedling tone was the same. I recognized it at once.

"Scandal, she's—I think she's flirting with you."

"I know." The cat closed his eyes tight and cringed. "You're the wizard, boss. Make it go away."

"Do you mean that she's . . . the way you told me she was going to get after a while? The thing cats can't turn on and off like humans?"

"Trust me, right now I'd trade seven of the eight lives I've got left for one giant 'Off' switch on that kitty." He opened one eye a crack and closed it tight after a quick glimpse of Mysti in all her furry glory.

"OORROO," she crooned at him.

I was confused. "Wasn't this what you wanted?"

"Not . . . really. Not now. And sure as heck *not like this!*" His whiskers hung limp and lifeless. "Look at her. Just look at her. For pity's sake, there's just so much one tomcat can handle!" He covered his nose with his paws and muttered, "Now I know how you feel, married to her. Feline or skinball, that Mysti's a whole lotta female."

"Scandal, why is Mysti getting down on her belly and rocking back and forth like that?" I asked. Scandal yowled in terror and hid under the table.

I could see that I was on my own. I returned to the books, but there were too many of them. The four I'd picked out for closer study were lost in the avalanche that happened when Scandal sprayed micro-fish all over the room. If I found a book I didn't need or want, there was hardly any space to put it aside without knocking over more books or squishing some fish. I caught myself examining the same book three times.

I laid my hand on the little water tank. "At least nothing happened to you," I told it. I stuck a book with the well-dried point of my borrower's wand as an experiment, hoping it would dwindle to doll-size and get out of my way. No luck. I stuck the nearest micro-fish with the wand, and it did shrink until it was an almost invisible dot on the tabletop. I was very careful to dab it up with my fingertip and drop it back in the tank.

I checked out our plight once more. I could either use my time for reducing and replacing the micro-fish one by one, or I could spend it searching these books of sorcery for a way to fix everything with one sweeping spell.

There was also the chance that I'd lose my head and dart back and forth between the two plans in a panic, accomplishing nothing. The micro-fish would die, the books would still be a hazard, Mysti would stay big as a horse, I'd never regain control of my Majyk, and Acerbia would solve my complexion problem by skinning me alive when she caught me.

Yes, that was a very good possibility.

"RRRROOONYAAAARRR?" Mysti's meows became more intense and insistent. She sounded so mournful that I decided the books could wait a bit longer. I went over and scratched her behind the ear. No matter how big she was, she still enjoyed the simple pleasures.

"I'm sorry, Mysti," I told her. "I didn't know the micro-fish would work on people, too." I thought about what I'd just said, then added, "But some of the fish *must* have hit me—I was closer to the tank than you were when Scandal sneezed. I wonder why I didn't turn into a giant?" I gnawed a knuckle, pondering the riddle. "Just one of those Majyk things, I guess."

"Logic," came a voice from under the table. Scandal poked his nose out, a wary eye on Mysti while he spoke to me. "Use logic, Kendar. Common sense. Don't just go saying, 'Oh, it's a Majyk thing, there *is* no explanation.' That's an easy out. You asked a good question and you're smart enough to find the real answer."

"How do you know I'm that smart?"

"You were smart enough to ask the question, that's how."

"Wellllll . . ." I was reluctant—there was enough to do without answering my own unanswerable riddles—but I knew Scandal would never let me hear the end of it if I didn't at least try. "Logic, huh?"

"Indeed, Captain." One of Scandal's eyebrows quirked up. "I think you will find the process . . . fascinating. Begin by stating the problem. Use a Number Two pencil. Do not write on both sides of the paper at once. Void where prohibited."

"All right. The micro-fish worked on Acerbia's books and on Mysti, but not on me and not on you."

"Good start. Also not on the furniture or the floor or anything else like that. Now if you can figure out what Acerbia's books and Mysti have in common that the other stuff, including us, *don't* have, you've got your answer."

I thought about it. I tried, honestly I did, but I came up blank. Hey, it was hard to think! The sound of Mysti's yodeling yowls and the thrash-thrash of dying micro-fish distracted me. "It's no use," I said. "This really *is* a Majyk thing."

"Precisely, Captain." Scandal flicked his ears forward.

"What—?"

"You have found the answer."

"All I said was it's a Majyk . . ." I paused. Majyk. Mortals could gather it up, but creatures like Acerbia and Mysti (and probably the micro-fish) were born with it. Acerbia's Majyk was like mine, yet different, the way Scandal and Mysti (in cat form) were also alike and different at the same time.

"*It's a Majyk thing!*" I exclaimed, triumphant. "Acerbia's Majyk. Her spells are all over her books and her micro-fish and Mysti, when she slapped that spell on her. But there's none of it on us or the furniture or the castle. That's it; that's *got* to be it!"

"Please, Captain, there is no need to be so emotional," Scandal said. "It is not logical."

"It is so! And stop calling me 'Captain.'"

"Sorry, pal." Scandal smiled. "I keep confusing you with my former human. Your answer's perfectly logical, and I'll bet my last anchovy it's right, too."

"I got the right answer?" I'd spent most of my time as a student at the Academy getting the wrong answer. I should have been thrilled at the change, but I wasn't. "Big deal. It only tells us why we got in this mess; it doesn't tell us how to fix it."

"That's what the book is for." Scandal didn't seem to be worried.

"*Which* book?" I cried, flinging my arms wide to embrace the whole chaotic room.

"The one you need," the cat said, still calm.

I could feel steam seeping out of my collar. "And which one is *that*? Where am I going to find it?"

"Like I said, Kendar: Be logical."

I sprang down and grabbed Scandal by the scruff of his neck, hauling him out from under the table. I held him so he had to look me in the eye and told him, "*If* you don't explain this any better, *then* I am going to throw you to Mysti. How's that for logic?"

"No, boss! Not that! Anything but that!" The cat writhed and squirmed. "You rat, you dirty rat, I'll squeal. Yeah, I'll turn stoolie. Just don't tell me kid brother I cracked, see? He'll think I'm yella. But I ain't yella! I ain't no stoolie! I ain't no squealer, you dirty screw. Nyaaa, nyaa, Big Scandal ain't no—"

"Here, Mysti!" I called, winding up for the cat-toss.

"*She's sitting on it!*" Scandal screamed.

I relaxed and looked at him. "That's the logical answer?"

"Aw, come on, bwana, you'd know it was if you thought about it. Back home, whenever you had something important to read or a special letter to send off, what happened?"

I put him down on the table. "I couldn't find it."

"And remember *why* you couldn't find it?"

"Because—because—" My knuckle got another nibble or two. "Because *you* were always sitting on it!" I flashed an accusing finger at the cat.

"You betcha. It's a Universal Truth that whenever you skinballs have something really important that you've gotta have right now, and you just can't find it, and you tore up the whole house looking for it, it's right under your cat's butt. Period." Scandal wasn't ashamed at all. "Call it instinct, call it obsession, call it a holy feline mission from God. Hey, what can I tell you?" He shrugged. "It's a cat thing."

I looked at Mysti's rump. It would take someone stronger than me to move it. "Mysti, would you mind getting up?" I asked nicely.

"NYOWWWW!" She rocked back and forth, kneading with her forepaws, but she didn't budge.

"Please, Mysti, you've got to get up so I can find a book. It'll help me change you back to the way you were."

The giant black-and-white cat only purred. It was like standing next to a furry earthquake.

Scandal sighed. "Forget it, Mister Manners. There's no talking to dames when they're like this. I'll handle it. We who are about to die salute you." He posed himself on the tabletop, opened his mouth, and called "C'MONOWWWWWWWWT! AWANA-SEEEEEEYAAAAA!"

Mysti was up and eager before the last note of his courting serenade died away. I made a fast grab for the book that was right where Scandal said it would be. "I got it!" I yelled to him.

"Praise Bast!" he yelled back, and dived out of Mysti's reach. The big cat sank down beside the table, looking extremely disappointed.

I paged through the book for some time. It was unpleasant work; the cover was smeared with squished micro-fish. Now and then I'd hear Scandal's voice piping up with, "Is it the one, boss? Is it? Is it, huh?" I didn't have the time to answer. I was too deeply into the book.

At last I closed the cover and sat back with a sigh. "So that's it."

"That's what?" Scandal asked, reaching out to paw my ankle gently.

I didn't reply. Instead I held the borrower's wand between my fingers and passed my free hand over it. There was a faint flare of Majyk and I was holding a full-sized metal wand. Big, it no longer looked like a straight pin, not even a gigantic one. The flat end was capped with a diamond as large as a cinnamon bun and the pointed end looked like it should belong to an assassin, not a wizard. Between the point and the diamond was a silver shaft etched with a design of frolicking lizards, their eyes picked out with chips of glittering black onyx. I held the wand at arm's length and waited for Scandal's reaction.

"Cooooool," he said, gazing upwards.

"I can do it," I said, more to myself than to him. "I *did* do it. The Majyk inside me is all together now and I can make it obey me again." I stared at the proof I held in my hand. The diamond sparkled, the lizards' eyes winked.

"How'd you do it, bwana?"

"Later," I told Scandal. I rose from the table and turned solemnly to Mysti. "Come here," I commanded her with a terse gesture of the wand.

"Oh, no you don't!" Scandal sauntered out into the open and set himself down between me and Mysti. "Every time one of you Majyk mongers gets the hang of things, you act like the heavens opened up and God Himself pasted a gold star on your forehead. Then you get all stuck-up and mystic and close-mouthed and not-of-this-earth. If you don't watch it, pretty soon you're gonna start talking in *cryptic utterances*, when you condescend to talk to us lowly mortals at all. Well, quit it! You didn't run any gantlets or pass through any ordeals. You didn't even qualify to be an Eagle Scout! All you did was figure out how to make it work. Can the woo-woo, Mr. Barnum, and *spill it*."

I could've refused, I guess, but Scandal wasn't just my familiar; he was my friend. "Mysti, stay," I said as I picked the cat up and put him on the table next to the book that had revealed so many mysteries to me. "The answer is in there," I told him.

He pawed it open to the title page. "*Hex and the Single Girl*," he read. "'Every Fairy's Guide to Cursing Your Way into Marriage.' Say, boss, are you sure this was the book that taught you how to—?"

"Not the book, what's *in* the book," I said, and flipped through the pages until I found what I was looking for.

A small card stuck up from between the pages in the chapter on

Real Men Don't Kiss Frogs: Turning His Other Girlfriends into Amphibians. Either Acerbia had used it as a bookmark or she'd just misplaced it. I passed it to Scandal.

"It's a membership card for Majyk Masters Anonymous," I explained. "It's got their twelve-step program printed on it. Basically it says to take things one spell at a time."

Scandal flattened his ears and looked doubtful. "Well, whatever wags your wand. If it worked for you, super."

"I think it worked for me." I looked at Mysti. "There's one sure way to find out."

"ARRRROWWWWW!" Mysti treaded furiously with her hind paws. She sounded like she was in pain.

"Go for it," Scandal commanded. "And *hurry*."

I leveled the wand at the huge cat's face, aiming it point-first right between the eyes. "I can do it, I can do it, I can do it," I whispered, focusing everything I had in me on the great diamond cap. I felt something at the pit of my stomach burst into wildfire and leap from there to my hand to the wand and across the gap to Mysti. Her mouth opened wide in a silent cry; then fangs and fur all melted into a glowing heap at my feet. When the glow faded, there lay Mysti just as she'd been before Acerbia's spell.

Scandal trotted over and sniffed the unconscious Welfie's masked face. "Next time ease up a little, Houdini. You're putting too much English on it. Head down, arms straight, eye on the crystal ball. The operation's not a success if the patient dies." He bounced back onto the tabletop.

I knelt beside Mysti and cradled her head in my lap. "Are you all right?" I asked anxiously. Her head lolled from side to side, and she moaned. "Did I hurt you?"

"Oh, I *do* hope you didn't hurt him." Acerbia loomed above us, wings outspread to their fullest span. Her own wand burned with a deathly white brilliance. "Goodness, what a surprise. Here I thought you were nothing more than what you seemed, Kendar. The world *does* need more sweet-faced idiots. But a wizard, and at your age—! To have accomplished so much, so young!" She cast her arms high, and all the books and micro-fish vanished. (Only the tiny tank remained on the table. From the corner of my eye I saw Scandal casually move so that it was hidden under his belly, behind his forepaws.)

"What a pity," the fairy went on, her eyes like stone. "What a great pity you shall also die so young, so painfully."

CHAPTER ————————— 23

"IT'S BAD MANNERS TO DIE WITHOUT RETURNING everything you borrowed first," Acerbia said, using her wand to point at mine. "I'll take that."

"I don't think so." My palms were sweating, but the silver lizards gave me a good grip on the diamond-capped wand.

"It's not nice to contradict a lady." The fairy's gaze shifted to Mysti. "I see you've been a busy little wizard. Nice work. You must have a good deal of Majyk to be able to undo one of my spells."

"I've got enough to take care of myself," I said, feeling uneasy. What was all this chitchat? Why didn't she just attack? I'd seen how Acerbia enjoyed toying with Wulfdeth. What did she have in store for me?

"I suppose I ought to call you Master Kendar, in that case. Kendar *is* your real name?" I nodded. "Good. You lied to me about so much else, I thought it best to ask." She waved her wand, and a plump, pink spangled cloud appeared behind her. She sat on it, swinging her feet like a little girl on a fence rail.

"I shouldn't be so angry with you, *Master* Kendar," she went on. "My sweet daughter speaks very highly of you."

"Anisella *is* your daughter?"

"Mine and Wulfdeth's, yes. We fairies don't often have children of our own kind—there are enough of us as it is—and we have half-human children even less often than that. I don't know how to describe my feelings when I found out I was going to have a baby." She rested the starry tip of her wand against her chin in thought. "I think 'disgusted' is closest."

"You didn't want a baby?" I was shocked. Mom was crazy for babies. She told Lucy and Basehart and me how she'd hoped to have lots and lots of them, except Dad was always off on long hunting trips. Then she'd sigh and add, "At least Wedwel saw fit to bless me with two normal children." She never was much good at arithmetic . . . I hope.

"My dear boy, why are you goggling at me like that?" the fairy asked. "Have I said something so horrible? You're hardly out of diapers yourself. How can you know what a burden children are?"

"To you, maybe." Mysti sat up, her eyes burning behind the black mask. "We Welfies treasure our little ones."

Acerbia rolled her eyes. "You Welfies treasure acorn cups and fungus. You live in giant *mushrooms*, for pity's sake! I wouldn't expect anyone like you to see children for what they are: loud, selfish, inconsiderate, cruel, attention-hungry creatures that always want their own way and pout when they don't get it."

"But enough about you," Scandal purred.

Fortunately, the fairy didn't hear his comment. "Of course I couldn't be bothered with a baby. Without me there to help him, Wulfdeth could hold onto a greased mirror more easily than he could ever hold onto the throne. As soon as I knew there was no doubt about my condition, I told him I was going to take a brief vacation. My excuse was a long diplomatic voyage Topside to give all the rulers there hand-painted beer mugs as a souvenir of Wulfdeth's coronation. Anisella was born while I was visiting Grashgoboum. Once *that* nasty business was over with, it was no trouble at all to hire a couple willing to raise the infant for me."

"You know what?" I said. "Listening to you talk about children, I'm no longer surprised that you put a curse on your own daughter."

Acerbia snorted. "Your wisdom is about as deep as a dry lake. Don't you understand? I was *provoked* to curse her. It wasn't my fault at all."

"Why did I know she was gonna say that?" Scandal asked.

"Anisella was born half-fairy and half-mortal," Acerbia told us. "Such children remain half-and-half until they reach maturity."

"Maturity is not a word I would use in the same sentence with Anisella," Mysti growled, so low that I think I was the only one to hear it.

"You know what she means," I hissed back, helping her to stand.

"When that time comes, a certain ceremony must be performed if the child is going to be made into a full-fledged fairy," Acerbia continued. "It is not a *nice* ceremony—quite inconvenient, expensive, exhausting, and messy. It is also extremely painful for the child. I gave Anisella's foster-parents detailed instructions for putting her through it. I even made certain they had a good supply of ointments and bandages to use on her afterwards, and potions for the pain."

"Gee, I know who *I'm* voting for as Mother-of-the-Year," Scandal announced. "This sure beats the heck out of a bat-mitzvah."

Acerbia's silky brows dived into a scowl. "They did not perform the ceremony at the correct time. Once the moment passed, it was too late; my child would remain a half-blood all her days. I don't know what they could have been thinking of. Perhaps they assumed that if the girl did not become a fairy, they could keep her as their own forever. They did jabber some nonsense about being fond of the girl. The nerve! I soon set them straight. The marriage curse was brilliant, if I do say so myself." She sniffed delicately. "Mortals are so selfish."

"Well, now that you're all one big happy family again, I guess all curses are off, huh?" Scandal asked.

Acerbia idly fluffed up her pink cloud. "Hmmmm? Oh. Yes, I suppose that I ought to remove the curse now. What's the use of having a royal princess around the house unless you can marry her off to a powerful king? It's the cheapest way Wulfdeth will ever get any military aid, and if we play our cards right, maybe Anisella's husband will die and we can add his kingdom to our own." Her smile told me that there was no "maybe" about it.

"Nice plan," Scandal remarked. "One problem."

"Yes?"

"Yoo hoo! Mummy!" Clad in a glimmering gown of blue and gold, Anisella sailed into the room. Her eyes fell on Mysti—her beloved "Blade"—almost immediately. With a joyful cry she flew to embrace the masked Welfie. Only a nimble sidestep saved Mysti from a hug so close it couldn't help but uncover her . . . little secret.

"Speak of the problem." Scandal was smug.

"Oh, Mummy, thank you!" Anisella burbled, clasping her hands. "Thank you, thank you, *thank* you for changing Blade back to the way he was! You're the best Mummy in the whole world and I love you!" She sprang for Acerbia, and because clouds can't sidestep as fast as Welfies, this time she hit her target.

"Ugh, stop, get off me." Acerbia pried Anisella's arms from around her neck. A scrap of cloud scrubbed off all the girl's exuberant kisses. "Goodness, child, you aren't some half-naked urchin now. You are the crown princess of Wingdingo! Try to remember that and show a little dignity."

Anisella looked down. "Yes, Mummy."

The fairy studied her daughter. "That dress looks all right on you. Is it comfortable to wear?"

"It's wonderful," Anisella gushed. "I never could wear anything made out of cloth before. Is it enchanted?"

"It's spiderweb silk. My own wardrobe is made from that material alone. You cannot stand to wear the coarse fabrics fit for commonfolk. That is your fairy blood at work."

"Do you know, I always wondered about that. It was so awful, not being able to wear dresses like the other little girls. Do you have any idea how dreadful it is to wear chain mail in the winter? Oh, I love this dress!" She twirled around, making the skirt flare and dance. "How sweet of you to give it to me, Mummy. I always wanted—"

"Anisella, don't babble."

Anisella stopped twirling. "Yes, Mummy."

"Don't bore me with tales from your past. We all have our own troubles."

Anisella's head drooped. "Yes, Mummy."

"And most of all, don't call me 'Mummy.'"

"But you *are* my mother!" Anisella raised her eyes, bright with tears. "Are—aren't you?"

"I am your mother. And your father's prime minister is an idiot. However, he is an idiot with lots of money, land, and powerful relatives. His wife, whom he adores, is a common *spamini*. You will not call him 'idiot,' you will not call her '*spamini*,' and you will not call me 'Mummy.' In fact, while you are under this roof you will never call anyone at court what he or she truly is. That's the first rule of royal etiquette. You may call me Acerbia."

"Yes, Mu—Acerbia." Anisella sniffled. Even Mysti felt sorry for her and in a moment of weakness she patted her on the shoulder.

"Don't cry," she rumbled in her "Blade" voice.

It was not a wise move. Anisella spun around and burst into tears on Mysti's shoulder. I took one look at Acerbia's stormy brow and tightened my grip on the silver wand.

"What's going on here?" King Wulfdeth was among us once more. His eyes narrowed when he saw Mysti. "Who is that man and why does he have his arms around my daughter?" he demanded.

"Don't worry, my love," Acerbia said. "Soon he won't have arms at all."

"He will so!" Anisella tossed her head. "Daddy—I mean, King Wulfdeth dear—this is Blade and I'm going to marry him."

"No, you're not!" Acerbia, Wulfdeth, Mysti, and I all shouted at the same time.

Anisella pouted. She looked just like her mother. It was frightening. "Why not?"

"Because a royal princess must marry the husband her parents choose for her," said the fairy.

"Because he's not good enough for my little girl," Wulfdeth said.

"Because he's already marrie—eeeeee—Because mortals can't marry Welfies unless the Welfie gives up his Welfinhood," I said. "Remember?"

"Oh, *nice* save, chief," Scandal congratulated me.

"Because I do not want to be married to—"

Mysti's particular objection got drowned out by the sound of Anisella stamping her foot. "I *can* marry a Welfie without him giving up his Welfinhood! My mother's a fairy, and that means I've got just enough of her blood in me to let Blade marry me according to the rules."

"Strike one," the cat muttered.

"Blade is fine, and honorable, and brave, and loyal," Anisella declared, facing Wulfdeth. "If that doesn't make him good enough for me, what does?"

"Now see here—" the king began.

Anisella rushed into his arms and started playing with his beard. "Pleeeeeease, Daddy?"

The king woofed a bit, but he finally said, "Tchah! Have it your own way, child."

"And the kid fights dirty. Strike two." Scandal fanned his whiskers out like a peacock's tail.

Anisella released her father's beard and fixed her eyes on her mother. The two women sounded remarkably alike when Anisella said, "If you don't let me marry Blade, I'm never going to marry anyone. Never. You can't make me. Once upon a time I took an oath to Dul, goddess of unicorns, and I'm not afraid to take another one. If I promise the goddess never to marry, she will protect me and you won't be able to do a thing about it, not with all your spells."

"I'm afraid she's right, my dear," King Wulfdeth said gently. "Gods and goddesses do outrank fairies. It says so in Master Droon's *Illustrated Guide to Beings Who Are All Much More Powerful Than Mere Mortals*."

"You needn't tell me." Acerbia ground her teeth. "My cousin Merwallow is a god and he never lets any of us forget it for a moment. Very well, if the girl insists on throwing herself away, let her." She folded her arms and sank into the loudest brooding silence I ever heard.

"Strike three, and the kid retires the side for all the marbles *and* the pennant," Scandal commented. "Now she's going to *Disneyland*!"

"Blade, isn't it wonderful? We can get married!" Anisella made another grab for Mysti and again was left hugging thin air.

I decided it would be a kindness to break the bad news to the poor girl. "Anisella, I think what Blade's trying to say by running away from you like that is—"

"—Welfies never touch their brides-to-be until the wedding itself!" Mysti announced. "It is an ancient and sacred rule of my people. From the moment I knew that my dearest wish was about to be granted—that my beloved Anisella was going to be my bride—I swore that I would not lay a hand on her before we were pronounced Welfie and wife." She blew a kiss to Anisella through the mask. Anisella tittered and blushed and cooed.

"Bless you, my children," said King Wulfdeth.

"Boss?" Scandal whispered. "Boss, you all right? Boss, close your mouth, you're getting spit on the rug."

CHAPTER ———————— 24

THE DUNGEONS OF KING WULFDETH'S CASTLE WERE just as neat and orderly as the town surrounding it. Every stone in the floor was identical to its neighbor in size and shape, every cell was perfectly square, the torches in the hall faced each other in mirror-image pairs, and there were exactly four men—or whatever—to a cell, one chained to each wall with matching shackles. King Wulfdeth was entertaining a lot of unwilling, unhappy guests down there when we dropped in.

Mysti, Scandal, and I tramped through the corridors, following our guide, one of the prison guards. He was a round-faced, jolly fellow who spoke at length about points of interest we passed along the way.

"—and on your right you'll see the famous Weeping Cell of Prince Borith the Somewhat Poorly Prepared." He fluttered his plump hand at a cell door like a dozen others.

"Prince Borith—I mean, Ramses is in there?" I peered through the grate on the door, but saw nothing inside but darkness. The cell smelled of cold, old stone—no scent of sheep or human occupation.

The guard chuckled. "Bless you, sir, not the Prince Borith who's to be executed next Frogday. This cell's where the *historical* Prince Borith was locked away for twenty-three years. It's the only one we keep empty, in his honor. He was a great soldier, statesman, scholar, and artist, and a devil with the ladies. In his day, he was so popular that every family named a baby after him—didn't matter whether it was boy or girl, animal or human—and the families that didn't have any babies to spare gave his name to one of their pets or house plants. It made for some mighty confusing times at the great Loupgarou Fair, I can tell you that, with so many mothers yelling for their own little

199

Boriths to come here right this minute and half the livestock
answering the call."

"If you Wingdingers lock up your *popular* princes for twenty-
three years, I'd hate to be *un*popular," I said.

"Here, sir, he was only popular with the *people*. 'Tisn't the
people who's got the keys to the royal dungeons, it's the king!
King Owmer was Prince Borith's older brother, and around
Borith's fifteenth victory parade he decided enough was plenty. He
told his wife that he was going to have Borith arrested and thrown
in the dungeons. Queen Ingigungobryth was a tender-hearted
woman and more than sisterly fond of Borith, so the gossip ran.
She stole to his rooms to warn him of the danger."

"But she was too late, right?" Scandal asked. "I bet King
Owmer's troops burst in before poor old Borith could grab his
sword."

The guard shook his head. "No, she warned him about two days
before King Owmer was going to make his move. Prince Borith
told her thank you very much, he was in her debt forever, and did
she know how fetching she looked in that dress? They were still
picking daisies when King Owmer's men attacked, as promised,
two days later."

"A sad tale," Mysti said, trying to sound manly about it. "And
so Prince Borith was flung into this cell, where he spent the next
twenty-three years of his life weeping. Thus the name."

"I do wish you tourists would stop trying to tell stories you
don't know beans about," the guard snapped. "No one did any
weeping in there at all. King Owmer ordered Prince Borith and
Queen Ingigungobryth tossed into the same cell, that's what he
did. He was a mean one, Owmer. He wanted Borith to suffer."

"By locking him up with the queen?" Scandal pricked up his
ears. "That sounds like the sort of suffering a guy could get used
to."

"You didn't know the queen. Owmer did. For the next twenty-
three years, no matter what the time, day or night, any guard who
patrolled this stretch of hall always heard the sound of Ingigungobryth jawing over poor Borith nonstop. She didn't let the poor
feller draw breath to get a word in edgewise, let alone to weep."

"If no one in there did any crying, why is it called the Weeping
Cell?" I asked.

"Well, it wouldn't be half so, whatd'youcallit, *poetical* to call it
the Nagging Cell, now would it?"

Scandal whipped his tail back and forth. "What happened when
the twenty-three years were up? Did Prince Borith die?"

"No, my friend; Prince Borith died twenty-*two* years after he was first locked away. Maybe twenty-one, no one's sure."

"You said he was locked up for twenty-*three* years!" the cat protested.

"I said he was locked up; I didn't say he was alive."

"It couldn't have been very nice for Ingigungobryth, that last year or two," I said. "Why didn't she tell anyone she was stuck in a cell with a dead man?"

"Ingigungobryth was still so angry with Borith that it took her a while to notice he'd slipped away. She called for the guards to come and dispose of him pretty quick after that, I'm sure. And that, my friends, was her salvation."

"Yeah, she could breathe easier, for one thing," Scandal said.

"Oh, there was more than mere breath at stake," the guard said solemnly. "It was fate, sheer fate at work. The queen was a mere bit of a lass when Owmer imprisoned her—no more than nineteen, the records say—so she wasn't hardly a hag twenty-three years later. Being shut up out of the sunlight in a nice, moist dungeon did wonders for her complexion—made it look like polished ivory, they claim—and the prison diet being mostly coarse-grained bread and cabbages and root vegetables kept her off sweets. Most queens, when they get up into their forties, they've got all soft and pudgy from so many royal banquets and their teeth look like gravel, but not Ingigungobryth. Her smile was dazzling, her body a dream. And her habit of pacing back and forth with chains on her wrists and ankles while nagging Prince Borith didn't hurt any either. Ah! What a woman!"

"If you say so," Scandal said. "You want my opinion, I don't think Dungeonetics is ever gonna catch on as a weight-loss program. Thinner thighs in twenty-three years is too long for most humans to wait. It's a shame she never got to strut that bod, though."

"But she did!" The guard's eyes were wide and sincere. "When she summoned help to remove the prince's body, the guard on duty at the time was a healthy young lad named Lundwyrm. He took one look at the queen, fell madly in love, and went right upstairs to bring her a little token of his affection."

"Flowers? Candy? Poetry?" Scandal asked.

"King Owmer's head. He dropped it at Ingigungobryth's feet. She told him thank you very much, she was in his debt forever, and did he know how fetching he looked wearing that armor? Afterwards, he was crowned King Lundwyrm and they lived politely ever after." He gave us an affable smile. "But this isn't getting you where you'd like to be, is it? Come along."

We marched on, past the place where the prisoners were beaten and tortured. Scandal bushed out his fur at the cages, the rack, the whipping post, and snarled, "Barbaric!"

"I should say *not*!" The guard bristled. "We here in the Dungeon Corps are very proud of our torture chamber. It's all run on a strictly scientific basis, not like your higgledy-piggledy Topside ones. I hear tell that your kings just toss a victim to the dungeon workers with no more instructions than 'Hurt him' or 'Hurt him bad' or 'Make him talk' or maybe 'Use your imagination.' Hunh! If I'd had any imagination, I wouldn't've gone into government work. In *this* dungeon we're given precise and accurate directions with each individual prisoner, and we're never without good, solid, professional guidance."

He gestured at a wall chart beside the rack that told the operator how many turns of the wheel to give each victim, based on that unlucky person's height, weight, and age. Whips and cudgels were laid out on a worktable in strict size places.

Scandal stopped to sniff at a skull. It was one of four arranged at the corners of the torture chamber. A fifth sat in a niche above the exit door, watching over a sign that said: THINK. I looked behind me and saw a sixth nested above the door we'd come in by. The sign beneath that one said: SMILE.

"A buck says there's a rulebook somewhere to tell these geeks how many lashes per customer," the cat said.

"We keep it in the front office," the guard said. "You can buy a souvenir copy on your way out. Let's move on."

It was a good thing we had a guide. Down here, where everything looked the same, we'd never be able to find our own way out and there wasn't anyone around to give us directions.

(Not that I'd ever ask directions. I'm an Orthodox Wedwellian. When I went home from Master Thengor's Academy for my Oath of Manhood ceremony, I had to swear before Wedwel's altar that I would never pick up a wet towel, use a needle and thread, or ask directions as long as there was a female nearby. There was also something about leaving the seat up, but no one's been able to figure out that part of the Oath for centuries.)

Hey, Kendar, this guy's not so bad, for a guard, Scandal's thoughts invaded my head. *Don't hurt him too bad, huh?*

Why would I want to hurt him at all? I thought back.

You'll have to, won't you? Just a little. When you bust everyone out of jail.

I'm not busting anyone out of jail, I let him know. *We're only going to get Rhett released. It was King Wulfdeth's wedding gift to Anisella.*

You're not—? Yo, ace, do I have to remind you that even as we speak—or think—a whole bunch of happy carpenters are expanding the public gallows in honor of next Frogday's festivities?

You don't have to remind me. I was right there with you when Mysti told us all about it. Acerbia decided it would be good for Wulfdeth's popularity if they combined the royal wedding with a mass execution.

Yeah, yeah. Tinkerbell's a natural-born P.R. whiz. So what are you waiting for? If you don't use your Majyk to slice through their chains and set them free, Ramses and Captain Lan and the others are all gonna be a bunch of woolly pendulums in less than five days.

Scandal, it's not so simple. I thought.

Sure it is! Use the Force, Luke.

Great, now I don't know what you're thinking *about either. Look, say I do open their cell doors and cut their chains; then what?*

Then they get away.

Away like out-of-the-castle away?

The cat flicked his ears. *You got a better away?*

And how do they get out of the castle? Fight the guards?

Yeah, with swords your Majyk makes for them!

How many swords? I asked.

How many pirates? he returned.

How many guards? I countered. *In the whole castle, I mean.*

Scandal's face fell. *Oh. But couldn't you use your Majyk to help the sheep fight their way out of the castle?*

And after we're out of the castle, there's the city. How many guards does Wulfdeth have in Loupgarou? How many Secret Police does Acerbia have prowling the streets? But say we get through the city gates; then *where do we go? Ramses isn't going to get his throne back by running away.*

Maybe not, but all he's gonna get if he stays here is a loooooong neck. How come you can't use your Majyk to whip up a couple armies to fight on Ramses' side?

Because I never got up to the chapter on How To Whip Up Armies in Mother Toadbreath's book, I replied. *Scandal, when I got back control of my Majyk, I didn't learn any new tricks.*

New tricks or old, you'd better have something up your sleeve, buddy-boy, or our fleecy friends are finito, *you betcha.*

The guard stopped in front of yet another identical cell door. "Here we are," he announced, jingling a heavy ring of keys. He had the door open in no time. "Shall I fetch your friend out or would you prefer to go in and get him?"

"You do it," Mysti said firmly.

"Ah, feared I might have secret instructions to lock the door behind you if you go in, hey?" The guard winked. "A wise precaution, lad. You may yet survive more than a few months as King Wulfdeth's son-in-law. My money's on you."

"Thank you for your confidence." Mysti gave it her iciest I-am-Welfie-you-are-mortal-scum pronunciation.

"No, lad, I'm sincere. I put down a month's pay on you making it all the way to your first wedding anniversary before the king kills you." He selected another key from the ring, said, "Won't be a moment," and ducked into the cell. He came out shortly later with Rhett.

The oracle looked terrible. Before, he'd always been gloomy but stuck-up about it. It was as if knowing how bad the future was going to be gave him a sense of power, even if it had a bitter taste. Now he looked just plain helpless and scared.

"Has it happened?" he asked, stumbling towards us.

"Has what happened?"

"The blood—the fire—the bleating—O ye gods, the awful, awful bleating!" He clapped his hands to his ears and sank down, groaning.

Mysti and I knelt beside him. "Did you have a vision?" she asked.

"Ruin," Rhett said. "Devastation. Destruction. Death from every side and from above. The streets themselves gone mad—mad, I tell you! The curse, the curse! Oh woe!"

"So far, so good," Scandal said. "Now could you be a little more specific? So far it sounds like just another Saturday night in New York City."

The guard clicked his tongue. "Poor man," he remarked. "He looks like he could use a nice lie-down and a cup of gawfee. It don't much settle your nerves, but if it's strong enough it burns them out so they don't trouble you anymore. There's straw on the floor of the cells where we're keeping the pirates—not often we get to double the food expenses to cover bedding as well. You could bring him into one of those and let him rest until he's feeling better."

Mysti's suspicious stare could have bored holes through stone. "This jeweled sword at my side is a gift from my bride-to-be," she said. "It may look like a toy, but I assure you it can deal death as swiftly as its less attractive sisters in steel. We Welfies are keen of ear and fleet of foot. Make one move to betray us while we are in that cell with our friend and we'll see if you like the taste of cold metal through your gullet, turnkey."

The guard twiddled the key ring. "You mean if I try to lock you up, you'll kill me?"

"Aye."

"Then why didn't you say so?" He tossed her the keys. "Here, now you needn't worry. All that jabber—hunh! They say Queen Ingigungobryth had some Welfie blood in her, and now I believe it. No one *but* a Welfie could talk a man to death."

We helped Rhett into the cell and laid him down on a pile of straw. He fell into a light doze almost at once.

"What's the matter with him?" one of the prisoners asked out of the shadows.

"Ramses!" I struck a spark of Majyk in my hand and brought it near his face. He and three of the sheep pirates were shackled to the cell walls by all four hooves. Their chains were just long enough to let them feed and tidy themselves. "How are you? Acerbia hasn't done anything bad to you, has she?"

"Does condemning me to death count?" He put a brave face on it.

"Don't worry, she'll never succeed," I said.

"Why not, wizard? Have you a spell potent enough to fight off that dragon of hers? If so, you might have used it in the Cheese and Crackers."

"Wizards don't do dragons," Scandal barged in. "Dragons are for heroes, even I know that."

"Do you need your familiar to make excuses for you, Master Kendar?" Ramses asked, then sighed. "If my own eyes had not seen you use your sorcerous powers on board the *Golden Fleece*, I would not believe you had any."

"Hey! That ain't no firefly he's holding in his hand right now, buddy," the cat snarled. "Just because he doesn't have enough va-va-voom to waste a dragon doesn't mean he's enchantmentally challenged."

"Very true. I apologize for being so touchy." Ramses' eyes were full of regret. "If I'd been raised the way a prince should be, I wouldn't go losing my temper over silly little things like a death sentence. I hope we can still be friends until I'm killed, Master Kendar?"

"No one is going to kill you." I put my foot down about that. "Blade has agreed to marry Princess Anisella—"

"Princess!" Ramses and the other sheep sharing his cell were stunned. "That sweet girl is Wulfdeth's daughter?"

"And Acerbia's." Now they were really shocked. "Like I was saying, Blade agreed to marry her, and as a gift to his darling child, King Wulfdeth set all of us Topsiders free."

"He thinks we're harmless." Scandal opened his mouth wide in a soundless laugh.

"He also thinks they're taking the first Topside-bound ship out of Port O' Morph," Mysti murmured.

"But what will you do?" Ramses asked. I didn't answer right away.

Scandal, check on that guard, I thought.

The cat waved his tail and strolled casually to peek out the cell door. *It's cool, big guy. He's leaning against the wall a few doors down reading "Ogre Dashing, Ogre Dear." It's one of the dirtiest books Raptura Eglantine ever wrote. He won't be paying attention to anything else.*

My sister Lucy does not *write dirty books!*

Okay, then it's one of the cleanest *books Raptura Eglantine ever wrote, especially that scene where the hero surprises the heroine in her bathtub and he's got a big barrel full of whipped cream and a penguin with him and she grabs a bottle of rose-scented oil and a couple of satin sheets and the sieve and they—*

Never mind!

"Master Kendar? Master Kendar, why are you blushing?"

"Never mind," I repeated aloud. "We're going to save you, that's what we're going to do."

"How?"

"Leave that to me."

"Ah. Aha. So that's the plan. Your whole plan. I see." He looked me straight in the eye. "You don't have any idea at all of how you're going to do it, do you." He didn't intend it as a question and he didn't say it as a question.

And I didn't have an honest answer to give him.

"Oh well, don't fret over it," he went on kindly. "If I'd wanted a safe life, I'd still be tending sheep back home with good old Thickskull Bertie. Go then, Master Kendar; go and do what you can for me. And even if you can't save me, I beg you, do your best to save my shipmates, especially Captain Lan and Lodda. He thinks I'm his brother, and to speak the truth he's been nicer to me than many a human ever was. As for Lodda, her faithfulness deserves a better reward then being hanged."

"I'll save them if I can. I can't promise any more than that," I said.

"One thing more, Master Kendar: I don't want to die a sheep. Although your powers can't touch Acerbia's dragon, can they at least—?"

"Whoa! You wanna shuck the sheepskin?" Scandal exclaimed. "*No problemo.* That's kidstuff for Master Kendar after the number he did on our pal Blade, there. Ripped Acerbia's spell off him like it was a mustard plaster."

"Ow," Mysti said drily.

"And get a load of the nifty doodad of mystic whatever he picked up along the way." The cat waved a paw at the diamond-capped wand, which I carried in my belt.

I took it out and held it up for Ramses' inspection. He and his cellmates were impressed enough to set up a chorus of "Ooooh! Aaaaah! Ohhhhh!" I aimed the wand at Ramses and mustered my Majyk the same way I'd done to take the cat-spell off of Mysti.

"I don't think this will hurt much," I told him.

"*No!*" Rhett sat bolt upright and lunged forward, knocking the wand from my hand as he sprawled in the straw. "You must not transform him now! If you do, the vision will mean nothing and all will be lost!"

"What vision? What are you talking about?" I demanded. "The one with all the ruin and devastation and stuff?"

Rhett stood up, his eyes unfocused, his arms hanging stiffly at his sides. When he spoke, it sounded like his voice was coming from somewhere far away:

"From the great mountains of the north
"A shepherd army shall come forth.
"With heavy crooks and warlike sheep
"They come to trouble Wulfdeth's sleep.
"They rouse the wrath of man and beast
"Who march to end the wedding feast.
"Now rings the sound from earth to sky
"And 'Death to humans!' is their cry.
"Their leader earns a hero's fame,
"Despite a lowly, mocking name.
"Though short of words, of stature slight,
"Thought of as really not too bright,
"This shepherd, skilled at bladderball,
"Will hazard much and conquer all.

"Let proud Acerbia despair:
"From sheepskin forth shall come the heir!
"The dragon's fire burns and sears;
"The victor's smile is bathed with tears.
"Make of my vision what you may;
"Merwallow here has said his say."

Mysti moved quickly to catch him as he collapsed. While she sprinkled his face with water from one of the prisoners' cups, Scandal fetched my wand back.

"Butterfingers," he commented, dropping it in my lap. He looked at Rhett, whose eyelids were fluttering. "Well, he sure ain't no Rod McKuen. What was *that* all about?"

"That was his vision. I don't know what it means, though."

"It means you can't change Ramses back into a human yet," Mysti said. "Didn't you hear? 'From sheepskin forth shall come the heir.'"

"Yeah, but a shepherd army?" Scandal was skeptical. "What kind of weapons do a bunch of shepherds have: anti-baaaaaalistic missiles?"

I didn't know what he was talking about, but I had a hunch I should have thrown something heavy at him.

"Hey, you heard the vision just like we did," I said. "If Rhett saw an army of shepherds, there'll be an army of shepherds."

"Yes," Ramses agreed. "And Thickskull Bertie's going to be leading them. It can only mean one thing—" His shoulders slumped. "I'm dead."

ChAPTER ———————— 25

ANISELLA STOOD IN THE MIDDLE OF THE GREAT HALL OF Wulfdeth's castle, Mysti at her side. It was funny to see her in a dress, with her flaming hair tucked neatly into a gold net, but I was getting used to it. King Wulfdeth was the sort of man who liked everything tied down, wrapped up, and fitted snugly into its proper place. I always thought you did that with boxes of books or stacks of logs, not people.

Anisella still looked lovely, as always. Only the tears in her eyes as she said goodbye to us spoiled the pretty picture of a princess and bride-to-be getting ready for her happily-ever-after.

"Goodbye, Master Kendar," she said, squeezing my hand. "I'm sorry you can't stay for the wedding."

"If you don't board this ship, there won't be one leaving for the Topside for months," I told her. "King Steffan needs me. And I have to tell him what happened to Blade."

"Oh yes, of course, Blade." Anisella glanced at Mysti. "Blade, dear, now that we're about to be married, do you think you could take off that mask?"

Mysti planted her hands on her hips. "So long as there is one corner of this wretched land where injustice rears its ugly head, I shall remain"—she thumped her chest—"a Blade for Justice! No."

"Its ugly head . . ." Anisella eyed the Welfie more closely. "Blade, darling, you know I adore you, and that nothing can ever change that, and that it's not what a person looks like, it's what's inside that counts, but, sweetheart . . . is there some other reason besides injustice that makes you wear that mask all the time?"

"She means are you the Welfie from the Black Lagoon under there or what?" Scandal loved to be helpful.

"If what is inside a person matters most, you need know no

209

more." Mysti pulled her shoulders back proudly, but not far enough to give anything away. I had to admire her. Considering the size of what she had to hide, she was doing a miraculous job.

Anisella's uneasy gaze wandered from Blade's mask to Rhett's face. The oracle was feeling better after his ordeal-by-vision. It had taken most of a day to get him back on his feet—a day we could hardly spare—but we needed him with us if we were going to go rouse that shepherd army. As Scandal himself said, "These shepherds are a superstitious, cowardly lot. If they won't march on the castle to save their rightful king's life, let's get Rhett to throw a few mystic conniption fits to convince 'em."

Rhett was wearing his traveling clothes. He no longer looked so impressive and superior as before. The old proud gloom was gone, replaced by something a lot more human.

Scandal swarmed up my leg and back to grab a seat on my shoulder. "Who'd'a thunk it?" he whispered.

"Who'd'a thunk what?"

"Him, Rhett, Mister Hotline-to-Tomorrow and don't you ever forget it. He went and got himself a broken heart. I didn't think he had a heart to break."

"Well, he loves Anisella."

"Sure, *now*." The cat licked a paw. "Anisella's a babe, no argument there. Lotsa guys fall for babes the same way they fall for cool cars and state-of-the-art stereo systems and—Oh, sorry. That stuff doesn't mean zip to you, Prince Valiant. Okay, let's just say some guys go for a gorgeous woman not because of who *she* is, but because of who they think *they* are. *Parlez-vous* status symbol?"

I remembered Mom and Dad arguing when he bought himself an expensive new hunting bow with the servants' wages. Mom gave him a dozen good, sensible reasons why he didn't need it. Dad had only reason to throw back at her: "I am Sir Lucius Parkland Gangle and this bow is no more or less than I deserve!"

"Rhett only wanted Anisella because people would think *he* was somebody special to have such a beautiful wife," I murmured. "Is that it?"

"Right in one. But that was then. Just look at the poor chump now. He thinks he's lost her, and all of a sudden—too late—he realizes that there are lots of pretty girls out there but only one Anisella. And it doesn't matter if her hair falls out or she loses her teeth or she gets fat, she'll still be the one for him."

I watched as Anisella took Rhett's hand in farewell. What Scandal said was true; it accounted for the change I'd noticed in the oracle's bearing and expression. Funny, but I was ready to swear there was something different about Anisella, too.

"Safe voyage, mas—I mean, Rhett." She held onto his hand a lot longer than she'd held mine.

"Thank you," he replied stiffly.

"Here." She took a thick gold chain from her neck and gave it to him, closing his reluctant hands around the treasure. "Please take this. When you get back to the Dregs I want you to sell it and buy yourself a new slave, or hire someone to come in and take care of things around the house. You don't know how to do anything for yourself, not even the shopping." Her mouth curved up, but her eyes couldn't hold a smile. "I don't know how you're ever going to survive without me."

"Neither do I." Rhett's voice was suddenly hoarse. He put the gold chain in his belt pouch. "Since it is your wish, I will do as you ask. I have long thought that a woman like you should always get everything she wants." He glanced at Mysti. "I see that you have."

"Yes." Her reply was so soft, I almost couldn't hear it. She looked at Mysti again and I saw a shadow flicker over her face.

"What's worse than not getting everything you want?" Scandal whispered. I shrugged, almost pitching him off my shoulder. "*Getting* everything you want. And watch it with the shoulders, Quasimodo. I'm not wearing my seat belt, you know."

"Rhett, we have to leave," I said. "Our ship—"

"Yes, yes, you are quite right, Master Kendar." He gazed deeply at Anisella. "Be happy, my dear."

"Is that—is that a prediction?" she asked.

"It is something that carries more weight than any prediction or the words of any god," he replied. "It is a wish from the heart."

"Goodbye, Scandal." Anisella scratched the cat behind his ears. He closed his eyes and purred with pleasure.

"Doll, no matter what happens, you listen to your old Uncle Scandal. I want you to remember one thing," he said.

"What?"

"Beautiful women need love too."

King Wulfdeth had ordered his kitchen workers to pack us a preview of the wedding feast we were going to be missing. "It's the least I can do for the men who brought my little girl home again," he said as we shouldered the bulging packs. "Your ship awaits. A good voyage."

There were horses to take us down from the heights of Loupgarou to the dock at Port O' Morph. I took a deep breath, gritted my teeth, and mounted up. It was amazing: I stayed on.

"Hey, look at me, Scandal!" I called down to the cat, who had chosen to walk instead of ride. "I'm a horseman! Looks like I do have a few new tricks on hand after all."

"Yeah, and it doesn't hurt that the horse you're on is built like a hammock and looks older than my Uncle Bernie's jokes," he replied.

Down at the docks, we rode past the *Golden Fleece*. There was a big sign next to the gangplank, two of Acerbia's Secret Police flanking it. It said that the pirate craft was going to be stripped and sold. A crowd of well-dressed cattle had gathered to view the merchandise and discuss how high the price might go.

"Looks like a bull market to me," Scandal said. "I'm glad Captain Lan isn't here to see this. It would break his heart."

"Here's your ship, friends," one of our escort said, indicating a fine sailing vessel a little larger than the *Fleece*. The crew were bustling here and there, getting her ready to sail. Most of the ones I saw were human, with a squirrel or two in the rigging and a fox keeping a keen eye on the cargo being shifted to the hold.

We gave our horses back to the guards and went up the gangplank, where a wolf in ship's clothing waited to greet us. "Welcome, grrrracious sirs," he said, doffing his plumed hat. "Welcome aboard the good ship *Siren*. I am Captain Talbot, at your service. We haven't any fancy quarters, being mostly a merchant ship—you'll have to share space in the fo'c's'le with the crew—but while the weather holds you're welcome to spread some bedding on the forward deck and dream under the stars."

We wandered towards the front of the ship to see how it was laid out. The *Siren* was a high-prowed vessel with the carved figurehead of a fantastic creature—woman from the waist down, manatee from the waist up—to watch over her path across the water. I was admiring it when Rhett came up behind me and whispered, "Now?"

"Now is fine with me." I adjusted my pack more comfortably on my back. "Scandal?"

"Yeah?" The cat perked up his ears.

"Abandon ship." I slung a leg over the rail and got ready to climb down, using the figurehead as a ladder.

"Say, Brainiac, I don't like to rain on your parade, but there's a thing or two wrong with the direct approach here."

"What's that?" I asked, clinging to the manatee's head.

"For one, you're about as good a mountaineer as you are a horseman. You're gonna fall off the side of the boat and hurt your feelings. For another, people are staring at you. You want

Acerbia's bullies to come see what all the giggling's about? The whole idea is to get away *secretly*."

"Oh." I clambered back aboard just as the captain came hurrying over to ask, "Is there something amiss, sirs?"

"I was just stretching my muscles a little," I said, trying to sound nonchalant. "I don't get much exercise, being a wizard."

"A wizard!" The wolf bowed deeply to me. "It is an honor to have you aboard." He hesitated, as if there was something more he wanted to say. "Would you—? I know you must be traveling for pleasure, not business, but still, would you mind if I asked you a professional question?"

"Go ahead," I encouraged him.

The wolf licked his chops nervously. "Not here. Come to my cabin." He started off and we all fell into line behind him. This was not what he had in mind. "Just Master Kendar, please."

Scandal and Rhett traded a perplexed look. "It'll be all right," I told them, slipping the pack off my back. "Wait here."

"Whatever you do, boss, don't tell him what big teeth he has!" Scandal shouted after me as Captain Talbot and I went below.

I returned shortly after, hauling a clumsy bundle with me. "Our problem is solved," I announced. "We'll be able to get off this ship with no trouble and no one noticing us."

"How's that?" Scandal asked.

"Captain Talbot himself will set up two sleeping mats and a basket in the fo'c's'le, cover them with blankets, and stuff a bunch of pillows underneath so it looks like we're sleeping. He'll give the crew the excuse that we're seasick, until the *Siren* is far from shore. Only then will he tell them the truth."

"Mighty nice of the big, bad wolf," Scandal remarked. "What's the catch?"

"No catch."

"C'mon, Kendar, I'm no kitten. There is no such thing as a free catnip mouse. What's in it for Captain Talbot?"

"Welllllll, I did do him one itsy-bitsy favor."

"'Yeeeeeesssss?"

"I turned him into a grandmother."

"You what?" Even Rhett was shaken by the news.

"I turned him into a grandmother," I repeated. "A *human* grandmother. He's always wanted to be one. A lot of the Underside wolves have the same problem. When he was younger, he ran with a crowd of granny-dressing wolves until the day they got arrested for stealing a bunch of flannel nighties from a merchant's stall. He promised his mother he'd change his ways, get an honest job, but the urge was too strong. He's really a grandma trapped in a wolf's body. I did what I could to help him. As soon as he returns from this voyage, he's going to find a little forest cottage and settle down to wait for the right granddaughter to come along."

"Wow," Scandal breathed. "You actually *changed* him? I didn't know you could do that."

"Sure, I can. I did the same for Mysti."

"Did not. With her, you just removed a shape-changing spell. For Captain Talbot you had to put together a shape-change of your own."

"Yeah?" I hadn't thought of it that way. This was a pleasant surprise. "Gee, I guess I did it because no one told me I *couldn't* do it. He's still kind of hairy, but he looks almost human. Come to think of it, he looks exactly like my Granny Gangle."

"Congrats on the new trick, old dog. So what's in the sack, Jack?" Scandal pointed at the bundle I'd brought up.

"Our disguises," I said. "Now all we've got to do is go below, put them on, and walk off the ship like that's what we're supposed to be doing."

Scandal padded up the bundle and sniffed. "There's something mighty familiar about this smell," he commented.

"I hate this," said Scandal as we made our way toward the town gates.

"Shut up and frolic," I told him out of the corner of my mouth.

"Cats don't frolic."

"You're not supposed to be a cat. You're a lamb. Try to remember that."

"My mama didn't raise her kittens to be mutton."

"Look, we're all in this together. Do you hear Rhett complaining?" I gestured with a hand blackened to resemble a hoof like Captain Lan's.

"Bear with this, cat," the oracle said from inside his sheep-suit. "This masquerade is necessary if we are to escape Port O' Morph undiscovered. Indeed, I foresee that these same disguises that you despise will be of great help to us soon."

"Not soon enough." The cat didn't look anything like the lamb he was supposed to be. Lambs don't stalk or sulk or lash their tails like miniature lions. "What I wanna know is where Captain Talbot got all these sheepskins he loaned us?"

"There are some questions even a man in my profession does not care to answer," Rhett replied with a shiver.

"If you won't frolic, at least try to whisk your tail around merrily," I suggested.

"You wanna know what you can do with my—?"

"Hail, comrades!"

We stopped in our tracks. There, in the middle of the street stood a group of lean young sheep dressed all in black tunics and trousers. A brown-fleeced ram wearing a thick pair of spectacles on his nose rushed forward to meet us while the others politely kept their distance.

"You must be the new ones from Brother Romney's group," he said, squinting at us. "I am Brother Wensley and I'll be leading this glorious mission. I see you've brought supplies for the journey. Excellent! I must tell you, though, it won't take as long as we originally thought. Brother Kerry has been lucky enough to get us all a ride into the very lair of the oppressors. It will only take us two days to reach the highlands instead of four. Isn't that grand?"

"Grand," I echoed.

"Now before we leave, I must ask you to take the oath. Raise your right hoof—the lamb doesn't have to—" He smiled indulgently at Scandal. The cat stuck out his tongue at him. "—and repeat after me: I do solemnly swear to uphold the cause of independence for my brothers and sisters in slavery. I will devote my life to their liberty and set them free wherever they languish in the chains of their oppressors. May this oath make me a brother to all who share this vision and these words. I will be faithful to my comrades forever."

We all repeated the words, including the "lamb." When we'd done that, Brother Wensley embraced each of us warmly and handed out badges from his belt pouch. I turned mine over and over in my hand. It showed a shepherd being clobbered on the head with his own crook by a sheep.

"Ramses' raiders," I said under my breath. Brother Wensley didn't hear. He bustled back to the others, probably to tell them that we were now officially part of their group. "Scandal, do you know what we've gotten ourselves into?"

"I sure do!" The cat was smiling. "A free ride, and the beginning of the end for King Wulfdeth."

CHAPTER —————————— 26

"REMEMBER, LET ME DO THE TALKING," I TOLD BROTHER Wensley. We crouched behind a boulder above a windswept mountain meadow and gazed down at a lone shepherd tending his flock. I gazed, Brother Wensley squinted.

"I'm not sure about this, Brother Kendar." The nearsighted sheep rocked from hoof to hoof. "That's a shepherd. Shepherds are the enemy."

"The only enemy this kingdom has is King Wulfdeth," I declared. "And the fairy Acerbia. Also her Secret Police. Sometimes the royal guards. It's probably a good idea to watch out for Torquil, too—that's Acerbia's dragon. And—"

"That's enough enemies for me. Oh, dear. Things were so much easier before I swore you into our group."

"No second thoughts, now. Once we took the oath, we became your brothers in the cause," I reminded him. "Listen, this is all going to work out so that everyone will be happy. When Ramses—Borith—becomes your king, I'll ask him to decree that from now on, sheep who can't speak in their own defense are only to be raised for their wool."

"Better to have your wool cut than your throat, I suppose." Brother Wensley sounded only partially convinced.

"You *have* to go through with the plan now." I wasn't going to let him back out; I couldn't. "Wingdingo's future is at stake."

"Yes, but it's so embarrassing, and to have to work with—*shepherds!*" Brother Wensley was torn between hatred and disgust.

I decided that it was time for me to do a quick review of the big speech Scandal had used on all the sheep that first night out on the trail. Praise Wedwel the cat was such a smooth talker or we might have been torn limb from limb when Rhett and I revealed

216

ourselves to be human. "Listen, do you or don't you believe in the liberation of animals?" My finger shot out a hairsbreadth from his nose.

"What a question! That is the whole purpose of our organization." He reached inside his tunic and brought out a little green book. I'd already seen copies of it many times on the trip to the highlands; the sheep all carried them and read pages aloud before bedtime. It was called *Out of the Stables and Into the Streets*, the work of a militant revolutionary cow from a good family. I don't know why Scandal kept calling it *Udder Discontent* or *The Quotations of Chairman Moo*. "It isn't just sheep, either. Wherever we find our poor, speechless brethren living under the yoke of oppression, we shall redeem them."

"And how about your poor, oppressed brethren who *can* speak? Is it right for the sheep of the countryside to enjoy freedom while the city herds must serve King Wulfdeth and his minions?"

Brother Wensley gave a nervous glance downslope to where the shepherd sat. "Things—things aren't all that bad in the cities."

"Aren't they? That's not what you said two nights ago."

"All I said was that—that it's getting harder and harder for a young sheep—even one with a university degree—to find a decent job. Everywhere you turn these days it seems like the humans have taken all the better positions and left us nothing but stubble. The last five places I applied I was told they were—what did they say?—'looking for someone a bit less fleecy.'" He struck a noble pose and added, "That's why my friends and I have so much time to devote to the cause."

"Which would you rather have? A cause or a salary?"

Brother Wensley chewed over the question. "To be honest, one doesn't meet many ewes in the cause. You're sure that if Prince Borith regains the throne, he'll undo all the injustices in Wingdingo?"

"He'll do it or die trying. You see, Prince Borith has suffered a few injustices himself. He knows what it feels like; it's not just a rallying cry to him."

The sheep sighed. "Very well, Brother Kendar. Let's do it and get it over with." He stripped off his clothing and folded it neatly, then laid his other belongings on top of the pile. Last of all, off came his spectacles. "Make sure you watch where I'm going, Brother Kendar," he said, getting down on all fours. "I don't want to break my neck, not even for the cause."

I picked up the walking staff I'd cut for myself and tried to get myself into a shepherd-y mood. It wasn't a real crook, but it was the best I could come up with. Whistling a merry tune, I led Brother Wensley down the slope towards our target.

"You can start bleating, if you want," I whispered to him.

"Oo! Ow! Oh! Yi!" he replied.

"Brother Wensley, I'm not a sheep or a shepherd, but I know that's not how you bleat. You sort of go *baaaaaa!*"

The shepherd downslope jerked his head around and stared at us. I drummed up a weak smile and waved. "Halloo, there!" I called. The shepherd merely stared at us for a moment, then turned back to his own flock.

"Not very friendly," I muttered so that only Brother Wensley could hear me.

"Oweee, oweee, oweee," the sheep responded.

"*What* is the matter with you?" I stamped the staff on the ground impatiently.

"All of this going around on all fours *hurts*, especially these." Brother Wensley sat back and held up his forehooves. "I'm not used to it. I have very tender feet."

"What do you want me to do? Carry you?" I hissed.

"Not a bad idea. We can pretend that I wandered off from your flock and twisted my ankle and there was a huge, wild bear ready to attack me, but you leaped in and fought him off bravely with only your staff as a weapon, and then you picked me up and carried me across the blazing wasteland, in search of the rest of the flock, who had all been kidnapped by an evil butcher and—"

Brother Wensley's weak eyes were gazing off blissfully into adventures only he could see. I squatted down and got his attention with a tap on the nose. "Where do you get your ideas?"

It was the first time I saw a sheep blush. "When I was at the university, I studied creative writing. Someday I hope to be published like my idol, Raptura Eglantine. Are you familiar with her work?"

"Oh boy."

"I do think that there's a vast, untapped market for more romances with sheep, don't you?" he asked, looking hopeful.

"Can we forget your epic and stick to the plan?" I demanded. "I can't carry you, and you can't go on yelping 'Ooooh, ow, oh' all the way downslope. The shepherd will hear you, and even if that is Thickskull Bertie, I don't think he's thick enough to believe a real sheep squawks about his feet. So bleat, all right?"

"What's my motivation?"

I shook his motivation right in front of his face so that even without his spectacles he could see how heavy it was.

"Baaaaa," Brother Wensley said.

"Hey!" the shepherd cried uphill at us. He sounded annoyed, his voice shrill. "You talking to that sheep of yours?"

"No, no, not at all," I called back. I gave Brother Wensley a nudge with the staff to get him moving towards our target again. When we were down on roughly the same level as the shepherd I added, "After all, who talks to sheep?"

"I do." He narrowed his eyes suspiciously. "We all do, up here. You don't look like anyone I know." He held his crook ready to use against me if I made any funny moves.

"You're right, I'm no one you know," I replied. "But if you're the shepherd I've been searching for, we do have a friend in common."

The shepherd pulled back, as if getting ready to spring at me or run away. He looked so very young—curly brown hair, dark eyes, beardless as an egg, all alone with the flock—no wonder he was scared. "Who do you think I am?" he demanded, trying to sound older, except his voice kept skidding off high.

"In the town we asked where we could find Thick—um—where we could find Bertram."

"That's my name. You're not from Loupgarou, are you?"

He named Wingdingo's capital city with the same cold dread we Academy students spoke of Master Thengor's private office. "I'm from the Topside," I said. Better to put it that way than to have him take fright and bolt. "I am a friend of Ramses."

"*Ramses!*" Astonishment and joy flashed over Bertram's face. He dropped his crook and clasped his hands to his chest, then blushed and ducked to retrieve the crook. "Uh, you see, sir, Ramses and I—we were best friends."

"I know," I said. "Ramses told me."

"What happened to him, sir?" he implored. "Please tell me. One day he just wasn't there anymore. All the village gossip said he'd gone to Loupgarou, but no one knew for sure, not even his parents. I didn't know what to think. I was so afraid for him! I imagined all sorts of terrors. I'm not much for visiting shrines and such, but I went down to Charbon, where they've got a temple to Ovejuna, goddess of shepherds, and asked her to look out for Ramses. Oh, why did he go away?" The poor fellow was starting to sniffle. "Was it something I said?"

"To be honest, according to Ramses you never said much of anything."

"That's 'cause I'm too ashamed."

"Of what?"

"My voice. It's so—so *flimsy*, like. Better to say nothing and have the other shepherds call you Thickskull Bertie than to speak up and have them call you girlie." A gleam of fire came into Bertie's eye and his hands tightened around his crook. "Though I'd just like to see 'em *try*."

"You sound like a fighter." I was hoping for something like that. "Ramses needs fighters on his side now."

"Why? What's happened?"

So I told him, and when I was done he said, "That's awful! Horrid! A crime!" He shook his crook high overhead and shouted, "By Ovejuna, the time has come to overthrow the evil tyrant and put the true heir back on the throne of Wingdingo!"

"You'll join us, then?" I asked.

"You couldn't keep me away. There's only one problem, though." He looked around, troubled. "I've got to bring along the sheep."

"Baaaaa, baaaa, baaa. *Now* can I get up?" Brother Wensley whined.

I had to do a lot of fast talking to prevent Bertie and Brother Wensley from turning their introduction into a declaration of war. Each one had his own burden of heavyweight grudges against the other, but I kept reminding them of our common cause until they stopped swapping insults and started saying, "Shut up" to me at regular intervals. Scandal would have been proud.

Scandal *was* proud when I showed up in the village tavern with Bertie and his flock tagging along after. "I knew you could do it, *mi jefe*." Plain compliments from the cat were rare. I enjoyed it while I could.

Rhett, however, cast a bucket of cold water over the whole thing. "This is the leader of the shepherd army?" He looked Bertie up and down. "Rather young, is he not? Skinny, too, I daresay. That tunic is positively swimming on him. I doubt a belt would help." He turned to me as if Bertie were a book he was through with. "How in Merwallow's name do you expect a mere child like that to save his own life in battle, let alone lead a—*Yagk!*"

"Like that," said Bertie, standing over a writhing Rhett. The shepherd lad had slipped his crook up between the oracle's legs and done something dreadful, but direct.

"Yar!" called a shepherd seated at another table. "Serves you right fer teasin' our Bertie! He don't say much an' maybe he's a bit slow, but he's also the best bladderball player in all the mountains."

"It's a fool what trifles with a feller who can use his crook that skillful, aye," said a second.

The tavern was full of shepherds, all enjoying a refreshing drink after a hard day. Ramses told me that sheepherding was a child's job, yet a lot of these lads were as old as me, some older.

"Why'd the idjit go an' provoke Bertie anyhow?" someone wondered aloud. Other voices added their votes to the question.

"Yes, and why's Bertie come in here for? Never did that previous. Always kept to the slopes, he did."

"And he *talked*." That seemed to be the greatest miracle to these people.

Bertie hopped onto a table. "Yes, I *talked*," he said, indignant. (Somewhere in the room someone giggled, then sneered, "*Girlie!*" A killing frown from Bertie put a swift end to it.) "It's past time I talked. Past time we *all* did. Look at you! Look at all of you, sitting there while your land suffers under King Wulfdeth's unjust rule. How many years has it been since we've had a killer for our king? Other lands don't put murderers on the throne!"

"Usual they puts theirselfs on it pretty good," a shepherd volunteered.

"I hear that the King o' Lower Weldwood was once caught tryin' to sneak out of a fancy banquet with some silver spoons in his pocket," his drinking companion said. "'Course it were his own banquet and his own spoons, but it's the thought what makes it so sordid, eh? They never did breed the royals too bright over in Lower Weldwood."

"Silence!" Bertie banged his crook on the table. "If you can't say something worthwhile, keep your mouths shut. When the Underside was formed, there were plenty of humans who lost the gift of speech. There was nothing anyone could do about that—the gods made it so—but what have you done, you who still *can* speak? Have you raised your voices to protest injustice? Have you said one word in defense of the innocent people arrested every day, in the king's name? Or have you only sat around jabbering about the herds and the weather and the price of wool while your land—*our* land—pays the price of your silence? Arise! Arise! The time has come! Let us help our true ruler cast down Wulfdeth the Usurper! Let us speak out and refuse to be silenced! March with me now, make yourselves heard, and truth shall prevail!"

All the shepherds in the tavern rose to their feet as one. Cheering loudly, they swirled around Bertie, swearing to follow him wherever he would lead them. Feelings ran so high that Brother Wensley and his group joined in with the cheering shepherds. Pretty soon they were all pounding one another on the back, hollering quotations from the little green book, and singing old sheepherding songs.

I helped Rhett into a chair. I knew he was still hurting, but I couldn't resist teasing him. "Well? What do you think of the skinny kid now?"

"I—I am not—surprised," he managed to get out. "All—*ow*—all things are as Merwallow revealed to me."

"You mean you *hope* all things are gonna turn out as accurate as the bit about Bertie," Scandal said. He watched the rejoicing throng of shepherds and sheep awhile and observed, "The kid rouses a good rabble. I can hardly wait to see what happens when we take this show on the road."

CHAPTER ———————— 27

"DEATH TO HUMANS! DEATH TO HUMANS!"

The giant cloud of dust barreled along behind us on the road to Loupgarou, and out of its heart came that awful chant.

"DEATH TO HUMANS! DEATH TO HUMANS!"

Scandal tightened his grip on my shoulder, glanced backward at the cloud and said, "You know, bwana, I don't want to upset you or anything, but do you think maybe we could teach them another cheer? Something like: Two-four-six-eight, who will we obliterate? Gooooo, *Wulfdeth*!"

"We don't have time," I said, panting as the tempo of our forced march sped up. "The sun's already up and this is Frogday."

"DEATH TO HUMANS! DEATH TO HUMANS!"

The cat went tsk-tsk. "You know what I really don't get? About a quarter of the mob we picked up *are* humans, and they're chanting as loud as anybody."

"Perhaps they reason that since they share the same cause with Bertram and his shepherd band, they ought to share all else," Rhett suggested.

"Yoo hoo, Rhett, Reality's having a call-in show and you're on the air: Bertram and his shepherd band are *also* humans! And stop calling them 'Bertram and his shepherd band'; it sounds like they should be playing gigs at bar mitzvahs."

"It's the sheep," I muttered, wiping sweat from my brow. I definitely did *not* want the army to overtake me, even if we were all fighting for the same thing. "They're the ones who started it, and the other animals and humans just followed their lead like they were all a bunch of—of—"

"Be easy, Master Kendar," Rhett said, sounding confident. "Merwallow's vision spoke of an army and, to be frank, no one

223

could call the few shepherds who originally joined with Bertram an army."

"Yeah, Rasputin's right," Scandal said. "Good thing for us it sorta snowballed on the way back to the city."

Snowballed? It was more like an avalanche. The road back to Loupgarou was downhill all the way and the progress of Bertie's followers drew plenty of curious looks from every village and town we passed through. While the shepherds marched on, eyes fixed on the distant goal, Brother Wensley and his sheep dropped out here and there, temporarily, to stir up the people. The people (and on the Underside, that includes the intelligent animals) listened. Then they thought over all the little and not-so-little ways life under King Wulfdeth stank. Next they remembered how good things had been under the rule of King Wulfdeth's murdered brother. It didn't take long before we were leading an angry mob.

"I hope the sight of them's enough to scare Wulfdeth off the throne," I remarked.

"Don't bet the mortgage." Scandal was the cold voice of reason. I *hated* the cold voice of reason. It upset my stomach. "Wulfdeth might want to run like a bunny, but he's got Acerbia at his back. I don't think he'll make a move without her say-so. The man is whipped."

"In that case, I hope our troops pick up some better weapons before we reach Loupgarou," I said. "The enemy has swords, spears, arrows, and I don't know what else. All these folk have got are shepherds' crooks and farmers' tools."

"Well, pass me the hot buttered hemlock and call me Socrates, but you know all the talk about beating your swords into plowshares—?"

"No."

"It works the other way too."

A smaller cloud of dust detached itself from the main one and went racing down the road ahead of us. "What was that?" I asked, shading my eyes.

"That looked like Brother Targhee," Rhett said. "He has run ahead to rouse the folk of the outlying farms. They will join our cause and march ahead of us, storming the city gates. Meanwhile, Brother Targhee will make further inroads, passing through the gates before the attack so that he may begin working amid the festive crowd. He will contact as many rebel sheep as possible, from Brother Romney's group and others. He will lead them in a flanking maneuver against Acerbia's Secret Police. He will not survive, but the stratagem will be a success. If the true heir regains the throne, his comrades will raise a statue in his honor. Birds will nest on his head and the city council will build a fountain at the statue's base ten years later. Five years after that, a young girl will be drawing water from the fountain when she will meet a handsome prince who is passing through the streets in disguise. They will fall madly in love, but her wicked uncle will never—"

I got a good grip on Rhett's collar and dragged him off to the side of the road. Startled by the sudden move, Scandal jumped off my shoulder. "Do we win?" I demanded.

"Do we win what?"

"The New York State Lottery, bozo, what do you think?" Scandal snarled. "You're giving us a peek into the future that's got the answers to everything except the biggie: Do we save Ramses and do we boot Wulfdeth and Acerbia out on their greedy rumps?"

"I do not know," Rhett replied. "Merwallow has not entrusted that information to me."

"Merwallow is also Acerbia's cousin," I told him.

"Indeed!" It was nice to see an oracle surprised. "Ah, that answers much. No wonder Merwallow could not tell me all. He and his divine siblings are descended from the same goddess who gave birth to the tribe of fairies: Isenbergina, Lady of a Thousand Whims."

"She makes him play nice with Cousin Acerbia, huh?" Scandal asked. "Which means not giving *too* many helpful hints to Acerbia's enemies?"

"That is so."

"Maybe. Or maybe your pal Merwallow's just getting his kicks by leaning over the railings of Paradise to drop some more mystical water-balloons on the heads of mortals."

While we were off to the side, arguing, the big cloud of dust surged past us. The shepherds came first, Bertie at their head, driving their flocks before them. After came the farmers and townsfolk who'd joined us on the way. There were some ordinary people in the crowd, but mostly I saw bears and pigs and foxes and deer and horses and cows and wolves—some of them still wearing frilly nightcaps—and even a transformed rappid or two, gnashing their long teeth ferociously. Brother Wensley's comrades were scattered throughout the mob, waving their little green books and leading everyone in the relentless chant:

"DEATH TO HUMANS! DEATH TO HUMANS!"

"Except Prince Borith! Except Prince Borith!" Scandal shouted at them. "And Rhett! And Master Kendar! And Anisella! And—!"

If they heard him, they didn't act as if his words changed

anything. All of a sudden I realized what we had to do: "We've got to get to Loupgarou ahead of the army. If they reach the city first, they might just go on a rampage. Innocent folk could be hurt."

"And how do you propose we get ahead of them now?" the cat asked. "Leapfrog?"

"Rhett, take off your cloak," I directed.

The oracle gave me a questioning look, but did what I asked. It was a big cloak, heavy and long. I stepped onto the middle of it and took a deep breath. "I did it before, I can do it again," I told myself out loud. I took the silver wand from my belt, held it point-downwards over the cape, and thought of Acerbia's twelve-step card. "One spell at a time," I mumbled. "Just one spell at a time." I closed my eyes and concentrated.

"And we *have* liftoff!" I heard Scandal's delighted cry. "Good work, Mandrake, that puppy is *airborne!*"

I opened my eyes and grinned. The cape was floating as high as the top of Rhett's head. I commanded it to land and it did. I didn't even have to close my eyes to do it. "What do you know? I don't need Mysti's help to make things fly after all."

"And I bet she's gonna be real thrilled to hear how much you don't need her," Scandal said.

"Oh, Mysti won't mind. She knows how to take care of herself. She'll be glad to know I can take care of myself, too."

"*Needing* someone isn't the same thing as being able to *use* her. Just ask any cat."

"I don't understand."

"Later. Now we've got to get ahead of Bertie's batallion." Scandal padded onto the cape and gestured for Rhett to do the same. "Ahead warp factor one, Mr. Sulu."

Once we were up in the air, we overtook the army easily. There were gasps and exclamations aplenty from below as the shepherds and their followers looked up wide-eyed, pointing hand and paw and hoof at the spectacle of the flying cape. The sight brought the mob to a shuddering halt.

"Gor! Them Topsiders is flying like they was birds!" one shepherd cried. "What's it mean, Bertie?"

"It means happy days are here again!" Scandal yelled down at him. "Don't you rubes know that everything takes a turn for the better when hemlines go up?"

"Free folk of Wingdingo, I am Master Kendar!" I shouted. Everyone knew what the title *Master* meant, but I made a lot of unnecessary waves and flourishes with my wand anyway, to make sure they were impressed and stayed impressed. "I have come all the way from the Topside with my companions to right an old wrong that has afflicted your kingdom for much too long."

The crowd below set up a loud muttering. I caught a few distinct comments like, " —took your sweet time about it" and " —mighty nice of them to go to all that trouble" and " —believe it when I see it" and "Wizards is expensive. This isn't going to show up on our taxes later, is it?"

"Now the hour is at hand," I continued. "We are all in this together. Right shall prevail over might. Justice shall triumph. We are all brothers in the same cause, no matter whether we are furred, fleeced, feathered, or fairly clean-shaven. Now is the time for all good folk to come to the aid of Prince Borith. But before we can march through the city gates we must—"

Scandal clawed urgently at my leg. "What is it?" I asked him crossly.

"Don't get to the point yet, boss. I think there's still a couple of clichés you forgot to use in your big speech." He leaned over the edge of the flying cape and hollered at the bewildered throng, "Listen up down there: Knock it off with the 'Death to humans' chant. There are plenty of humans in the ranks right now, and plenty more in Loupgarou who'd be happy to join us. They are not—repeat, *not* going to do it if you bunch of Doctor Doolittle rejects make them think we're out for *their* blood. The only blood we want is Wulfdeth's, got it?"

The crowd shuffled their feet and looked embarrassed. "The hamsters started it!" someone called.

"I don't care who started it, you stop it. Now pay attention: Master Kendar's got some more wizard stuff to say." He turned to me, smiling. "All yours, hot-shot."

I tried to recapture the bold, dramatic tone I'd used before, with no success. It was gone, banished by Scandal's interruption. I decided to carry on the best I could. "We're going to fly on ahead of you to the city," I told everyone. "We'll be able to help Brother Targhee if he runs into any problems clearing the way for you. We also ought to get there as fast as we can because we don't know just when they're planning on having the executions."

A shepherd cupped his hands to his mouth and bawled out, "Yer a wizard, ain't you? You can stop them executions all by yerself!"

"No!" I shouted back. "No, I can't. Not alone. But I *can* put up enough of a fight to keep your rightful prince alive until you get there. Farewell, for now. We'll meet again!" I waved goodbye with my wand and commanded the cape to fly on.

We reached the gates of Loupgarou and found them standing wide open. Not a guard was in sight, not a citizen, no one. It was all very suspicious.

"Looks like Brother Targhee beat us here," Scandal said.

"Impossible," Rhett said. "I saw him still on the road as we flew over. Master Kendar, where is everyone?"

"I don't know, but I have an idea." I made the flying cape land and gave it back to Rhett after we got off.

"Keep it," he said, pushing it away. "You may have need of it soon."

"Another vision?" Scandal asked.

"No, not 'another vision.'" Rhett mocked the cat in singsong. "By Merwallow's incredibly self-indulgent and capricious powers, why must you always assume that anything I say comes from a vision? I do have *some* original thoughts on occasion."

"Stop quarreling, you two," I said, fastening Rhett's cape around my neck. It looked like a heavy piece of goods, but it felt light as a breeze on my shoulders. "We have to find out what's going on."

I didn't know the layout of Loupgarou very well, but I did know the way from the gates to the castle. King Wulfdeth's men had escorted us that way when they took us down to the docks at Port O' Morph. Now I led Rhett and Scandal back towards Wulfdeth's stronghold.

We hadn't gone far before we heard it: the sound of a large crowd pressed into a small space. A little way farther on and we saw a wall of backs blockading the street. People and animals and more people stood packed like bundles of kindling wood with no room for a snake to slip through between them. Like islands in the sea, merchants' stalls were the only things to break up the crowd.

"Hey, get your souvenirs of the royal wedding!" a lively young otter cried, holding high a pair of painted dishes. "Special today, buy one, get one free. Yes, buy a plate commemorating the wedding of Princess Anisella and Blade the Welfie and get one commemorating the executions of the evil sheep pirates! Come on, ladies and gents, don't be shy. How are you gonna get your grandchildren to believe you were here if you don't buy a souvenir?"

I rushed up to the otter's stall. "Has it started?" I asked. "The executions, I mean."

"Naw, they've still got their paws full with the wedding," he said. "They've set up the altar on the same scaffold where they're going to hang the sheep." His bright eyes darted left and right before he whispered, "Between you and me—and if any of the lady Acerbia's creepers overhears this, I never said it—this is just like that old skinflint King Wulfdeth. Tax us to the bone, then scrimp when it comes to his own daughter's wedding. There's supposed to be free wine running out of the public fountains. Ha! He's got his guards watching 'em, ready to throw you in jail with a big, fat fine for drunkenness if you take more than a swallow. And what's more—"

"Thank you very much," I said in haste. "We have to find a way to get closer to the altar now."

"Hi! Don't rush off, sir." The otter thrust his wares at me. "Still lots of time to buy a nice souvenir to take home to the missus."

"His missus won't need any souvenirs to remember *this* wedding," Scandal said.

We backtracked into the deserted streets, and once again I spread the cape on the ground. "If we fly low over the rooftops, we might not be noticed," I said. This time, instead of standing on the cape, I lay down on it. Rhett was about to do the same when Scandal cried, "*Watch it!*"

"What? Where? Someone coming?" I looked everywhere, and saw nothing dangerous or even strange. "Wedwel's sacred hip, Scandal, have you lost your mind?"

"Better my mind than that egg," the cat returned.

"*What* egg?"

"This one." Rhett looked guilty as he took a carefully wrapped object out of his belt pouch. When the cloth was unrolled, there lay a common hen's egg with big blobs of red sealing wax at either end. "The cat gave this into my keeping just before we left the castle."

"Why?"

"I do not know." Rhett weighed it in his palm. "It feels heavier than you would expect."

"It oughta or I'll sue." Scandal whisked his tail back and forth the way he did when he was particularly proud of himself. "You were about to lie down on top of my secret weapon. Boy howdy, would you ever have been sorry! Okay, you can give it to Kendar now."

Rhett offered to pass me the egg, but I wasn't so sure I wanted to take it. "What's so special about this egg?"

"Ask me no questions and I'll tell you no lies," the cat replied. "Well, maybe I'll tell you a few lies, but just to stay in practice. I went to a lot of trouble to create this baby. I even"—he lowered his voice—"I even used *Majyk*. Just a little. That spell for making things float is so darned easy, you'd have to be an idiot not to—Oh, sorry, boss. Nothing personal. Go on, take the egg."

I took it, rolling it over in my hand. It did feel heavier than a normal egg, and the telltale tingle of Majyk clung to it. "How does it work? What does it do?" I asked.

"You throw it, and it cuts your really big problems down to size." The cat got onto the cape and announced, "All passengers requiring special assistance or traveling with small animals may board the aircraft now."

We sailed towards the castle, hugging the rooftops of Loupgarou. No one looked up, all of the spectators too busy trying to worm themselves a little closer to the action. When we reached the row of houses bordering the great square, I made the cape settle down on the shingles. Lucky for us the roof wasn't too steep. We had the best view anyone could want of the royal wedding.

There stood the altar on the scaffold, just as we'd been told. The king's guards formed a living fence around it, to keep the people a good distance back. Under the gallows, Captain Lan, Ramses, and the others awaited their doom. King Wulfdeth and Acerbia sat off to one side of the platform on gilded thrones. The king wore a splendid set of regal robes and a fond expression; the fairy just wore spidersilk, a fortune in gems, and a pout.

"Why has she got that green balloon tied to the back of her chair?" Scandal asked.

"That's no balloon," I said. "That's Torquil. She's keeping him small."

"Cheaper to feed at the wedding reception, huh?"

Anisella was a lovely bride. Anisella was a lovely anything. She and Mysti stood on the gallows, beneath a row of ribbon-bedecked hangman's nooses, and listened to a gorgeously dressed priest pronounce them Welfie and wife.

Scandal pretended to sniffle. "I always cry at weddings. How about you, boss?"

"Cut it out, Scandal."

"Awww, c'mon, you old softy! It's not every day your wife gets married!"

"Shhh!"

The priest clapped his hands, and two pretty little boys in blue robes came forward, each carrying a silver bowl. The priest dipped Anisella's left hand in one, Mysti's right hand in the other, then clasped them together. Brown goo dripped down.

"Ah, it is the sacred mud," Rhett commented. "This ritual comes at the very end of the ceremony. The hands of the bride and groom will be trapped within when the mud hardens. This symbolizes faithfulness, and how time will only make the bond between husband and wife stronger."

"One of the choir boys is making mud pies out of the leftover faithfulness," Scandal announced.

The priest next raised his hands and declared, "Behold, the Princess Anisella has now become the wedded wife of the Welfie called Blade. No power exists strong enough to break this bond, save death itself."

"And now for the entertainment!" King Wulfdeth sprang from his place, rubbing his hands together. "Bring out the prisoners!" he commanded.

The guards obeyed instantly, hustling the prisoners up the scaffold stairs. I saw Captain Lan stumble when his pegleg knocked against one of the steps. Without thinking, Lodda lunged forward to help him, but her paws were tied. I heard her whine with frustration. In no time at all, the sheep pirates were lined up under the row of nooses. Last of all came Ramses, led to the center of the platform by the hangman himself.

"Hitch them up and hang them high!" King Wulfdeth shouted.

"Not so fast, Your Majesty," the priest said, a huffy edge to his words. "We have not *quite* finished the marriage ceremony."

"What more is there to be done?" the king demanded, impatient. "I gave the girl away, they drank the ceremonial wine, ate the ceremonial herring, played the ceremonial match of Haxi-Chaxi, jumped over the ceremonial stack of dirty dishes, did that ooky thing with the mud—I sat here through all that goat-dribble, sometimes I even woke up and paid attention, and now I want to get on with the hanging. What's left?"

Snowflakes fell from the priest's lips. "Only the part where I ask if anyone knows a good reason why this marriage is a mistake. If someone does speak up, we must hear his reasons. If they are good ones, we must then decide whether it is the bride's or the groom's fault that we wasted all this time on the wedding. Then we kill whoever's to blame. It is a fine old tradition, much beloved by the gods. Skip it and you get locusts."

"All right," the king growled. "Do it. But if anyone says one word against my daughter, there's going to be an extra noose with a surprise occupant, and I don't mean Anisella."

The priest threw his arms wide. "If anyone knows any cause—"

"Ow! Please be more careful where you're flinging your hands,

Revered One," Ramses told the priest. "You smacked me in the
eye."

"Sorry," the priest said automatically. "It's too crowded up here.
Some people don't know how to wait." He glared at the king, then
lifted his arms more cautiously. "If anyone knows any cause why
this marriage should not receive the blessing of the gods, let him
speak or—"

"I do," said Mysti.

A murmur of astonishment ran through the crowd. Anisella
began to tremble. Wulfdeth's expression was indescribable. Even
Acerbia looked like she'd been turned to stone.

The priest was puzzled almost beyond words. "Are you—are
you sure, lad? If you accuse your new bride of any wrongdoing,
the law says she must die for it." Wulfdeth gave an inarticulate
roar. "But I don't think she will be the one to pay that price."

"I am a Blade for Justice," Mysti said simply. "In the name of
justice, I cannot be married to this woman."

"Why—why not?"

"Because I am already married."

The crowd gasped.

"To Master Kendar."

The crowd choked.

"*Daaaaaaaddeeeeeeeee!*" Anisella wailed, throwing herself
into Wulfdeth's arms.

CHAPTER ———— 28

THE SQUARE AND THE STREETS WERE IN A TURMOIL. Whispers, murmurs, and all sorts of shocked chatter flew. The priest grabbed his young helpers by the hand and hastily dragged them out of harm's way. King Wulfdeth stood speechless, his arms full of weeping Anisella. He cast a pleading glance at Acerbia, whose first shock was quickly crumbling into a look stormy enough to put half the kingdom under water.

"Is this a joke?" she rumbled, rising from her chair and unfurling her wings with a snap.

"I speak the truth," Mysti replied. "If Master Kendar were here, he would tell you the same."

"Well, I heard they did things differently on the Topside, but this—!" Wulfdeth was appalled. Anisella just howled.

Acerbia's lips curved into one of her most evil smiles. "In that case, I am doubly glad I didn't remove the curse on Anisella."

"You did *what*?" Wulfdeth roared.

"Did *not* do what, darling," the fairy replied, smooth as butter. "I did not remove the curse that doomed the first to wed our daughter. A mere precaution. I was going to lift it if I became convinced that this—this Blade-person was to be trusted. Never turn your wings to a Welfie, Mama always said. She was right."

"You fool! That curse also dooms whoever *gives* the girl in marriage!" the king shouted.

"Don't be silly, love," Acerbia said. "It's my curse and I can make it jump through hoops, if I want. I'll just lift the part of it that dooms you and leave on the part of it that dooms *him*." She gave Mysti another killing look, then waved her wand at the royal guards. "Seize him."

Mysti drew her sword. "Do your worst."

"Happy to oblige, sir," the nearest guard replied, and threw himself at her.

"Well, there goes the clash of steel again," Scandal said as we watched Mysti slice, slash, and sliver her attackers. "Boss, you think maybe we oughta lend a hand?"

Rhett answered for me: "If we do, we will destroy the element of surprise that Bertram's army might need most desperately if they are to win. I must say, I admire Blade for uttering such a stunning lie. It will serve us well, buying time for the oncoming horde."

"Who asked you?" Scandal spat. "The oncoming horde's gonna oncome real soon now, but how soon? They may have a hard time fighting their way through those streets. Did you get a load of the crowds? Not only is all Loupgarou here, I think they also emptied Port O' Morph. We've gotta stall the hanging more than we've gotta hold onto the element of surprise. If we don't, they'll string up Ramses and the rest right after they take care of Mysti."

"Mysti?" Rhett echoed. "Who is Mysti?"

"Uh-oh." Scandal would have bitten his tongue if his teeth weren't so pointy. "I guess the cat's out of the bag now, huh?" he said, looking at me.

"What Blade said was no lie," I told Rhett.

"You mean you are married to—?"

"Yes, we are married. Blade's real name is Mysti."

"And Mysti is a *girl* Welfie's name," Scandal added. "So pull your eyes back into your head; you may need them later."

"A girl Welfie?" Rhett was flabbergasted. He watched while Mysti jumped up, seized one of the nooses, and swung from it while she fought off six guards at once. The people cheered. "But that means—"

"Yep. Anisella's all yours. Minus the curse." Scandal winked.

"The curse? By Merwallow, Master Kendar, this is terrible! The curse will fall upon your wife!"

"No, it won't," Scandal objected. "Mysti's female, so she and Anisella can't really be married, so that means no curse on Mysti for marrying her. But because Anisella *did* go through with a wedding ceremony, that means the curse is fulfilled, or canceled, or neutralized, or void where prohibited, or—"

"But the curse said that it would doom whomever married Anisella!" Rhett argued. "It did not specify that she had to wed a male. Therefore, whether or not Mysti *can* be Anisella's husband, she still married her, so—"

"Yeah, but because Mysti was already married to Kendar at the time, it doesn't really—"

I whipped the cape around my shoulders while the two of them were still wrangling over the terms of the curse. All I could see was that even Mysti's expert swordsmanship was no match for so many of King Wulfdeth's men. They kept coming, swarming up the scaffold, pushing the prisoners aside. Captain Lan, Lodda, and most of the others were shoved over the edge. They landed heavily on the paving stones below. Fortunately for them, the gallows wasn't built too high (probably another example of King Wulfdeth's miserliness, saving money on lumber). They stumbled to their feet almost as soon as they hit the ground. Only Ramses remained where he was, too close to the center of the platform to be pushed off.

I bent down and tucked the trailing ends of the cape firmly into the tops of my boots. "All right," I said to myself, taking a deep breath. "Either this is going to work or it's not. If not, I'm a pancake, but I have to try. One spell at a time, that's all I've got to remember. Here goes." And I stepped off the edge of the roof into air.

The cape billowed out behind me like a sail, the flying spell lifting it, it lifting me. Someone in the crowd glanced up and saw me as I swooped towards the scaffold.

"Look! Up in the sky! It's a bird!"

"It's a *big* bird. Got a spare hat I could borrow?"

The guards paused in their battle to stare up at me as I flew to perch on the centermost gibbet. Mysti took advantage of their distraction to take a few more of them out of combat. I turned off the flying spell and balanced on the crossbeam, holding my glittering wand high. "In the name of justice and right, stop the execution!" I shouted so that everyone could hear. "The evil reign of King Wulfdeth the Usurper is at an end. Behold your true prince!" I pointed the wand at Ramses.

Majyk engulfed him, peeling away the fleece like the rind of an orange. His hands were still tied (one spell at a time, you know), but he stepped out of the sheepskin as a full human being. (Fully clothed, too. I admit I was a little worried about that.) The people cheered again. King Wulfdeth looked nervous.

"You idiots!" he bawled at his guards. "What are you standing there for? Kill him!"

"You'll have to reach him first!" Mysti yelled. A swift cut of her blade and Ramses was free. He stooped swiftly to pick up a sword belonging to one of the dead guards and set to helping Mysti fight off the rest.

From up on the gallows crossbeam I could see a long way down the streets of Loupgarou. The crowd was agitated, but not too far off I saw major turbulence pushing through the mob from several directions. They were here! The shepherd army, the rebellious peasants, the cityfolk that Brother Targhee had stirred up to revolt! Already I heard the fierce sound of infuriated bleating. It rolled down the streets like thunder, making strong men turn pale.

"For Borith! For Borith!" came the cry from a host of throats, animal and human, as the first battle-maddened sheep burst into the square.

"For Borith!" new voices answered. The crowd parted willingly before the onrushing attackers. "Never did like Wulfdeth's foreign policy anyhow. For Borith!"

I spied Bertram and his comrades wading through the mob, brandishing their crooks. "Throw down the traitor Wulfdeth!" Bertram shouted. His voice might have been high-pitched, but it carried. "Bring back Prince Borith, the son of our murdered king!"

"For Borith! For Borith! And how about that tax Wulfdeth put on beer, hey? For Borith!"

"For Borith! For Borith, and better schools for our kids!"

The royal guards were terror-stricken. They held their posts only because they were frozen to the spot. The people in the front ranks didn't wait for the army to reach them before striking out at King Wulfdeth's troops. This revolt had been a long time coming. Some of them wrenched the guards' own weapons from their hands and gave them back the sharp way. The guards defended themselves, but they were floundering.

I aimed my wand lower, and the ropes holding the sheep pirates helpless frayed into a thousand threads, then snapped. Captain Lan uttered a bellow of triumph.

"Baa'arrrrh! At 'em, lads! Fer the honor o' the *Golden Fleece!*" Like Ramses, he seized the sword of a dead guard and led his crew against the king's men from the rear.

King Wulfdeth's troops were being slaughtered. "Kill him! Forget the others and kill him first!" the king ranted, pointing madly at Ramses. "If he dies, they've lost everything!"

A fresh troop of guards stormed the square from the castle, heading for the scaffold to obey their master's command. Bertie let out a shrill whistle and thumped his crook soundly against the flank of a huge ram. The beast bawled and charged right at the invaders, the rest

of the herds pounding recklessly after him. The king's men went
down, crushed beneath wave after wave of woolly destruction.

"You *men*! Do I have to do everything myself?" Acerbia snarled
an order, and throughout the crowd her Secret Police stripped off
cloak and cape and hood to reveal themselves and draw steel.

The spectators shrieked in fear and outrage. Some struggled to
get away. Those who had daggers or knives handy pulled them out
and turned on their startled assailants. No doubt it was the first
time the people had fought back, and the Secret Police weren't
expecting it. I thought I saw Captain Thukwad rise up in the midst
of a knot of females. Unfortunately for him, one of them was the
she-bear from the Cheese and Crackers. Her heavy paw came
down hard on top of his skull. It wasn't pretty.

On the scaffold, Mysti and Ramses fought side by side, toppling
all comers. The guards they didn't kill outright they shoved or
kicked over the edge to the waiting swords of Captain Lan and his
crew. When they had swept the platform clear, Ramses fixed King
Wulfdeth with a dark look.

"Now you'll pay for my father's death, villain!" he cried, his
sword leveled at the false king's heart.

"Daddy?" Anisella whimpered, clinging to Wulfdeth's chest.

"Not now, dear, Daddy's busy," the king said quietly, moving
her behind him. He drew his own sword. "I should have done this
when you were in your cradle."

"Yes, it would have been easier for you then," Ramses sneered.
He lunged for Wulfdeth and the duel began while all around them
the cry resounded, "For Borith! For Borith and less unemployment!"

"I'll give you less unemployment!" Acerbia screeched. A shaft
of Majyk zinged from her wand into the midst of the milling
sheep. There was a tremendous blast, fleece flying everywhere.
"I'm going to destroy as many of you miserable traitors as I can.
Anyone who survives can have a job. Is that less unemployment or
isn't it?" A second blast leaped after the first. Rams and ewes took
to the sky, landing on the crowd below with deadly effect. People
screamed and fell back under the bleating bombardment. Acerbia's
men made the most of the confusion, moving in with club and
blade.

The fairy glowed golden with rage, her slender body wrapped in
a blazing, crackling shell. She cast bolt after bolt of power at the
crowd, sometimes several at once. "Wulfdeth and I had a nice little
kingdom going here. *We* were happy. Why couldn't you Topside
troublemakers leave well enough alone?" She glared up at me and

threw a shield-sized disc of Majyk. It knocked me from my feet. Quickly I called up the spell that made my cape fly, but the cape's hem had come untucked from my boots. The cape flew and I dangled, choking on the tightly fastened neck. Acerbia's laughter battered me.

As I struggled, I saw her switch her attention to Ramses, who was forcing Wulfdeth nearer and nearer to the edge of the platform. The sheep pirates circled below like a school of hungry sharks. One more step and they would have him. Captain Lan's hook glittered and Lodda bayed for blood.

"Oh, no you don't!" Acerbia cried. "I didn't waste the best years of my life making Wulfdeth king just to have some jumped-up mutton-minder kill him!"

One spell at a time, I thought, fighting the cape. *Just one spell at a time.* I made an effort and wrenched the neck-clasp open. Air rushed into my grateful lungs. I was very happy for the few moments before I hit the pavement head-first.

Through swimming vision I thought I saw the fairy's wand trace a burning path across the sky. A small green balloon came floating to her hand, growing bigger and bigger the closer it came.

"Nay, I'll not have ye summonin' up yer great fireworm again, lady!" Captain Lan clambered up the scaffold as nimbly as if it were the rigging of the *Golden Fleece.* "By this good blade, I swear ye'll cast no more wicked spells with yer pretty head sliced from yer shoulders, baa'arrrrrRRRRRRGGGGHHHH!"

A gust of incredible heat poured over the square, a blinding flare, and the smell of roasted mutton filled my nostrils. In the distance I heard Ramses' heartbroken cry, "Lan! Lan, my brother!" then a loud thud and King Wulfdeth's victorious cackle.

"Boss! Get up, boss!" Scandal tapped my face insistently with his paw. "This is not the time for a nap. Wulfdeth just hit Ramses upside the head with the flat of his sword. Our prince is o-u-t and soon to be d-e-a-d."

"Huh?" I mumbled.

"The pirates are too stunned to fight anymore. Captain Lan got barbecued by Acerbia's dragon. There's poor Lodda, sprawled over the body, howling her heart out. The guards are closing in. Mysti's trying to stave them off until the sheep can recover, but she's only one Welfie and her mask keeps getting twisted around over her face."

I sat up, shaking my head. "How did you get down from the roof?"

"I jumped."

"From so high?" I was horrified.

"Big deal. I always land on my feet."

Oh yes, I'd forgotten that.

"Now get *up*," the cat urged. "We need you. Acerbia's mounted on her dragon and she's trying to turn everyone in Loupgarou into crispy critters. See there?"

I couldn't help but see. Torquil was bigger than before. His body blotted out the castle, his wingspan covered the sun. Acerbia straddled his neck and rained down stroke after fiery stroke from her wand into the rebels. The dragon shot streams of flaming breath wherever the fairy directed. Many on our side were fleeing, others grimly holding their positions. The guards and the Secret Police took heart and renewed their assault. On the platform, King Wulfdeth gloated as he held a limp, unconscious Ramses by the scruff of the neck. Mysti fought on, braver than any warrior from the old legends, but she was beginning to tire. The common sheep galloped around and around in panicky circles, getting in everyone's way. Over all, the dark shape of the flying cloak dipped and soared like a gigantic bat.

A shaggy body fell beside me. It was Brother Targhee. "Until all are free, none are free," he rasped, and died.

"Here, Master Kendar, let me help you up." Bertram offered me a small brown hand. I stumbled to my feet, clutching my wand. "Master Kendar, we're being driven back," the shepherd lad said softly. "Can't you use your powers in our cause?"

"You bet he can!" Scandal bounced with glee. "Go ahead, Kendar, blitz Wulfdeth, zap Acerbia, blow that overgrown Godzilla out of the sky! Biff! Wham! Zowie!"

"I can't," I said.

"Kaboom! Ping! *What?*"

"I can only do this one spell at a time," I reminded him. "If I don't, I lose control of my Majyk. Like Master Thengor did right before he died, remember? It was hovering over him like a big cloud and—"

"Like that cloud?" The cat motioned with his eyes for me to look up.

I did, and I knew. "Acerbia's using too many spells at once!" I exclaimed. "That's why she's glowing."

"And check it out, champ, her wand's the thing. Ever see her without it? Her Majyk's on the verge of running wild; the only control device she's got is the wand . . . Kendar, baby, Acerbia's the camel's back and you're about to become the last straw."

"Uh-huh." I rubbed my chin, gazing up at the sky. "And I know just where the last straw's going to drop, too." I cupped a hand to my mouth and hollered, "Acerbiaaaaaa!"

The fairy heard. She pulled the dragon up short out of a flame-run and turned his head in my direction. "Hello, little wizard," she said in the too-sweet voice I'd come to hate. "Don't be impatient. I'll get to you all in good time."

"*Now*, Acerbia!" I thrust the wand straight at her. "Leave the others alone and fight me now."

"I'd love to—" She launched another sizzle of Majyk from her wand at a shepherd. "Really I would"—a fountain of fireballs went spinning away into the crowd—"but Torquil is having such fun"—she and the dragon both whipped ribbons of flame over the heads of the people—"that I hate to cut it short." She giggled.

"Oh, *stop* it, Mummy!" Anisella stood with fists clenched at her sides, the picture of boiling wrath. "You leave Master Kendar alone *and* you tell Daddy not to hurt Ramses!"

"I'm sorry, precious, but—ugh—*Mummy* can't do that," Acerbia replied. "Mummy and Daddy have to kill the nasty mans so that our little princess can live happily ever after. Don't you worry your pretty little empty head about it."

"Oh, shut up, you nasty thing! Your idea of happily ever after is me married to someone you pick. Well, forget it! I don't *want* to live your happily ever after!" Anisella stamped her foot. "I don't want to be a princess, if it means killing anyone!" She tore the gold net from her hair and flung it away. "If you don't let them go, I'll run away and you'll never see me again! Try to marry me off to anybody *then*!" She ripped off her spidersilk gown and stepped out of it. She was wearing her old chain-mail outfit beneath. The square echoed with the sound of male jaws hitting the stones.

"Don't go to the trouble of running away, sweetie," Acerbia told her daughter. By now the cloud of Majyk around her had swollen like a dry sponge plunged into water. "There's a *much* simpler way for me never to see you again." Her wand rose, shimmering with fire.

Wulfdeth dropped Ramses' body. "Acerbia, no! Not our daughter!"

"Oh, don't snivel, Wulfdeth," the fairy said, out of patience. "There are plenty more where she came from. Next time I'll raise the brat myself, if I must. Maybe then we'll get one that's smart enough to realize that Mother knows best."

She loosed the destroying spell just as I released some Majyk of my own.

Three screams shattered the air.

CHAPTER ———————— 29

KING WULFDETH'S SCREAM OF AGONY DIED WHEN HE did. He slumped down on the platform, a hole through his chest.

Anisella's scream of terror changed to sobs of purest misery as she knelt to cradle her father in her arms.

Acerbia's scream of indignation was muffled by the flying cape that had dropped over her head at my command. In her panic, she windmilled her arms, lost her grip on the star-tipped wand, grabbed for it blindly, and slipped from Torquil's neck. The cape fouled her wings too completely for her to spread them and fly under her own power. She squeaked when she hit the ground.

A good-sized cloud of Majyk floated in the space where Acerbia had been the moment before the cape dropped. Torquil sleepily turned his heavy head to sniff at it. It was nothing good to eat, so he simply puffed a little smoke at it and it dispersed in a thousand different directions. For an instant I thought I heard the sound of giggling.

A hush fell over the square, a silence broken only by those who wept for the dead. The fairy's fall and Wulfdeth's doom had yanked the rug out from under the battle. The shepherds, the townsfolk, the guards, the peasants, and the Secret Police all stood around staring blankly at one another, weapons dangling at their sides. One of the guards raised his sword in a half-hearted attempt to chop an unarmed peasant in two. The peasant just growled, "Leave off them monkeyshines, you," and the guard slunk away.

"Plates!" The young otter shouted, weaving through the shambles. "Get your commemorative plates here! Sure to be a collector's item! Nice fresh memorial plate to the late King Wulfdeth's memory!" He climbed up the scaffold and nudged Ramses with his paw. "Plate, Your Majesty? A little something to remember the day by?"

Ramses groaned and held his head. "What happened?"

"You lived long enough to be king, Prince Borith," Mysti said. "And now that justice has been served—" She pulled off the black mask. "My, that's a relief!" She shook out her curls and stretched her combat-weary arms back. Far back. Back far enough so that Ramses and everyone else couldn't help but notice that—

"You—you're a *girl*!" he gasped.

Anisella uttered a strangled cry, then began to laugh hysterically. Mysti crossed the platform and squatted down beside her and patted her on the back until she calmed down.

"I'm sorry," she said sincerely. "I couldn't tell you." As an afterthought she added, "I can't be sorry about what happened to King Wulfdeth, but he was your father and—"

"He loved me." Anisella stroked the dead king's cheek. "For years and years he didn't know I was alive, but the moment he found out who I was, he loved me just like that. No questions. Being his daughter was enough. Enough to make him die for me." She bent over King Wulfdeth's body, and even I could see the tears fall. "Daddy . . ."

A snarl snapped my attention away from the scaffold. Acerbia yanked the cape off her head and crawled out, glowering. She looked worse than my brother Basehart after a night in the town tavern. "You . . . *moron*!" she gritted at me.

"Awww, and here we thought she wasn't gonna be a good loser," Scandal said.

"You took my Majyk from me, you fool!" she shrilled. "No, you did worse than take it; you wasted it! Scattered it to the four winds!"

"Good," I said. "Majyk's too dangerous to leave in the wrong hands."

Two of the shepherds stood beside me, holding the fairy's wand between them. "Now?" they asked. I nodded curtly. They broke it and let the pieces clatter to the paving stones.

"Remember, whoever has the bigger part gets his wish," Scandal said.

Acerbia's voice sounded like something that hauls itself out of an old tomb, dragging chains behind. "Do you realize what you've done?"

"He has fulfilled Merwallow's prophecy!" Rhett shouted from the rooftop. (Unlike Scandal, he had no safe way of getting himself down.) "He has restored the rightful heir to the throne. He has—"

A spurt of flame struck the tiles to Rhett's left, making him jump and go skidding off the roof. Lucky for him, he shot out a hand and clung to the gutter. There he dangled, feet kicking nothing. The dragon soared high, the nasty, cold sound of his laughter tumbling in his wake.

"Rhett!" Anisella exclaimed. She laid King Wulfdeth's body aside gently and was on her feet in an instant. "Hang on, Rhett, I'll save you!" She became an auburn-haired streak of light as she raced across the square.

"My Majyk was the only thing controlling Torquil!" Acerbia hollered at me. "Any properly educated wizard knows that unless they have a master, dragons are stupid, sly, malicious beasts who love to set things on fire just to watch them burn."

"Oh, and is that why you sent your own child a dragon's egg for her birthday?" I demanded. (I was trying to distract myself from what she'd said. Me, a "properly educated wizard?" Not if you saw my grades at Master Thengor's Academy.)

"They're all right if you raise them from eggs," she shot back. "It's the ones that grow up in the great western desert that are so hard to manage. They're the reason we've *got* the great western desert! That whole region used to be the great western rainforest until the dragons moved in. Ugh, just *look* at him!" She pointed upwards.

Torquil was doing a lazy loop-de-loop, smoke dribbling from his nostrils. He rolled over and stretched his snaky neck down as he studied the city. Puffs of flame dotted the sky. He was laughing again. Dipping his right wing, he glided lower and bathed the castle gate with fire.

"Hi! Leave my castle alone, you miserable worm!" Ramses had recovered and was on his feet, wigwagging a sword at the dragon. "If it's a fight you want—"

The dragon turned one glowing eye towards the man on the scaffold and almost casually sent a stream of flame to overwhelm him. It fell short of the mark, but Ramses reeled back, pushed by a wave of infernal heat, and pitched off the platform. He landed with a hideous snapping sound and lay still.

"You . . . *dragon*! You hurt Ramses!" Bertram yelled, choking on tears. Holding his crook overhead with both hands he charged at the monster. Torquil was startled into higher flight by this insane attack, but once he had put some air between himself and Bertram, he acted as if he were ashamed to have fled before such a puny foe. His scaly brows knit in anger. Slowly and deliberately, he landed in the square.

"Uh-oh," Scandal said. "Now he's done it. Now he's gone and

made him mad. This isn't going to be any quickie flame-broil job. Torquil's going to make this death last."

"How do you know?" I asked.

"I recognize the attitude."

"I can't let that happen," I said. My wand shone in the sunlight as I tried to get it in line with Torquil. That wasn't hard. Once earthbound, the dragon was a fine big target. I couldn't miss him if I tried.

"Wha—?" I stared at my empty hand. The wand had vanished. I darted an accusing glance at Acerbia. "Where is it? What have you done with my wand?"

"*Your* wand?" she sneered. "Oh, I like that! I told you when I gave it to you, it was only a borrower's wand. It was due to be returned today, so it went back to where it belongs: my apartment in the castle." She pursed her lips as the dragon stomped closer to Bertram. "If Torquil leaves us a castle."

"Skip the wand, fearless leader!" Scandal yelled. "You don't need anything like a wand to make your Majyk work."

"You're right." I narrowed my eyes and straightened my belt. "A wizard's gotta do what a wizard's gotta do." I stalked towards the dragon, calling up the Majyk within me as I went. It was a wonderful feeling, a feeling of power, a magnificent feeling of—

Oh well, why lie about it? It felt like holding back a big burp at a fancy dinner party.

"Torquil!" I shouted. The beast knew his name, or else the sound of my voice got his attention. His head swerved away from Bertram, towards me. This was it. I wasn't going to get another chance. Wandless, I raised my hands and sent a wave of Majyk at the monster. I was going to lift him up, throw him far out to sea, and make him explode when he got there. I put everything I had into it.

Everything except common sense. *One spell at a time, you stupid ratwhacker!* Too late, I remembered the rule that let me control my Majyk. Lifting and heaving and blowing up a dragon the size of Torquil was three spells, at the very least. The brightness pouring from my hands splashed and splattered all over Torquil's scales, making them glow but not doing much else. Again I heard the creature's wicked laughter.

A slim, agile figure vaulted over the dragon's tail and ran to stand between me and the worm, jeweled sword in hand. "Mysti! Get out of the way!"

"I don't think so," the Welfie replied, never taking her eyes from Torquil.

"Listen, don't worry about me; I'm safe," I argued. "Even if I can't fight him off, he can't kill me."

"No, he can just crush you with one paw and leave you to go on living without a single whole bone in your body. Or he can sear you alive and see how you like that sort of pain. Sorry, Kendar. I am a Blade for Justice. I can't let this happen."

"I thought this 'Blade for Justice' stuff was just a disguise you used."

"It was, at first. Now I'm thinking of making it my career. I'm tired of doing nothing but sitting around the palace, munching bonbons and reading Raptura Eglantine romances all day. Now stay back and let me work. It's part of my job to defend the defenseless and help the hopeless."

"Don't you mean help the *helpless*?"

"Yes, but I know you." She attacked Torquil's flank.

The dragon saw her coming. I think it amused him to have so many human insects going after him at once. He spread his wings, flapped them twice with a force that knocked all three of us off our feet, and rose just out of sword range and shepherd's-crook reach. The clouds of smoke rising from his nostrils changed from white to gray to black, mottled with sparks and flecks of flame. His eyes took a leisurely aerial survey of the square. You could almost imagine that he was thinking—

"Run! Run!" Acerbia cried. "He's going to blow! He's going to burn us all where we stand!" She would have escaped, except for the two burly shepherds pinning her arms and her wings. Everyone else who could move took her advice, but the streets were too narrow and there were too many people. All of them would never be able to escape in time when Torquil drowned us with fire.

I tried throwing another spell at the beast—just one, this time. I settled for the one that would make him explode into tiny pieces. I prayed they'd be tiny enough to do no harm when Loupgarou got drenched with bits of dead dragon. My Majyk hit Torquil's glowing side and turned to vapor. What in Wedwel's name was wrong?

"You must've done something to his scales with that first shot, Kendar," Mysti said, watching the dragon circle above us. "Now he's immune to your Majyk."

"To mine . . ." I could hear the rush of indrawn air as Torquil filled his lungs before the ultimate fiery blast. "But maybe not to Scandal's."

I dipped into my belt pouch. The wax-sealed egg lay in my palm. Scandal told me to use it when I had a big problem I wanted to cut down to size. If this didn't qualify, nothing did. I flung the egg at Torquil.

Did I ever tell you about how none of the other students at Master Thengor's Academy of High Wizardry ever wanted to have me on their basteball team? They told me I threw like a girl. This is not fair. I throw much worse than any girl I've ever met.

The egg went high, but not high enough. It reached the top of its flight and dropped straight back the way it had come. "Get away! Get away!" Scandal shrieked. "Don't let it hit you! Run!"

"Um?" I said.

There was a whizzing noise, the sudden smell of sheep, and a *nok* near my ear. Bertram had come running in, crook outstretched, to intercept the egg. His crook connected solidly. For a miracle, the egg didn't break. Instead it zoomed back up into the sky, higher than I could ever hope to throw.

"Just like making a save in bladderball," Bertie told me with a grin as we watched the egg soar. "Easier. You really don't want to get splattered with what's inside the bladder we use, you know." It hit Torquil's ribs with a healthy splat.

And suddenly the dragon was covered with micro-fish.

Micro-fish? a tiny, petrified voice inside my head squawked. *But when they hit something touched by Acerbia's Majyk, they don't cut it down to size; they make it get—*

Bigger. The fish grow on impact and make whatever they hit grow along with them. One micro-fish can turn a doll-sized booklet into a volume too heavy for one man to carry. A whole egg-full of micro-fish hitting a dragon that was big as a house to start with meant . . .

Yipe.

Torquil swelled up and kept on swelling. The effect started at the spot where the fish first struck him, and spread. Micro-fish were popping up to full size all over the dragon, forcing his scales apart like ivy roots cracking the mortar of a wall, making the scales themselves inflate like bubbles. The dragon's throat expanded from the size of a young sapling to a forest giant, his bellow of terror going from simple roar to castle-shaking soundquake. His shadow rippled a blanket of darkness over us until it stretched from the gates of Loupgarou to beyond the breakwater of Port O' Morph harbor.

Torquil's belly peeled and popped, the underscales breaking off and falling on our heads as the monster continued to grow. People stopped running away. There was nowhere safe left to run. If the dragon landed now, all Loupgarou would be rubble and jelly.

I knotted my fists in powerless rage and screamed, "Scandal, why in Wedwel's name do I ever listen to you?"

"Shut up and listen to me!" the cat hollered back, two glowing eyes in the dragon's shadow. Majyk arced and forked from the tip of his tail to the points of his ears. "Get your Majyk in gear and be ready to push when I give the word!"

"Push? Push what?"

"A shopping cart, a baby carriage, your *luck*, ningnong, whaddaya think? The *dragon*! One good sorcerous shove out to sea or we're all dog food. Get ready . . ."

Through the rain of shattering scales I heard Mysti yell, "There! I see an opening!" She pointed at a patch of Torquil's belly where all the scales had fallen away. "I think I've got a clear shot." She took her sword in both hands, ready to throw it like a spear.

"Mysti, don't throw it!" Scandal bounced on stiff legs, his tail bushed out and rigid. "It only worked for the prince in *Sleeping Beauty* because it was a flippin' Disney cartoon! Kendar, get set . . ."

Mysti gave a grunt and flung the sword.

"*Now!*"

My Majyk and Mysti's sword both hit Torquil just as the dragon uttered a bloodcurdling roar and—

What's the opposite of "blow up"? Not "blow down"—I know that much. But what Torquil did looked like the way a piece of paper crumples in on itself when you throw it into a fire. Crushed, the dragon plummeted. He would have crashed on the square below if my Majyk hadn't met him halfway down, like a paddle meeting a baseball, and launched him far out over the water. The sound of a mighty splash rode the seawind back to shore and all the ships docked at Port O' Morph rocked and rose high on the swell. That was the last of Torquil.

But not entirely. Mysti's sword struck Torquil just an eye blink before my spell did. The Majyk sheathing his scales wasn't enough to ward off a blade, definitely not strong enough to stand against a blade for justice. The sword stabbed deep, biting in the edge of the bald patch and shearing off a sliver of scale half its own length, twice its sharpness.

A lot of detail for me to measure with my eyes in an instant when so much else was happening? No. I didn't see how big or how sharp that scale dagger was until later, after the dragon had sunk into the sea. I had plenty of time to notice it then.

It stood, still glowing with its portion of my Majyk, lodged in Mysti's heart.

CHAPTER ———————— 30

"HERE YOU ARE, MASTER KENDAR, SIR," SAID THE DUN-
geon guard. "This is the cell, right next to the famous Weeping
Cell of Prince Borith the Somewhat—"

"I know."

He snorted as he bent to open the lock. "No need to be snippy,
sir, I'm sure. I merely thought that you might find it interesting,
seeing as how our own beloved Prince Borith has been restored to
us. Pity 'bout what happened to him, though, now ain't it?"

I said nothing. At least Ramses (I still couldn't think of him as
Borith) was alive. True, his legs would be useless for the rest of his
life, thanks to Torquil's malice. The fall from the gallows had
broken his back. "A carry-chair's better than a coffin," I muttered.
I thought of Mysti, cold and pale, laid out with care in a gold and
glass coffin that was one of the treasures of Wingdingo. The prince
insisted that we take it to transport her body home. It was carried
aboard the *Golden Fleece* under the watchful eye of Captain
Lodda herself. We would set sail as soon as the coronation was
over.

"Shall I wait here, sir?" the guard asked, holding the cell door
open for me.

"Please. This won't take long." I went into the dark.

They hadn't chained Acerbia to the wall like a common
prisoner. She sat hunched in one corner of the cell, scorning the
chair that Anisella had requested for her use. The soft mattress that
was another of her daughter's gifts lay slit open and gutted in
another corner. She didn't give any sign she was aware of my
presence. Only when I called her by name, did she raise her head.

"What do you want now, little wizard? My wings?" There was
still plenty of the old venom left.

"You can keep them."

Her laugh was thin and brittle as the winter morning skin of ice on a dishpan's surface. "That's about all you've let me keep. My wand, my books, all that was left of my Majyk, even my poor dear Wulfdeth's life—all these you've taken from me. Why stop at wings?"

"No ordinary cell would hold you if I hadn't drained the last of your Majyk away," I reminded her needlessly. "And as for Wulfdeth, you took his life yourself."

"It wasn't my fault!" Her eyes blazed. "You're to blame, you and your interfering Topside friends. If you hadn't come here uninvited, my Wulfdeth would never have seen that atrocious girl. Who told the fool to give his life for hers? Now she's still alive, but he—Oh, you're to blame!"

I decided not to bother pointing out that the only reason Acerbia herself was still alive was that Anisella had begged Ramses to spare the evil fairy. And who could ever say no to Anisella?

"I'm not here to argue any of that," I said, feeling nothing but ice inside me. "I've come to invite you to the coronation of Prince Borith."

"Me?" The fairy's eyes flew wide with surprise. "They want me there? They trust me?"

"Without your Majyk and with a pair of guards to keep an eye on you, it isn't a question of trust."

"Guards . . ." A calculating look stole over her face.

"No one you know," I told her. "The first thing that the prince did was to dismiss all of Wulfdeth's men and to arrest all of yours. All that were left." It felt good to say that.

"Then I assume I'm supposed to be present so that everyone can mock me," Acerbia said sourly. "They'll point and whisper—the fine lords and ladies of the court who used to kneel and simper before me. Perhaps they'll even throw a piece of fruit or a rotten turnip in my face if they think it will buy them their new ruler's favor."

"Not as long as your daughter is there. The prince has made her captain of his new troop of royal guards. He was very impressed when he heard how she climbed up the front of that building to rescue Rhett and brought him down slung over her shoulder. I don't know if Anisella will ever be able to love you the way she wanted to, Acerbia, but she'll never be able to hate."

The fairy made a wry face. "Just let me do my hair."

As she was pulling the comb through the straw-laced tangles she said, "So Wulfdeth's gone and no one's to blame. Not you—you never raised a hand against him—and not me—I was trying to kill someone else entirely and he merely got in the way. His death must be only one of many things that . . . just happened."

"What things?"

"You coming here, bringing Anisella, stealing my wand, my tank of micro-fish—"

"Scandal did that."

"Clever kitty. How did he manage to hide it in that egg?"

"He's got Majyk of his own. I encouraged him to use it. He did. He used it to help him spirit the tank out of your apartment and pour the water into that eggshell he prepared."

"With your encouragement, as you say. And you finding the prince after I'd gone to so much trouble to hide him from the world! But none of it's your fault at all. It was fate, chance, the roll of the dice, the whim of the gods—" She looked me full in the face. "Can you tell me which is worse, little wizard? Knowing that you're blameless but helpless in the hands of the infinite, or knowing you do have the power to influence how things happen, even if it means that sometimes you're responsible for the results?"

Results like Mysti's death.

· "If you're ready, let's go," was all I said to her.

Scandal met us at the entrance to the great hall where the ceremony was going to take place. "Lookin' good, Tinkerbell," he told Acerbia. "Being locked up for a zillion years agrees with you."

She doled out one of her cool, unfriendly smiles. "It hasn't been a zillion years, clever kitty. It may never be. Wingdingo's got its precious Prince Borith back again, but look at him! Can he mount a horse, fight with a sword, lead his troops in battle? You can't do any of those things when you're trapped in a chair."

"I guess not. Looks like he'll have to stick to the old peace-and-prosperity angle instead." The cat turned his tail to the fairy. "Come on, Kendar. I got us a pair of good seats up front in the No Sneering section."

The great hall was filled with row after row of benches with an aisle running up the middle. Most of the seats were packed. Respectable merchants from Loupgarou rubbed elbows with scruffy tavernkeepers from Port O' Morph; highland peasants chatted with bankers and men of law, shepherds consorted with sheep.

They'd built a long, low platform all along the front wall. Even though it was covered with blue velvet and gold brocade, it gave me a shuddery reminder of the scaffold. Ramses sat enthroned, wearing only a loose white tunic of the thinnest fabric. Eight nobles stood to his right, Bertram to his left. The slender shepherd was very handsome since he'd been bathed and had his thick, curly hair washed and trimmed.

"Where'd Bertie get that black eye?" I whispered to Scandal.

"Aw, one of the other shepherds teased him about how pretty he looked and they got into a fist fight. You oughta see the other guy. Bertie really packs a wallop, and he's got a quick temper."

Bertie's temper looked ready to explode again any time now. He wasn't used to the fine new garments his old friend Ramses had given him to wear today. Obviously itchy and irritable, he kept scratching the back of one leg with the other foot when he thought no one was looking. Behind him was the priest who would conduct the ceremony and Anisella, holding the prince's sword.

"Why's Ramses sitting there in his nightgown?" Scandal asked as we settled into our places of honor.

Rhett had the seat next to the cat. "That is no nightgown," he said. "The coronation demands that the new king be sprinkled and anointed and dusted and washed and perfumed and in general messed up with many different ceremonial substances. There is no sense wearing one's good clothes for that."

I thought I heard someone crying in the row of seats behind me. I turned around and saw an elderly couple wearing fancy clothes that didn't quite fit them. The woman sniffled on her satin sleeve while the man patted her on the back and said, "There, there, Mother," over and over again.

"Is anything wrong?" I asked.

"Oh, 'tisn't such a much, lad," the man answered. "Mother's just so proud of our Ramses, it's come out tearful."

"You must be Ramses' foster-parents!" I exclaimed.

"Er, aye. So we must, if the lad's to—"

"He's *hurt*," the woman wailed. She sounded angry about it, under the tears. "Going off foolish with not a word, racketing about with pirates, teasing death a hundred times at sea, then nigh getting his full of it when that horrid dragon—Oh! When I think how close we come to losing him, and for what? A crown? There's simpler ways to come by one of those gewgaws."

"There, there, Mother," the old man said.

"Don't you there-there me! You know it's true. Didn't your own brother Thestos go off and win himself a whole kingdom just on the coin of that pretty face of his, and kissing some royal chippy who hadn't the sense to sidestep a poisoned spindle? Now he's *King* Thestos of Belacan, and no one the wiser that he used to be as much a lowly shepherd as ever you or the boy was. Ramses might've done the same—them princesses are always sticking their fingers where they don't belong. Instead there he sits, and there he *will* sit forever—not to walk nor run nor dance again in this world." She was overcome with loud, gurgling sobs.

"There, there, Mother." Her mate patted her on the back some more. "Our Ramses never did know how to dance."

A flourish of trumpets silenced us all. The priest motioned for his assistants to bring out a large table set with an array of bottles, boxes, basins, and at the very end, the royal crown of Wingdingo. Last of all, one of the little boys came up carrying a cumbersome, silver-bound book which he and a companion held open for the priest's eyes.

There was a slight disturbance in the back of the hall. An immensely tall, radiant being strode down the aisle and took the vacant seat on Rhett's other side.

HELLO AGAIN, said Merwallow. He smiled at us, especially at Rhett, and winked at Anisella. I THOUGHT YOU MIGHT LIKE TO KNOW THAT I WAS VERY PLEASED WITH THE WAY YOU DELIVERED THAT LAST PREDICTION, he told the oracle. IT WASN'T IN VERSE WHEN I GAVE IT TO YOU. NICE TOUCH. SO, I HEAR YOU'RE GETTING MARRIED.

Rhett blushed and said nothing.

COME, COME, DON'T BE BASHFUL. THAT'S WHY I'M HERE. I HAVE A WEDDING GIFT FOR YOU. REMEMBER THAT SILLY OATH OF RENUNCIATION? WELL, I'M WILLING TO FORGET ALL ABOUT IT IF YOU ARE. TELLING THE UNVARNISHED TRUTH CAN BE AWKWARD ANY TIME, BUT WHEN YOU'RE MARRIED IT CAN BE DOWNRIGHT FATAL.

"But what about my business?" Rhett asked. "Are you taking away my powers as an oracle too?"

NO.

Rhett grew suspicious. "Is that all you have to say? 'No'? Are you not going to disguise your answer in mystic terms and cryptic utterances?"

WHAT PART OF 'NO' DIDN'T YOU UNDERSTAND?

The priest cleared his throat loudly, attracting even the attention of the god. Merwallow waved at him in a chummy way. YOU GO RIGHT AHEAD AND CROWN BORITH. DON'T MIND ME.

"Thank you." The priest let a hint of sarcasm slip in. He raised his hands. "My children, we have gathered here to witness the coronation of our beloved Prince Borith, rightful heir to the throne of Wingdingo. Before we begin, I call upon the gods to grant him many happy years as—"

WHO? Merwallow asked.

The priest lowered his arms. "Who what?" he snarled.

YOU SAID YOU CALL UPON THE GODS TO GRANT HIM MANY HAPPY YEARS. I'M SURE THE REST OF US WILL BE PLEASED TO HONOR YOUR REQUEST AS SOON AS I BRING HOME THE NEWS, BUT WE WILL NEED TO KNOW THE FULL, LEGAL NAME OF THE PERSON YOU'RE RE-QUESTING ALL THOSE HAPPY YEARS FOR. TO PUT ON THE CERTIFICATE OF MORE-OR-LESS ENJOYABLE LON-GEVITY, YOU KNOW. THAT'S WHY I NEED TO KNOW HIM WHO.

"*Whom.*" Rhett corrected him discreetly.

Merwallow frowned at his oracle. GODS MAKE THEIR OWN GRAMMAR.

"If you'd been listening, you would know that we were requesting a long and happy life for our beloved Prince Borith of Wingdingo," the priest replied, becoming even more annoyed with Merwallow.

WHO? the god repeated. He reached a hand inside the dazzling radiance wrapping him and pulled out a small tablet that glowed with a weird green light. It emitted a series of beeps as he punched it several times with his finger. OH, Merwallow said at last, after studying the tablet's surface. NO, SORRY. WE CAN'T OBLIGE YOU AFTER ALL. THERE IS NO SUCH PERSON AS PRINCE BORITH OF WINGDINGO.

"*What!*" There wasn't single soul present who didn't join in that shout of astonishment.

Merwallow sighed. LOOK, YOU CAN SEE FOR YOURSELF IF YOU LIKE. IT'S ALL RIGHT HERE IN GREEN AND PURPLE: THERE IS NO PRINCE BORITH OF WINGDINGO. THERE WAS ONE A LONG TIME AGO, BUT HE DIED IN THE FAMOUS WEEPING CELL, NAGGED TO DEATH BY QUEEN INGIGUNGO—

The great hall burst into a thousand babbling knots of people. Ramses sat immobile, his face a study in confusion. The nobles who had so lately fawned all over him now stood giving him the sort of mistrustful stares rich folk give the beggar they catch going through their refuse heap. The priest was desperately flipping the pages of his book, seeking an answer to a question he didn't know.

The elderly couple behind me started arguing with no one in particular that even if Ramses wasn't Prince Borith, he still deserved the throne.

In the midst of this tumult, I saw Bertram leave the platform with the air of someone with a nasty chore that he just wants to get over with and forget. He returned holding his shepherd's crook. Using two hands, he pounded the heavy staff on the boards until the booming restored order in the hall.

"All right, that's enough!" he bawled, his voice skirling high. "I didn't get all scraped and scented, like a market-day lamb, just to stand here forever while you mudheads let some silly, second-class godling throw the whole place into an uproar."

SECOND-CLASS GODLING, AM I? Merwallow growled. HOW WOULD YOU LIKE LOCUSTS IN YOUR YOGURT?

Bertie's reply was to make a rude sound with his tongue. "I say we go on ahead with the coronation. So what if Ramses isn't Prince Borith? He's smart and brave and kind and the best man I ever met. You are, you know," he said, turning a strangely tender look on Ramses. "During the battle, when you fell off the platform and we thought you were dead, I wanted to die, too."

"Uhhhhh . . . Thank you?" Ramses responded dubiously.

"But if he's not Prince Borith, he shouldn't be king!" I objected. "The Mystic Balance won't be set right until the true heir is back on to the throne. We've come a long way to restore your rightful ruler—Mysti *died* for it! Don't tell she gave her life for nothing!"

"You think she was the only one who died?" Bertie countered. "You think Ramses wasn't ready to die for it, too? Anyway, you heard the god: There *is* no Prince Borith!"

THAT'S RIGHT, Merwallow said, nodding.

"You see?" Betram gave the whole hall a smug look. "So since there's no Prince Borith to put on the throne, we might as well—"

OF COURSE YOU MIGHT HAVE ASKED ME WHETHER THERE'S A *PRINCESS* BORITH.

This time the god's pronouncement was too breathtaking for anyone to exclaim *What?* again.

The priest was the first to recover, being used to gods and their ways. "O Greatness, isn't Borith a boy's name?"

NOT ALWAYS. AT THE TIME OF THE HISTORIC PRINCE BORITH THERE WERE PLENTY OF GIRL CHILDREN GIVEN THAT NAME. SOMETIMES THEY SPELLED IT WITH A FINAL "E."

Rhett tapped the god on his shining elbow. "*Is* there a Princess Borith?"

MAYBE THERE IS AND MAYBE THERE ISN'T.

"Is—is she alive?"

NO PROMISES.

"How can we find her?"

ASK ME NO QUESTIONS AND I'LL TELL YOU NO LIES.

"Curse it, Merwallow, there is a difference between cryptic utterances and merely being snide! *Will* you stop playing games and give us a straight answer?" Rhett stormed.

WHY SHOULD I? I'M JUST A SECOND-CLASS GODLING, ACCORDING TO *SOME* PEOPLE WHO HAVE NO MANNERS AND A BAD TEMPER THAT WILL PROBABLY GET WINGDINGO INTO A DOZEN WARS BEFORE SOMEONE TEACHES HER THAT IT'S NOT POLITE TO SPEAK TO GODS AND PEOPLE AS IF THEY WERE HER DIRTY OLD SHEEP.

"My sheep are *not* dirty!" Bertram shouted, and rushed the god, waving the heavy crook overhead.

All Merwallow said was, OH, FOR PITY'S SAKE, BORITH, ACT LIKE A LADY. He vanished.

So did Bertram's clothes.

The ladies shrieked, the gentlemen covered their eyes, and everyone else stared.

"Hoi! Thickskull Bertie's a *girl*!" one of the shepherds hooted.

"Bertie's a *girl*?" came the resentful echo from another shepherd who had two black eyes, a bloody nose, and a split lip.

"Bertie's . . . a girl," Ramses marveled aloud. He tried to rise from his chair, but couldn't. With a moan of frustration he used the arms of the throne to push himself upright, only to topple forward with a crash.

Bertie gave a little scream and rushed to help him up. "Oh, Ramses, I'm sorry! You've hurt yourself again on account of me!" she cried.

"No, no, don't worry about it, Ber—Borith—*Princess*." Ramses leaned back in her arms and faced the facts. "Wow, you really *are* a girl!"

"My foster-parents made me swear an oath never to reveal what I really was," the lady replied. "They said I'd be in danger if I did, but they never explained why. All those years with you and the sheep, I rather hoped you'd figure it out for yourself, but you never did. And to think you called *me* a thickskull!" Her tone softened. "But whatever you called me, you *did* like me—just a little?"

Ramses was downcast. "All those years . . . Oh yes, I *did* like you, Ber—Your Majesty. A lot. In fact there were times when—"

He blushed. "But now I'm like this, and you're a princess. I guess it's too late now."

The princess lifted his chin. "Not for me," she said, and kissed him.

"I don't know about the rest of you, but I haven't got all day," the priest said, and plopped the royal crown on the princess's head while she and Ramses embraced. "We can catch up on the other parts of the ceremony later. All hail our new monarch, Queen Borith of Wingdingo!" The hall rocked with cheers.

"Love the hat," Scandal said. "But it doesn't match the rest of her outfit at all."

CHAPTER ———————— 31

"MASTER KENDAR! YOO HOO, MASTER KENDAR!" SOME-
one on the dock was calling my name.

Scandal trotted across the ship's deck to where I sat beside
Mysti's glass-and-gold coffin. It was too bulky and fragile to be
stowed below safely, but Captain Lodda's crew had rigged a
canopy over it and done what they could to keep it from sliding
across the planking once the *Golden Fleece* got under way.

"Someone's paging you, pal," he said. When I didn't answer, he
persisted: "Look, there are some things all the Majyk in the world
can't do, or Master Thengor would still be alive today. Other
things just happen. It's not your fault she's gone."

"Whose fault is it, then?" My eyes were stinging from all the
crying I'd done.

"If I give you the answer to that, will it change anything? Hey,
I'm not telling you not to grieve, just that the pain's big enough as
is. You shouldn't go looking for reasons to make it hurt more."

I gave him a hard look. "What can you know about pain? Can
cats even cry?" I asked.

"After some of the stuff you humans put us through over the
ages?" he replied stiffly. "Burning us as witches, drowning our
kittens, putting out poisoned meat, dumping us in rivers, throwing
rocks, hitting us with cars and leaving us to die by the roadside?
If we ever could cry, you sucked all the tears out of us long ago."

"Scandal . . . I'm sorry." I gathered him into my lap and held
him close.

"I know, kid." He rubbed his head under my chin. "That was
just the hurt talking. You know I miss her too. There was this
special way she had of knowing just where I needed to be
scratched and—Don't get me started." He leaped out of my arms

and headed for the gangplank. "Come on, it's Ramses' mother calling you. Don't make a lady wait."

One of the crew was just helping the old woman aboard when we got to the gangplank. Behind her came a tall, handsome, muscular, fair-haired, blue-eyed young man dressed in splendid clothes and wearing a gold circlet on his head. He carried a heavy traveling trunk as if it weighed less than a cabbage.

"Master Kendar, I'd like you to meet my nephew, Prince Boffin of Belacan," Ramses' mother said. "He's the fourth son of my dear Lambert's brother Thestos—you know, the one I told you about at the coronation?"

"Yeah, the royal kiss-up," Scandal said before I could reply.

"Hullo," said Prince Boffin. "I'm going to the Topside. Amn't I, Auntie?"

"Yes, dear, of course you are." Ramses' mother patted his golden cheek, then motioned for me to step aside with her. Scandal tagged along, leaving the prince standing there like a very good-looking hunk of meat with eyes.

"Boffin's a good boy," Ramses' mother said. "But he's Thestos' fourth son. His oldest brother gets the kingdom, and the other two are smart enough to take care of themselves, but Boffin . . ." Her voice trailed off and she smiled apologetically.

"Nothing between the ears but a 'For Rent' sign, huh?" Scandal commiserated with her. She didn't deny it.

"He *is* good-looking, though. Gets it from his father. Our Ramses favored Thestos, too—very regal-looking, both of them. No wonder he convinced himself he was really Wulfdeth's kin when that man came to our—"

I didn't want to think about Wulfdeth or Acerbia or anything connected with Mysti's death. "What about Boffin?" I asked, cutting her off.

"Well, since he can't hope to have a living handed to him, and he certainly can't hope to make a living with his brains, he's going to the Topside to seek his fortune."

"Too bad he's not twins; he could hire himself out as bookends," Scandal said.

Ramses' mother only laughed at the cat's sally. "Master Kendar, all I ask is that you do what you can for dear Boffin on the voyage over—prepare him, advise him, tell him what to watch out for once he's on Topside land. Be a *friend* to him. Please."

"So what am I? Chopped liver?" Scandal puffed out his furry chest. "Don't worry, lady. We'll look after Prince Boffin."

Ramses' mother left the ship a happy woman. She was hardly down the gangplank before I confronted the cat.

"Why did you agree to that? I don't want to be a friend to that dumb hulk!"

"No, you just want to spend the whole voyage sitting next to Mysti's coffin until you stop feeling sorry for her and start feeling sorry for yourself. Do it, if that's what you want, but if Mysti was here, she'd give you a boot in the pants and tell you to get on with your life."

I glanced at the gleaming coffin. The gold fastenings holding the glass panels together shimmered with a hint of Majyk. No matter how long the voyage, Mysti's body would reach the Topside perfectly preserved. Lying there, she did look ready to open her eyes at any moment, get up, and kick me just the way Scandal described. Only the sliver of dragon's scale embedded in her heart ruined the illusion.

"All right, Scandal," I said. "I'll do it for Ramses' mother, and for you . . . and for Mysti."

Captain Lodda barked commands, and the *Golden Fleece*—no longer a pirate vessel but a respectable ship under the protection of Queen Borith herself—cast off from her moorings and headed for the open sea. The turrets of the castle were a blue-gray smear on the horizon when Scandal said, "Want to get started?"

We found Prince Boffin at the rail, gazing back at the retreating shore of his homeland. Scandal hopped onto the rail to his right side; I leaned on it to his left. He smiled at us and we smiled back. I hoped I didn't look as stupid as I felt.

"Hello, Your Highness," I said, trying to sound like I was glad to be there. "I'm Master Kendar Gangle and this is my friend Scandal."

"Hullo," Prince Boffin said. He continued to smile.

"So . . . I hear you're going to live on the Topside," I said, trying to start a conversation.

"Uh-huh, uh-huh, uh-huh." His head bobbed like a bubble floating on water.

"Any ideas about what you'll do when you get there?"

"Uh-uh." His blue eyes were as vacant as a baby's.

"I'm a wizard, myself; Chief Wizard to good King Steffan of Grashgoboum. I could introduce you to the king if—"

"How'd he get to be king?" Boffin asked suddenly.

"Huh? Um, I think he was born to it."

"It's not fair!" Prince Boffin slammed his fist on the rail. Poor Scandal almost jumped overboard.

"Wh—what's not fair?"

"How you get to be king. It's not fair that there's only three ways: Either you're born to it, like my brother Prince Helftwig, or you marry into it, like Cousin Ramses." He fell into a sulk.

I tapped his arm. It was like poking at an anvil. "You said *three* ways. What's the third?"

"Three?" Perplexed, he ticked off twos and threes and fours on his fingers until the answer stumbled into his head by accident. "Oh! Oh, that's right, *three*. Third's how Dad did it."

"You mean kiss a sleeping princess?"

"Uh-huh, uh-huh, uh-huh. That, or something else magical. Back home I heard say that King Cadric of Pelata's grandpa was just a wandering salt merchant from Port O' Lyn until he came across this big rock with a sword stuck in it. Well, you know what they say about Lynmen: They'll steal anything that isn't nailed down, and that sword wasn't. He yanked it right out and the next thing he knew there were all these maidens dressed in floaty white gowns singing and dancing all around him. At first he thought they were some ungodly foreign sort of police force, so he punched a couple of them flat before the others told him that they were only welcoming their new king."

"That must've made him happy," Scandal said.

"No, *then* he thought this new king they were talking about was going to have him imprisoned for sword-stealing, so he knocked down a few more of the ladies and tried to run away. The ones that were left grabbed him, punched *him* flat for a change, and when he came to, they explained that the *he* was the one they were welcoming because of what he'd done with that sword. Then they hit him again and asked him what he thought. He thought it was a dead stupid way to pick a ruler, but a very fine chance for him to sell off his salt at the best price, so he took the job. Of course King Cadric doesn't like anyone to remind him about the whole business; hardly can bear to look at the salt cellar during meals, too." He giggled.

"You know, Boffin, I think I see your problem," Scandal said. "No opportunity for royal advancement, that's what."

"Huh?"

"No chance to get to be king."

"Ohhhhh. Uh-huh, uh-huh, uh-huh."

"Yes, there's only so many enchanted princesses to go around. Supply and demand, free market economy, cheap foreign sorcery undercutting local enterprise—"

"Huh?" This time it wasn't Prince Boffin who didn't understand, it was me.

"When no demand exists, create a demand," the cat went on. "When the old watering hole dries up, dig yourself a new one. This kissing business is old hat, a glut on the market. It's time for something fresh, something new, something different! Move with the times and you'll do all right. Fall behind the times and you'll fail. Move *ahead* of the times and you can write your own ticket—"

Prince Boffin stared at the cat, fascinated, but my eyes were starting to close. "I'm tired," I announced. "If you want me, I'll be below." They didn't even notice when I left.

In my cabin, I stretched out on the bunk and closed my eyes. I must have fallen asleep, because all of a sudden I dreamed of a familiar voice—one I never expected to hear again outside of dreams.

"Kendar?"

"Mysti?" I replied sleepily.

"Kendar, it's me."

"I know." I kept my eyes closed. I didn't want to wake up.

Strong hands seized my ankles and yanked me out of the bunk onto the floor. "Ouch!" I yelled, my eyes wide open.

"Is that all you've got to say?" Mysti loomed over me, hands on hips.

"Hi, boss!" Scandal stuck his head through the cabin doorway. "Surprise!"

"Wha—wha—wha—wha—?" I couldn't get up off the floor or make my jaw stop flapping.

"Hullo." Prince Boffin came in without being asked. "I did what Scandal said. You know, about trying something new? If kissing worked for Dad and pulling a sword out worked for King Cadric's grandpa, I thought I'd try doing both at the same time. Too bad this wasn't a real sword." He dropped the sliver of dragon's scale into my hands. It still glowed with Majyk. "But it worked!"

"I'll say it worked!" Mysti laughed out loud. "And even after, when he found out I wasn't a princess, Boffie was *such* a good sport about—"

" 'Boffie'?"

Mysti went on as if I hadn't said a thing: "—since I'm not a princess, so he can't marry me and become king, I promised him an introduction to Raptura Eglantine when we reach the Topside. I think he'd be the perfect model to pose for her book covers. She always uses that fellow Curio, but there's nothing wrong with a little variety. It's the least I can do." She slipped her arm through his. "Isn't it, Boffie?"

"Just a minute!" I protested. "Aren't you forgetting something?"

Mysti batted her eyelashes at me. "What?"

"You're my *wife*."

"No, I'm not. We're not married anymore."

"We're not?"

"I was dead, remember?"

Scandal cocked his head at her. "No fooling? You guys use that 'til-death-do-us-part rule here too?"

"I should hope so!" Mysti said. "Except for vampires and tax collectors." She snuggled closer to Prince Boffin. "Let's go back up on deck, Boffie, and watch the sea serpent races."

I heard Prince Boffin's eager "Uh-huh, uh-huh, uh-huh," trail away after them.

I stared, bewildered, at the dragon's scale in my hands, then turned to Scandal. "What happened?" I implored.

The cat heaved a massive sigh. "What can I tell you, chief? It's the old, old story: Boy meets Welfie, boy loses Welfie, boy gets cat." He stepped into my lap and began to purr. "Sounds like a happy ending to me."

Shadow Novels from
ANNE LOGSTON

Shadow is a master thief as elusive as her name. Only her dagger is as sharp as her eyes and wits. Where there's a rich merchant to rob, good food and wine to be had, or a lusty fellow to kiss...there's Shadow.

"Spiced with magic and intrigue..."–Simon R. Green
"A highly entertaining fantasy."–Locus